A Grain of Wheat

A Grain of Wheat

Joseph Robert Jacobson

Elm Hill

A Division of
HarperCollins Christian Publishing

www.elmhillbooks.com

A Grain of Wheat

Published in Nashville, Tennessee, by Elm Hill, an imprint of Thomas Nelson. Elm Hill and Thomas Nelson are registered trademarks of HarperCollins Christian Publishing, Inc.

Elm Hill titles may be purchased in bulk for educational, business, fund-raising, or sales promotional use. For information, please e-mail SpecialMarkets@ThomasNelson.com.

Publisher's Note: This novel is a work of fiction. Names, characters, places, and incidents are either products of the author's imagination or used fictitiously. All characters are fictional, and any similarity to people living or dead is purely coincidental.

Library of Congress Cataloging-in-Publication Data

Library of Congress Control Number: 2020900762

ISBN 978-1-400330416 (Paperback)
ISBN 978-1-400330423 (Hardbound)
ISBN 978-1-400330430 (eBook)

DEDICATION

To Carolyn, my lifelong Kay.
To Ann, my real live Cecilia.
To Theresa, my Third Angel.

And with my heartfelt thanks to the excellent support staff at Elm Hill Books.

Author's Foreword

In June of 2018, after the death of Carolyn, my wife of nearly fifty-three years, I discovered a small box squirreled away in a storage trailer on our farm. It contained a carbon copy of the manuscript of this book. I opened the box for the first time in fifty-six years and began reading out of curiosity. I was alternately shocked, blown away, and deeply moved by what I read.

I recalled that a good friend of mine had submitted it to a publisher in 1962 when I was studying in France and had received a rejection slip. Reading it fifty-six years later, I think I understand why. I immediately went to work on two sections toward the end of the book, both abbreviating them and reshaping their contents. I then submitted the manuscript to our daughter, Theresa, to get her take on it. She made a couple of good suggestions which I have incorporated into the new laptop version of the manuscript.

"Dad," she said, "this has to be published. I can't believe you wrote it so long ago. This is as good as anything we read in English literature. People need to read it now more than ever."

Book One was written during the summer of 1961 when I was serving as a lookout fireman stationed on Loon Creek Point in what was then the Primitive Area of the Challis National Forest in central Idaho. Books Two and Three were written in the following months during my senior year at St. Olaf College in Northfield, Minnesota. I then transferred everything from my longhand scribble onto a typewritten manuscript with a carbon copy. The job was completed by the end of the school year. Once it was done and commended to my friend, I never laid eyes on it again until last June. That's when it blew me out of the water.

The main characters in the book are inspired by real people, as are many of the minor characters. Many episodes throughout the book likewise reflect actual happenings. Of course, as author I assume full responsibility for the form they take in a work of fiction. It has been tempting to revise it more than I have. But as an old man, I am loath to tamper with the fires and passions of the youth I once was.

I hope our daughter is right. I hope that you are drawn into the story, that you will laugh and cry, and that in the end you will be glad you read it.

Joseph Robert Jacobson, Autumn, 2018

Prologue

At first I was more than puzzled that Dr. Stephan Pearson was calling on me to spend his last days with him, but I soon realized that under the circumstances I was the only person to whom he could turn. He needed someone who could understand and represent fairly his relationship with my cousin, Cecilia Endsrud, and who could interconnect with some accuracy the events of the subsequent course of his life. I see all this now, but when I received from him the following telegram, I was thoroughly baffled as to what the chairman of the Department of Physics at my alma mater, Christiania College, wanted with me at a time like this:

APRIL 27, 1960

DEAR PAUL

PLEASE COME TO MY HOME IN ST MARK AS SOON AS POSSIBLE STOP I NEED YOU VERY MUCH STOP I BELIEVE I AM RIGHT IN ASKING YOU TO DROP EVERYTHING AND COME STOP I SHALL PROBABLY HAVE DIED BY THIS TIME NEXT WEEK STOP BY COMING YOU WILL PREVENT THE ONLY TRUE GOOD IN ME FROM DYING WITH ME STOP

STEVE

Needless to say, I was at his side the following morning.

Over the next few days he used his very last reserves of strength to pour out to me the story he felt so compelled to tell. I hung on every word he uttered and took copious notes. It helped that I was already acquainted with its broad outline and in certain places also with many of its details. Verbatim accounts, of course, have had to be reconstructed, but many of them I jotted down while still in the fever of the spirit in which Steve related them. Thanks to his phenomenal memory, I am sure that many conversations appear here substantially as they occurred.

I am not a professional author, yet I do not present this work with apologies. For I am certain that its own inherent strengths will more than compensate for the literary shortcomings of the one who recorded it.

Stephan Pearson's pilgrimage through life, though unique in so many ways, can be seen in other ways as a template for the still unfolding pilgrimage of modern Western society. In that sense it touches almost every one of us. The big question mark is whether our society, before it is too late, is capable of coming to terms with what it took him a lifetime to learn. Only God knows.

Book One

I

Lars Pearson was a great chuck of a man, a tall broad-shouldered, ruddy Norwegian whose lanky frame was filled out with massive bands of muscle acquired from many hard years of wheat farming. His thinning hair was tossed back in wavy shocks and added the dignity of experience to his imposing stature. Before he reached fifty years of age, his face was already deeply furrowed with downward-tending lines. The beating prairie sun and the punishing wind had permanently bronzed and leathered his skin. But it was his eyes that were unquestionably the most riveting, almost frightening, feature of his countenance, strained as they had been through the years into a perpetual squint. What those burning eyes of Lars Pearson discerned from their narrow slits, God only knew. It was as though he was making an intense study of everyone and everything he beheld. Even people whom he met only casually came away with the disconcerting feeling that they had just been analyzed by someone whose X-ray gaze had cut through to their most buried secrets. In short, his were the eyes of a man whose vision was resolutely fixed on some point in the distance, and his was the frame of a man who tirelessly strove to reach that point.

It was not without reason that people looked with awe on Lars Pearson, for more than once he had perceived, exposed, and even exploited the diligently concealed motives of others. He was not above capitalizing on others' misfortunes to acquire more land and wealth for himself. By the end of World War One he was in full possession of six sections of land, including the farms of several hapless former neighbors. Lars Pearson's ambition had made him a far wealthier man than his immigrant father had been, although not a perceptibly happier one. Setting and achieving new goals and surmounting new challenges seemed to be merely the food that kept him alive, for he did not appear to derive lasting satisfaction from his achievements. His plans were the stuff on which he thrived; once they had become accomplishments, they meant little to him. He simply could not sit back and enjoy the fruits of his labors. He was a man who was constantly looking ahead as far as there was anything to see. No wonder he was always squinting.

He had one overriding ambition in life: he would leave his son a prosperous and respected land baron, not the toiling serf of the soil that his father had left him. His son would not have to sweat as he had!

Of quite another sort was Julia Olsen Pearson. She too was the child of a poor hardworking immigrant Norwegian farmer, but it happened that her father, Ole Olsen, had come to the end of his days without sons or direct heirs to whom he could hand on his farm. This was how Lars came into possession of one of his acquired sections of land, some years after he had married Julia.

Young Julia had been swept quite off her feet when Lars started courting her. She was fair-skinned, slight in stature, and all woman. Hers was a reserved sort of haunting beauty that was emitted mostly from her tender deep-blue eyes reminiscent of a bank of early morning mist rising slowly out of a woodland lake into the pure dawn sky. They were dewy and gleaming, and they seemed to hold an enigma, telling only half of what was behind them and filtering their every message through a veil of melancholy before letting it seep out into the world. Now and then the veil lifted, and this Lars succeeded in doing often during their courtship. They were openly enchanted with one another. The current of Lars' innate enthusiasm for life swept her out of her melancholy; for although she never was able to subscribe fully to the ambitious vision that sustained his spirits, she could not escape being infected by the spirits themselves.

Any misgivings she might have had simply could not survive in the heat of their young love.

For his part, Lars had been plainly bewitched by the mystery that always seemed to be lurking just beneath the surface of Julia's soft beauty. As with all things, he consciously set himself to conquering her affection. Even Lars, sturdy and self-confident as he was about everything else, trembled and stammered the first time she agreed to go with him to a Sunday afternoon outdoor meeting. But soon both of them entered into that blessed synthesis that feels like love—their hearts leapt anxiously within them when they were together, and yet their being together felt as natural and unaffected as a bee in a flower on a warm spring day.

Theirs was not a protracted courtship. In those simpler days people made decisions and wasted no time in carrying them through. At what point precisely it was that Lars' vision morphed into an unrelenting obsession and Julia's veil drew back over her eyes again it is impossible to say. What can be said is that the fusion of these two very different people did not last very long. Lars was still mystified and sometimes deeply discouraged by Julia's withdrawal into herself, and Julia was still awed and occasionally even inspired by Lars' vast resourcefulness. The cords of their hearts had been tied somehow together, but not the direction of their wills. They recaptured only rarely brief flashes of the mutual sincerity they enjoyed at first, sometimes in the intimacy of lovemaking; but more often it was the very emptiness of these "intimate" moments that cruelly revealed the widening gap between them.

There was yet one more difference which their courtship had minimized. Julia was acutely aware of the obligations placed upon her by her religion. God was good but just, in her mind. Her contemplative nature easily succumbed to the almost mystical forces of the Great Central Plain whose interminable expanses could swallow a man and well-nigh digest him too. It could suck him into its wind-whipped treeless bosom and batter him with the brute rage of its storms. It could parch him under the blistering fire of its sun and gnaw him with the desolation of its emptiness until he would bear on his body and in his soul all the scars and calluses inflicted over the years. And it had a voice that whispered in the grass and whistled around the lonely buildings and almost never fell silent: "What is man that Thou art mindful of him? What is man that Thou art mindful?… What is man?… What is man?…"

Julia Pearson could not escape that voice. She knew well how insignificant man is, and each manifestation of God's goodness towards him struck wonder and apprehension in her heart—wonder at the greatness of God's gifts to unworthy man and apprehension at the smallness of man's gratitude for these undeserved gifts. She was plagued by the question: How much ingratitude does it take to trigger the righteous wrath of God?

In Lars, on the other hand, there was little of this awe. During their courtship he had gladly gone to church because he could sit next to Julia, and he had patiently listened to her musings about the spiritual realm without really connecting to them. The overall effect of her musings on him was to increase his desire to protect her from the perils and uncertainties he was sure she was imagining. It attracted him to her more than ever. He was just the man for her: it was second nature to him to calculate his risks ahead of time and know pretty well what his chances were of succeeding. The lion's share of Lars Pearson's fate lay in his own powerfully capable hands. With him she would soon realize how little there was to fear.

After their marriage, Lars lost interest in weekly church-going. There was often something more important demanding his attention. Julia grew fearful for his soul, and as success followed success in the realization of his ambitions, his Day of Reckoning seemed ever more imminent to her. A man could not forever ignore God and get away with it!

A son was born to them on May 20, 1901, in their second year of marriage. Julia's labor was long and arduous. In the absence of a doctor, it was probably Lars' experience with cows calving in the spring that saved the life of both mother and son. Julia was a very long time in recovering from it.

They named their son Stephan Lars Pearson.

Stephan Pearson, thought Julia. *That is a good name. Our son will be as strong and God-fearing as St. Stephan the Martyr.*

Stephan Lars Pearson, thought Lars. *Now there's a real name, fit for the next lord of this estate!*

II

Growing up as an only child in the middle of the empty prairie must be desolate under any circumstances, but for Stephan Pearson the desolation was intensified by an empty home. Ever since he could remember, his father had been gone all day every day and his mother had taken refuge in an inconspicuous corner of the large farmhouse as soon as her chores were over, leaving him to fend for himself. He heard his father speak only when a friend came to call, usually on some farm business. The few words beyond the absolutely necessary that he heard from his mother usually came in the evening as she tucked him into bed. She would sit near the foot of the bed and join him in his bedtime prayers. Then she would address him for a few moments in low tones of furtive admonition. She spoke of things he did not really understand. She would say things like, "Listen, Stevie. It doesn't please God to think only about how to raise more wheat so you can get richer." Very often, bending low over him to kiss his forehead, she would preface the kiss with a remark like, "Stevie Boy, when you grow up you will think about what makes God happy, won't you?" And he would fall asleep with confusing and vaguely suggestive thoughts turning in his head.

A large part of the tragedy of his home life boiled down to the fact that each of his parents had a distinct idea of what he should become, but both of them lacked the foresight to set aside their preoccupations long enough to put some effort into igniting their respective ambitions in him.

Lars' driving ambition was to leave his son a well-established farmer, but he did nothing to interest him in farming. The two were nearly strangers. They never worked or played together. Steve learned nothing of the joy and satisfaction of a job well done. The impression his father made on him was of a restless, tense, fundamentally unhappy man. There always seemed to be something demanding Lars' immediate attention. After all, tomorrow would be soon enough to start teaching the boy the ropes of farming. Being a man of means, he had enough hired help to look after the normal chores on which most farm boys were raised.

Julia Pearson was equally ineffective in laying a foundation on which to build her aspirations for the lad. In her mind she had a picture of Steve growing up to become a God-fearing professional man who would not be continually tempting the patience of God by endlessly pursuing his own personal ambitions. Perhaps he would be a pastor or a doctor whose whole purpose would be to please God and serve people. But her little evening pep talks succeeded rather in sowing the seeds of discord and suspicion in his heart. It didn't take him long to realize that the prongs of her words were aimed at his father, but he had no clear idea why. And the example of her apparent helpless submission to the kind of life she despised inspired in him no confidence in whatever way of life she espoused. That was just the trouble—she was so resigned to the oppressing situation in which she found herself trapped that she had long since ceased to espouse anything actively. The message one might glean from her life was that most people are evil, not many people understand this, and those who do are very sad. She failed on the whole to give Steve any reason to suspect that under some conditions, life can actually be meaningful and enjoyable.

Not until he entered grade school in town did he discover entirely on his own that it was actually possible to enjoy life from time to time and to forget the bitter melancholy that normally hung over it. This was an epochal discovery for it released him, at least momentarily, from the two dominant forces in his life—the constant state of tension and strain he experienced in his father and the perpetual solitary sadness he experienced in his mother. Thus he virtually stepped out of the frame of reference of both parents neither of whom had any concept of a life driven by diversion. His father's life was driven by his ambitions. His mother's life was consumed by her pessimism. His life, meanwhile, was increasingly defined by seeking out pleasurable experiences and reproducing them whenever possible.

Stephan developed a sort of schizophrenic personality that automatically adapted itself to sudden changes in his environment. Away from home he was an entirely different person from the person he was in the cheerless atmosphere of the big cold farmhouse. As he grew older and began to see his parents' behaviors as two concentric ruts going nowhere, he became ever more restless at home. Time and again he would bound off across the prairie early in the morning on days when there was no school and not return until suppertime or later. Nobody had much of an idea of just what he did in those long hours all by himself but, from the hints picked up by his friends, it became generally known that he was a sharp observer like his father and comfortable in his own company like his mother.

Old Lars Pearson unwittingly aggravated the disintegrating situation in the home by providing Steve with anything he asked for—a horse and tack, a rifle, riding clothes, and in 1915 a spanking new Model T Ford. The ungainly thing was soon seen sputtering and roaring around the countryside like a mad monster, raising great billows of dust in its wake. Stephan Pearson needed no destination to induce him to leap into the stately machine and take off down the lane. All he needed was a ringing tension building up in his muscles and a hint of the sensations of power and freedom he would feel behind the wheel. He was plainly the envy of every less fortunate lad for miles around.

Among his friends he was known as the quiet one who was game for anything and who was never so animated as when he was at the center of a prank. Reflective of his amusements during this period of his life are the numerous clever maneuvers he engineered from time to time, all of them calculated to embarrass the ridiculous as he conceived it. I recall from our college days one such event which he recounted for us one evening with a mixture of enjoyment and pain.

One day he and a group of cronies succeeded in greasing a husky piglet and slipping it just before closing time into the high school library when the librarian wasn't looking. A set of chains and a padlock on the main door finished the job. Then they hid in the bushes outside a window and watched what happened. As he told it, three spindly young females and the old librarian let out a scream, flew to the door and, finding it padlocked, leapt on top of some tables. Meanwhile, the piglet, no less alarmed than the women, made quick work of some lower shelves in the nonfiction and took frantic refuge in the reference room. Then the boys ran around to the other side of the school, pretending to come from the opposite direction. Overhearing the terrible racket, they notified the principal that something was apparently wrong in the direction of the library. Following the panic-stricken man to the trouble spot they quickly assessed the situation, cursed the scoundrels who would do such a thing, and offered to break through the glass in the door. The desperate man nodded. Stephan grabbed a nearby chair and smashed a large hole in the glass panels of the door. The boys ducked inside and made off after the porker.

Catching a slimy mass of slithering and squirming flesh is no easy task under any circumstances, especially when the mass is as terrified as that poor piglet was. But, as Stephan told it, the boys made rather more work of it than necessary. By the time they finally wrestled it out of the library through the shattered door, it had liberalized its education in almost every subject offered by the library. Herding it out through the main entrance, Stephan called out to the principal not to worry about the door: his dad would replace it. And he did.

This masterpiece of strategy was just one of the many mostly harmless pranks of which Stephan was the chief—and normally the anonymous—tactician. He would usually dream them up while he was supposed to be doing something distasteful to him, like working in the library on an assignment on "The Life and Times of Alexander Pope" in the presence of the prim and proper spinster librarian and her prim and proper helpers, when the inspiration for the greased pig came into his head. The funeral director, an especially annoying teacher, a visiting evangelist, several prominent businessmen, one conceited fellow student, and other appropriate candidates as well, all found themselves on the butt end of some unexplainable and embarrassing turn of events sooner or later, skillfully engineered incognito by Stephan.

To his teachers as well as to his pals, he was the quiet one who rarely tended to business. Some of them were inclined to consider him a dull pupil, for in those days most people took it for granted that intelligence and industriousness went hand in hand. Nevertheless, he did remarkably well on his tests, considering how seldom he studied. Occasionally he even displayed unusual sensitivity. His English teacher, for example, was fascinated by his compositions which displayed not so much grammatical perfection and sentence balance as originality and lucidity of thought. They were always scratched-out first copies, a practice of which she never succeeded in breaking him. There was something about his unique approach to any subject which placed them in a category all their own. Once she assigned the prosaic theme, "My Favorite Animal." Most of the class chose the horse for its beauty and strength or the bee for its cheerful dedication to its work or the dog for its faithfulness. But Steve chose the cowbird since it didn't have to worry about finding its food (it simply followed the cows around) or raising children (it cleverly laid its eggs in other birds' nests) or getting an education (instinct provided it with all it needed to know); therefore it could spend all its time doing what it felt like doing, not just a few brief moments of it. This viewpoint, which ignored all traditional virtues and aesthetic considerations, was something of a shock to the teacher. But, after all, this was Stephan Pearson. She regarded him as one of her more interesting problems.

The lone exception to this record of jagged mediocrity was mathematics. On the average day the subject simply presented no challenge to him, but on special days something about it sparked his curiosity and drew him ineluctably in, way in. In either case, he was always leap years ahead of the class and the teacher when it came to grasping principles and applying them. By consistently outthinking and outfiguring his mathematics teacher, this indifferent young man baffled him even more than he baffled his English teacher. This was the only noticeable indication in his school days of the budding genius buried within him.

"Friends" he had, as we have noted. Yet he never knew one soul in the first nineteen years of his life with whom he felt completely at ease. This state of affairs was rendered all the more unnatural by the fact that his restless agitation when forced to do something disagreeable to him betrayed a continuous and progressive inner disturbance that cried out for help, or at least a listening ear. But his experience at home made him suspicious of everyone's motives. Survival, not resolution, was the *modus operandi* of his family. You kept your convictions largely to yourself, observed the necessary domestic forms and rituals, and did nothing to disturb the artificial crust that held everything together. To Steve this became the template for how he understood society at large. Each man carried on his private thoughts behind his personal barricade and presented to the world only the cold symmetry of the barricade itself. It was unthinkable to him to probe into the secret world behind someone else's barricade or to admit anyone else into the secret world behind his.

It was in this frame of mind that Stephan Pearson graduated from high school and took a look at the world. Although he had no idea what he wanted to do, his mother did. She enrolled him in Christiania College for the coming year. It would be a story in itself to relate how this single tangible fact jolted old Lars from his dreams for Steve and forced him to face the stark truth of his neglect. Realizing in his soul's soul that Steve would never be a farmer, his life became the pathetic tale of a man whose all-consuming goal in life has been shattered but who from sheer force of habit continues to plod doggedly onward towards where it once was.

Steve, for his part, was neither excited nor dismayed by the prospect of attending Christiania College. After high school was over, he had hovered in the air of indecision just long enough to appreciate the value of having something to do, some place to go.

Thus it was that in the fall of 1919, Stephan Pearson began his student years at Christiania College in St. Mark, Minnesota, there ostensibly to prepare for a life of professional service in accordance with the wishes of his mother, but really because he had nothing better to do.

III

The fiery beauty of autumn had long since faded away. No longer was the rolling hilltop campus of Christiania College crowned by the dazzling scarlet of symmetrical maples or the more regal purple of twisted oaks. The piles and ridges of wind-driven leaves were gone too, buried under the accumulation of two late-fall snowstorms. The temperature was already taking those deep plunges so characteristic of Minnesota winters, and the wind was sweeping as usual across the barren fields and whipping over the crest of the hill on which Christiania stood. Fine particles of icy snow cut like shredded glass into the face of anyone brave enough to venture out across the naked campus. The challenge of a long hard winter had arrived with its clean fair-handed fury. The hardy country folks accepted it head-on, leaning into the wind in their thick fur-lined coats or huddled around their fires indoors. The cold on the outside served to concentrate the warmth on the inside, and the forbidding brutality of nature tended to intensify the intimacy shared among friends and family members.

But for one young man on the campus of Christiania College, this was a period of creeping disintegration. To all outward appearances, Stephan Pearson was very little changed from his high school days. He was still the quiet one wherever he went, still an enigma to his professors. They did not know quite how to interpret the nervous detachment that often descended on him during their lectures: Was he daydreaming, bored, or pursuing some line of thought suggested by the lecture? He was still attracted to the ranks of those fellow students who made a practice of severing their ties to the college every weekend and just letting themselves go. But he was not always comfortable in their company either.

Among his friends in those days was Tom Mahler, a tall, sturdy, handsome veteran of the First World War who was taking premedicine in the hope of following in his father's footsteps. He roomed across the corridor from Steve and seemed to enjoy Steve's company on his weekend excursions into the countryside around St. Mark. Since St. Mark was his hometown, he was acquainted with several farmers in the area who made a decent home brew. More often than not, they were joined by such lads as Lute Odegaard, a quick-witted farmer's son from Western Minnesota, and by Steve's roommate, Ted Bjornson, the tall lanky son of a South Dakota Ford dealer. The recent passage of the Prohibition Amendment and the firm stand Christiania College took against intoxicating beverages added measurably to the attractiveness of these weekend excursions.

But the normal course of the average day provided Steve with numberless irritations. Each morning the entire student body was required to gather in the chapel for a full half hour devoted to worship and instruction. In one form or another, the students were regularly reminded of their Christian duty to be good stewards of the God-given talents entrusted to them, which was synonymous with their duty to study diligently and get a solid liberal arts education. Was not the Parable of the Talents ample evidence that squandering our gifts will earn us the wrath of God? Steve sat through such counsel impassively. He could barely stomach harangues of this sort. They ran so counter to the observable facts of life. His dad would admirably have filled their bill, and yet he was just about the least happy man Steve knew. People who toiled and ground their lives away had to die in the end just like anyone else, and most of them never experienced a day of true enjoyment all the while. This kind of talk was so annoying to him that he wrote off whatever good there might have been in other aspects of chapel and came to look on it as a choice time to catch up on his sleep in a rear pew.

And then there was that cursed obligation to sit through sixteen hours of didactic droning each week. And they took attendance in those days! So he would sleep until the last moment every morning, skip breakfast, and saunter off to his first class. Between classes he would meet some buddies in the Tiger's Haunt and play checkers or eat ice cream. Every chance he got he would abandon the campus altogether, taking long hikes through the fields, even in bad weather. Occasionally he would skim through a textbook, but ordinarily he spent his time doodling away on a blank sheet of paper, drawing cars, horses, math formulas, war scenes, and intricate designs of all sorts. Sometimes he merely sulked around his room in seething agitation, as though he were about to burst.

The only courses that interested him in the slightest degree were his mathematics and science courses. He frankly despised his required religion course taught by a young Th.D. who enjoyed displaying the shock value of his newly acquired skills in what he "modestly" called higher criticism.

In a word, Steve's life was torn between a myriad of things that disgusted him and a mere handful of things that he enjoyed. If he had had his way, he would have turned his back on the former and spent all his time on the latter. But that was impossible. Wherever he turned he was ensnared by distasteful obligations: his textbooks were always staring at him, his schedule was always glowering at him, his professors were always nagging him, his mother's letters were always admonishing him. At times his disgust would turn to rage and he would seize the nearest book and hurl it to the floor or storm out of his room and charge blindly down the hill out into the open fields.

For the first two or three months, the weekends transformed him into a different person. In the company of his pals he felt free to set loose his wit and unleash his mischief. There was always plenty of beer and cigarettes to create a convivial mood on the farms where Tom Mahler took his buddies. Before winter set in, they rented horses and rode all over the place or hunted small game in the many nearby woodlots. But when Sunday night came, they had to be cautious not to betray the faintest whiff of beer on their breath when they returned to the college, and on Monday morning it was back to the same old grind. The Stephan Pearson of the school week and the Stephan Pearson of the weekend remained separate personalities until somewhere around Thanksgiving time. Then for some reason Steve began having a difficult time throwing off his sulkiness and wearying disgust when the weekend came. With the grim blanket of sloppy snow that set a limit to what you could do on weekends came a heavy feeling of the futility of it all. It smothered him wherever he was. He was constantly fidgeting, anxious about everything. His barricade was being breached on every hand. He was finding it more and more difficult to hide himself behind it, more and more difficult to keep his true feelings of disgust from showing.

Just before Christmas recess, the boys decided to have a free-wheeling party at the Brennan farm within walking distance of the hill. Joe Brennan was a middle-aged bachelor who welcomed the weekends the boys spent at his place every bit as much as the boys themselves did. He had no qualms about their proposal to invite some girls to this party.

Steve, however, didn't know any girls well enough to feel comfortable about inviting one. The stringent moral code of his hometown made normal interaction of teens with the opposite sex almost impossible. In addition, there was his extreme reserve in dealing with other people in general, resulting in a lack of enthusiasm on his part for the party from the start.

His strapping roommate Ted Bjornson finally took a hand in the matter of getting him a date. Thus, on the evening of the party Steve found himself escorting a willowy blond Swede named Sue Olson who, Ted had assured him, could be trusted to keep their secret and to inject some wit into the occasion. Steve himself felt anything but witty that night, having undergone that same day a comprehensive English examination and a test covering the first two hundred fifty pages of his religion textbook. The whole pointless nonsense of it all was still gagging him as he trudged through the snow to call for Miss Olson. During the mile-long walk into the wind to the Brennan farm, Sue made several dead-end attempts to provoke a conversation. But Steve's terse answers never offered more than a literal one- or two-word response to her questions. He seemed much more annoyed with himself than with her.

The spacious farmhouse was amply provided with all the attractions calculated to furnish an evening of pleasure at every level. The beer flowed from the kegs in a steady stream, as did the music from the fancy new Victrola. There was laughing and dancing—forbidden by the college—and general gaiety. Steve knew he should be having a good time, but for the life of him he just could not dive into the stream of the evening.

As the evening progressed, he discovered that what Ted had described as Sue's wit was really the babbling of a scatterbrain. The lithe female, who towered over him by a good three inches, insisted on dragging him relentlessly around the dance floor while the Victrola spewed forth an unebbing tide of raucous sounds. Between dances she probably consumed more beer than she had ever seen in her life before, growing more obnoxious and, frankly, indecent by the mugful. Her prattling questions and her increasingly parasitic physical proximity became for Steve a major invasion of his privacy, an uninvited intrusion into the sanctuary behind his barricade. He was rapidly coming to despise her and even more to hate himself for his inability to have a good time when everyone else seemed to be having one.

A few hours and several beers into the evening, Lute noticed that Steve was far from his normal self. Sidling over to him during a pause in the music, he said with a facetiousness slightly tainted by reproof, "What's the matter, old boy? You don't seem to be having any fun."

Steve looked him in the eye and smiled weakly, "Yeah. It's a great party."

Then the music started belting again and Lute returned to his date. Steve looked up and saw Sue wobbling towards him with another glass of beer in her hand and a foolish grin on her face. She winked at him and nodded in the direction of the bedroom from which a couple was at that very moment emerging, as if to say, *It's our turn.* Sick, he wheeled about and made a rush for the door. Everyone was stamping on the floor in time to the blaring music. He pulled open the door and made his escape out onto the porch. The icy air met his flushed face. He stood there for a moment, glowering into the noiseless white night. Then, grabbing a handful of snow from the railing, he flung it out into the darkness.

"No!" he shouted. "No! No! No!"

IV

The Great Northern passenger train was rumbling and swaying over the rails of North Dakota that stretched without a ripple or a curve as far as the eye could see. In the winter these rails were the scene of a continuous battle between drifting snow and the traffic of trains, a battle which was usually won by the traffic. The heaps of snow on either side lent to the tracks the appearance of two silver rivers in the bottom of an alabaster canyon. Looking out of the window of the train was like looking at a blank movie screen, and when the drifts receded enough for the passengers to see beyond them, it was only more of the same anyhow.

The train was gathering speed now after having stopped at Minot to pick up a load of students and other holiday guests heading back to Minnesota, Wisconsin, and Illinois. Among them was a young man slight of stature whose parents had brought him a long way through the snow to meet the train. He had clambered into the last car somewhat hastily and left his parents a little stunned by omitting the usual departing signs of affection. Just now he was slouched down in the front seat of the car staring motionlessly at his feet.

For a long time he sat there oblivious to the clicking and clacking of the coach wheels over the rails and the irregular swaying of the carriage. By offering no resistance to it, he looked more like a permanent fixture than a transient passenger. Perhaps an hour went by in which he remained deeply engulfed in another world, a disappointing world to judge by the occasional grimace or shudder that interrupted his otherwise expressionless state of torpor.

Then without warning he sat bolt upright and peered out the window. There was nothing to see but glaring featureless white. He reached up onto the baggage rack above him and retrieved a heavy sheepskin coat with a large hood. Stepping out into the aisle he pulled it on, walked swiftly to the rear of the coach, and shoved open the door. Stepping out into the platform, he slammed the door shut and found himself in the forbidding isolation he was seeking.

The platform was slick with ice. The gale force of the kicked-up snow in the train's wake beat against his exposed face. He spread his feet apart, tightened the cords of his hood, and lowered his head into the blast. For a moment he seemed reinvigorated by the change, but before long he was mumbling to himself and growing restive within the confines of the platform.

"What a vacation!" he muttered sourly. "What's happened to everyone? They've all turned into masochists!"

With that his mind moved in turn from one of his former high school cronies to another.

Take Gus Gunderson, for example. What on earth had come over him? All of a sudden now he was your aspiring student! Gus! The same fellow who only last spring had joined Steve in making elaborate plans for this coming summer to take off for California in Steve's Model T! The whole idea had been to get away from schools and farms for once in their lives and see the world. Gus had been just as fed up with the whole business as Steve was. And now here he was, loud-mouthing about all the opportunities for a career and advancement to be found in some new field called sociology. All you needed was your doctor's degree and a pinch of curiosity and you'd have the world by the tail. Oh sure! As far as Steve was concerned, Gus could collect a hundred doctor's degrees to hang on the wall of his stuffy office and spend the rest of his life in a lousy classroom if that's what he wanted. Let him slave away and die! That was his business. But Gus!... Why Gus?

It was hard for Steve not to feel betrayed.

And Al Holte and Miles Holverson and even the little Bohemian Johnny Maier, all of them going out of their way to impress the folks back home with how educated they had become. They had all run around town with a disdainful "Did-you-know-that-such-and-such?..." expression on their faces, for which they forfeited all the good times they had delighted in a few short months before. They couldn't be really enjoying now what they detested then! They seemed almost like robots, as though the more they tortured themselves the better they liked it. What had got into them?

And what do you make of the Hansen twins? They used to be just about the wildest fellows in the old gang! They had always been game for anything. Sometimes the rest of the fellows even had to restrain them or they'd have got into real trouble. Now what had happened to them? Steve would not have believed it if he hadn't seen it with his own eyes. They had gone into the funeral business as junior partners with Mr. Lien! Steve had gone over to their place one evening to see if they wanted to have an old-time reunion with some of the boys at the Maier farm. Their response to his invitation was still haunting him.

"We'd really like to, Steve, but imagine the bad publicity if word of it got out. We can't afford the risk."

Bad publicity! Those black suits they always wore now and those mustaches they were trying to grow said it all. They were draping themselves in a living death from top to bottom.

At least Pete Jorgensen hadn't changed, thank goodness for that! Or Shorty Samuelson or Bob Wolfe. Several times during the Christmas break the four of them had got together and made a noble effort to resurrect the past. Or so it seemed to Steve. The other three had no trouble enjoying themselves as they always had; but, of all things, even in this setting Steve could not shake off the black cloud that had been hanging over him ever since Thanksgiving. The fellows talked about the same things they had always talked about before—horses, women, pranks, cars, sports, and the like—but now there seemed to be a gulf of some kind between Steve and his pals, for no good reason that he could figure out. Oh, he had lost himself in many a good four-handed game of poker and had laughed heartily at many a good joke the fellows had cracked, but in the long run things just didn't seem quite right. Perhaps the absence of most of his former chums made a deeper impression on him than he realized, but perhaps there was more to it than that. The jokes often related to things that had happened since Steve had left home. The conversation often wound through dry trivialities about which he had not thought for many months. But it was more than that, a trace of something in Steve lurking way beneath the surface. What was it? A shadow of contempt? No! Surely not contempt. How could he ever be contemptuous of them? They weren't choked by inhibitions, they didn't care what people thought of them. They were Steve's own kind. They did what they felt like doing. They avoided drudgery. Life would be an enjoyable affair for them. They had been born, they would have fun, and they would get old and die. How could you be contemptuous of that? You couldn't! You couldn't look down on them!

"Well, in that case, old boy," Steve demanded of himself out loud, "what in the world were you feeling?"

Could it be that he himself had changed? Maybe he would never again know what it meant to free himself from the strait jacket of dull routine and fly away into real freedom. Curse the institution, the people, the way of life, the secret forces that kept driving him further away from the one solace he knew! Curse them all!

"It's robbery!" he shouted into the cold air. "Downright robbery!"

Just then the train gave a lurch and Steve, who had momentarily let go of the railing, was nearly thrown off the slippery platform. He grabbed it and jerked to a halt inches from disaster. Pulling himself along the railing, against the sharp blasts of the wind, he made his way back to the center of the platform and braced himself in place.

Recovering his breath, he muttered to himself, "That felt a lot like what Mom and Dad did to me during the break. Only she was trying to push me off one side of the platform and he was trying to push me off the other side. And I was hanging on to my railing for dear life!" This led him to muse for a little while on what his parents had just put him through.

Steve had never known his mother to be so animated. From the moment his parents picked him up at the railroad station, she had not ceased introducing him to everyone as her wonderful son who was studying up at Christiana College to prepare for a life of Christian service. This introduction had never failed to evoke ohs and ahs and no little amazement from the simple town and country folk who had known Steve before. For his part, Steve made no effort to conform to her new image of him; but he was already used to being passive in her presence, neither affirming nor denying anything she said. To the continuous round of questions she kept posing him when they were alone, he offered short inconclusive answers which she seized upon and magnified in her imagination all out of proportion to what he had actually said. If this had been the extent of her impositions, he might even have borne them with a measure of charity.

But the crowning imposition came the day before he was to leave for college when his mother presented him with a brand-new seminary catalog that had just arrived in the mail. Only the joy that lit up her beaming eyes when she coyly presented it to him prevented him from exploding on the spot into a volley of profanity. She winked at him and kissed him on the forehead, leaving him to fondle his new treasure in private. As soon as she was gone, he stumbled into the big chair in the corner of the room and sat there sulking for a full half hour, holding the stupid thing enclosed in his clammy hands.

His father had been an even greater enigma. In the span of his life up to that point, Steve had probably not been with his father or heard him speak to him so much as he had in the past two weeks. Lars took an uncharacteristic interest in everything Steve had been doing while away at college. He asked him all sorts of questions about what the farms were like in the neighborhood of the campus—their size, what crops they grew, how many cattle they grazed, etc. When Steve happened to allude to all the wood lots around the college, his father exclaimed in disbelief,

"You don't mean to tell me there are actually trees out there growing on good farmland! What's the matter with those people?"

It was a funny thing. Throughout the Christmas holiday, Lars had gone into town only once on business. The fourth day that Steve was at home—it was Christmas Eve—his father put his massive arms around the lad's slender shoulders and took him out into the barn. They walked about in the drafty building for a while, surveying the horses and cows and examining the equipment stored in there. Then Lars suddenly stopped right in the very middle of the barn and said in a low rumbling voice trembling with emotion, "Steve, my son, you know that in less than four years all of this will be half yours." Once again he put his big arms around the shoulders of the dismayed young man and they both walked over to the barn door. Surveying the snow-covered expanses that stretched beyond the meandering line of willows in the creek bed beneath the barn, Lars squinted and declared with conviction, "That will all be yours before long, my boy, as far as you can see. It takes a good man to run a huge estate like this, a better man than I am. I'm glad you're getting an education. You're learning how to think better than I can. Of course, your old man will be able to give you a few helpful pointers when you get back here. But I've always said the day was coming when farming would call for an educated man!" He gave Steve's shoulders a big squeeze.

Steve's shock at his father's self-assured words had been tempered only by his shock at his father's apparent affection for him. But inwardly he was no less angered by his father's assumptions than by his mother's presumptions. He would like to have had a dollar for every time Lars had suggestively dropped a comment about Len Carlson, one of Steve's boyhood buddies, and his dad going into partnership on their farm, which wasn't half the farm Steve was in line to get. And, by golly, if the young fellow wasn't planning on marrying the Pedersen girl in the spring! Didn't Steve think that was dandy? Steve had nodded his assent and mused to himself that this was the same Len who had cursed farming as a boy and dreamed of moving to a big town when he grew up.

There goes Len, he had thought to himself.

Thus the vacation had limped by, a dark memory to be forgotten as soon as possible. Steve's ruminations left him exhausted. He felt deserted by some of his friends and strangely alienated from the rest of them. He felt tossed into the frying pan by his mother and hurled into the fire by his father. All he had wanted to do was to fly away anywhere like a bird, but he was caught in the snare of his parents' dreams for him. On top of that, it felt as if his wings were broken from all his internal flapping to get free of the snares. If so, he would never have what it takes to rise into the air again. Surely his spirit was not broken beyond repair! No! No! Maybe it would still heal.

"But how can it heal when it is being forever savaged?"

With that, his thought wound down and his mind was left more with the taste of what it had just chewed over than with its substance. It was bitter and pungent, but slowly it melted away. He fell into a depressed trance, blindly staring at the snow whizzing past him.

After a few minutes the door opened onto the platform and an elderly conductor stepped out, bucking the wind with the top of his cap.

"Say, young man!" he shouted over the shrill blasts and the clacking wheels. "Don't you think you'd better come in before you freeze to death?"

Steve looked around him and for the first time realized how terribly cold he had become. His face was numb. He started to shiver all over.

"Yeah," he said stiffly. "I guess I'd better."

V

It was a mock sun that rose and fell over the January drifts, slicing through the brittle air and glaring off the fresh snow, a cold impersonal glow illuminating the fairyland world outdoors. The sheer storybook beauty of those days, their visual enticements coupled with their physical remoteness, lent an aura of unreality even to the places that were very familiar to the students in more clement weather. Deep snowdrifts buried their favorite haunts and obliterated the meandering woodland paths down which young lovers aimlessly strolled in the springtime. At times, though, the new-fallen snow accentuated the delicately suspended objects on which it fell: each tiny black twig supported an identical white twin so that from a little distance, the branches looked like so many pairs of matching doilies not quite perfectly lined up.

All of this physical unreality out of doors had the effect for most students of helping them concentrate on the very real demands of their studies indoors. Adding to this effect were the approach of final examinations and the heavy load of assignments given by some professors in a scramble to complete the prescribed courses. The month of January was truly a time of intellectual ferment on the campus of Christiania College.

But in Stephan Pearson different forces were at work. For him, reality whether outdoors or indoors seemed to hang intangible in the air during this month so cruelly calculated by nature and man to be conducive to nothing but studying. By itself, the fact that the outdoor world was an untouchable chimera and the indoor world an imminent day of reckoning no more drove him to his books than an impending squall drives a ship's captain into his lifeboat. While everyone else was sitting hypnotized before a stack of books, Steve was pacing to and fro, tugging as it were on the bars of his cage.

The better part of a month had passed since Steve had caught his hacking cold on the rear platform of the Great Northern passenger train. This evening he was in his room all alone, slouched down in an overstuffed chair with his feet up on the windowsill. It was almost pitch dark, but dim rays from a streetlight across the lane were filtering in through the windowpane and casting a dull luminescence over the area where he was sitting. He gazed absently out into the scene before him that was being formed and re-formed by the compelling hand of a driving snowstorm. It was nine thirty at night. Across the ravine through the slanted streaks of flying snow, he could just make out the windows of the library, all ablaze with light. From each tiny window marking a carrel cell in the "stacks" a beam pierced the night, and under each beam was a student laboring away.

For many nights recently Steve had been left alone in his nearly deserted corridor. His roommate, Ted Bjornson, had been caught up in the general panic that swept over every class of freshmen about two weeks before finals when he discovered to his serious alarm that he had most of a semester's work to cram into fourteen days. At first he had sat chained to his desk day and night, putting up with Steve's thoughtless agitation. But when he started coming down with Steve's cold, he took refuge in the library on the pretext that he had some reference work to do there.

Tom Mahler, the veteran across the hall, always had been a diligent student except on weekends. Although, as we have noted, he aspired to follow his father's footsteps into the medical profession, his modest intellectual gifts required him to work hard to qualify for medical school. Steve thought of him as almost schizophrenic: unapproachable during the week because he was so caught up in his studies, and the life of the party on weekends. He could shed academia like a cloak for a day or two and pour himself into whatever form of amusement was on offer. Women were the only topic on which he could almost always be approached, a field of interest which he seemed to have developed to a fine art in Europe during the war. But now, with finals right around the corner, even that topic took a backseat. He plodded along day and night in a stupor, spending even the weekends in the library and returning to his room each night all played out but without a word of complaint. To Steve he was a total self-contradiction. What drove him on? Didn't he have a brain in his head? Couldn't he see that he was slaving away to prepare for a future that was bound to be as dull as his present?

A funereal pall had descended over the dormitory that night: it was as silent as death. Only the whining of the wind around the sharp corners of the building and the rattling of the windowpanes broke the silence. Steve sunk lower and lower into his chair, sucking on his pipe that had long since gone cold. The immense emptiness around him played with the tangle of emotions within him. His lips were tense and dry, a persistent scowl deformed his features, his watery eyes were compressed into a squint. He sat there, a knot of dull sensations, staring into the blackness. His mind sluggishly stirred around in the brew of bitterness within him whose individual components had long since blended into one acrid pottage.

Then, as though in response to a new turn of thought, he sat up a little straighter and relit his pipe. His eyes opened wider as the new thought took root. He spent only a moment or two rolling it around in his mind. Then he got to his feet, walked over to his desk, thumbed through a small pile of papers in the semidarkness, and pulled out a couple of sheets. Before he could change his mind, he was tapping on the half-open door of the room next to his.

"Come on in," I called, surprised that anyone would knock.

Yes, I was Steve's neighbor during his freshman year, but up to this point I hardly knew him. This is a strange fact, I must admit. But it can be explained by his reserved personality and my natural reticence. If it had not been for one happy fact, I might never have become well acquainted with anyone in the dorm. But this one fact brought many of the guys to my room and provided the incentive for Steve's nocturnal visit as well. As it happened, my high school education included Latin, German, and French which put me in a position to help a number of friends struggling with one of these languages.

But even more than that, my study of other languages gave me a good grasp of English, and so I was able to help even more friends by checking over their essays assigned in any subject for grammar and syntax. I learned a lot from this, both about the subjects of the essays and about their authors. At term-paper time the task became almost unmanageable, but I never had to turn anyone down.

"Come on in," I repeated before turning around in my chair to see who it was. Throwing a period on the end of a sentence, I looked about to see Steve walk through the door, papers in hand. "Why, good evening, Steve," I exclaimed in mild surprise. "Have a seat."

He walked over to the soft chair next to my desk and sat down. It was a congenial place for friends to sit while I went over their work. Steve perched himself on the edge of the chair holding the sheets of paper on his knees.

"You wouldn't happen to have a few minutes to look this over, would you?" he asked hesitantly. "Doc Rasmussen assigned us this paper and said he expects it to be perfect."

"Sure. Let's have a look at it."

Steve leaned back in the chair and pulled out a cigarette. "Do you mind?"

"Not a bit." I noticed he had thought to close the door. In those days, smoking infractions were rather severely dealt with at Christiania. Glancing at the pages I asked, "What topic did he assign you?"

"Oh, anything. Anything at all. Just so it contains between three and five hundred perfect words. I've never been strong in grammar. That's where I may need some help."

"One thing I learned from studying all those languages, especially Latin, was English grammar."

He laughed politely and a little cynically. "You really enjoy that stuff, don't you?"

"Well, not exactly. Let's just say that since a fellow's got to take *some*thing in all this schooling folks seem to think we need, you might as well take what you least dislike, especially if you figure you can get some use out of it in the future." I was touching only the fringe of my real sentiments.

"Yeah, I guess so," Steve said slowly. My reply seemed to have caught him a bit sidewise. It wasn't what he had expected.

For the next few minutes I was engaged in reading the following essay which I happened to recover after Steve's death in a trunk filled with memorabilia:

> One drab day not long ago when low heavy clouds were hanging motionless in the sky, I was sitting at my desk trying to study our religion assignment. Even before opening the textbook my head was as muddled and thick as the air outside, but after I started reading it got even worse. Page after page was consumed by the author in dissecting the hair-splitting reasons why Paul's Epistle to the Ephesians could not have been written by Paul himself, but had to have been composed by a loyal disciple a generation later. As he built his case, he became increasingly sure of himself and impressed with his own brilliance.
>
> He went from one scrap of evidence to the next, wringing every drop of proof he could out of each one. He reveled in his confident assertions and in everything they implied. Not only did the poor man actually expect his fellowmen to plow through all this stuff, but he took it for granted that they would swallow it all. The crowning insult came when he made a big issue of Paul's personal references to himself in 3:1–13, claiming that these were totally out of character for the apostle. Even I knew that he had said the same things about himself in his First Epistle to the Corinthians, but our author never even alluded to this fact in his three-page effort to prove his point.
>
> That's when I slammed the book shut and stalked out of the room

into the lavatory. "Who the devil cares who wrote Paul's Epistle to the Ephesians?" I spit out bitterly.

I returned to my room fuming and headed over to the desk. But something stopped me in my tracks. Lying there on my bed looking up at me with lazy drop-shaped eyes was a little grey kitten. How she had got there I couldn't even guess.

"Well, well, well," I said to her. "Look what happens when I leave my door open a crack. Here you are all curled up on my bed. What do you care whose bed it is?"

The kitten yawned and stretched.

I sat down beside her. I stroked her under the chin and ruffled her behind the ears. Instantly she started purring. Then she closed her eyes and stretched out her neck, her little head swaying from side to side. Moments later she drifted off into a catnap.

"Nothing ever bothers you, does it?" I confided to her. "You always have more than enough food, you're never bored, you fear neither life nor death, you don't study for exams, you're contented wherever you are.......

"Why didn't God make us all like you?"

Long after I was done reading the essay and correcting its few errors, I sat there staring a hole through it. One by one its implications dawned on me. I was dumbfounded by what it was suggesting and bewildered by its climax in the last line. A passionate prayerful desire welled up within me to find out who this Stephan Pearson really was and to get to know him.

At length I made a weak attempt to say something. "This ought to satisfy Doc Rasmussen." I meant it from a grammatical point of view, but it sounded like I meant more than that. I felt awkward and foolish.

"No problem with the grammar and sentence structure."

That was worse yet. I prayed in my heart for the grace to say something helpful.

"I suppose it would be rather serene to be a little kitten," I offered cautiously. "But I wonder whether a kitten is capable of the joy we can experience as human beings.... Yes, I suppose life must pose fewer problems for a cat than for us, but wouldn't that limit a cat's capacity for achieving something really good?" I was speaking suggestively, more ruminating than preaching.

"Sometimes it's hard to find any good things in life," mumbled Steve. "And when you do find some, all people want to do is take them away from you."

"That's true often enough.... Could that mean that the only reliable source of happiness for us is to enjoy giving good things, including ourselves, to other people, rather than letting them take them from us?"

"Like homework?"

"O sorry. I guess I'm thinking about different things than homework. Homework falls into the category of stuff demanded of us whether we think it's worth the effort or not. No, I'm thinking of life in general. It seems to me that a person's life can't be worth much if you haven't found something bigger than yourself to give it to, right? For me, that means giving it to God. If we get all wrapped up in ourselves, we make a pretty small package. But if we unite our destiny to something much bigger than we are, we grow with it. I'm not sure kittens were created for something as big as this."

Steve looked at me quizzically. The expression on his face told me that I had said more than he was capable of absorbing. An awkward silence ensued. I returned his essay to him, repeating that I thought Doc Rasmussen would be very satisfied with it. He got up and with a word of thanks, he left the room.

VI

Within a week-and-a-half after Steve's night visit, finals were over for another four months. Tensely he endured this artificial period of time. It took a great effort of self-constraint and apathetic resignation for him to subdue the throbbing forces in his soul, but he had had a lot of practice at subduing them during his upbringing. He was like the protagonist in one of those Greek tragedies whose dynamism the Fates have so succeeded in thwarting at every turn that he is finally reduced to impotence and remorseful prostration before them. Steve certainly did not embrace the course of events which necessity thrust upon him, but neither did he fight it. He simply submitted to the unavoidable.

The semester break was spent at Joe Brennan's farm with a number of the fellows. They filled their days with eating, sleeping, drinking, card-playing, and the like. Several times a day Steve yielded to the impulse to strike out on his own across the snowy fields to the woods on the far end of the farm, there to stamp about concealed by the trees and out of earshot of his friends who would have been baffled by the stuff that came out of his mouth.

It was from an entirely unexpected source that trouble suddenly broke in on him two days after the second semester began. He stumbled onto it early one morning well camouflaged in an innocent-looking white envelope in his post office box. Taking the envelope into the Tiger's

Haunt, he sat down at a table in the corner and opened it. It contained a note typewritten by a student secretary:

> "Dr. C. B. Larson respectfully requests the presence of Mr. Stephan Pearson in his office this afternoon between the hours of three and five o'clock. Thank you."

Steve, confused by it, reread the note several times before remarking out loud, "What in the world does he want with me?" For the rest of the day he was plagued by this question until at four-thirty he decided to bite the bullet and get it over with. He trudged haltingly across the campus to Old Main and climbed up to the third story where the Mathematics Department was housed.

The door to Doc Larson's office was ajar, as though he was expecting someone. Through the crack in the door, Steve spied the middle-aged professor bending over a desk and engrossed in a stack of papers. He had almost decided that this was not a good time to disturb him when the gray-haired man sensed his presence and looked up.

"Ah yes, Mr. Pearson. I was expecting you. Come in and sit down," he said with a sharp precision. Running his fingers quickly through his tousled hair, he lost no time in getting down to business.

"Mr. Pearson," he began. "My colleague, Dr. Brockhaus, and I have been surprised and, well, quite impressed by your showing on our final examinations." He was now measuring his words one by one. "As a matter of fact, you would have written a perfect examination for me if in your haste you had not misread the fifth problem on spherical trigonometry and made it much harder for yourself. Still, if I had stated it the way you construed it, your answer would not only have been correct but—and I do not say this lightly—a stroke of genius. And Dr. Brockhaus tells me your only errors in the physics final occurred where solving a problem required memorizing tables of specific gravities and that sort of thing. He was forced to conclude that you had never even opened the textbook."

The professor paused. Steve sat impassive before him. He pressed on to make his point.

"Now, Mr. Pearson, if you had bothered to submit your daily assignments or had shown any interest in your work during the semester, I would have been compelled to give you an A. But, young man, in view of your record, what do you expect me to do?"

It was a question demanding an answer. Steve, of course, had not wasted a moment of thought on it up to this point. The question hung in the air. The silence was getting embarrassing.

"I don't know, sir," Stephan said weakly.

"Well, I don't know either. But that's not actually the reason I asked to see you today. Mr. Pearson, tell me this: What are you really interested in? What stirs your juices?"

Another unanswerable question for someone whose spurts of eloquence were confined to paper and whose honest response was, in any case, unthinkable at the moment. Steve had a feeling that the longer it took for him to find some kind of an answer, the more likely he was to get a drawn-out lecture from Dr. Larson. But nothing came to him. He squirmed nervously in the chair, his eyes glued to the floor. Finally he stated with as much conviction as he could muster, "I like nature and the out-of-doors, and animals, especially horses."

"That's just fine," retorted the educator. "So do I. Everyone needs an avocation. But what are you planning to do with your life? What is your vocation? Let me be frank with you. It would be criminal of you to squander your God-given ability. That's true of everyone, of course. But when we are talking about an extraordinarily rare and priceless treasure such as you have been given, young man, it becomes doubly criminal to squander it. What you have been given is not just yours. It is the common property of all mankind. I don't think I've ever had a student whose natural gifts in mathematics approach yours. You've got to harness those gifts and put them to work in a productive way. It's time for you to start digging in, my boy. Life is too short to throw away on frivolities. Sure enjoy them from time to time, but don't make a career out of them. If it sounds like I'm pleading with you, I am! What will it take for you to discover your true calling in life?"

Dr. Larson had said his piece. The blank expression on Steve's face said it all. He was wasting his breath.

"You may leave now. But at least give some serious thought to what I have just told you. We are here to help and encourage you. I'm telling you point blank, Mr. Pearson, I would be only too grateful for the chance to do that."

Steve got up, thanked him perfunctorily, and walked out of the frustrated professor's office, but not out of his mind.

And indeed it would be true to say that he stalked about in Dr. Larson's mind for the rest of the year. The devoted professor joined hands with Dr. Brockhaus in a relentless effort to arouse in Steve some sense of his "obligations to God, to society, and to himself." The peace of anonymous obscurity was no longer a luxury available to the taciturn young man who, in the classroom, always chose to sit as far away from the action as he could get.

VII

Although it was muddy and messy everywhere, no one was complaining. Large patches of snow still dotted the fields, but each day a revitalized and rejuvenated sun squeezed a little more cold rushing water out of them and dumped it into the low places. And when the low places filled up, new streams were born leading to gullies and ditches, whence the turbid waters raced on into swelling creeks and streams. Doughty flowerlets fragile to behold were breaking through the snow crust and heralding days of profuse color ahead. The grip of frozen death was relaxing and the whole world was warming to life again.

Away out in a field more than a mile from College Hill, a strange figure was sloshing through the sloppy snow, every now and then breaking through thin spots and sinking deep into the mud. He looked ridiculous in his tattered work jacket, his faded pair of Levi's, and his floppy galoshes.

From the moment he had stepped out of the dorm that morning, Steve had known what he was going to do with the day. Giving a shudder at the mere thought of Dr. Brockhaus' 10:20 physics class, he went back inside, slung his .22 over his shoulder, and headed into the nearby woods for a day of squirrel hunting under the streaming sun. How could anybody with real blood in his veins resist the invitation of such a glorious day? So now there he was, trampling over the fields towards the large wooded tract of land on the Anderson farm where they had told him he was always welcome.

And what a day for hunting it was! The trees, still barren of their leaves, offered little cover for the acorn-fattened squirrels. Arriving at the edge of the woods, Steve stopped to look it over. The untouched contour of the forest floor, the untamed tangle of trees, stalks, bushes and vines, and the startling depth of the blue sky all drew his heart free from its usual shroud and set it on edge.

That morning he took many trick shots and left many easy ones, giving the squirrels what he considered more than a fair chance. Often he just sat down on a high spot free of snow or on a fallen log and took in his surroundings. This total change of environment exhilarated him and the freedom he felt here cheered him up. The cloud of gloom that had hung over his soul for so long gradually began to dissipate. Immersed in the goodness of his immediate surroundings, he forgot about all the things that had kept him depressed. He felt so much a part of this special world that for a little while it actually seemed to him that he could possess it forever. At noon he skinned a squirrel, sprinkled salt on it, and roasted it over a crackling fire. It was mouth-watering.

As evening approached, he gathered up the fourteen choice squirrels he had shot and carried them down to the Anderson farmhouse. He knew that they were very fond of squirrel and that ever since their children had grown up and left home, their many chores left them little time for hunting. With a measure of pride and satisfaction, he presented his collection to them. Old Anna beamed from ear to ear.

"Ya, and I vass yust commencin' to get very hongry for dem!"

They wouldn't let Steve leave the farmhouse until he had eaten all the roast squirrel and other fixings he could hold.

He took off down the road back to the college at that time of dusk when the world seems to recede in all directions, leaving the observer alone with his thoughts. The whirr of the wind and the noise of the day's activities cease, and a man must make his own music. It was still early enough in spring for the sun's mellow influence to vanish the moment it dipped below the horizon and for winter to return for the night. But just now the air was still tangy and crisp, the earth warm and soft.

Contentment and indefinable peace reigned in Steve's soul, quickened by the aftertaste of a successful adventure.

Then behind him, in the distance, he heard the soft erratic hammering of an engine. It grew gradually louder as it bore down on him. Looking over his shoulder, he could make out in the twilight one of those motorcycle contraptions American soldiers had discovered in Europe during the Great War. It was wallowing and splashing grotesquely through the slosh and mud. Steve had to laugh out loud. The only other motorcycles he had ever seen were sleek black darts racing along well-graded roadways, leaving a trail of dust in their wake, a far cry from the sight before his eyes now. Mud and water were flying in all directions. The machine was clawing hungrily at what was supposed to be the roadbed. The rear wheel was sliding around in the ruts formed during the heat of the day by the traffic that had passed over it, and the front wheel was responding to the driver's skillful efforts to hold the thing on the road and keep it from bogging down.

It didn't take long for the cycle to overtake Steve. He stepped a respectable distance off to the side, but the cyclist had caught sight of him and pulled to a halt. "Hi there!" he shouted. "Don't you live on the east end of the dorm?"

"Yeah!"

"Well, come on! Climb aboard if a little mud doesn't bother you. It'll soon be dark. I'm heading up there right now."

Nothing could have struck Steve's fancy better. The perfect end to a perfect day!

"You bet! What's a little mud?" His heart swelled up within him as he swung onto the rear extension of the seat. Cramming his .22 between himself and the driver, he grabbed onto the rings on the back of the seat and planted his feet on the footrests.

"Better hang on to me around the guts. It gets a little tricky with all these ruts. By the way, I'm Craig Olafson, from St. Paul."

"Steve Pearson. North Dakota."

"Good to meet you, Steve."

Craig shifted into gear. The engine roared. Steve plastered himself to Craig's back and they were off in a spray of muddy water. On up the road snorted the laboring cycle, careening from side to side. For one of the two riders straddling its back, these wild moments were to epitomize for months to come what life should be all about, an unforgettable dream, a symbol of true freedom, a heady blend of inner peace and life on the edge.

It was all totally beautiful for Steve—the smooth embracing flow of cool air around his head and ears, the reassuring swell and ebb of the engine, the thrill of surmounting all the challenges that came along, the flying mud, the splashing, the sliding around, even the noise. As they roared up the hill and swung through the stone gate into the upper campus, Steve's heart swelled with pride. This was life!

Craig pulled the cycle up behind the dorm. Not a few curtains drew back as they sputtered to a stop. He gunned the engine a couple of times to clear her out and then shut her off. A deafening quiet encased the two of them. Through the ringing in his ears, Steve overheard the affectionate comment, "Well, baby. It's a shame I've got to sell you. A fellow's got to pay his way somehow."

Craig turned to Steve who had hopped off the cycle. "Hope you don't mind a little mud there. At least you're home before dark."

"Not at all. I've been wallowing in it all day."

Now for the first time the two young men were looking at each other face to face. There was a moment of muffled silence and surprise. Then they burst out laughing, and they laughed themselves sick and silly.

"Naw, a little mud never hurt anyone!" Craig proclaimed.

"Maybe you should open a beauty parlor that offers mud packs."

"Do you think they'd approve of my way of applying them?"

They stared at each other for another minute or two. They couldn't stop laughing and smarting off.

At last Craig announced with a touch of urgency in his voice, "Hey! I've got to clean up for my date tonight!"

"Sounds like a legitimate excuse to shed this stuff. Thanks for the ride."

"You bet. Any time. See you later."

They parted company, Steve heading to the east end and Craig to the west end of the dormitory. Steve flew up the stairs to his room on a cloud, trailing clods of mud behind him. That night he joked with Ted, his roommate, in a way Ted had never seen before. But he was genuinely weary now, limp from head to toe. So for the first time in months, after he had taken a hot bath, he fell into bed before ten o'clock and slept like a baby until the alarm went off in the morning.

VIII

When Steve awoke the next morning, the brightness of the day immediately cheered him and reminded him of the previous day. The air was every bit as fragrant and the sun every bit as glorious as on the morning before. Nothing could have been further from his mind than the dingy atmosphere of the classrooms he so despised. As a matter of fact, he was among the first in line for breakfast. There was something about the whole appeal of things that gave him an appetite. A hearty breakfast seemed the order of the day.

Who knows what prevented him from taking off across the countryside once again? When he stepped out of the cafeteria and inhaled the clean air, his spirit soared. In his mind's eye he was back in the woodland where life went on in a harmony of desire and duty because its creatures were all doing by instinct exactly what they wanted to do. Watching a couple of early spring robins peck around in the damp lawn in front of him, he imagined their joy in possessing the bright wide freedom of the whole world. And then he looked around and thought of man.

Why did man alone have to build walls, make unnatural laws, deprive animals of their freedom, and make a slave of himself? It might be understandable if some greater animal had robbed him of his liberty just as he had robbed the horse. But man had made a slave of himself! He had made his own bit and bridle. And if he was slave only to himself, then what's to prevent him from setting himself free?

"Nothing!" Steve exclaimed out loud.

The rest of the morning he found it easy to live out his newfound conviction. It's not that he rebelled against what was going on around him, nor did he openly oppose his teachers. Rather, it was the woodland itself, with its carefree spirit and elemental satisfactions still burning like a fire within him, which held the classroom, the professor, and subject matter at bay and made them simply irrelevant.

At 10:20 he went to his physics class. Right off the mark, Dr. Brockhaus was visibly irritated by Steve's unexcused absence the day before. He opened the class by letting fly a well-aimed dart in Steve's direction which missed its mark because its mark was elsewhere in spirit. In the course of the lecture, Dr. Brockhaus asked Steve two easy questions to which he received no answer because Steve never even heard them. The student next to him had to jab him in the ribs and the question had to be repeated. The second time this happened, the professor took a deep breath and said in a cold tone of voice, "Mr. Pearson, you will remain here after class is dismissed."

This jolted Steve abruptly out of his reveries and back into the classroom. "What a way to die!" he flustered to himself.

And it was as though he had just died. A moment ago he had been living his dream, and now it was gone. In its place there remained the cold propositions he had formulated in his well-ordered mind to make sense of his dream. The scenes and smells that had been dancing around in his head now suddenly were reduced to tableaux, lifeless murals, mounted laboratory slides, information you could put into a dusty textbook. The old shroud dropped on him like a curtain and smothered him in darkness again.

Class was over. Dr. Brockhaus was shuffling some papers around on his desk as the students filed out. Steve approached him slowly. When the other students were gone, the professor looked up and said, "Mr. Pearson, what is the matter with you?"

A long pause ensued.

"I was just beginning to think we were making some progress with you. Am I wrong? Do you have no sense of obligation to those who fought and died to make our world a better place? Doesn't it matter to you at all that a lasting peace is within reach, that democracy is giving the whole human race a chance to move up, that men with your ability are more needed now than ever?"

Silence.

"Young man, I know what you did yesterday," the professor went on more gently. "I know how difficult it can be to concentrate on your studies in the springtime. I was young once too, you know. But you can't just spend your life yielding to your whims. It's fine to indulge them in the right time and place, and in the right amount. But it is just plain foolish to choose them over the effort it takes to stick with things that are much more necessary but not as much fun. You don't want to spend your whole life darting around after butterflies. You may not realize it now, but most of the good things you take for granted on every level, others have worked hard to place at your disposal. It's the duty of every one of us to do the same thing for those who come after us. Remember, there's a big difference between being truly happy and just having fun. Working to add something good to the rich cultural store that supports us all is the only path to happiness."

Steve was seething within. Here was a man so obsessed with "culture" that he failed utterly to see that "culture" was the very wall that penned man in, the very bridle that made him a slave. What did he know about life on the other side of the wall? All that mattered to him was adding to the wall, making it harder for people to escape. The job of the superintelligent is to shore up the wall and pen everybody else in, like cattle in the stockyards, is that it?

Steve was too furious to talk. Dr. Brockhaus turned back to his papers. Stephan Pearson stormed out of the room, his beautiful world in a shambles and his orderly mind deeply offended.

Back in his room he sulked and fumed. So great was his agitation that he finally had to turn to paper and pencil to get it out of his system. He wrote feverishly in a large scrawl all the convictions that had distilled in his mind that morning. He saved the paper and put it in the bottom drawer of his desk. For the next several months it remained there, a symbol of the lucidity of his reasoning based on real experiences and a silent justifier of nearly everything he did.

He had scarcely finished writing and had just started to pace up and down the room when he heard a familiar roar coming from beneath the window. Down below he saw Craig winding up the engine of his motorcycle to go somewhere. A ripple of excitement passed over Steve.

"If only every day could be like yesterday," he heard himself saying out loud. "Then life would be life."

The memory of his thrilling ride through the dusk over the muddy roadway drew a pained smile across his face. It was a crooked smile that incorporated both what life could be and what life actually was.

"If only...," he mused. "If only...."

He settled back in his overstuffed chair and listened to the sound of the cycle fade away in the distance. Shutting his eyes he tried to envision the day before, but succeeded only in evoking bits and pieces of it. Then all at once this bit came to the surface: "Well, baby. It's a shame that I've got to sell you. But a fellow's got to live somehow."

Steve sat up, startled. What was that all about? Did Craig actually say he had to sell the cycle? A shaft of light broke into the gloom and all but drove it away in an instant.

"Why can't I buy it?"

It seemed forever until Craig got back. Was he out there right now selling it to someone else? What if he came back without it? An hour passed. Two hours. And then, through the opened window, he heard the sound he was longing for. He ran down the steps to meet Craig just as he pulled into the parking stall. Trying to appear relaxed, he sauntered over to him as he was shutting off the engine.

"How's she purring today?"

"Smooth as ever. Polished her up this morning. It took a good hour to get all the mud off."

"That's not hard to believe. I'll bet you're not too happy about having to … did I hear you say sell her?"

"O yeah." Disappointment was written all over Craig's face. "I owe the school over a hundred dollars before the end of the semester. That's what I get for buying a motorcycle with my college money, I suppose. But it was worth it even for just half a year."

"Do you have any prospects—for buying it, I mean?"

"Well, there's a couple of fellows in Minneapolis, but I don't know…."

"How much are you asking for it?"

Craig's interest perked up. "Well, I paid over two hundred dollars for it, but I'd be willing to part with it for a hundred and fifty."

"Would you be willing to take fifty now and a hundred within a couple of weeks?" Steve was not even trying to hide his excitement.

And that's how Stephan Pearson acquired the motorcycle that ultimately altered the course of so many lives.

IX

The rest of the school year involved Steve in a constant effort to escape as often as possible from doing things he hated. It helped that it was spring. Whenever the walls seemed to be closing in around him like the jaws of a mammoth vise, he leapt onto his cycle and fled into open spaces in a cloud of dust. Steve made the woods his backyard and the country roads his private pathways, all aimed at reliving his one perfect day.

It was a strange fact that the more he employed his cycle to drain off the pressures swelling within him, the more he succeeded in stirring them up. The only relaxation he could count on came when he was on the move. His rides did succeed in momentarily smothering the fires of frustration within him, but like a shovelful of coal on a bed of smoldering clinkers in a furnace, their long-term effect was to generate more heat and energy than ever. Returning to the dormitory in the evening was a growing disappointment. The pangs of emptiness quickly caught up with him. As long as he was on the run they trailed out behind him like the dust he was raising, but as soon as he stopped they were all over the top of him, right down into the pit of his stomach.

By the time school was at last over until fall, Steve had developed a firm concept of what he wanted to do that summer. He had long since concluded that the only thing preventing him from reliving the carefree happiness of his first spring day in the woodlot was having to come back to face on a daily basis people who were committed to enchaining his will to theirs. The answer? Get as far away from such people as you can. Find a place deep in the northern woods where you can spend the entire summer in harmony with nature in all its simplicity and undemanding routines. Leaving most of his things packed in a trunk in a store room at Christiania, he took his bedroll and a few other essentials and set off for home to get some money and pacify his parents.

Lars was bitterly disappointed when he found out that Steve had no intention of spending the summer on the farm. He had already lost most of his hope that Steve would succeed him, and this dashed the rest of it to pieces. Julia too was heartbroken. But Steve, displaying considerably more initiative than his parents were used to, insisted that having a variety of experiences was part of a good education and that next summer he might well decide to stay home. So Lars gave him enough money to last him through the summer, and then some.

Taut as the string of a bow, the arrow poised, young Stephan Pearson roared off one early morning for parts unknown. Rolled into a compact bundle and lashed to the rear fender of his cycle was everything he thought he would need for the whole summer—a bedroll, a long-barreled revolver, a few clothes, a cooking kit, and some toilet items. Stuffed under the lashing was also a lunch his mother had given him at the very last moment. Inside the lunch was a tear-stained note that read, "Please, darling, if you get lonesome, come home."

Get lonesome? He already was! Had he ever been anything else? Lonesome was normal.

His first idea was just to keep going until he came to the "perfect spot" of his mind's eye: a cool stream in a wilderness far from human interference, flowing lazily through rolling hills and towering trees, in a glen filled with lush vegetation and prolific berry bushes, with animals and signs of animals everywhere. There must be thousands of places like that in northern Minnesota, and one of them would be his, he told himself as he headed in an easterly direction.

As he drove along, he had to force himself to slow down. What was there to hurry? There was no reason here for entertaining the morbid thoughts that he had tried to escape from all year. After all, none of the people he encountered along the way in stores or gas stations was out to force him to do anything. Calm down! Take it easy!

As it happened, Steve spent the rest of June roaming around in northern Minnesota. First he went to Warroad near the south shore of Lake of the Woods. He was tempted to stop right there, but a little voice inside him said, *No, this is not far enough away from the lumber industry and tourists.* So he drove east to Baudette and then south through the wilderness to the Red Lakes, encountering a few startled Indians on horseback along the way. This country pleased him in a way, but it was not exactly the kind of terrain where he could expect to find his "spot." The trees were scrubby and the undergrowth was scraggily, and it was flat as a pancake. He often stopped along the way as he slowly wound down. He knew his "spot" was ahead of him, somewhere. That's all that mattered. It was a happy few days for him.

When he arrived at a point east of the southern shore of Lower Red Lake, he turned east along a small winding road not much more than a fire lane. He followed it through the tiny hamlets of Northome and Effie and into the wilderness beyond. And there one morning as he was chugging along the narrowest road he had thus far encountered, the motor of his cycle gave a couple of coughs and a sputter and stopped dead. He tried in vain to restart it. Nothing obvious appeared wrong to him. So he decided to walk the cycle in a leisurely way on to the next town, Togo, where he would get a mechanic to look at it. He had just passed Deer Lake. That meant, according to the map, that he was over halfway to Togo from Effie.

He had not foreseen how much sheer sweat it would take to lug the bulky machine down the lane. Each little rise, not even noticeable when the cycle was running, seemed like a mountain now. As the day progressed, he was assaulted by thirst, dust, and weariness and discouragement. His canteen was not large enough to last between streams. The cycle sunk heavily into the loose sand at many points along the way. His arms and legs ached from the nonstop effort. The sun beat down on him pitilessly. When evening came, he was still a long way from Togo, tired, hungry, dirty, and without much food. Despite himself, he was starting to feel irritable and disenchanted. The sun had already sunk beneath the horizon when at last he came to a much needed brook where he soaked his legs in the cool water and drank deeply. Then he loaded his revolver and walked up the brook in search of his supper.

Nothing presented itself. Chipmunks scurried around. A hawk circled high overhead. Nothing edible was to be seen—no grouse, no rabbit, no squirrel, not even a raccoon. So in the last faint glow of daylight, he followed thc stream back to the cycle and made supper of a raw carrot and a few crackers. Then he stretched out in his bedroll for the night, pretty disgruntled.

The next evening, hungry and bone-weary, he finally nursed the dead cycle into Togo. But Togo was nothing more than the place where his trail crossed an equally obscure trail! Marking the spot almost ceremonially was a small log cabin with a stable behind it. Thank God there was a light burning in the cabin. Steve took heart and rapped on the door. An old geezer with a full white beard and white hair covering his shoulders answered the door and listened in rapt disbelief as Steve explained what had happened.

"Shonny," he said toothlessly. "I ain't heerd of nothin' sho dadbing shtoopid ash that in all m' born daysh. Ya mean ya trushted that ther contraption to bring ya through thish here wild land without nothin' happ'nin? Well, I shpect I gotta put cha up fer the night. I sure dunno wha cher gonna do with that ther contraption."

The two of them scarcely exchanged another word all evening. Steve got the distinct impression that his host thought he was crazier than a hoot owl. He served him up a warm dose of some kind of stew in a badly cracked bowl which tasted pretty good, finished off with a cup of something like coffee. The old duffer's eyes never left him until they turned in for the night. It was all pretty awkward, but also comical in its own way. Steve stretched out on the dirt floor in his bedroll, aware that he had intruded uninvited on the old man's privacy, but also that he really needed him and was genuinely grateful to him.

In the morning he gave the old fellow his revolver and some money as security, rented an ancient buckboard from him drawn by a haggard draft horse and loaded his motorcycle onto it, tying it down as best he could. The old man told him his best bet would be to head for Virginia which he could find by traveling east to the first intersection and then turning south "fer a good peesh." It proved to be a long and tedious haul.

It took four full days to reach Virginia. Steve lived on a sack full of baking powder biscuits supplied by his host. The old horse rarely exceeded one mile per hour. Once in Virginia he was another week-and-a-half getting the parts shipped up from Duluth for the mechanic to install, a week of pure misery for him. Virginia represented Steve's worst nightmare: the destruction of wilderness to appease human greed in the name of progress. Everyone there had pinned their destiny on the ugly scar of the open-pit mine. The only virtue in the whole place was their carefree disregard for the Prohibition Amendment. Steve appreciated that.

It was a full two-and-a-half weeks before Steve pulled up in front of the cabin in Togo with the horse and buckboard. He had been tempted to sell the old nag and the wagon and move on, but the thought of forfeiting his revolver and much of his money was enough to induce him to return. The old man had just about written off the old plug and the wagon as losses and chalked up the revolver and the money as gains when Steve pulled up in front of the cabin. After staying the night with the old man and thanking him sincerely for doing what he could, Steve fired up the motorcycle first thing in the morning and set out.

Steve had only one thought when he set out—to put that wretched country behind him as fast as he could. It had been a long and clumsy three weeks that had contributed nothing to his goal for the summer. He would look elsewhere to find his "spot," and it wouldn't be in Minnesota.

X

The next couple of days carried him blindly out of Minnesota and into Wisconsin via Duluth and Superior. Very little else registered with him but the roar of the engine and the blur of the trees as they whizzed past him. Exploring the byways no longer appealed to him as it had before his misadventure, and the main roads seemed to lead him from one "Virginia" to another, each belching smoke into the air and tearing up the terrain to make someone rich. It was getting urgent for him now: he just had to get away from all that. He whipped through the north-western tip of Wisconsin in a day, drawn on by his very ignorance of what lay ahead. Another day and he was halfway across Upper Michigan: Ishpeming, Negaunee, Marquette, and beyond. The wide clear expanses of Lake Superior were now lying before him, but even then he did not stop to have a look.

Around him now towered his rolling verdant hills. Beside him tumbled his crystal brooks. On both sides of him were his berry patches laden with fruit. But none of it registered with him.

It was late afternoon and he was halfway between Marquette and Munising when clouds began to gather over the lake and move in towards land. A storm front formed above the water, drawing a dark curtain across the horizon as it sped towards the shore. Waves were already sending spray over the road and the still air hung in breathless expectation of what was coming. Then it hit. A vicious gale caught Steve broadside. He gripped the handlebars fiercely to keep the cycle on course. He lowered his head into the driving rain and hurtled on through the sudden darkness. The lake heaved and waves battered the rocky shoreline right next to the road. Steve was drenched. Then came the lightning and thunder. Locals call it "the Lake effect." It can come out of nowhere and happen at almost any time.

Steve didn't realize that he was speeding along behind the storm front and thus lodging himself within the most torrential section of the downpour. His first glimpse of Munising was veiled by gray sheets of rain, denying him a view of one of the most serenely beautiful towns in the North. He was oblivious to its sturdy quaint homes and saw nothing of the crescent of majestic hills that abruptly rise at the end of its short streets or of the sea of azure glass that normally stretches out deep and pure before it. He roared right through the heart of Munising in the belly of the storm.

Just east of town the highway swung inland and the shoreline receded northward. In less than an hour twilight and darkness closed in, trapping the young cyclist in the even blacker delirium of the unabated storm. His sense of direction abandoned him. All he really cared about was pressing ahead, staying on the move. He was stone-faced and stiff-armed. He plowed on through the night until an erratic flash of lightning happened to reveal a narrow trail that disappeared into the dark forest north of the road. Benumbed and soaked, on impulse he swung off onto the trail and plied his way along it, dodging ruts and gullies as best he could. Guided by blind determination alone, he fought his way ever higher into the blackness. At a fork in the road he took the narrower one. Up and over a great hill and down the other side he went, then up and over a smaller one, bouncing through the trees and over the rocks in the trail. Then suddenly as he was descending a steep slope a little too fast, he ran head-on into a tree fallen across the trail and flew off the cycle into a bed of drenched leaves. And there he lay. The shock of the fall had fortunately shut off the engine and now only the sound of the storm could be heard, moaning in the treetops.

Presently it stopped raining and the thunder grew more distant. The moon came out and, beaming down onto the forest floor, it glittered in each standing drop of water and lit up the figure of a young man in a shiny leather motorcycle jacket lying fast asleep on the ground.

XI

The gray hues of the morning came while the thick fog was rolling and billowing upward. By the time the sun had been over the hills for an hour, only light wisps of steamy mist were seeping out of the matted forest floor and swaying to and fro with the breathing air. Little woodland creatures were scurrying about rectifying the damages and reaping the benefits which the storm had left in its wake. One busy chipmunk, her cheeks budging with food and her head bent low, was scampering back to her nest as fast as she could go along one of her normal pathways home when she collided nose-first into a fleshy mass sprawled out in the ground. The collision alarmed her more than it did the mass. She looked up, jumped back, and scurried off on a wide detour.

The other party to the collision, namely Stephan Pearson (or more accurately his left cheek) stirred sluggishly. He seemed about to roll over when one of his eyes opened a slit. Then the other one opened. Both of them blinked. Then they both closed again. Stephan Pearson muddily conjectured that he must still be dreaming. Then he opened both of them wide and sat up.

He was halfway down the slope of a large hill, sitting in deep soft turf and surrounded by a whole world of emerald and azure. Before him spread a broad basin that was almost completely enclosed in verdant hills covered with lofty pines, maples, and oaks and carpeted with lush undergrowth. Directly in front of him to the north was a V-shaped opening in the wall of encircling hills through which he could see the placid blue waters of Lake Superior stretching out into a horizonless distance. Springing from somewhere on the hillside behind him was a rushing brook that tumbled to the bottom of the basin and cascaded down towards the lake through the V. He could hear deer romping around in the creek bed beneath him, and at the tips of his fingers was a patch of blueberry bushes burdened with plump, succulent berries. Steve sat there taking it all in for many minutes and then ventured in wonderment: *I spend a month looking for this spot, and then I stumble onto it in the dark. It's perfect. Why would you ever want to leave it?*

For many days he acted as if he never would. The first day, after checking the motorcycle for damage (everything on it was working fine) and for leaks in the upended jerry can (it was still full of gas), he moved what little property he had down the hill about a hundred feet to a flatter piece of ground near the creek. Right off the bat he decided that all his hunting would be done outside the hollow. Nothing should be allowed to disturb its peace and harmony. He could fish in the brook and eat the fresh berries that were all around him: blueberries, raspberries, a few remaining strawberries, blackberries, thimbleberries, gooseberries, currants—they were all there. Firewood was no problem, nor was drinking water. Everything was virtually at his fingertips, with no irrelevant obligations to distract him. Joyfully he set about the task of making this place his home.

The first few days he did some exploring. He followed the stream back up the hill beyond the hollow, discovering to his great satisfaction that small game abounded, especially squirrels, rabbits, and grouse. He didn't even have to hunt for them: they came to him if he sat still for a few minutes in the grass under a tree. He had only to wet his fish hook in a quiet pool to catch a gourmet meal of rainbow trout. He had no need to garner bergamot leaves for tea since patches of the plant were everywhere to be found, along with wood sorrel and wintergreen to munch on.

He also busied himself by constructing a small lean-to out of saplings where he could roll out his bedroll and store his few belongings in the two small weatherproof cases he had brought with him. He built a makeshift latrine nearby adjacent to a large patch of milkweed, nature's toilet paper. The pond just below the campsite served as his bathtub. He dug a garbage pit several hundred feet to the west where wild creatures could clean up his leftovers without confronting him. Within a week this place felt more like home to him than any place he had ever lived in before.

On the evening of his seventh day in the hollow, he stretched out on his soft bed of white-pine needles as night began to fall and watched the stars pop out one by one. The flames playing in the embers in the fire pit set the shadows of the trees dancing eerily in the stillness. A hawk was spiraling round and round overhead. Was he looking for supper or was he just having fun? At this hour of the evening, probably just having fun. Whip-poor-wills were calling to one another from the far edges of the hollow, their strident age-old song attesting to the timelessness of the present moment in this timeless place. Lying there, Steve was drawn into an all-pervading sense of the rightness of things. The troubles and dissensions that people create for themselves were not to be found here. They seem so big when you're in the middle of them and so tiny when you're not. A warm breeze blew lightly in his face and fanned the glowing coals of the fire.

"This is life," he whispered.

And, lo, he was asleep.

XII

One morning a few days later, Steve took a notion to hike up the creek as far as he could go, but he had not gone very far when he was attracted to the unusually jagged face of a ridge off to his right. Not being at all pressed to follow his original plan, he decided instead to clamber up to the sharp crest of the ridge and have a look around. In a matter of minutes he was commanding a spectacular view of a sweeping panorama for many miles in all directions. It was most reassuring for him to see nothing but heavily forested hills as far as the eye could see in three directions and nothing but water as far as it could scan to the north. And no sign anywhere of those robbers of the peace and freedom of such marvelous Worlds Apart as this—the human race!

Then Steve studied the terrain immediately around him. What had seemed like a sharp peak from the bottom was in fact the lopped-off end of a ridge sloping gently downward on the other side of the face. The shoulder of the ridge itself ran down to an obscure point in the distance like a well-tended shady lawn. It was bordered by giant spreading hardwoods interspersed with pines and cedars, a perfect arbored lane. The sight of it so fascinated Steve that he spent the rest of the day roaming all the way down the ridge and back, exploring its spur shoulders and admiring its grace. A bear was feasting in a raspberry thicket. Deer were almost everywhere. He even found a large patch of late-season strawberries in perfect condition. As the sun began to lean toward the horizon, he made his way back up to the summit, shot a fat young squirrel, and roasted it over a fire.

He was about to begin feasting on it when he heard a crashing noise coming straight towards him through the thick undergrowth along the ribs of the ridge. He froze. Unfaltering it broke its way through twigs and stalks. It couldn't have been a bear or a deer. The light breeze was taking the smoke from his fire in the direction of the noise. This was not an animal stealthily stalking him. Now it was very close. He reached for his revolver, got up, and swung around to face the beast head-on.

A great silver husky came crashing out of the underbrush onto the open ridge top and amiably loped up to Steve, wagging its tail vigorously. Steve's mouth dropped open and his revolver dropped loosely around his trigger finger. At first he was at a loss what to say. But when the big soft eyes of the beautiful dog met his own, he exclaimed, "Well, hello there! So you want to join me for supper, eh? This is your lucky day. I have more here than I can ever eat."

That evening and for the rest of the summer, Steve shared every meal he cooked with his new friend whom he called King. Sometimes it was King himself who brought them their meal, usually a grouse, but once it was a huge wild turkey. Steve marveled that he was just as willing to share his catch with him as Steve was to share his catch with King. King especially loved trout.

Steve and King became bosom buddies. The great dog accompanied him wherever he went, sleeping near him at night and roaming with him during the day. He was entirely silver and white except for a patch of black under his powerful neck. He had the keen intelligent look of a wolf, but there was nothing cruel or cold about his eyes. He seemed to talk through them. And through them Steve rediscovered his tongue. Or truer yet, Steve discovered for the first time that he had one.

Every day Steve did only what he was inclined to do after the manner, so he told himself, of all the other creatures in the hollow. He hunted or fished when he was hungry. He hiked and climbed when he was curious. He spent hours observing his neighbors—playful catbirds, voracious pileated woodpeckers, grazing deer, flitting warblers of many kinds, and those always endearing chickadees. If he was hot he bathed in his bathtub, nibbled by curious trout if he sat still. If he had something to say, King always listened with a most knowing look in his eyes. But King didn't mind at all if hours went by with nothing said. And hours did go by in which Steve was perfectly content to sit and absorb. King was the perfect companion—ready for action at a moment's notice but content to lie low when Steve was deep in thought.

Truth to tell, Steve was starting to love King.

How tiny is the worm on entering the apple, almost too tiny to be of concern. Its work is scarcely noticeable as it bores down into the crevice around the stem. Even when it is inside there seems little cause for worry: the apple hangs plump and firm, a beauty to the eye. But in the core the worm is silently gnawing out an ever-widening cavity around itself. Every day the worm grows bigger and hungrier. And while the apple on the outside preserves its symmetry and grace, on the inside it grows hollow and putrid.

With comparable insidiousness a tiny worm now bored its way into Steve's soul and began to burrow down into its core. It was the old worm of restlessness. As long as he had been occupied with building his campsite, the worm had had no opportunity to attack him. He had been too busy making things just right for his summer of idleness! With all his energies enthusiastically enlisted in fulfilling his longed-for goal, there was nothing left over for the worm to feed on. But once his goal was achieved and the time had come to sit back and let life come to him, the worm of restlessness attacked. It was barely noticeable at first, but one morning early in his third week in the hollow, as the grays of dawn were slowly spreading, something happened that changed everything.

Steve, sound asleep, was jolted to life by an outburst of howling and barking from King. The poor dog was stamping and leaping around in a mad frenzy. Steve jumped up. And then he saw it.

The whole campsite was alive and creeping. Scores of embattled ants were crawling all over King. Steve's first impulse was to get them off the dog. He called him to one side, off the battleground, and brushed the ants off King's face and ears. Then he picked and pulled them out of his thick hair until not one was left. The bewildered dog charged up the hill to watch from a safe distance. In the nick of time Steve grabbed his bedroll and duffle bag, carried them up for King to stand guard over, and rushed back down to the campsite. In the few moments this took, he returned to find the ants swarming all over his cooking utensils. And in the few seconds it took for him to rescue these, the horde engulfed the lean-to. Having salvaged all he could, Steve backed off to watch the carnage.

The arena of the most active conflict was ten or fifteen feet wide, he guessed, and maybe twice as long. At the head of the moving column were the retreating ranks of the colony on the defensive. They were much larger than their attackers, likely wood ants that had colonized a large rotting snag. They were formed in a tight phalanx around one enormous ant measuring at least an inch in length, their queen.

Mildly surprised at first that the larger more fierce-looking ants were in retreat, in surveying the whole battlefield he soon discovered why. They were vastly outnumbered by the smaller variety whose strategy seemed to be most frustrating to their larger cousins. He never saw them engage the giants head-on or singly, but from each side and in groups of two or three. The furious wood ants would snap in one direction only to be nipped from the other. The earth ants, as he supposed they were, seemed to know that to fight alone was suicide. And as there were enough of them to win by attrition, they contented themselves with wearing down the enemy, crippling him bit by bit. The unfortunate earth ant that got in the path of a pair of the huge jaws of a wood ant was instantly severed in two.

Spellbound, Steve became curious about what the path of battle looked like behind the advancing ranks. He had no trouble tracing the wreckage down the hill, over a log across the creek, along the opposite bank, right up to the catastrophic event that had occasioned it all. In the wind the night before, a mammoth snag filled with wood ants had apparently snapped off its base and landed directly across the top of a very large mound of earth ants. The two colonies doubtless had blamed each other for their respective disasters and gone on attack. The ensuing battle must have been apocalyptic. Decapitated bodies of earth ants littered the ground all over the site, overwhelmed at first. But then as both colonies vacated their homes to join the call to arms, Steve surmised, the tide began to turn. Just beyond the mound the carcasses of wood ants were liberally sprinkled among the earth ants, but they were not decapitated. They were stripped of their limbs, often still alive as indicated by their antennae waving in the air. If he brushed a blade a grass between their jaws, they snapped them together and hung on. Walking back to the lean-to, he noted that the proportion of the dead from each colony was about the same as the proportion of those that were still alive and fighting. This did not bode well for the future of either colony, he mused. And all over a misunderstanding....

All day he kept track of the battle. At some points it appeared that the tide was turning the favor of one of the combatants, but then it would seem to swing in favor of the other one. Steve learned that the wood ants were retreating not because they were being outfought in the long run but because that was the only way they could hope to engage the pressing earth ants one on one. They were like boxers with one killer punch who were constantly backing off from the annoying flurries of their opponents, until one of them got careless and exposed himself to the fatal blow. In the process, of course, they were often simply overwhelmed. The phalanx around their queen had thus far proved a complete success. No earth ant had yet seriously attempted to break through that powerful line of jaws. No side of Her Majesty was exposed, no limb vulnerable. But as the conflict wore on, it was becoming evident that in the end only the phalanx would be left to defend their queen. Over time numbers were proving the decisive factor in the battle surrounding the phalanx.

By two o'clock in the afternoon only the phalanx of the wood ants remained, and their queen. Steve had followed the battlefield all the way up the hill to the place where the trail leading into the hollow petered out. "So they're going to make their last stand on the roadbed, are they?"

Steve muttered out loud. "They don't know and they don't care that I'm watching them, or that I could put an end to it all with a few twists of my heel. This is too weird…."

Before long the earth ants had disabled every wood ant except those forming the phalanx around the queen. The remnant of their once countless host, still an impressive number, gathered for a mass attack on the phalanx. Steve counted about eighty wood ants against three or four hundred earth ants, all of whom lost no time in charging the living wall of defenders from all sides as a body. The first row in the phalanx cut down the foremost chargers as fast as they came. Behind them were more, and still more, cascading forward over the bodies of their comrades. Attacked from all sides, there was no direction in which the phalanx could retreat any more. The second row of the phalanx swung into action as earth ants scrambled over the first thrashing row. Soon the third row was in the fray. A small tight circle of wood ants fell out of their rank in the phalanx and closed in around the queen. Bedlam raged on every side. Even with their losses, the earth ants still vastly outnumbered their larger opponents.

Bodies of earth ants flew in every direction. But as the conflict shifted around on the roadbed, limbless or mostly limbless wood ants were left helpless in its wake. The inner circle around the queen and her few bodyguards was now the only portion of the phalanx left intact. They gave it all they had in Her Majesty's defense. The ranks of the inner circle were thinning. The earth ants took immediate advantage of this and closed in on the queen herself. Her tiny bodyguard defended her valiantly. No earth ant had touched her yet, and for a short while it looked as if she would be safe.

It didn't take very long, however, before the bodyguards had all broken rank and were engaged in individual combat and the queen was forced to defend herself. Breathless, Steve watch the end approach. He had no idea who would win. Pieces and segments lay twitching everywhere. Active battle was raging only right around the queen. Five wood ants against eleven earth ants! Three wood ants against seven earth ants! One partially crippled wood ant and the queen against three earth ants.

But these odds were unfair. The queen and her valiant knight made quick work of two of the earth ants, but this permitted the third one to slip around behind them. In one fell slash the gallant but doomed earth ant crippled one of the queen's legs and turned and snapped off the only remaining leg on the right side of the wood ant. The queen whirled around and easily decapitated the earth ant.

Et le combat cessa faute de combattants.

"They call that a Pyrrhic victory, King," Steve mumbled, shaking his head as he watched the queen hobble from one helpless wood ant to the next in search of a surviving escort. "Now what will she do?"

They watched as she dragged herself into the undergrowth beside the roadbed, presumably to wait in comfort for death to overtake her. Leaving her to her solitary reflections under the leaves, Steve trudged heavily down the hill.

"Should I have killed her? Would it have been an act of mercy? It was all so senseless. So much death and destruction for nothing."

That night after supper around the campfire, King came over to Steve where he was sitting with his back up against a tree watching the moon rise over the hills. The great dog lay down beside him, put his head in the young man's lap, and looked up into his eyes.

"I'd give anything for a pencil and paper," Steve said out loud. King whined in sympathy. They sat in silence for a long time. Every passing minute gnawed away at a cavity forming deep in the core of Steve's soul. He should do something about what he had just witnessed, so it wouldn't all go for naught, all that pointless suffering and death. It had taken up his entire day. There had to be a reason he'd watched it all.... O really?... Really!

He gazed off into the lowering darkness. A light moved along the horizon out on the lake. The whip-poor-wills were bouncing their calls off the valley walls again. The owls and the hawk and the gurgling stream and the glittering stars were all there, right where they were supposed to be. There was the breath of air on the glowing coals, a breath that ran its cooling hand across Steve's brow and then disappeared into the evening stillness. But tonight, for some reason, it didn't fill him. He moved over and lay down flat on the ground gazing upward. King lay his head on Steve's bosom. Steve nudged it gently into the hollow spot he felt down in the pit of his stomach somewhere. This was a new feeling for him. It didn't feel good, but it didn't exactly feel bad either. It was sort of heavy and hollow at the same time, and the more beautiful the evening became in its silence and in its sounds, the heavier and the hollower it got.

That night Steve had a dream. King was in the dream and so were the ants, and the forest, and the deep evening. But there was something else in that dream, something that went straight for the hollowness in his heart and filled it as it had never been filled before: a woman was in his dream too. And not just any woman.

XIII

Vaguely she shimmered in and out of his dream's eye, an elusive, haunting apparition of tantalizing beauty. No, she was not a Greek goddess or a Nordic nymph whom to behold stirred up only erotic sensations. Hers was rather the softer beauty of a compassionate heart, of a pure heart overflowing with love and an intense concern for others—including Steve, the ants, and the whole wide world. She hovered at a little distance from him, never looking him straight in the eye but yet encompassing him somehow within her aura. Her golden shoulder-length hair, her full brown eyes, and her slender form slightly stooped as in sorrow, all of her, yes, all of her seemed to be shimmering and wavering behind a thin veil of tears, tears he sensed were there because she was seeing into his heart and feeling the pathos which the ant war had plunged him into. But it was clear that her tears were not just for him. They were also for the ants and for the world, tears of love and, in a most mysterious way—as Steve later struggled to describe it—tears of unrequited faithfulness, leaving him to wonder if he was in fact the faithless one over whom she wept. Hers seemed like a love as faithful as King's, but infinitely deeper. Even in the dream his heart broke because he knew that from her point of view he was closer to the ants and the world than he was to her, detached from this heavenly Maiden and yet tenderly touched by her. There she stood before him, fading in and out, alone but illuminating everything, motionlessly beckoning, a solitary figure of irresistible charm in search of a love to respond to her own. Everything within Steve screamed "Yes!" in the dream. But in the dream he was paralyzed. He could not move. The gulf between her and him remained.

Her gentle melancholy sorrow grew more painful by the moment, especially as Steve could not get to her and the ants would not cease fighting. This pushed him over the boundary of dreamland and he awoke to find himself on the point of sobbing. So he let himself go and sobbed sweet tears into his bedroll. He was too moved even to ask himself what it all meant, but there was a wondrous satisfaction in it somehow, an infilling.

He couldn't get the image of his Phantom Maiden out of his head. Her slender trembling beauty and especially her tears bathed him in thoughts and feelings entirely new to him. This time when he drifted off to sleep it was into her arms and a warm and guiltless love.

Steve spent the entire next day walking under the halo of his nocturnal visitor. She muddled, soothed and disturbed, and excited him all at the same time, giving rise to a level and quality of restlessness he had never known before. He didn't know what to do about her, and he had no idea what to do about the ants. But he had to do something! She had wept over them! And, in the end, so had he, thanks to her.

A dismal and awesome heaviness hung over him because of those ants. He knew that what he had witnessed was important or she would not have been weeping over it. He also knew that there was nothing he could do in the hollow to bring any good out of it. And so, it seemed to him, she would continue to be sad, all on account of him. Sometimes in those first days after the dream all of this struck him as irrational, but most of the time it didn't. Most of the time, whether he was walking noiselessly along woodland trails in the full glory of the daylight or lying motionless under the canopy of stars at night, the image of two highly organized nations that had lived side by side in harmony for years annihilating each other under his very eyes over a misunderstanding kept reappearing in his mind's eye. It was as though she wouldn't let him forget it.

That was because he could not forget her! Over and over again when he should have been absorbed in the glories and harmonies of his immediate surroundings, he found himself drifting off into another dimension in search of his nocturnal Maiden. Her silhouette appeared everywhere, it seemed. Once he imagined he was actually seeing her behind a clump of chokecherries. It startled him—it was so realistic. But these vivid moments disappeared like soap bubbles in the air. Try as he might he could not escape from her, and most of the time he didn't try very hard. He had fallen in love. It was that simple.

These two strange new impulses (the one to tell, the other to love) grew within him unbidden as the days went by. When they were in control of him, they became pure torture for him. Of course, given a bit of distance from them, his rational mind saw the folly of the whole business of letting a dream run your life. It was all insane nonsense. The price of trying to make something rational of that crazy dream would be to deny everything he had discovered to be true the previous year, and so help him, that would never happen! Why should he care whether anyone heard about the ants or not? He had no duty to the world he had intentionally left behind, a world that was just like the ants in so many ways. It was as useless to try to get a message across to the world as it would have been to try to get the ants to stop killing each other. People would think he was crazy for trying.

And what reason could there possibly be in the real world for getting tangled up with a woman, any kind of actual woman? They lure you in and then they chain you down. You'd always be at cross-purposes with each other under a veneer of social conformity. It'd be the end of your freedom.

Let's get this straight! It's plain stupid to think you have to tell something to the world that it can't hear anyway and to dream endlessly about someone somewhere out there who can't possibly exist. So settle down and recover the joy you had in this hallowed place until you got stupid. All the rest is delusion.

The tensions that this tug-of-war produced in him, he recalled years later, became unbearable. All the reasoning in the world did nothing to subdue his two new obsessions. He got furious whenever he found himself impervious to the many delights all around him just because his imagination had run wild and taken him somewhere else. The forest and its treasures hadn't changed. He had changed. He had no one to blame but himself.

For the remainder of Steve's time in the hollow, King played the humble role of making his Spectre Maiden believable. The dog's selfless love and unquestioning devotion went to work on Steve. If a dog could be like that, surely she could too in real life. Even when Steve was all twisted up in his own thoughts and self-recrimination, the great silver husky would never make demands on him or complain about being neglected. On the contrary, his long-suffering and constancy found their way deep into Steve's heart, reshaping it ever so slowly into a believer in a new sort of love, a love he could begin to respond to now in kind if he ever found it in a real person.

But you're such a frog, he told himself in his clearer moments. *Even if she is out there somewhere, why would she pay any attention to you?*

XIV

Solitude and an inescapable idea are the perfect formula for creating an obsession, and nothing destroys peace faster than an obsession. Steve's new yearnings became irrepressible. He acquiesced so readily to fantasies about the beautiful Maiden now living within him almost all the time that his ability to disown her almost evaporated. The joy of his evenings was spending time with her because it was even easier in the evening to let his heart smother his mind than it was during the day. These evening meetings of theirs satisfied something inside him that he hadn't known was there until his night of dreams. But they left him in turmoil afterwards. His heart and his mind were no longer flowing in united opposition to a senseless world. Rather, they were clashing with each other now, each declaring the other insane for the opposite reason. His heart told his mind: *Look where you are! How are you ever going to find her here?* His mind told his heart: *Look where you are! You've got everything you need right here.*

On the first day of September 1920, the cacophonous firing of a motorcycle engine rent the pristine stillness of the early morning air in a wooded basin some twenty miles east and north of Munising, Michigan. A young man was chugging up the hill on an overburdened cycle, while a large silver husky was anxiously leaping up and down beside him. The young man was staring down at the passing ground directly in front of the cycle. The leaves and the grass were swimming behind a blurred film of tears. When he reached the crest of the hill, he hesitantly stopped and looked around into the hollow from which he had come. The bright and dark hues of the valley danced together in the tears that distorted his vision. Ardently he pressed the magnificent dog to his side and held him there for dear life with trembling hands. In a soft voice he whispered into his ear, "It's not your fault, King. I'm so sorry. It's all in me." Then he released the dog, straightened up, and shouted across the valley at the top of his lungs, "It's all in me!"

It was all in him as he wound through the forest to the highway, all the confusion and despair. What was driving him out of the heaven of his dreams into the world of his nightmares? Why was he leaving his mind back there to pursue his heart out here? What was forcing him to do that?

King followed him out to the highway and raced along behind him, falling farther and farther back until he collapsed into the ditch, overcome by exhaustion.

XV

The first days of autumn brought to the campus of Christiania College a wave of rejuvenation and cheer. Its dormer windows, both literal and figurative, were thrown open and an embracing gale of fresh wind flushed out its musty old corners. In the cafeteria, around the registration desks, in fact just about anywhere you looked there were long lines or little clusters of self-conscious blushing freshman women floating about seemingly unattached. And wherever this was the case, it was a safe bet that there would be loose groups of upperclassmen, at first backed off surveying the new crop as a whole, then cautiously moving in for a closer look at the most attractive flowers among them.

An air of expectation, bustling activity in preparation for the days ahead, animated every nook and cranny on campus. As yet the trees and the grass were green, but crisp fall breezes were even now stirring playfully through them, chasing away the stifling idleness left behind by the hot days of summer. It was the time of year when old people begin to wonder whether they will be able to "weather out another one" and young people can hardly wait for ice to form on the rinks and snow to blanket the toboggan runs. Scholars are anticipating the delights of leaning back in an easy chair before an open hearth and savoring a good briar pipe and the likes of Soren Kierkegaard, while the sound of the winter wind whistles harmlessly through the eaves. And since the young people on campus greatly outnumbered the elderly and the scholarly, anticipation of happy days ahead was written all over their faces and gave bounce to their step.

It was the time of year when the attention required of you to look after the endless details of registration, settling into your dorm room, and meeting your roommate and a lot of other totally new people kept you excited and on your toes.

Almost everyone was in an upbeat mood.

Even Stephen Pearson was being drawn back to Christiania, but it was by the same forces that had driven him out of the hollow back into the world. He had spent three days at home before setting off for St. Mark on his motorcycle. The long hours on the road were giving his mind and his imagination plenty of opportunity to take off in almost any direction and to pursue it to the very end.

Some of his time on the road his thoughts were darkened by his rational disenchantment with himself and his hopes. What had gone wrong? Surely not his basic logic! He was just as convinced as ever that choosing a life of meaningless and disagreeable toil was pure idiocy. He also knew that almost everyone expected you to do exactly that, and that if you did cave in to them and do it their way, you were doomed to a life of slavery and perpetual discontent. The secret was never let yourself get trapped in a situation that prevented you from doing what you wanted to do. If you got caught in that trap, your life would turn into one endless grind of drudgery. That's exactly what it had become for his parents.

Perhaps, he mused, this explained why the summer had gone sour on him! Let us assume that on the first of June he really wanted to be in just the right "spot" in the wilderness. What guarantee was there that he would want the same thing on the first of August? Give him one good reason why he should feel obligated to be tied to June's dream in August? A person had to reckon with the likelihood of a change in desires! It was wrong to assume that his desire to live in the wilderness, no matter how strong it may have been, was a permanent desire. He wasn't built like the motorcycle which burned only one kind of fuel. His engine burned many kinds of fuel, today this, tomorrow that. A person had to do what appealed to him <u>when</u> it appealed to him and not feel obliged to stick with it when something else appealed to him more. You had to move on! That was the secret. There was a lot of truth to Tom Mahler's belief, which he had probably picked up in Europe, that "the most important things in life are just a matter of taste."

"All right, then!" he concluded dozens of time as he rolled along the highway, salvaging what he could from his experiences of the summer. "I will NEVER AGAIN chain my tomorrow to today's desires."

Thus hardened and resolved he raced along the gravel highways, vexed with himself for having failed to recognize this obvious principle from the start, but equally determined to hang on to it from now on. This meant that he had to view with great suspicion that inner force that had drawn him out of the hollow and was continuing to draw him on now completely independent of his will. But a traveler has many unguarded moments in which things can sneak up on you unnoticed until it's too late. The steady drone of his engine would gradually wear down his hard-won resolve, to be replaced effortlessly time and again by those warm and increasingly familiar sensations of "her." Sometimes King and sometimes the warring ants also appeared out of nowhere in his mind's eye, all mixed up with bits and fragments of his freshly articulated principle for a happy life. All of this tumbled around in his mind like garments in a revolving clothes dryer, contradictory thoughts and images endlessly colliding with one another and going nowhere. And hovering over him, and even beside him, the mysterious presence of his Spectre Maiden, intangible but more real than all of the rest of it put together.

When Steve pulled up at Christiania just in time to register for his classes and receive his room assignment, a shudder of excitement surprised him. He had no idea what to expect, but something was going to happen. He could feel it in his bones no matter what his head told him.

Three days later he was sitting at a corner table in the cafeteria with his three friends—Tom, Lute, and Ted. They had acted glad to see him again. Just now the three of them were surveying the new "crop" of freshman women in the supper line as it inched its way through the door.

"Hey Ted!" Lute Odegaard nudged his big friend. "Get a load of that doll just coming through the door. Remind you of somebody?"

"Yeah. Geraldine Simpson from Sioux City," he replied in his deep deliberate tone of voice. "Boy, oh boy!"

"Yup. That's who I was thinking of. I'll bet she's got legs like Geraldine's too."

"You would know?"

"She don't remind me of anyone or anything I ever saw before," injected Tom. "And I've seen a lot. That gal's in a class by herself."

"Look at that figure, would you!" marveled Lute. "All the clothes in the world can't hide what she's got."

The flaxen-haired beauty in question now looked straight at their table. Ted turned red, Tom politely tipped his invisible hat, and Lute waved at her and mouthed the words, "Hi, honey!" She flustered an instant, smiled back at him, and pretended to be distracted by something behind her.

Lute turned around and with a broad grin said, "Well, Steve? Don't tell me that one didn't do something to you!"

"Sure did. Made me spill my soup when you waved at her," he replied dryly, dabbing his lap with a napkin.

In fact, Steve had not been paying much attention to what was going on around him. As usual, he had been lost in thought.

The line at the door inched on, providing a continuous source of material for conversation for the three more vocal friends. For this one it was the face, for that one it was the figure, for the next one perhaps the smile, and on and on. Lute was getting so worked up that he declared his serious intention to date them all during the year so as to "savor each one's special charms."

Sure! reacted Steve bitterly within himself. *And someday you'll latch on to one of them who will latch on to you, and it will be downhill all the way from there.*

The talk was beginning to disgust him.

"Hey, Steve! There's a cute little number just your size!" Lute blurted out, nodding at a six-foot-plus Amazon ducking in the doorway.

"Looks to me like she has enough upfront for a half a dozen ordinary girls," Ted observed with his usual candor.

"Yeah, Steve'd get lost just trying to……."

Suddenly Steve's ears began to ring. Instantly the crude comments of his friends faded away. Every muscle in his body seized up. The cause of this was the young woman who was just seating herself at the table directly in front of him. His face flushed beet red. He couldn't take his eyes off her. For him there was suddenly no one else in the room but her.

"O my God!" he gasped.

XVI

Poor Steve!

There he sat, stone deaf to Lute's coarse humor and right back in the heart of his night of dreams. Someone had played a dreadful trick on him, someone who knew his heart inside out and had transformed his Spectre Maiden into flesh and blood not six feet in front of him! All the floodlights in the world were trained on him as he sat there paralyzed, unable to move or speak or even think.

There was no doubt about it. This was the woman of his dreams. The resemblance was uncanny. Her salient features that had struck him so indelibly that night were all there before his eyes. Every one of them! She was sitting across from him, not exactly with her back towards him, but off to the right a little so that he could see a hint of the profile of her face. The last thing he wanted was for the guys to divine his secret, so he shifted his eyes to his soup bowl and stared at it blankly, stealing furtive glances up at her without moving his head.

Her golden hair fell to just above her slender shoulders in soft flowing waves, in a word, altogether right, just like what he could see of her face. Everything about her struck him as wondrously pure and mild. Her skin was radiant and bronzed from the summer sun, contrasting joyously with her hair. Her blouse was the solid blue of a deep woodland pond in early evening, and her full skirt was a clean white except for a bit of embroidery work around the hem. Her movements were flowing and graceful. When she spoke, the gentle sound of her voice melted his heart. Once he caught her looking to the left and smiling at a table companion. It was a warm and inviting smile. It sent shivers up and down Steve's spine.

Tom was the one who picked up on what was happening to Steve. He had seen that first look of incredulous astonishment on Steve's face and had followed it to its object at the next table. Curious, he studied her with his usual unconcealed frankness. Yes, she was quite a dish, all right. It was understandable that someone like Steve might give her a second look. *She's nothing that Lute or Ted would go in for,* he told himself, *except for that face and hair and that nutmeg complexion. They want those top-heavy models. This one probably has very dainty breasts that turn up on the ends a little like her nose. Those two licentious louts have to have plenty of beef to be happy.... Man, that face of hers is gorgeous, though. And what a smile! She seems so innocent, and so, so beautiful....*

He turned and winked at Steve who was too absorbed in his own world to wink back.

The fellows were in no hurry to get out of the dining hall that evening, for obvious reasons. It was a good thing. Steve was virtually chained to his chair. After some twenty minutes the girls at the opposite table shifted around a little and rose to leave. Steve watched her get up and lift her tray. His heart skipped a beat. She was a good two or three inches shorter than Steve's five-foot-nine-inch frame, yet she truly was a long and lovely angel.

"Come on, Cecilia," he heard someone urge.

"Sure. I'm coming," she replied, low and eager.

An angel, yes! marveled Steve to himself. "*My* angel," he said out loud but very softly, his eyes watering up as he watched her gracefully move away.

It would be truthful to say that from this moment on, Steve's former dream world became his new reality, and his former reality simply faded away into irrelevance.

XVII

So it was "Cecilia," was it! The perfect name for an angel.

That evening Steve forgot all about his daily motorcycle ride. A walk was the thing instead, he decided. Just what he needed to settle the queasy feeling in his stomach. So he picked up an impressive-looking volume from the top of his desk and strolled as nonchalantly as possible out of the room. Ted looked on with mild surprise. He wasn't used to seeing Steve move with such urbanity.

Well, where should he go on his walk? He could walk across the campus past the women's dorm to Old Main. Then he could walk down the hill, circle around through the woods, come up again on the trail behind the women's dorm, and walk past it to the library. If he was still in the mood for a walk, he might just as well stroll from there over to the chapel well beyond the women's dorm and back to the music hall on the other side of the women's dorm. And, of course, there was that nice old bench to sit on halfway between the music hall and the women's dorm in the event he needed a little rest by then. After that he could saunter back to his room past the women's dorm and the science hall. Yes, that sounded like a good workable plan—lots of good healthy exercise!

"It would be good for me to do this every evening after supper," he told himself halfway through the first lap of his little trek.

As it turned out, he never did get as far as Old Main, for just as he was approaching the women's dorm, the door opened and out came

Cecilia with an armload of music. Steve stopped in his tracks. Be danged if his fool shoelace hadn't come undone! He bent over and fumbled around with it for a few moments. By the time he had rectified the situation, Miss Cecilia was slowly making her way along the arbored lane not ten paces in front of him.

Her head was bowed slightly in thought. Steve could tell that her mind was working on something, perhaps one of the pieces of music she was carrying. She was in no hurry. Gracefully making her way along the path to the music hall, with the setting sun playing in her golden hair, she did look very much like a celestial visitor to earth. I myself had often seen her in just such a disarming pose and truly wondered if she was of earth or of heaven.

It was only a couple of hundred yards from the women's dormitory to the music hall. In less than a minute she turned to the right onto the short walk that doubled back a bit and led to the entrance of the great fortresslike edifice. This gave Steve a very good look at her face. Suddenly he was caught short of breath. A lump formed in his throat. Luckily, he wasn't far from the old bench where he could sit down until he got his wind back.

The cacophony of sounds pouring out of the windows of the dozens of practice rooms in the music hall that evening flowed together for Steve into a glorious symphony.

Leaning back into the bench, Steve reasoned, *I think I'll just read this book for a few minutes here before it gets too dark.*

He opened the book and gazed off into the distance. Little matter that what he was holding was a dictionary. Littler matter still that it was upside down!

XVIII

Truly Cecilia Endsrud was both a lyric poem and a full symphony. Every little thing she did possessed a soft lyrical quality to it, and yet the total effect of it all was as impelling as a grand symphony. The folks in her hometown, Meadowville, Minnesota, all knew her because she was the pastor's daughter, and they adored her. She was one of those special people who are always welcome and never out of place no matter where they go, but whose arrival always seems to come as a delightful surprise. Such were her unaffected ways that even if she had walked unannounced into the saloon on the edge of town, I am sure its patrons would have been curious about what had brought her there but glad to see her. Folks had got used to seeing her almost anywhere. She seemed to have a sixth sense when you had a special need, and she would unobtrusively slip in and out of your life, leaving something behind just for you.

Of course she was markedly different from her classmates in high school. But it was not a difference that created a cleavage between her and them. I am told that a full score of them considered her their best friend. She had a way of striking a responsive chord in almost everyone. Especially kids who were unsure of themselves, or who were relegated to the fringe for whatever reason, gravitated to her because in her eyes they were somebody, and they knew it. Yet, paradoxically, everyone knew she could spend hours out in the fields and the woods walking all alone and talking softly to herself, and no one who knew her found it the least bit odd. Spotting her in the distance strolling along slowly, her hands crossed behind her back, they might remark, "Oh, it's just Cecilia," and all would be explained.

"Just Cecilia." Anyone else would have set the town gossips buzzing time and again. But it was "just Cecilia": Cecilia, whose organ preludes these past five years had brought most people to church early so they wouldn't miss them, not as showpieces but as the ideal medium for preparing the heart for worship; Cecilia, who might be expected to carry flowers in the same hour to the ailing mayor in his sprawling mansion and to frail Mrs. Wilson recovering in her hovel from bearing their eleventh child; Cecilia, who always had a glow about her whether she was with people or off by herself. There was a connection, folks seemed to know intuitively, between the warmth she shared so spontaneously when she was with people and the warmth she absorbed from God in her frequent times alone with Him, often out under the open sky. No one really begrudged her that time alone. Naturally, a few considered her "uppity," but they had to keep their opinion to themselves. If they expressed it, every one jumped to her defense. "It wouldn't do any of us any harm to do a little more thinking and praying ourselves," they might say.

Her father and mother had named her Cecilia after the patron saint of music. Both of them possessed an enthusiastic love of good music. Both, in fact, were responsive to harmony and grace wherever they found them. But in Cecilia this family characteristic took on a different form. She had little tendency either toward her mother's musical ecstasies or toward her father's joyous raptures. In her, music was more like a steady current flowing through her soul, absorbing into itself all the joy and beauty, the grief and sorrow she encountered along life's way. That is why I refer to her as both a lyric poem and a grand symphony, tenderly responsive to the smallest trifle and weaving all the trifles together into a whole. A person experienced something inescapably musical just by being near her.

She had always been a thoughtful and sensitive child. But when she was fourteen she had an experience that, among other things, made her even more thoughtful and aware of the people around her. She had been given a small New Testament for her Confirmation but had accorded it scant use over the next several months. Then one day she said to herself, "I think I'll just sit down and read the whole Gospel of Luke because it's the one that begins with the beautiful Christmas story. It's true that I get to hear a passage from one of the Gospels every Sunday in church, but wouldn't it be grand to find out how they all fit together?"

So she took her New Testament out into the meadow with her on that warm summer day, made herself comfortable on the grass under an old oak tree, and opened it to Luke. She told me later that she had to stop often in sheer awe of what she was reading, and to let it sink in. When she was done, she couldn't move for maybe half an hour. Then she rolled over onto her knees, happy tears running down her cheeks, and prayed, "Jesus, take all of me. I'm yours."

I am quite certain that from that moment until the day she died, she never knew what it was like not to belong to Jesus.

At this point I am sorely tempted to digress for a page or two and comment on the metamorphosis of my cousin from a playful little girl in pigtails to a young woman you couldn't take your eyes off. We saw each other only once a year due to the distance between the town in northwestern Wisconsin where I grew up and Meadowville in central Minnesota. The only realistic way of making that trip in those days was by train, requiring two transfers. But we made that pilgrimage every year solely for the joy of spending a week with the Endsruds. Uncle Irv was my mother's brother, the pride and joy of her childhood. And Aunt Ellie was one of the most gracious women I have ever known. The year she nearly died giving birth to Cecilia, my mother took off immediately to be with her, leaving me in the care of my grandmother for several weeks. That created a bond that was renewed every summer about the time of the second haying. Dad would turn his general store over to Mimi, his assistant, and we would all set off for Meadowville to help Uncle Irv on the parish farm which he worked.

As it happened, we could not make our annual trip during the summer of 1916 because Dad had fallen off a ladder and broken himself up pretty badly. But the following summer he had recovered enough to resume our yearly visits.

It is strange how you tend to assume time has stood still when you haven't seen friends for a while. I myself had grown at least a foot since our last visit, but I still pictured Cecilia as the scrawny kid I had known two years before. Was I in for a shock!

It took me two full days before I could start treating that queenly woman as my cousin again. Gone were the days when, in youthful innocence, we "played house" or rolled around in the grass, tussling and tickling each other to the point of exhaustion. Neither of us had a sibling, so we made the most of our week together each year.

And that part didn't change once we'd got used to the new reality that she was a girl and I was a boy. We'd never noticed that before. So although it took more than two minutes of hide-and-seek to reconnect this time, in the long evening walks we took to our old haunts all over the countryside we bonded again, and Jesus was a big part of it for both of us.

I grew to cherish certain things that I noticed about her now for the first time. She had just a hint of the hereditary idiosyncrasies that marked her as an Endsrud. Her nose turned up ever so slightly, her cheekbones were just slightly higher than usual, her chin had a very slight slope inward. Somehow these little touches set off her delicate features from anyone else's and gave her overall loveliness a unique quality. She was the only person in our whole extended family with silky blond hair, but she shared with all of us the ability to tan well in the sun. And since she loved the sunny meadows and being out-of-doors, her face and arms were always a healthy hazelnut brown. To look at her made you love life!

To look at her! Those sparkling brown eyes made especially for that angel face! When she was happy, joy danced in them. When she was sad, they were deep wells. They were the unshuttered windows of her soul. She did not know what it meant to be secretive. She had never had any reason to be. She had always been loved just as she was.

This is the Cecilia I remember so well—sitting beside me on the barnyard fence talking together quietly, but often also in silence; ambling along beside the woods across the meadow, her head lowered in meditation; fondling a tiny lamb or feeding a nervous chipmunk; trouncing on the hay in the overloaded wagon on the way back to the barn; picking up a dirty little kid on a street corner and planting a kiss on his forehead; gliding nimble fingers lightly over the piano keys and singing softly; or just smiling at me through those bright brown eyes of hers for some reason now long forgotten. I have to admit that more than once, I regretted the fact that we were first cousins.

She was now a freshman at Christiania. The congregation had raised a hundred and fifty dollars so she could go and "study up on music." She must be sure to come back at Christmas time and play the organ for the Christmas pageant and let them listen to the new preludes she was going to learn at Christiania.

Of course she would be back at Christmas time, she assured them. She loved her God, her family, her friends, and her music.

Of course she'd be back.

XIX

The next three weeks were by all odds the strangest weeks Steve had experienced in his twenty years of life. His motives, impulses, and feelings were tumbling all over each other. He did the most unusual things! Nothing he said really fit into the context of what was going on around him. And nothing he said came out crisp and clear. As he walked along every evening on his chosen path, the ground receded from beneath his feet.

It is amazing how many things a fellow can find out about a girl in the space of three weeks without ever asking anyone. For example, he can stumble over the fact that on Mondays, Wednesdays, and Fridays she eats lunch at 11:30, whereas on Tuesdays, Thursdays and Saturdays she does not eat until 12:15, meaning that she must have an 11:20 class on those days. He can even discover that on Mondays and Fridays, she passes him on the staircase between the second and the third storeys of Old Main, provided he is "detained" after math class for a moment or two; that during chapel she nearly always sits on the right-hand side of the nave near the front except on Wednesdays when she arrives late and quietly slips into the balcony to avoid disturbing anyone; that every evening between 7:00 and 7:30 she walks from the women's dorm to the music hall, often detouring briefly into the woods near the door; that she then proceeds up to the fifth floor where the practice pipe organs are located and for an hour sends a torrent of music out through one of the windows up there; and that she begins almost every day by getting up at the crack of dawn and striking out across the fields behind the dorm on a hike that can take her as far as Mill Creek and back before breakfast. The singular thing about these data is that they all came to him, apparently out of nowhere, with no particular effort on his part.

In this way each day was furnished with its own high points. When one of them occasionally failed to happen (for example, not passing her on the staircase when he should have), his heart sank. Was she sick? Had she dropped that class? Was she detained by that handsome fellow she sat next to in class? Well, as long as she was happy.... Sometimes a lump formed in his throat at the thought. Once he actually said, "Oh phooey!" loud enough to attract a puzzled look from the people around him.

Phooey it indeed! That's what he told himself times without number when he thought about how hopeless it was to think that a fellow like him could ever attract the attention of a woman like her. He tried to console himself with the thought that women were just trouble. He had seen what a woman could do to a man. He'd been warned that the first sign of love is the last sign of wisdom. You had to really be on your guard. He remembered all the nagging his father had to take from his mother. There wasn't a woman in the world who would shut up when you were tired of her and spruce up when you wanted her. They just tied a man down for the rest of his life. Who wanted that?

But none of this applied to his Cecilia! How defenseless this left his heart! She was for him the crown of creation, the fusion of all that is good and alluring in womanhood with that extra something from Above which his Spectre Maiden had possessed. He couldn't think about her without being swamped by that warm ache in the midsection and that feeling of helplessness all over his body so familiar to anyone in love.

This, of course, led him back to the one huge incongruous fact that glared at him: he was worried about warding off a creature as lovely as Cecilia!?! What was there about his mousy face to warrant even a glance from her? If she knew he was worried about her dominating him, she'd just laugh and think he was crazy. Poor Cecilia! She had no idea she was causing him so much anxiety. Her only guilt was her innocence; her only blight was her grace.

But for the moment a few very simple joys sufficed to make his days bright, brighter than they'd ever been before. Just to sit facing her from halfway across the cafeteria was all it took to warm his heart. Just knowing she was there, that's all. With the studied regularity of an old man set in his ways, he sought out the hardwood bench near the music hall every evening at 7:00, there to "study" in the sharp crispness of the autumnal air, just to be there when she walked past. Of course, he took great pains "for her sake" to avoid drawing any attention to himself. But surely it did no harm to imagine that she was really sitting there next to him on the bench. They might even be holding hands! It must be wondrous to feel her beside you, to have her hand voluntarily enclosed in yours.......

"Get over it, man," a little voice inside him chided. "It's never going to happen. Who do you think you are?"

Day by day he was winding himself up tighter and tighter, growing ever more addicted to his bitter-sweet narcotic. He knew very well that this was all going to go nowhere, but he was powerless to stop it. Why would you ever want to put a stop to the one thing that is injecting into your life something altogether new to you, and totally wondrous—a compelling reason to get up in the morning?

XX

About this time something happened that jolted Steve out of his routine and hurled him back into the throes of chaos.

"What do you know about that blond chick, Cecilia Endsrud?" Tom asked casually as he swept up the four discards in a game of pinochle. The four men were sitting around a table in the dormitory lounge at the end of the hall.

"Never heard of her," Lute responded quickly, sizing up his chances of making three-seventy this hand.

"Me neither," drawled Ted. "How come?"

"Oh, just curious. How 'bout you, partner?" he inquired of Steve across the table.

"Seems nice," Steve managed to choke out, recovering his breath.

"'Nice,' the man says! Would you listen to him? He calls her 'nice'!"

"Well, what do you call her?" demanded Lute.

"Une merveille!" Tom lingered on each syllable, enunciating even the mute e's.

"All right, Johnny boy. So you were in France. Now say that in plain English."

"A miracle! A wonder!" Tom translated unperturbed.

"Well then, how come I haven't seen her?"

"You're too busy eyeing the broads to notice her. This one's got class."

"Now that you're an old man of twenty-four who's played the field and is ready to settle down and domesticate, you're looking for class, eh?"

"No. Now listen, seriously. She's about five foot six or seven. She's got wavy golden hair like you've never seen before and smooth tan skin that makes you drool. She's got soft brown eyes that make you wilt, pretty crescent lips, and a neat slender body with just the right amount of curves. That's my idea of a real woman!"

"Listen to the poet!" cried Lute.

"Yeah," chimed in Ted, closing his eyes to get a better picture of this woman.

"And he," exclaimed Tom pointing at Steve, "he calls her 'nice'!"

"Well, what did you expect from Pearson? Some sort of dreamy rhapsody like yours?" Lute demanded.

"Of course not. But 'nice' doesn't cut it. Not in any way."

"So what do you plan to do about her, a big handsome brute like you?" Ted teased.

"That's just what I've been wondering. This place is dying a slow death. And there she is, and here I am. It doesn't make sense not to do something about that. Another thing—I'll bet a fellow would have to be kind of careful. They say she's a preacher's daughter."

"So that's the one you mean, is it?" The light suddenly dawned on Lute. "I'll admit she's got a real pretty face, but that's about all she's got."

"Get your mind out of the gutter for a change, would you?" Tom was visibly annoyed. "You don't have to be a cow to be a woman."

"Well, I didn't know you went in for that type, that's all. Another thing you'd have to watch out for"—Lute lowered his voice—"she's Mork's cousin. Haven't you noticed them hanging out together a lot?"

"Now don't you say nothing against Paul," Tom declared defiantly. "He checks over my French assignments, you know. I'll bet he'd be glad to see me dating his cousin."

"All right! All right! No offense intended, big fellow. But a word to the wise...," he concluded guardedly.

"Don't worry about me.... Well, Steve buddy, looks like we got them that time. They'll never make three-seventy now."

Nobody had noticed that Steve's face had gone feverish and that he was struggling to control the tremors in his hands.

"Yeah. Looks like we got 'em," Steve concurred.

Five minutes later all the fellows except Steve had sauntered back to their rooms. It was 11:00 p.m. Steve slouched down low in the davenport. His eyes were vacant, glazed, staring a hole through the wall in front of him.

All at once he jumped to his feet and tore down the stairs. There was a loud roar in the parking lot. A lone motorcycle wheeled out the driveway and ripped off down the hill. The ear-shattering racket hung in the breathless air for many minutes before fading into the stillness of the night.

XXI

It was 8:00 the following Wednesday evening. A half-moon lay low on the western horizon in the receding aura of the long-set sun. Dry leaves were scraping lifelessly along the sidewalks and lanes and were piling up in the eddies of trees, gutters, and even the old oak bench on which Stephan Pearson was nervously fidgeting.

Where on earth could she be? he asked himself anxiously. *She's looked so unbearably pretty these last few days. Makes you fall all apart on the inside.*

This led him into a series of vague and inconclusive musings about his weird life these past weeks. But as the darkness deepened around him, it also deepened within him. This was the one time each day when he could count on seeing her. She never failed to emerge from the women's dorm, stroll past him to the music hall, and mount the stairs to her organ perch high above him. It hadn't taken him long to distinguish the sound of her organ from all the other sounds coming from the building. He had grown to depend on this evening routine for his inner sustenance, and now that for the first time it hadn't happened, he felt more ravenous than if he had skipped a meal.

Where are you? he moaned inwardly.

As time wore on and she didn't appear, his worry over her also became disgust with himself. Self-doubt began tormenting him again.

This is so stupid, he chided. *Whether she comes or doesn't come, just look at yourself. You're behaving like a fool. Get up and get out of here!*

With that he grabbed his book and fled the bench. Soon, however, he had slowed to a normal walk. He was aching all over and about as crestfallen as he could get. Maybe there was something wrong with her? Maybe she was sick?... No, not likely. He had seen her at supper. But then, he had noticed that she'd eaten only a few mouthfuls before getting up and taking her tray to the rack. She had seemed a bit flustered at that.... Those music students were an odd lot. Perhaps there was a special concert or recital in Minneapolis. He knew the train left shortly after supper. Yes, that was probably it! He felt relieved to hit upon such a logical explanation for her absence.

I hope she's having a good time up there, he said to himself with resignation.

At that moment he stepped out from under the trees into a flood of light coming from the auditorium. *What's this all about?* he wondered, recalling as quickly the announcement in chapel that morning that the Drama Department was staging an English production of Schiller's *Cabale und Liebe* that evening.

Sounds like a real thriller, Steve told himself.

Students were now pouring in toward the auditorium from every direction. But the main flow was on the broad sidewalk from the women's dorm that ran roughly parallel to the little used trail Steve was on. He was glad to be out of the traffic. Near the entrance of the auditorium, however, the trail and the sidewalk converged. Steve was tempted to turn off the trail and walk around the auditorium through the trees to avoid the crowd, but something prevented him. So he continued straight ahead towards the crowd.

He was nearly at the intersection of his trail with the sidewalk when his blood froze. Coming down the walk and destined to converge with him were Tom Mahler and Cecilia Endsrud! The handsome young ex-soldier was walking straight and tall with a broad grin on his face. And at his side, her arm through his arm, radiant and glowing as usual, was Steve's angel.

Steve's legs turned to lead weights. He wanted to run away, but his feet kept plodding forward on their collision course. Robotlike he lurched forward. Closer and closer and closer.

"Evening, buddy!" Tom sang out across the well-lit ten feet that separated them. "Heading for the play, too? Cecilia here tells me it's a real tearjerker. Poisoned lemonade and everything."

"No, no. Just out for a walk," Steve squeezed out.

Cecilia was looking at Steve full in his mournful face. A gentle smile played on her lips but it looked to him as though there was a question mark in her soft eyes. There was nothing condescending about it, just the merest hint that Steve's sorrow was touching her now as it had touched his Spectre Maiden on that night in his dream. It was almost a look of understanding. It was too much for Steve. It lasted for the briefest instant, and then they were past him.

He dropped his head, turned away, and stepped off into the obscurity of the trees. *There's your quota for life*, he moaned. *She's just* too *much for you.*

He couldn't go back to the dorm. Instead he wandered down into the town and out into the countryside. He paced around in the blackness of the now moonless night. Finally, wearied in body and soul, he returned to the dormitory by another route.

The play lasted rather late into the evening. The women had been issued special passes at the door so that they could get back into the dorm "not later than 11:30 p.m. on pain of forfeiting similar privileges in the future." By 11:45 half the fellows in the men's dorm were congregated in their respective lounges discussing, surprisingly enough, the relative merits both of their dates and of the play. Apparently, those men who really cared about their dates had been really shaken up by Schiller's tearful tale, while most of the girls had sobbed quietly into their handkerchiefs for the better part of the last two acts.

Lute and Ted had decided to forego the play and stay in the dorm.

When Steve came absently trudging up the staircase, they were both sitting in the lounge listening intently to Tom's play-by-play account of his date. Steve slipped past them into his room without greeting them, but he left his door ajar.

"And she sat there next to me, her shoulders quivering and the tears streaming down her cheeks just as unashamed as can be. I was too embarrassed to look at her, but I sure wanted to. I did get a chance to steal a look at her once. She looked at me and I could see she had taken the whole thing into her heart. It was awfully sad, all right.... You can't imagine how gosh awful pretty some girls are when they have tears in their eyes. I had the strongest urge right there to take her in my arms and tell her that everything would be all right."

"That's what I'd have done," boasted Lute.

"Not with her you wouldn't have! This little chick has got a built-in something-or-other that draws you in and then holds you at arm's length even though you want to grab her and squeeze the living daylights out of her."

"Oh, I see. One of the magic kind, eh? Well, you held her hand at least, didn't you?"

"Well, ah, as a matter of fact, you fellows just don't get it. She's a good girl, a really good girl. But you just wait until Christmas. By then I'll have her doing cartwheels around my little finger!" Tom swelled up with confidence.

"Listen to him talk!"

"Don't be too hard on him, Lute. A great big handsome brute like him will just bowl that innocent little farm girl over in no time flat." Ted enjoyed poking fun at Tom whose muscular frame and classical Nordic features would have impressed even Miss America.

"Now don't you be too sure about that. He's not dealing with one of those man-hungry French broads that were running around on the loose after the war. A Minnesota preacher's daughter is nothing like them."

"Lute, would you shut up. It might just be that I wouldn't want to treat Cecilia like one of them."

"Yeah. And it might just be that you couldn't."

"You just listen to me now!" Tom's wrath was aroused. "It isn't a matter of 'can or can't.' Some things are a matter of 'want to or not'!"

"Well, I'll bet you anything that you can't take her by Christmas." Lute was needling Tom along solely for the satisfaction of seeing his friend's fair face turn scarlet. Nor was he disappointed. He knew exactly which of the ex-soldier's buttons to push.

"Listen here! I'll do whatever I decide to do! If I want to, I will. If I don't, nobody can make me."

"All right. Fair enough," Lute said coldly. "If you're still going with her two weeks from now, guaranteed that you'll want to. And if you are, I'll bet you can't take her by January second. See, I'll even throw New Year's Eve into the bargain. If you quit going with her before the two weeks are up, the bet's off."

"Well, screw you both. I suppose I'll have to show you." At midnight there must have been something about the voluptuous prospects of this bet that seemed especially attractive to Tom who had had a generous foretaste of such things in France. "What do you want to make of it?"

"Two to one," said Lute, feigning the cool detachment of a businessman. You win, I pay you fifty dollars. You lose, you pay me twenty-five."

"It's a deal, by golly!"

"Shake."

"Shake."

"Well, I'll be the son of a three-legged centipede," drawled Ted, marveling at the rapidity of the transaction.

That's all Steve heard. He wanted to slam the door shut so hard that the dorm would rock. Instead he eased it shut until it clicked. He could not stand still. He paced up and down the room, bumping into his chair and kicking the bunk. He was seeing red. It was all he could handle to hear them kicking his precious Cecilia around like a piece of garbage. Sure! That's how those guys always talked. They were always needling each other, and bets had come and gone and been forgotten about more times than you could name. But this was about Cecilia and they sounded dead serious! Couldn't you just see a handsome chunk of a man like Tom following gullible, trusting Cecilia around day and night like an innocent little puppy dog? Those "guileless" features on that sculpted face of his that could look so wounded, so hurt, so maltreated? It would be so easy for her to fall for that. She was so trusting she'd have to be tottering on the brink of disaster before she'd realize she was in danger. It was unthinkable! They were treating his angel as if she were their plaything! Her! Their plaything! And she'd be the last one to catch on.

Steve flung himself down on his bed in a heavy sweat.

But what could a little runt like him do against the bold honest face of a hunk like Tom Mahler? Not a thing came to mind. Steve felt utterly helpless. It is not too hard for us to understand that in his state of mind, the most obvious solution to his dilemma seemed the most remote to him.

He lay there fuming long after Ted had come to bed and long after the lights had been turned off. Everything was tumbling around in his head—his miserable lot, the whole institution of womanhood, the unspeakable gall of anyone conniving to harm his Cecilia, and the overwhelming need he felt to plant himself somehow smack dab in front of her to defend her at any cost. The only thought that didn't occur to him that night was the startling truth that until a few weeks ago, he would have been utterly incapable of entertaining any such need to defend anybody.

XXII

Two nights later, Stephan Pearson was again sitting on the old bench beneath the nearly naked maples between the music hall and the women's dormitory. About half an hour earlier Cecilia Endsrud had passed by and, recognizing him from the night of the play, she had greeted him in a cheery voice. This had taken him by surprise. He had managed to return her greeting without betraying any special concern for her. It's not easy to speak in a normal tone of voice to someone you hold so tenderly in your heart, especially when you know full well that she is according you only a passing thought. *I am sharing the light she beams on everybody*, Steve had told himself ruefully. *But the light I am beaming on her is the only light I have ever beamed on anyone.*

Right now the lilting strains of Bach's "Fantasia and Fugue in C Minor" were floating lightly out of the center window on the fifth story, the only window in the building that was still open in spite of the briskness of the evening air. Steve did not know the name of what she was playing, but it sure performed wonders in his heart! It made him feel so close to her in spirit, and so furious with Tom.

This led him to think about yesterday at supper. Tom had walked up to where Cecilia was sitting and had politely asked whether the seat next to her was reserved for someone. She had blushed a little and just as politely motioned for him to be seated. The rest of the meal for Steve was like watching a tragedy unfold. From two tables away he had observed

Tom executing and directing a most successful conversation, guiding it into what appeared to be a bashful repartee in which he was mildly unctuous and persistent and she was innocent and coy, or so it seemed. The oil of experience fairly oozed from Tom's lips as he bathed Cecilia in discreet compliments backed up by his impressive chivalry. And, clever lad that he was, he had carried her tray for her back to the dirty dishes rack near the kitchen door, pretty well obliging her to wait for and walk out with him. When Steve had left a few minutes later, they were still talking together under the arbor in front of the cafeteria.

The same thing had been reenacted this very night, but this time Tom had joined her in the cafeteria line even before they were seated.

And as if that weren't enough, there was what had happened at chapel this morning. Steve had mounted the steps of the balcony to his usual unobtrusive perch only to look down and see Tom Mahler escorting Cecilia down the aisle! During the service Steve had watched with growing repulsion Tom's newfound devotion. His piety reeked with ulterior motives. Steve could almost smell the stench of Tom's effort to impress Cecilia with his virtuousness. It was all Steve could do to stay to the end of the service.

But the final crushing weight that was bearing down on Steve was Tom's daily reports to his friends about his encounters with Cecilia. He came close to admitting straight out that everything revolved around the age-old challenge of virtue. He seemed fixated on the glories of the conquest of chastity. Tom was a wily chap, to be sure. As he put it to the guys, for him Cecilia had it all—a thrilling challenge for the moment and a supremely satisfying companion for life. From the way the ex-soldier was talking, Steve had got the idea that his strategy in the short term was to overwhelm Cecilia's resistance by arousing her passions to a fever pitch, and in the long term to spend the rest of his life savoring her exquisite beauty at his leisure. Steve had listened to all this from inside his room, door ajar, where he sat seething.

But now, the wondrous sounds coming through the window high above him drew Steve back into the present moment. They were being produced by Cecilia's nimble fingers and agile feet, all of it issuing from her beautiful spirit. He was so glad she always opened her window. *She must love fresh air*, he mused. *That way her music can fly as freely as her soul!*

"O my angel! If only you knew what danger you are in!" cried out his inner voice.

At that moment he looked around and saw me approaching him down the lane. A possibility must have suggested itself to him the moment he saw me.

"Evening, Paul! Good evening!" he exclaimed with uncharacteristic energy. "Why don't you sit down here for a minute? It's a lovely evening, isn't it?"

"Sure is," I returned, taking my place next to him. "I was just bringing this piece of sheet music up to my cousin, but I don't imagine she'll be going anywhere for a while."

"No. Not for another half hour," Steve assured me.

That little phrase, spoken off guard, told me everything.

"I, ah…," he began, stammering for words. His lips parted several times and clamped shut. I was beginning to get the picture.

To break the silence, I said, "That's her playing up there right now."

"Yes, I know…," Steve shot back.

This was getting very interesting. I could see that Steve desperately wanted to tell me something but was much too nervous to spit it out. So I suggested we listen to the same "Fantasia and Fugue in C Minor" that she was just beginning to play over again.

"She wants to play this work at Christmas for the people back home in Meadowville. She loves to play Bach, and this is her favorite of all."

"I can see why," Steve replied dreamily. He seemed a little more relaxed. "There's places in it you can't hear without tears coming to your eyes," he offered.

So we sat and listened.

To this day when I hear this work well played, a little scenario comes into my head. The lilting and lyrical opening section of the Fantasia suggests to me two young lovers in a small rowboat out on a calm sea one moonlit night. Their world is magically flooded by the cool beams of the low-lying moon whose mystical purity blends with the swelling passions of their love and sanctifies it. Very gradually and ineluctably the heart-pain of their love builds up and up to an almost unbearable climax before subsiding, leaving the two of them trembling expectantly in each other's arms.

All of sudden, with the outbreak of the Fugue, a vicious squall descends on them. The sea turns into a monster. The moon and the stars disappear. The little rowboat is pitched and tossed around wildly by the breakers. The lovers cling to one another in terror, the sea-spray whipping their faces. For a brief moment, everything calms back down and the moon peeks through the racing clouds. But the squall has saved its worst furies to unleash upon the lovers now. The breakers tower and crash around them again. Four celestial trumpet blasts signal the approaching end as a giant sea bears the quivering craft and its two passengers aloft and dashes them to bits on the rocks below. Then in a powerful restatement of the theme, the squall proclaims its bloody victory. The whole thing is an emotional wringer for me. I never did ask my cousin what it meant to her. But I know it meant something because she played it with such passion and feeling.

Well, Steve and I sat on the bench speechless. Whatever it meant to him, I could see he was deeply moved. And ready to talk.

"Paul," he began confidently. "You're a reasonable fellow. And besides, you're Cecilia's cousin and she's partly your responsibility. She'd have good reason to listen to you."

He looked at me intently, then almost desperately. A look of hopelessness came over him. Turning his face away from me, he muttered to himself, "Oh, crumb. What am I saying?…"

"What is it, Steve?" I asked gently.

He turned his head back toward me slowly, fixing his pleading eyes on mine. "You've got to protect her, that's all. You're her cousin."

He would gladly have stopped there and left me to figure out the rest.

"Of course I will, Steve. But why does she need to be protected?"

Steve sat silent for several moments. He looked up into the trees, bit his lip, opened his mouth hesitantly, and spoke.

"Tom—Tom Mahler, that is—is a fine fellow in his own way and all that, but…." And he went on to recount in concise phrases all that had happened in the past week: the talk around the pinochle game, the wager after the play, the ploys Tom was using on Cecilia, the risk she was in, and more. In quoting the language the fellows had used in describing Cecilia, he took no pains to spare my sensibilities. The only factor he left out was the very one that was most obvious to me—that he had a huge personal stake in what might happen to Cecilia.

Cecilia was to me both a cousin and a woman. We loved each other very dearly. And so I was more than mildly alarmed to hear what Steve had just told me. But I had great confidence in Cecilia's ability to sense danger and handle herself well. I was more moved by Steve's impassioned concern for her welfare than I was about Cecilia's alleged plight. He had obviously never before faced anything that had aroused such powerful emotions in him. I could tell from the way he referred to Cecilia throughout his account of her plight that for him she was "way up there" and he was "way down here," that the most someone like him could hope for from someone like her was to get a glimpse of her from time to time and take some joy for himself in her happiness and her beauty.

I am not sure precisely what inspired the idea in me. Perhaps I saw something in each of them that could bless the other. I don't know. But whatever it was, after pondering his words for a few moments, I looked straight at him and said, "Why don't you take her out?"

"Me?" Steve looked flabbergasted. Looking down at his tendinous body and holding out his arms helplessly, he tried to tell me without words how absurd the very idea was. In point of fact, he was paralyzed by overawe and fear of failure.

"Steve," I said firmly, taking hold of his shoulders. "I guarantee you that what you have is worth far more in Cecilia's eyes than what Tom has."

I paused and went on. "I'm not going to say anything for a while about what we just talked about, maybe never. But thank you for alerting me to the situation. I hope you can see your own potential for solving this problem." With that I smiled at him, noting the stunned expression on his face. I got up, patted him on the shoulder, and left him in a daze with the words, "The key is in your hands, Steve."

I'm not sure I've ever quite forgiven myself for saying that.

XXIII

The reader need not conjecture what was Steve's next move. As Cecilia and I were leaving the music hall, I heard the roar of his motorcycle thundering out of the parking lot on the other side of the campus. It seems that Steve could untie the knots of his troubles only when the clean sweep of cool air was rushing through his hair and when the surging of the engine was drawing off his excess energy.

With him Steve took his warm bedroll and his .22 caliber rifle. He knew only that to the west of the college were densely forested hills. All that mattered was to get to those hills where he could find a little peace and quiet. He ached all over as he bucked his way toward the Mississippi River Valley. His cycle could not fly fast enough through the darkness. But his spirit was hurtling forward even faster.

Deep into the night the road took a plunge down into the hill country. Trees closed in on it from both sides. Still Steve roared up and down the hills. Then, approaching the crest of a steep slope, he spotted a little-used path cutting off to the right. Following that, he skirted the top of a horseshoe ridge until he observed in the moonlight a small glade not far below the path. There the hillside leveled off a bit before dropping sharply into a boxed-in valley. He stopped, grabbed his bedroll and rifle, and descended to the clearing. The dry grass and fallen leaves made a superb mattress.

As he sank to sleep, a rosy tint on the eastern horizon was already beginning to cast a flush over the forest.

XXIV

Real sleep lasted only a couple of hours for Steve. Broad daylight brought with it the climbing sun in a cloudless sky that beat down through his thin eyelids and stirred up a host of grotesque dreams from which he awoke in fits and starts, and back into which he limply slipped time and again. From different directions the dreams all converged on a most distressing single motif as Steve went in and out of semiconsciousness. At last he'd had enough. He threw back his bedroll. "Can't a fellow have a little peace even in his sleep?" he demanded.

Dragging himself into the shade of an ash tree, he leaned back against its trunk. A dull headache befuddled his mind. His eyes were aching and bloodshot. The hollow pain that had been pressing on his chest for days now was eating at him worse than ever. It seemed to be this pain that had spawned his dreams, each of which, having staged its particular drama, receded back into the pain from which it had come and magnified the pressure on his chest.

Fragments alone were left now. Whatever larger context they may have once fit into was lost forever. But, oh how they cut him, these fragments. This one, for example. How it hurt!

He was alone in a corner somewhere—was it in a bar? Straight across the large room from him was a noisy crowd of eight or ten rowdies about his age, gathered around one small table and lustily singing "Gaudeamus igitur juvenes cum sumus!" They were laughing boisterously in the heady afterglow of many beers. A gayer picture of unbridled youthful lustiness was never seen. Steve was staring at them from a distance, almost contemptuously, until he saw something else in the picture. God knows he saw something else in that picture! Sitting in the very center of this half-drunk mob, her head bowed slightly and cocked to one side, was his Cecilia! In her misty eyes Steve could see a deep well of infinite pity for the men around her and what they were doing to themselves, a pity that lay her wide open to the filth they were obviously planning for her. From his dark corner Steve's heart strained to reach her, but he was rooted to the spot, doomed to watch them take whatever liberties they wanted with her.... Next thing Steve saw, they were walking past him, leading her away. She was not resisting, oblivious to their intentions, still pitying them, even loving them with those soft misty eyes. He had the impression that she had often been violated by them already, but had never lost her compassion for them. Guileless, chaste, spotless, though defiled over and over again, and likely ridden with disease. Cecilia, Cecilia! And Steve powerless to move.

Recalling this scene as he sat under the ash tree, tears streamed down his cheeks.

And then there was this fragment

He was at a church meeting, but all over the floor around him a regular orgy was going on. Across the sea of milling heads, caressing limbs, and squirming bodies he could see into the far corner of the room. And there she was again, standing apart from and above the slime going on around her while yet in its very midst. The same back-slapping rowdies were saucily poking at her and coaxing her to follow them to the door. In her eyes again Steve could see only pity for her abusers. Her pure heart raised her soul above her abusers' ravages, but left her body helpless. Steve had to get to her! He scrambled through the sea of bodies, pushing and shoving against the twisting mass. As often as he cleaved a passage forward, he was forced back. Desperately he struggled against the tide until he finally broke out into the open area where he had last seen Cecilia and her tormenters. But now they were not there! Panicking, he searched the room for any sign of her. Where was she? What had they done with her? Frantically he asked someone what had happened to them. The informant simply pointed to a door across the room in the direction from which he had just come. And there Steve caught a glimpse of her being led away into the night.

Steve's head slumped to his breast. He shuddered. Only one more fragment occurred to him as he sat there. It was very short and very sharp.

It seemed he was walking down a narrow cobblestone street in an Old World town. He stopped before a mossy set of stone steps leading directly down to a heavy oaken door in the foundation of a large mansion dating from the Middle Ages. Somehow he was aware that his Cecilia was inside. Just as he was about to descend the steps, a crooked old woman with a cackling voice shuffled in front of him and rasped, "No! You can't go in there!" He looked up and realized he was on the threshold of a brothel. Its windows were closed and barred, and Cecilia was behind them.

"Am I sane?" Steve whimpered. "How can I even dream such a thing?"

His dreams weighed on him like blocks of concrete. Awake or asleep, there was no doubt about it: he was obsessed by the thought of Cecilia's impotence in the face of dangers which she was too naive and too innocent to recognize in time. This was exactly what Tom was counting on! On top of that, Steve was clearly also obsessed by the thought of his own powerlessness to help her despite his knowing what she didn't know! Whenever he closed his eyes and thought of Cecilia, the real Cecilia, he could not escape the truth that she was in clear and present danger, or the truth that he, Stephan Pearson, had been told that he was the person in the best position to do something about it.

It was the tightness in Steve's throat that eventually drew him out from under the tree and sent him off toward the cradle of the ravine in search of a spring of water. He had to follow the spring bed down the hillside several hundred feet before coming upon a little trickle of water in a recess where a mass of roots supported the top of a small ledge of rock. Here, under the lip, icy water dripped and oozed into a clear pool about two feet across. He grimaced before lapping up the icy water, knowing it would drive nails into his throbbed temples.

He closed his smarting eyes until the pain subsided. Then slowly lifting his head, he watched the tiny stream trickle down the lush gully. About a hundred and fifty feet below him, his attention was arrested by a giant fallen white pine. Many years before, it had been rooted up by high winds and stretched out across the gully, forming above the streambed a sturdy bridge about five feet in diameter. Trudging down to it, Steve examined it all the way around and discovered it was still as solid as the day it had fallen. He scrambled up the side of the ravine to the base of the trunk and walked out to the center above the creek bed.

A muted happiness ran through him for having found so suitable a place to be so sad. The situation had about it something of the precariousness of life itself as well as its solid reality. Steve pondered the paradox of his own position on the trunk. If he took a long leap upcreek, he would land safely. But let him just slide effortlessly off the log downcreek and it would mean certain disaster. He sat down facing downcreek.

At the bottom of the ravine in the distance was an isolated farm. The thought crossed his mind that if a man had to farm at all, this was the ideal place for it, in contrast to the featureless prairie where he had been raised. But such thoughts didn't occupy him for long. Sitting still, his head automatically dropped to his chest under the burden of the night's dreams. The hollowness in his heart was hurting again. Involuntarily he reached out for a hand that wasn't there. He groped for it a bit and then sank back into his pain.

After a while he reached into his back pocket and pulled out a folded sheet of paper. He held it in his hands and stared at it without opening it. Then, fumbling, he unfolded it and began to read. It was the statement of the lucid convictions he had come to the previous spring after his day in "paradise." He had stored it in the bottom drawer of his desk and had grabbed it on impulse on the way out of his room. It was his Declaration of Independence, his window to that one perfect day, his point of departure for all future hopes for happiness. It read:

It is to me a great insoluble mystery that all men in this world without exception choose to harness themselves to a daily routine of drudgery and endless misery. I can understand the horse's plight, brute victim of the whims of a higher intelligence. But who has enslaved man if not man himself?

I am not very wise and I have no desire to be. But one thing appears to me to be so obvious that I despise every man who fails to see it. It is this: all other creatures in the natural state do only what they instinctively want to do. Only man when left to himself hedges himself up, walls himself in, clamps himself down. What he calls "duty" is nothing but a fear inculcated in him by others who never cease to make demands upon him, a fear which he himself nurtures and reverences and which thus becomes his self-constructed prison.

You ask me about the duties of animals in nature? It is true that they are responsible for feeding and raising their young, but who lays this responsibility on them? No one! Are they tied down against their will? Certainly not! They fulfill their needful obligation because their instincts make them want to. And I set it forth as a fact that if man had not harnessed and bridled himself as he has, he too would by nature fulfill this, his one needful obligation and let the rest go hang.

Yes, birds feed and tend their young, but they also perch high in the treetops and sing their hearts out just because it feels good. And they soar through the clouds and flit about in the bushes just for the fun of it. Man has wrecked life for himself by adding to his one real obligation a host of imaginary obligations and has thereby robbed himself of the natural joy in life which all other creatures know.

Since this strange and scarcely curable disease has infected all humanity, the only sane course for any man who seeks the only sane goal in life—namely, happiness—is to sever himself from the diseased body and start all over on his own. Only

> thus can he rid himself of superfluous obligations and unnatural duties and follow the harmonious course of nature. To this I pledge myself: let no man stand in my way!

After he had finished reading it, he sat gazing off into the distance. Whatever world he had been in last spring, he was in a different world today. That world was way back then and way over there. This world was filling his heart to the breaking point right here and now. There may have been some truth to what he wrote back then, but the way back into that world for him was now forever blocked by one lone figure with the face of an angel, standing defenseless before him. In fact, the roads from Steve to about anywhere were all blocked by her. She was everywhere for him. Wherever he turned, there she was. And there he wanted her always to be.

What can one say about the rest of that day? It was one long soliloquy punctuated by periods of sheer silence. He found himself talking to her, about everything. And listening to her. And just looking at her in his mind while she smiled back at him. The hours passed like minutes until a rumbling growl from the pit of his stomach drew his attention to the fact that the sun was only half an hour above the horizon.

All at once he felt a surge of energy in his legs. They wanted to leap up and charge up the hill and leap onto the cycle and race back to Christiania and Cecilia!

He jumped to his feet, was off the log in a few long strides, and ran up the hill on the crest of the surge of power in his legs. Nothing could stop him. He skimmed over the creek bed, straining forward to get back to where he belonged. But, alas, his empty stomach had the last word. His legs suddenly turned to rubber. He tottered and sank to the ground, head throbbing and stomach growling. The taste of blood was in his throat from his overstrained lungs. He was definitely not going anywhere in that shape.

He needed to calm down, fetch his bedroll and rifle, shoot a squirrel or a rabbit or a grouse, eat and drink his fill, crawl in the sack, get up at the crack of dawn, and then drive back to the Hill.

Sleep came easily that night. It was a deep undisturbed sleep that lasted until just before dawn. Then, for the briefest moment they were sitting beside each other on the old oak bench. Their arms were touching, their fingers interlocked. She felt so warm. "Look," she said softly. "I want to show you this." He woke up without finding out what "this" was. But he was curious to know.

His head was clear, his eyes felt soothed. He lay there in his bedroll for a few moments savoring the joy of feeling himself so near to Cecilia. Then he got up, impelled by a surge of excitement, and prepared to leave. Soon the motorcycle was speeding back to Christiania. Steve knew now both what he had to do and what he wanted to do, and for a change they were beautifully merged into one. His heart was light and eager, in spite of the hint of fear that remained embedded within him. But its slow burn was no match for the fire in his heart.

XXV

It was already past noon when Steve chugged up the hill and pulled into the parking lot behind the dorm. He jumped off the cycle and charged into the dorm. He had work to do!

First of all, he had to find out what was available on campus that he could ask her out to. And then he'd better get right at it before Tom did. Let's see.... Where can a fellow find out what he needs to know? Of course! The bulletin board outside the post office! That should tell him! So off he trotted, his head in the clouds.

The bulletin board was a big arrangement that looked like an outhouse with only a back wall and a large overhanging roof. A fellow could scrutinize its various notices quite inconspicuously. At first he felt good about that, being the private guy that he was. But then it dawned on him: *So what? Who cares if the whole world knows?*

Let's see....

> Monday night—Canadian legislator to speak. Topic: "Four Reasons Why Russia Will Remain Depressed for at Least a Century"

Lovely. What's on Tuesday?

> Tuesday night—Estonian cosmetics demonstrated by two native Estonians. Recommended for home economics majors

We're getting better....

> Wednesday night—"The Philological Affinities of the Primitive European Dialects to Modern Basque as Shown by Certain Alleged Entomological Ties with the Finno-Ugric Language System: That this Hypothesis Is Untenable." Second in a series of five lectures.

Can't you just see the crowds lining up for that one?

> Thursday night—The Annual Minneapolis Symphony Orchestra Exchange Concert, featuring the works of Brahms

That's it! She'll love it!

And with that thought, Steve's heart skipped a beat because the next step was no longer just preparatory. It was the actual thing. He now had to approach her and ask her out. Not tomorrow. Today! Right now! O my God!

Up until this very moment he had been borne along by the power of his vision, with no thought of how he would handle its practical side. Sitting on the big log yesterday and feeling her hand in his all afternoon had made it seem so easy, so natural. But now suddenly he was back down on terra firma. His legs felt like lead weights. He, little mouse-faced Stephan Pearson, now had to talk to the real Cecilia Endsrud and ask her to go out with him to this concert! His throat tightened up. He swallowed hard. Beautiful Cecilia with the silky golden hair, the heart-melting smile, the graceful form, the kindest eyes he'd ever seen. He took a deep breath, blinked hard, and headed back to the dorm.

It was 2:30 Sunday afternoon. It would not be proper for him to call her until at least an hour after supper, maybe even not until 7:30 or 8:00. Being Sunday, she would not be in the music hall at that time. Five hours, and what could he do with himself? Goodness, he was hungry!

He went up to the room. Ted wasn't there, so he swiped a few crackers from his roommate's larder and downed them hastily. Time to go for a walk! So he left the dorm and strolled around the campus aimlessly.

What an afternoon of highs and lows for Steve! It boiled down to this: When his mind was on her, his spirit soared; but when his mind was on himself, his spirit sank. Sometimes it seemed as though she was walking right next to him at that very moment, kicking through the leaves on the ground and humming a cheerful melody, as he'd seen her do so often on the way to and from the music hall. It had been so easy to talk to her when he was sitting on that big log. Would he get all tongue-tied now when she wasn't present only in his imagination? He'd have to say something! If in his meanderings he happened to pass by a window, he'd sometimes glance into it to see if he was still as homely as he had been yesterday and the day before, and his heart would sink when he saw the answer. Imagine! Him! Steve Pearson the troll, having the gall to expect a princess like Cecilia to accompany him to a concert and the effrontery to expect that she might enjoy his company so much that she'd do it again, and again, and again, until....

Imagine!

At last suppertime came. Steve had no heart this evening to watch Tom play his little games with Cecilia, so he waited until the very last minute to duck into the cafeteria before it closed. On the way in he spotted Tom and Cecilia out of the corner of his eye getting up to leave. He turned his head the other way and shuddered. He hurried to get into the dinner line so they wouldn't pass him on the way out, avoiding Tom's cocky greeting and her awkward attention. All he could handle for supper was a bowl of soup and some crackers.

After supper he walked circuitously back to the dorm, fearfully, like a soldier approaching a beachhead. It was 6:30. The hour was almost upon him. Could he actually bring himself to do it? Would he buckle under the pressure? Back in his room he collapsed onto his bunk.

Out in the corridor the fellows were jabbering again, just when he needed a little peace and quiet. Why did it always have to be that way?

Now it was 7:15. Steve was no readier to call her now than he had been forty-five minutes earlier.

"Rats!" he mumbled, picturing handsome Tom leaning over lovely Cecilia as they exited the cafeteria.

"Rats!" he mumbled again, recalling what his reflection looked like in the windows.

"Oh," he sighed, just thinking of her.

"I tell you, she loves me! She absolutely loves me!" Steve's head cocked. It was Tom's booming voice out in the corridor. He stiffened, aghast.

He'd never thought of that. What if she loves him? What if she really loves him?

"Don't give me that bull." It was Lute. "I'll bet she's just putting up with you and too polite to tell you."

"I told you it wouldn't take him long to win her over. Who can resist a big handsome brute like him?" Ted put in, half serious, half teasing.

"Ha! I'll bet it's a long day before she goes out with you again!" Lute was right in there as usual, feeding Tom the old taunt.

"You wouldn't want to place a bet on that now, would you? I've got every social function on campus that she'd be interested in plotted out for the next month."

"I still say it'll be a long day."

"How would you like to make that long day one hour, say?"

"One hour! Listen to him. He thinks he's already got her in his back pocket!"

"O shut up for once! I'll bet you clod-hoppers don't even know there's going to be a first-class symphony concert here this Thursday. It's just her thing."

"She'll be there, all right. But you won't."

"One hour, I say. One hour. Just to show you low-brows what a little culture can do, I think I'll go over to the women's dorm right now and sew this one up with her for Thursday. See you in an hour, chumps!"

With that he strode down the stairs in a huff.

Steve sat bolt upright. It was now or never! He hadn't a moment to lose. Thank God for those new intercom phones they'd just installed to link the buildings on campus.

He stumbled out into the hall and grabbed the receiver. Then he slammed it down again. What was he thinking? He couldn't have Lute and Ted listening in on this. Breaking into a sprint, he raced down the corridor to the phone at the far end. What would he say? Who cared! Just so he said something.

He seized the receiver and put it to his ear.

"What building would you like, please?" a sing-songy voice asked.

All out of breath he swallowed and stated as calmly as he could, "Put me through to the women's dorm—the women's dorm, please."

"Women's dorm," sang out another voice a moment later.

"May I speak with Ce—Cecilia Endsrud?" he faltered.

"Just a moment, please. I'll see if she's in."

If she's in, if she's in…, the words echoed in his head. Now he was panting! How would he ever be able to say anything to her? What would he say? What time did it start again? Was it 8:15? Yes, 8:15. All right, 8:15!

"Hello, sir. She'll be here in a moment."

In a moment, just a moment. He was shaking like a leaf. His mouth was dry. His brain was muddled. How dare an animal like him even speak to an angel like her?

"Hello."

The voice was sweet and soft, with just a little lift of curiosity in it.

Steve's heart was thumping like a jack hammer.

Pulling himself together he stammered, "Hel-Hello. My name is Steve Pearson. I … I…," he faltered, the pit of his stomach caving in.

She didn't let him flounder long.

"Steve Pearson? Sure! You're the one who likes to study in the fresh air and has to put up with my blaring organ every night just because I like fresh air too. I've been wanting to apologize to you for some time."

"Apologize? But I like your music very much. That is, it … it helps a person to study to music…."

He was still flustered, but it relaxed him a bit to know that somehow she knew who he was. (I admit I had told her.) And the sound of her gentle voice! She honestly seemed glad he had called her!

"Still, I should be more thoughtful of others."

"You really like music, don't you?" It was the first phrase to fall out of his mouth naturally.

"O yes. I've never tried to explain it. Some things are too wonderful to put into words. How about you? Do you like music?"

"Yes. I don't know much about it, but some music makes me very happy, like robins singing early in the morning, or like hearing you play the organ in the evening. It's all so beautiful."

She giggled. "I don't try to vie with the robins. They're in a league of their own."

All at once it occurred to Steve that they were talking about music and he had called about a concert.

"Cecilia," he said. "I found out today that the Minneapolis Symphony Orchestra will be having a concert here on Thursday. I called to ask you if—you—would—go—with—me."

He'd said it! The last five words barely made it out of his mouth. But he'd said it!

"Of course I would, Steve. Thank you for asking me."

"O thank you, Cecilia," he whispered through the huge lump in his throat. "It starts at 8:15. Can I call for you a little before eight?"

"Sure."

She could tell he was all choked up, and so she got him off the hook by saying cheerfully, "So I'll see you tomorrow evening on your bench?"

"You sure will. Good night, Cecilia."

"Good night, Steve."

Steve stumbled his way back to his room and fell on his bed. Everything inside him had turned to goo. A smile broke out on his face so broad that it nearly ripped his lips. His heart was filled to the bursting point. Stephan Pearson had just died and risen from the dead.

XXVI

A few minutes later Steve heard a disturbance in the hallway. Lute and Ted were standing at the head of the staircase grinning curiously at Tom who was stomping up to the lounge. He brushed past them and made a beeline for his room, shaking his head and muttering, "I'll be a monkey's uncle, so help me, I'll be a monkey's uncle…."

Lute and Ted looked at each other, shrugged their shoulders, and sat down to wait for Tom to come out. In a few minutes he emerged from his room, still in a state of shock, and stumbled into the lounge, groping for a place to sit down. Lute shoved a chair under him and waited impatiently for his big friend to say something.

"I guess the bet's off."

Tom was too dead serious for Lute to crack a joke, so he waited for him to open up some more.

"I walk up to the reception desk as usual and ask for Cecilia Endsrud. The receptionist says she's on the phone so I'll have to wait a minute. I sit down. After a few minutes she comes in beaming like a full moon on an August night. We talk for a minute or two and then I ask her to the concert. She thanks me and says all bashful-like that someone has just asked her and she has said yes. I guess I just blurted out, 'Who?' without thinking. She says, 'Your friend, Steve Pearson.' I reckon my jaw must have dropped a good six inches. I was speechless. She stood there fidgeting, pretty as a picture. God, she never looked so beautiful. All I said was, 'Well, have a good time.' Then I excused myself and walked on out of there."

The big fellow dropped his chin into his hands and stared blankly at the wall. Then, like Caesar crying out, "Et tu, Brute!" he moaned, "Steve!... Buddy!... Steve!..."

Lute and Ted were as shocked as Tom was. There was dead silence.

"Well," Ted said at length in his slow drawl, "I reckon finally Steve has really done something."

Two heads nodded up and down. Even Tom had to concede that at long last Steve had "really done something."

XXVII

Steve was floating in heaven that week. For the first time in his life, there was actual substance to his longings, a merging of reality with his dreams. She was no longer his Spectre Maiden. She was his date for Thursday night.

His well-meaning professors could not fail to see the new glint in his eye and his unprecedented zest for life. They knew all about that glassy-eyed dizziness, that spurting response that has nothing to do with the question asked, that bubbly good-heartedness that rises above anything distasteful or disagreeable in anyone. They'd seen it many times before. It was unmistakable. It made you wonder what the world would be like if everyone were always in the first flush of love.

Monday morning they didn't take their eyes off one another from the moment they caught sight of each other on the staircase between the second and the third storeys of Old Main. They didn't say a word as they passed each other. They didn't have to. The vibration between them said it all. That evening she stopped at his bench. He stood up and they shyly exchanged a few words with each other. On Tuesday evening she sat down for a moment or two. On Wednesday evening she sat down for several moments. They didn't really say much to each other then, except through their eyes. Neither of them was embarrassed by the silence. They were just finding out what it was like to be near one another.

The music that came from that center window now seemed even

fuller and sweeter to Steve. It bore his heart up with it into the treetops where it was floating. If it was doing this for him, he wondered, what must it be doing for her, its creator? For him, he supposed, it was all about her. But for her, doubtless, it was all about the music.

From where he sat he could not discern her frequent glances out the window to see if he was still there. It was just one of those things: she did it almost without thinking.

XXVIII

It was Thursday. All day long Steve walked around in a daze. The only thing on his mind was Cecilia and that he was going to be with her all evening. He was so wrapped up in his thoughts that he even passed her in front of the chapel without noticing her. She watched him go by deep in thought and then let out that cute little giggle of hers which used to erupt from her all by itself when something struck her as funny.

By evening he was in a nervous trance. As he went about the clumsy business of preparing himself for the date, he mumbled various admonitions to himself. If he could only keep himself under control, everything would be all right. Just so he didn't do anything foolish. Just so he acted natural and normal. Just so....

"Well, you can start by putting the right shoe on the right foot!" he exclaimed as he pulled his left foot out of his right shoe.

Getting into his suit was a challenge. It had been so long since he'd worn it that he'd almost forgotten what went where. By 7:00 p.m., however, he was all ready to go, freshly showered, hair combed back, shoes polished, everything as shipshape as a sailor taking his first shore leave.

He was glad to be ready early. But now he had fifty minutes on his hands. He couldn't go for a walk. He'd feel foolish all duded up like this. He couldn't go to the women's dorm without being conspicuously early. Then he had an idea.

"Why not drop in on Paul?" (I had moved downstairs that year.) "Maybe he can give me a few hints."

So he came down to my room and knocked on my door. I was beginning to think about getting ready for my own date to the concert.

"Come on in," I called.

Steve walked in self-consciously and said, "Evening, Paul."

"Boy, don't you look sharp tonight! I know one young lady who's going to be mighty pleased when she sees you."

He grinned sheepishly. "I have a little extra time here. Thought I'd see if you'd … well, maybe sort of…." He fumbled around with his hands in his pockets.

"Give you a few suggestions?"

"Something like that."

Regarding him more closely, I was thankful he'd come to see me before heading over to the women's dorm.

"Well, to begin with," I said gravely, "do you always wear your necktie inside out?"

Incredulous, he stepped in front of the mirror. Sure enough! Big as a billboard, there was the label facing outward, and there were the frayed tucked-under edges of the cloth running up and down the center. When he saw this, his eyes popped. Then a broad grin wrinkled up his face.

"That would have been plenty hard to explain!"

"O, my friend. She would just have giggled and patted you on the cheek."

This time he took care to tie it looking into the mirror. A dark frown flitted across his brow. I knew he was comparing his plainness with Cecilia's beauty. I could see him thinking to himself, *Fancy clothes don't make a homely guy like me handsome. Won't we look ridiculous, her and me strolling down the lane? Me and my pointed nose.*

When he had finished retying the knot, I remarked, "Don't let Hollywood see you."

A pained smile met me as he turned around.

"She must have told you about our date."

"Of course. And about the one you rescued her from."

"Really?"

Silence.

Then, "I'm so grateful."

He collapsed into my easy chair.

"Mind if I just sit here for a few minutes?"

"Be my guest. I'll just get ready for my date."

Ten minutes later he rose to go.

"Thank you, Paul," he said as he disappeared through the door.

A moment later he reappeared in the doorway.

"Thank you," he said again.

XXIX

It was twenty minutes to eight when Steve mounted the steps to the main lobby of the women's dormitory. He was early after all, but not too early. He'd just sit and wait in the lobby for ten minutes or so. A funny flighty feeling curled up his stomach as he sank into a large overstuffed chair. He felt somehow out of place watching the men come in, give their dates' names to the receptionist, and casually stand around in the waiting area until their girls arrived and signed out.

"So that's how it's done," he noted.

The big hand on the clock above the entrance crept toward the ten. The closer it got, the more glued he felt to the chair. His stomach was definitely acting up now. Was he going to be sick? Not if he could help it! Now the hand had undeniably reached the ten. The moment had arrived.

Trying to imitate the well-practiced men, he sauntered up to the desk, asked for Cecilia Endsrud, went over to one of the big pillars, and leaned against it for support. Remember, act natural. But nothing felt natural to him! No matter where he put his hands, they seemed out of place. In his pockets, dangling free, by his side, folded, one in a pocket and the other dangling free, nothing felt natural. She'd be coming down any second now. He had to settle down, get himself under control. He had to quit freezing every time he heard a girl's footfall on the stairs. Just think clearly. Keep your balance.

With all of this going on in his head, he hadn't noticed her silently descend the staircase. Now all at once he looked up and there she was, standing across the lobby from him waiting in line to sign out. She was smiling at him. She was the only girl whose escort had not leapt to her side the moment she appeared in line. Unattended as she was, Steve noticed several of the men eying her over, probably wishing they could work out an exchange of dates for the evening, he thought.

Even at that, Steve could not move. He felt transfixed as by a light from heaven. He couldn't get his eyes off her. Everything about her was so right. She stood there just as she had in his very first dream of her—so pure, so otherworldly, so very kind, and so indescribably beautiful. In his dream he hadn't been able to get to her, but now she was quietly motioning him to come and join her.

And he did, drawn by her warmth. "Hello," he said, looking into her eyes.

"Hello," she said, looking into his.

XXX

In the course of that evening I am sure Steve committed many faux pas, but in a sense both he and Cecilia were oblivious to the stricter requirements of social convention. What mattered to each of them was the genuineness of the other. There was nothing fawning about the way they treated each other. Steve's almost paralyzing awe of her became a different kind of awe in her disarming presence. There was nothing ill-at-ease about it from the very first moments of their being together.

As they walked down the arbored lane to the concert hall arm in arm, Steve felt very proud, very unworthy, and very happy. They said almost nothing until they came to a little clearing in the trees. There Cecilia stopped and pointed to a small bright constellation off to the northeast of them. Leaning close to Steve she said, "That's my favorite formation. Folks call it Cassiopeia, but I call it Tiny Dipper. No matter what time of the year or what time of the night you look into the stars, you always see it."

Steve caught the wonder in her voice.

"I've noticed that too. Isn't it wonderful?"

They walked on.

In the gaily-lighted auditorium, one of Steve's friends from his physics class ushered them into a couple of seats halfway down the center aisle. As he handed Steve their program, he winked at him and Steve winked back.

Soon the lights dimmed and the curtain rose on the orchestra. A tingle of excitement rippled over Steve. This was going to bring joy to his Cecilia and that alone, with or without the music, would bring him joy. The conductor strode to the podium, greeted by a respectful ovation. On the downbeat the orchestra broke into Brahm's "Symphony Number One."

The first movement sustained Steve's mood of anticipation. It was a good work on which to begin the program. He could see that Cecilia was really getting into it, and he dearly appreciated all the time it gave him to sit next to her. It felt so good being so close to her surrounded by this glorious music.

Somewhere in the middle of the second movement, Steve and Cecilia happened to shift around at the same time so that their shoulders and upper arms pressed against each other. Neither of them moved. Steve could now feel the rise and fall of her chest as she breathed. He closed his eyes and let his head slump slightly forward. It was almost too much for him, this miracle. This was no phantom, no apparition. He was touching the real her, close and warm and alive.

During the third movement, an overpowering urge timidly lifted his hand to the armrest close to Cecilia's. It lay there palm down for two or three minutes. Then, in a lull in the music, he felt her soft strong hand gliding smoothly towards his, also palm down. Lifting his hand ever so slightly, she slid hers under his. Their fingers interlocked. They almost stopped breathing. The mere touching of one another in this simple way mysteriously portended to each of them a hint of a wondrous future in which they could be forever connected, forever one. Neither of them had ever been even close to this place before. This was wholly new territory for them. They remained interlocked like this until the very end of the symphony and only released each other reluctantly when they stood up for the applause. They looked at each other during the applause, began to understand, and were totally dumbfounded.

During the next section of the program consisting of a number of smaller lyrical works by Brahms, their hands came together all by themselves.

The final section of the program was the magnificent "Variations on a Theme by Haydn" in whose soaring interwoven melodies and harmonies their quickened hearts took flight. In the resounding affirmation with which this work closes, all they could think of was where this new and untested love of theirs was leading them, to a climax that would fulfill their lives for time and for eternity.

There was not much time to loiter after the long concert. The girls had to report into the dormitory within fifteen minutes of its conclusion. Steve and Cecilia spent fourteen and a half minutes strolling hand in hand under the stars. They said almost nothing. The current flowing through their fingers said it all. Accompanying her all the way up to the front door, Steve faced Cecilia and took both of her hands in his.

"Good night, Cecilia," he choked out.

"Good night, Steve," she whispered.

They squeezed their hands very tightly and Cecilia ducked into the door at the last second.

And each of them went their separate ways that night with their heads spinning.

XXXI

The next evening Steve was at his bench earlier than usual, gazing up into the sky. The day had vanished behind him in two bright flashes of lightning, the first when he passed her on the staircase and looked into her bedazzled eyes, and the second during chapel when she looked up at him sitting in the balcony and their hearts touched for the briefest instant. The rest of the day had been a blur.

When Steve lowered his eyes from the sky, there she was walking towards him down the lane, her arms burdened with a stack of music. Approaching him, a solitary figure in the twilight, she was for a moment indistinguishable from the angelic woman of his dreams. He got up and walked towards her, beaming shyly, to greet her. She too had a sort of sheepish look on her face that easily betrayed the stirrings deep within her. They strolled to the bench and sat down.

The air was nippy, but it served to sharpen their sensitivities. They looked at each other, groping for words they didn't find and couldn't express. That's the way they were, those two, often smiling at each other and not saying a word.

Cecilia broke the silence.

"At nine o'clock we could go for a walk, if you want to."

"Where should we meet? Right here?"

"Yes. Right here."

She rose to go.

"See you at nine o'clock."

"At nine o'clock, right here."

Cecilia proceeded on to the music hall and up the steps towards her big organ on the fifth floor.

As she was mounting the stairs, she heard a familiar sound and stopped. The noise was coming from a nearby cell and was a rough simulation of the "Grieg Piano Sonata" I was struggling to master at the time. For a few moments she stood on the landing indecisively. Then recognizing beyond doubt my own peculiar musical blunders, she came over to the door of my cell and knocked on it. I stopped playing and answered the door, surprised but pleased to see her.

"May I come in for a few minutes, Paul?"

"Of course," I replied, pulling the piano bench out a little so that we could both sit down on it. She opened her mouth several times, but nothing came out.

I knew she wanted to tell me something, and I had a pretty good idea what it might be. She sat there staring at her lap and rubbing her hands together slowly. Then without looking up she said in a low tone, "Paul, I don't know what's the matter with me.... I've been feeling so funny the past few days." She looked up at me pleadingly.

The poor girl was in dead earnest. Confusion was written all over her face. I had to bite my lip to keep from chuckling. With an air of deep concern, I said, "Oh? Do you think you're sick? Do you hurt anywhere?"

"Not really," she answered, shaking her head in perplexity. "Just kind of all over. Just a funny feeling as though I'm not myself. I'm not really sick. And sometimes I feel very well, even better than usual.... I don't know...."

She shook her head, thoroughly puzzled.

"Do you feel feverish ever?"

"Yes. Now and then I feel very feverish and get chills and run short of breath." She stopped and looked up at me. "Paul, what's wrong with me?" she pleaded.

"Well," probed I, "do you feel these symptoms in connection with any traceable pattern in your life? Do they come and go, say, with something special you eat or some special time of day or after something especially strains your eyes or … or whenever you think of someone special, or come near someone special?"

Her head popped up like a cork. She shot back, "Paul! Whatever do you mean by that?"

Grinning mischievously, I looked her straight in the eyes, which were as big as saucers, and said, "I mean are you in love, you silly thing?"

I'll never forget the expression on her face when the light dawned. She just sat there rocking back and forth, speechless, her mouth wide open. Slowly she raised her hands to her mouth to cover its gaping hole. Then she nodded her head slowly up and down.

"So all those corny songs aren't corny after all," she concluded in awe.

Next thing I knew she had jumped to her feet, planted a big kiss on my forehead, and flown out of my cell like a bird from a cage. A little later when I opened the window for some fresh air, I heard the most ecstatic organ music rolling out of the wide-open window above mine. One enraptured young lady was lifting that old organ to new heights of rhapsody.

She was, after all, a very simple ingenuous girl at heart, beautiful and innocent beyond words, and as thoroughly shaped by the love of Jesus as anyone I have ever known. And I knew from this point on that she was no longer "my" Cecilia.

XXXII

Steve did not move from the old bench between 6:45 when he got there and 8:45 when Cecilia unexpectedly appeared next to him. She had been unable to finish her allotted time on the organ in spite of the fact that the good people of Meadowville were paying for it. So, feeling uncommonly spritely, she had sneaked out the back door of the music hall and crept up behind the old bench fifteen minutes early to surprise Steve. But when she took stock of his unwary innocence she couldn't bring herself to startle him too brutally, so she simply stepped out of nowhere beside him. That was startling enough! Poor Steve jerked around like a released slingshot and looked up into her teasing eyes in pure astonishment. She just stood there twinkling back at him, unencumbered by music books and luscious enough to eat. He bounced off the bench and, catching her capricious spirit, declared, "No fair! That's guerrilla warfare!"

"All's fair…," she began, grinning back at him. Then she sucked in her cheeks a little and wavered back and forth with her hands behind her back, looking very elfin.

"As you say," declared Steve with conviction, catching one of her hands in his and holding it lightly. Then he gently but firmly turned her around and started her walking down the lane. She responded happily to this good-natured display of pseudo-authoritarianism: it exactly suited her mood. They looked at each other and melted together under their little joke.

As they strolled down the path in the quiet of the cool night, an impregnable assurance of the rightness of it all bound them together. It was so much what should be, so divinely appointed, so very good. Although it was totally new to them both, totally unlike anything they had tumbled into until now, it felt to them as if they had been created for this from the beginning, as if they had never been strangers. It felt as if they had known each other for always and needed only the right occasion to solemnify what already was. Up and down the campus outskirts they strolled like partners in a dance, paying no attention to where they were going. Steve led, without realizing it, and she followed, trusting Steve to lead her well.

After some time they stopped on a seldom-used set of stairs leading down the hill toward a building that had burned down some years before. Around and beneath them spread the rolling countryside, just bright enough under the first quarter of the moon to resemble a vast snapshot negative and just dark enough to preserve the mystic envelopment of night. Their eyes wandered over the panorama. A light breeze fanned their cheeks. Their thoughts zeroed in on the same target, and they knew it without saying a word.

The minutes passed and strangely enough Cecilia began to sense in Steve a kind of withdrawal from the warm circumference of their little circle. She was just beginning to worry about this when Steve haltingly opened his mouth and said:

"I will never understand why *you* … *you*…,"—Steve hesitated—" I will never understand why *you* would take a second look at a frog like me."

Her hand squeezed his. The silence of the next few moments cut off his breath entirely. Her hand held onto his so tightly that it almost hurt. Poor Cecilia had no idea what to say. How could Steve even think such a thing? Her heart was pounding, her breast rose and fell. There was only one answer that came to her at that most tender moment. Turning squarely towards him, the dim moonlight revealing the plea in her eyes, she raised her arms and entwined them behind his neck. He clasped her around the waist and drew her bosom into his chest. There was a moment of stillness, and then their lips met in a long and warm and moist kiss that effectively sealed their destiny. They would be together forever.

After the kiss she rested her head on his shoulder and closed her eyes. He entwined his head and neck around hers and held her there while love washed over them both in its purest and rarest form.

From that moment on, it was evident to all that Stephan Pearson and Cecilia Endsrud were destined to become husband and wife.

*****

I will admit that at the time I wondered how all of this could have happened so quickly. Of course, I knew nothing then of Steve's odyssey which had left him so helplessly ready to respond to Cecilia and to love her. But Cecilia? I think we can thank Tom in part for setting her up for her rapid and wholehearted response to the new Steve, the Steve who had already begun to emerge from his wilderness encounters of the previous summer a changed man even before he laid eyes on her.

I cannot claim full accuracy in my account of the reasons why they bonded so quickly, but I can confidently claim it in reporting the fact that they did.

And I know, because she told me, that Cecilia was quick to recognize and strongly affirm Steve's latent genius. She also found in him an exceptional sensitivity and kindness without realizing that she herself was the source of it.

XXXIII

During the month of November, Steve and Cecilia were, as I saw it, the two happiest people on campus. Day by day as they continued to grow into each other, they fell more and more in love. Those two had a knack for being completely themselves as individuals and at the same time completely united in their love, which only served to enhance their mutual enchantment with one another. Their oneness came from the way they gloried in their differences as well as in their similarities which bonded them all the more. To describe for me what their love felt like to him Steve once used the analogy of a colloidal suspension in which the parts remain distinct but are fully integrated, as opposed to a compound in which the parts dissolve into one another and lose their identity. Steve was in a state of awe at the fact that such a love was even possible, and when he tried to explain it to Cecilia in these terms as they sat together on their bench one evening, she simply responded by looking him straight in the eyes, nodding her head and planting a big kiss on his forehead. They never forfeited the awe in which they held each other. Nothing about Cecilia disenchanted Steve. Whether he was calling for her at the women's dorm or waiting for her on the old bench, his heart skipped a beat every time he caught sight of her coming towards him. But Cecilia was no less in awe of Steve, as her frequent little stopovers at my practice room made clear to me. She marveled at his intellect, especially at the way things came together so smoothly in his swift mathematical mind, as well as at his ability to respond instantly and deeply to anything, large or small, that was truly beautiful.

In spite of their surface differences, they shared some powerful cohesives. One of them was their response to "little things" unnoticed by most of us, things like Cassiopeia, or the rhapsodic singing of the birds, or the silvery magic of the moonlit countryside. Cecilia's love for the passion of the music of Bach matched Steve's admiration for its mathematical purity, and each enhanced the other, sending down ever deeper roots of appreciation in both of them for his music.

During those few all-too-short weeks in November of 1919, to meet either of them alone was to encounter the very definition of "happiness." To meet both of them together was to discover everything that is meant by "bliss."

Every morning they met in front of the church to attend chapel together. It felt so good to stroll down the aisle to "their" pew, to sit side by side before God and the whole world, to share the same hymnal and to sing the same hymn. Steve especially enjoyed the praise hymns. Praise was in his bones. God was so close to him when Cecilia was sitting beside him holding his hand.

But it was the evenings, the cool still November evenings, towards which their whole days tended. Then it was that they soaked each other up, mostly in silence as the well-matched pieces of their souls interlocked, almost physically, through their entwined fingers. A little ritual developed. They'd meet at the bench, give each other a hug, and sit down side by side. Then with Cecilia holding onto his hand, torn between her love for him and her duty to use her practice time well, Steve would rise from the bench without releasing her hand and walk her to the door of the music hall. Giving her a light kiss on the forehead, he'd gently nudge her through the door. Then he'd return to the bench and sit there listening to her organ music roll out through the open window until he couldn't stand it anymore. It was usually around 8:30 when he could no longer resist the urge to join her. Into the music hall he'd go and up the staircase to her chamber on the fifth floor. Quietly he'd slip through the door and there she was, his beautiful Cecilia, making beautiful music. As the days grew shorter and the air grew nippier, he found himself worrying about how cold it was getting in her room, so he'd quietly move over to the window and shut it. The first time he did that, she looked around at him without stopping the music and said very softly, very coyly, "Thank you, my love. Now that you are right here, I don't need to have the window open anymore."

Poor Steve! It was a good thing she looked back at her music or she would have seen his eyes fill with tears.

As for Cecilia, these silent visits from Steve towards the end of her practice period became a "minimum daily requirement" for her happiness. On the one occasion on which he was detained (by me!) until a few minutes after nine o'clock, he found her kneeling in fervent prayer next to her organ bench. She couldn't disguise her relief when he appeared in the doorway, almost flinging herself into his arms.

But normally their evening rendezvous were examples of exhilarating simplicity. Steve would stealthily step through the door "so as not to bother you" and stand behind her admiringly for several minutes. She would pretend she hadn't noticed him and continue playing until the end of the piece. Then she would pivot on the bench and look him straight in the eye as if to say, *You can't fool me!* He would kiss her on the forehead and either stand back to watch and listen or else head over to the pipe chamber to nose around in there while she was playing. The cubbyhole that housed all the ranks of pipes fascinated him. Each rank from the great sixteen-foot Bourdons to the tiny pencil-size flutes was arranged in the same slightly lopsided symmetry. Steve wondered what the purpose was of hiding such beauty in a dingy closet. At 9:00 they would leave the musty chamber and descend the stairs out into the starlit night.

That gave them an hour before Cecilia had to report in to the women's dorm. They thrilled at the prospect of having a whole unencumbered hour of strolling around together with nothing else to do but hold hands and talk. Steve felt no compulsion in these intimate moments to drag her through the world he had been living in before the past summer and her miraculous intervention in his life. Maybe someday, but not now. He was, on the other hand, intensely interested in knowing every detail about how she had become the angel she was. And since speaking about Jesus came to her so naturally, he learned from her bit by bit an entirely different way of experiencing and practicing the faith that he had grown up with. His walks with her in the evening were in some ways much like the walk of the two disciples with Jesus on the road to Emmaus on the day of His resurrection, in which "their hearts burned within them" as He opened the Scriptures to them (Luke 24). Steve, to his own amazement, soon found his heart burning not only for Cecilia but also for her God.

He was at first taken aback a little by her frequent stops in the middle of nowhere just to tell God how much she loved Him. Any little thing could trigger it—catching sight of the last fires of the sunset in the clouds, or marveling at the shimmering waves of the aurora borealis above their heads, or shivering at the distant hooting of a great-horned owl, or even just feeling Steve tenderly squeeze her hand. She'd close her eyes and ardently whisper, "O my dear dear God! I love You so much!"

Steve never really got used to this, but he loved it.

Cecilia was not excessively bothered by how new all this was to Steve. She sensed how receptive he was, how sincere in every way. She noted that his joy in attending chapel with her was growing into more than the joy of simply being with her. He was starting to enjoy God! It was only a matter of time before Jesus would do for him what He had done for her. And then he would grow! Oh, he would grow! There was so much in him, and soon he would give it all to Jesus.

One afternoon while Steve was in the physics lab, Cecilia and I bumped into each other on the library steps. She looked at me, smiled, and then looked up into the sky, with that distant dreamy gaze in her angel eyes. She spoke slowly, weighing each word.

"You know, Paul," she began, looking very lovable to me, "great spiritual truths within people are like trees. They all begin as tiny seeds planted by Jesus in the right place at the right time. They grow slowly but surely. God is so patient with us. It would be cruel to whip a little sapling because it isn't yet the giant pine it will become. It could even die from the whipping and never become great at all."

She turned towards me, still focusing her eyes in the distance. "Crops have to have a chance to grow after being seeded. You can't harvest them right away. We should be thankful to see the tiny sprouts and then believe in what they can become. If we are patient, we will wake up one morning and see a ripe harvest as far as the eye can see."

I got the message. Her only job as she saw it now was to love Steve with all her heart and to enjoy being with him. God would do the rest.

I hardly knew the Steve I experienced that month. Gone was the Steve of the essay he had submitted to me for "correction," the melancholic Steve groping for a way out of his incessant frustration with all of life. He did share with Cecilia indirectly something about the great disillusionment that had been his life until she came along, but only by way of helping her to understand why he loved her so much and treasured her and her love more than he could ever tell her.

It remains only to mention that in the course of this month, Steve's motorcycle was transformed from a release valve for his frustrations into a release valve for their swelling love. Cecilia, so secure in herself, had always been one to try new things—to test the brink of a cliff, to climb a tree to the very top, to find out what was on the other side of a hill or a closed door. She seemed a bit of a paradox that way. If there was a view to be seen, a bug to be examined, a breeze to be caught, that was all the reason she needed to take a little risk. Once, in the days before she met Steve, I caught her sitting sidewise in the window of her organ chamber five stories above the ground, who knows why? And so it came as no surprise to me the first time I noticed them scoot down the hill together on Steve's contraption.

The spice of the brisk wind in her face, the steady assurance with which Steve maneuvered the vehicle, the very notion of riding down a smooth road straight towards an invisible point off on God's horizon, and of course the delightful obligation of holding onto her Steve very tightly endeared the black machine to her at once. She eagerly awaited each Saturday noon when they would set out with a picnic lunch for parts unknown.

In short, it is unimaginable that any two young people could have been more thrilled and awed by one another than Steve and Cecilia were. They were a rare combination. Everyone who knew them was deeply happy for them.

Even Tom Mahler got over his bitterness and reaffirmed his friendship with Steve when he saw the effect Cecilia was having on him. "I'm happy for you, Steve," he told him one day. "Cecilia must be a miracle worker."

"She is," Steve replied, swallowing hard.

And of course old Drs. Brockhaus and Larsen were confident that at last their intransigent protégé was beginning to see the light.

XXXIV

Cecilia had sent such glowing letters about Steve home to her parents that by Thanksgiving they were very receptive to her suggestion that he come home with her and spend the holiday with them. Their confidence in the judgment of their daughter was almost boundless, and their curiosity to meet the young man who had so thoroughly won her affection led them to write him a friendly invitation.

When Steve received their letter, he ripped it open voraciously and read its contents with unconcealed surprise and delight. Apparently he had been accepted by the Endsruds sight unseen solely on the weight of Cecilia's love! Almost at once little flinches of apprehension began to coil and spring around in his stomach. Would the real Steve match the image of him that Cecilia had projected to them, filtered through the rose-colored lenses of young love? Would he have to struggle to wear the thin mask of polite conformity just to keep their image of him from shattering? These fears haunted him on and off until finally just two days before they were due to leave for Meadowville, he confided them to Cecilia.

She giggled. He looked so serious.

"I'm sorry," she said, realizing that he was serious.

"Take a look at me," she instructed, staring him in the eye.

He stared back at her.

"They're used to me, aren't they?"

That's all she needed to say. If they could love Cecilia with all her strange ways, maybe they wouldn't have any trouble with Steve and all his strange ways.

And so the vacation came. Each holiday a special train for students used to run from St. Mark to the Twin Cities on the old Minneapolis, St. Mark and Southern Railroad. Its timetable was so arranged that leaving St. Mark on Tuesday evening, it arrived in Minneapolis to make a connection with the Great Northern passenger train heading northwest. Steve and Cecilia were thus able to travel the one hundred thirty miles from Minneapolis to Meadowville in three short hours, arriving at 11:00 p.m. As the train pulled into the station, Cecilia snuggled up to Steve in the seat, squiggling with nervous excitement. He squiggled back.

They were the only two passengers to get off at Meadowville. Uncle Irv and Aunt Ellie threw their arms around their daughter and smothered her in kisses, despite their usual Norwegian reserve. Then they turned to Steve. The pastor firmly grasped his hand and, looking him straight in the face, smiled and said with conviction, "Welcome, Steve! It's a privilege to have you here with us for Thanksgiving."

Steve saw clarity and goodness in the pastor's eyes, and in his clean oval countenance he perceived an honest man. Heartily he replied, "Thank you for inviting me. I am very happy to be here."

Ellie took his hand in hers and also welcomed him warmly. Steve's nervous fears were already melting away.

Only then did Steve look around and notice, of all things, that a circle of people had gathered around them in spite of the late hour. Nobody offered any excuse or apology for showing up to welcome Cecilia home. Steve stood back in wonder as people descended on her from all sides, each one receiving a moment of special attention from her. They had many questions for her, but he noted that she had just as many for them! Then, inching back a couple of steps towards him, she reached out and, taking him by the left hand, drew him into the circle. A hush fell over the excited little mob.

"This is my Steve. You'll love him."

Then looking first at Steve and then at the people, "These are my friends. You'll love them."

In the long silence that followed, waves of love washed over them both. By this time, tears were flowing down Steve's cheeks. "I know I will," he beamed at her friends through his tears.

On the way home as the three Endsruds were cheerfully bringing one another up to date on matters close to their hearts, Steve reflected on Cecilia's reception. It was easy to see why everyone loved her. She gave herself so genuinely and so generously to each and all. There was nothing effusive about her, nothing that smacked of meddling. Each person simply received a special portion of her caring heart. This made him love her all the more and marvel that she loved him.

When they arrived at the parsonage, everyone sat around eating cake and drinking coffee. The happy parents had so many questions for Cecilia about college and friends and music that she had a hard time fitting questions about some of her friends edgewise into the conversation. They could have sat there talking until dawn.

At last Aunt Ellie looked at Steve, who had scarcely said a word, and exclaimed, "Gracious, Steve! I imagine you're really enjoying all this small-town gossip!"

Everyone laughed. Steve was, in fact, thoroughly enjoying this "gossip." Like a rose his Cecilia was continuously opening before him, growing more beautiful in his eyes by the moment. All he needed to be very happy was to watch her in action and listen to her.

At any rate, it was time for bed. The spacious frame house had more rooms in it than the Endsruds ever needed during their twenty-six-year tenure in Meadowville. Steve was introduced to the genial atmosphere of his bedroom towards the rear of the house upstairs.

He undressed and fell limply into the ample mattress, tugging the fresh sheets up under his chin. The words came out all by themselves, "O my dear dear God! I love You so much!"

The old clock on the mantle downstairs struck two.

As he closed his eyes and sank into slumber land, there was his Cecilia smiling at him, not far away but right there close enough to touch. A shiver of joy shook him from head to toe. And he was asleep.

XXXV

From the first twilight moments of wakefulness the next morning to the last flickerings of consciousness the next evening, Steve found himself in the warm embrace of a happy family operating with a gracious simplicity that seemed to be altogether natural and effortless for them. Nothing was a burden, nothing a drudgery.

From the very first moments, lying there stretching and yawning, Steve had to pinch himself to ensure that he was not dreaming, that he was actually waking up in the guest bedroom of the family of his real-life Spectre Maiden. Descending to an eight-thirty breakfast, his first glance into the kitchen told him that this was no ordinary household. Unseen, he stood back from the doorway and observed the two women of the house busy with the baking. Cecilia was elbow-deep kneading dough, wrestling with the unruly stuff like a pro, slugging it mercilessly and hurling it down into the massive bowl. Already every available square foot of surface area in the kitchen was concealed beneath a dozen varieties of gastronomic delights—fresh bread and sweet rolls, coffee cake and cookies, *lefse*, *sunbuckles, julekaka,* and other mysterious delectables. The aroma they gave off was heavenly. This was going to be one amazing Thanksgiving!

Cecilia was tugging and pulling at the springy dough, oblivious to Steve standing there watching her, with great amusement. After a few moments he chuckled out loud. Her head swung around.

"I can see I'd really be in for it if you and I ever got into an argument," he said with mock seriousness.

Cecilia wheeled around. "What was that?" she exclaimed. Then, catching the impish glint in his eye, she hefted the whole wad of dough to her shoulder and pretended she was going to throw it at him. "Catch this, you stinker!"

During breakfast Steve's curiosity about the paradise of pastry by which they were surrounded was partially slaked by the information that it had been their tradition for some years now to share their Thanksgiving dinner on Thursday with a large family of friends. Ellie suggested that Cecilia and Steve might like to do a little shopping after breakfast to round up a number of last-minute items on a list. That way they could see some townspeople and Steve could meet more of Cecilia's friends. The two young folks jumped at the idea.

For Steve, it proved to be a repeat of the night before at the railway station. As he accompanied his beloved in and out of the lives of almost all of the people they met, he stood back and marveled. Everywhere they went they were accosted in a friendly manner by people connected in some special way to Cecilia. Steve couldn't get over the fact that the relationship of each person to her seemed to be uniquely their own, and on many different levels. Furthermore, all veils were dropped in her presence. She had a disarming effect on everybody without even trying. It is impossible to overstate how deeply this phenomenon moved Steve.

(The night after they returned to Christiania, he came down to my room and carried on for over an hour about it, citing one example after another.

"She can't help but love people, anyone," he marveled. "It was so obvious just from watching her. Paul, I love that woman so much, everything about her…." His voice trailed off.

"So do I, Steve. And for the same reasons.")

The shopping was over and they returned home. They found Ellie humming a tune and washing the last bowls from the morning's work. Steve noticed that this little woman was just rotund enough to give the impression of merriness. He could tell that she loved doing things for others. She was, in fact, ever baking pies and cakes for the pastor to present to the parishioners and townspeople on his pastoral visits. ("Here's a little something for you that the Mrs. sent over with me.") Another evidence of her desire to make others happy was the fact that, unlike Steve's parental home, the parsonage looked very much lived in, not lived on. She kept it clean and reasonably neat, but she was not a fastidious housekeeper, like Julia. She simply could not find the joy in sweeping and dusting her own house that she found in baking or sewing or gathering eggs for someone else.

She and Steve took to each other from the start. She liked his reserve when he was around people. He was no show-off. That made him a good companion for Cecilia. She took note right away, as only a woman can, of the many little signs of his love and respect for their daughter, but she also appreciated that he didn't fawn all over her and was cautious not to be too demonstrative in public. Her intuition told her that he was both sensible and self-possessed, traits which in her mind were associated with humility. If he was as brilliant as Cecilia had made him out to be, this would stand him in very good stead. Steve, for his part, saw in Ellie the kind of person he never stopped wishing his mother would become.

Lunch consisted of warm rolls and freshly churned butter along with plenty of cold milk and two kinds of pickles. In the course of the meal, Steve learned still more about the family they would be sharing Thanksgiving with the next day, just enough to make him scratch his head. They were going to consume two ducks, two fat chickens, and a large pork roast!

As they were finishing the meal, Ellie said to Cecilia, "Honey, the folks want you to play the organ for our Thanksgiving service tomorrow morning. I forgot to mention it last evening. You can do that for them, can't you? Mrs. Myrholm said she'd like a break for one day."

"Sure."

"They'd like you to play one of those new preludes you've learned at college. Just to see if their investment in you is paying off," she added with a twinkle.

Cecilia blushed and looked over at Steve who looked puzzled. She had not told him about her financial support from the congregation.

Ellie picked up on this and explained the arrangement to Steve. A lump formed in his throat. He looked at his Cecilia and shook his head slowly.

"Why don't you and Steve walk over to church this afternoon and practice?" Ellie suggested. "The choir is going to sing the Harvest-Home song for their anthem and they're going to come early to run through it with you in the morning."

And so Cecilia and Steve spent the rest of the day by themselves in the church. It was a large frame structure that seated over three hundred worshippers on the main floor, and another fifty in the choir loft. Well-nigh everyone in town belonged to the church, and farmers for miles around also claimed it as their spiritual home. Pastor Endsrud conducted two worship services every Sunday morning during his twenty-six years in Meadowville, separated by a Sunday school hour for children and adults.

Within the sanctuary all was at rest. Steve was very content just to sit in one of the pews in the choir loft close to the organ and soak it all in—the holiness of the chancel with its life-size altarpiece depicting the Good Shepherd bearing a lost lamb home, the intricately wrought Communion Rail forming a half-circle around the altar itself where the faithful knelt to receive the Body and Blood of their Saviour, the elevated pulpit from which sounded forth the Word of God for all to hear, the structure of the nave with its vaulted ceiling which could not have been the work of an amateur, but most of all the glorious music pouring out relentlessly, now loud, now a mere whisper, from the hidden pipe chamber at the touch of his beloved's fingers and feet. For a long time he sat there staring at her graceful and strong movements over the keys and the pedals. At length, he could not help himself any longer. He got up, slipped around behind her on the organ bench, and enlaced her chest in his arms, breathing so hard she could feel it all the way to her toes. The music stopped. She tilted her head back. He tilted his forward and swung himself onto the bench beside her, facing backwards. She leaned into his arms. And they kissed and hung on to each other like that for what seemed like an eternity, eventually relaxing and letting each other get back to what they had been doing before, sort of. Not a word was said.

Happening in this Holy Place and in these holy circumstances, this lengthy embrace was almost the equivalent of marriage vows for them. That's how both of them described it to me separately the following week with not a trace of embarrassment.

This organ console was home to Cecilia. Mrs. Myrholm had given her lessons on it since she was eight years old. She knew the stain on each of its yellowed keys, the tone behind each of its plunger stops. It did not take her fingers long to accustom themselves once again to the stiff tracker action: each range of pipes was manually operated from the keyboard which had to be fastened to the side of the pipe chamber. After electricity came to town, you no longer needed to have somebody sitting behind the chamber to pump the bellows with his feet whenever you wanted to play it. An organist had to have powerful hands to last through an entire service. But Cecilia loved the old organ and affectionately compared the quality of the sounds produced by its pipes to those of the latest models back at Christiania.

Towards evening they left the church and skirted around the edge of town so they could stroll hand in hand without stirring up gossip.

The evening was spent quietly around the fireplace in the living room. A cold early winter wind was whining outside, but inside all was peaceful. The day had been so busy, but now serenity reigned in the Endsrud home. The pastor was sitting in his favorite easy chair to the right of the hearth. Ellie was in another chair to the left. And on the rug in front of the hearth Steve and Cecilia were sitting beside, or rather, discreetly interlocked with one another.

"If you weren't here, Mom and Dad would be sitting over there with their arms around each other," Cecilia said into Steve's ear just loud enough for all to hear, pointing to the love seat behind them directly facing the hearth. The pastor winked at Steve and nodded, and everyone had a good laugh.

Taken as a whole, this end-of-the day ritual broke entirely new ground in Steve's heart. He'd never experienced anything like it. The conversation ambled along dealing with things some people would call trifles—a new baby in the parish, the Thanksgiving Communion Service in the morning, the illness or the recovery of a friend, the sick calf in quarantine out in the barn, and such like.

At about 9:30 the family got out three well-worn hymnals from the bookcase and sang hymns. Steve's voice blended well with the rolling tones of the pastor and his wife and the full chords Cecilia struck on the piano. Nobody needed to tell him that his spirit was also beginning to blend with theirs effortlessly in a marvelous way. Then Pastor Endsrud opened the big family Bible and read the appointed passage for the day from St. Mark's Gospel about the Sower and the Seed. Cecilia looked up at Steve and he looked down at her, and she knew in that moment beyond a shadow of a doubt that his heart was fertile soil where the seed was taking root.

A family prayer followed, simple, direct, and not very long. Each one offered to the Lord what was on his or her heart. First the pastor, then Ellie, then Cecilia, and then it was Steve's turn. He didn't hesitate for a moment.

"My dear dear God. I love you so much. I love Pastor Endsrud. I love Ellie. And I love my Cecilia to the bursting point. Thank You, thank You, thank You!"

His voice cracked. That was all he could say. Pastor Endsrud intervened, "Our Father who art in Heaven…."

And everyone went off to bed, reminding each other that tomorrow would be a big day.

Could it be any bigger than today has been? Steve asked himself as he mounted the staircase to his bedroom.

XXXVI

Stalks of corn, chubby pumpkins, shocks of grain, knobby squashes along with many other fruits of the rich Minnesota soil flanked the altar and sentineled the pews of the Meadowville Lutheran Church the next morning. Bulging ears of golden corn adorned the altar rail and hung from the windowsills up and down the side aisles. The matured products of God's providence and man's patient toil were assembled here in prodigious array, and the festive hearts of the people were ready to render thanks for what they of themselves could never have wrought.

Steve had insisted that Cecilia's "patrons" would surely respond to her rendering of Bach's "Fantasia and Fugue in C Minor." And respond they did! The church was full to the brim fifteen minutes before the service was scheduled to begin. I have heard this work performed many times over the years, but never with the passion and lyricism with which Cecilia invested the Fantasia or with the energy and drama with which she flew through the Fugue, even on that tracker organ. The power in her hands must have been prodigious. When she was done there was dead silence in the church, silence which reigned until the service began. Steve told me that people were almost too astonished to breathe by what they had just heard. But when it came time to sing the first hymn, they raised the roof.

The service itself was elevating, unpretentious, and replete with gratitude to God, not only for the good harvest and its attendant blessings but also for the safe return from the war of several young men in the parish. Worshippers went home mindful of the responsibility incumbent upon them to share their abundance with others and in that way they would be feasting today in the aura of the law of love.

Back in the parsonage after church, Ellie and Cecilia scurried about in the kitchen to prepare for the guests due to arrive on foot at noon. The pastor and Steve were ordered to relax in the living room where they would not be underfoot. Luscious aromas from the belabored cast-iron stove wafted throughout the house, bearing promise of the banquet to come.

At five minutes to twelve there was a timid knock at the front door. Pastor got up and opened it. In trotted the thirteen Wilsons—father, mother, and eleven children ranging from four months to fourteen years of age. Steve did a double-take. Immediately the Endsruds swung into action.

First Cecilia and Mrs. Wilson exchanged places on the spot, the former descending into the swarming brood of children, the latter escaping into the kitchen. Next Pastor Endsrud shed his normally reserved demeanor and became positively aggressive—teasing, poking, and playing all at once. Steve watched the smaller children jump up and down beside Cecilia and the pastor, impatient for their turn to be tossed in the air or tickled in the tummy or just plain hugged. By some miracle they managed to relate to Mr. Wilson and the older children at the same time, encouraging them not to try to keep the littler ones in line and make them "behave themselves." They were all welcome just as they were. Steve now understood why Ellie had thoughtfully removed anything of value that playful kids might harm. The house was virtually kid-proofed!

Soon Steve was sucked into the rollicking maelstrom. The look of pride in Cecilia's shining eyes when they stole a glance at one another as he was kneeling on the carpet tussling with two giggling kids said everything. It did not actually require much resourcefulness to amuse these children, he discovered, just a lot of energy. Snatch up one and toss him in the air, push another one down and tickle her in the ribs, listen thoughtfully to the carefully chosen words of a quiet one while balancing a rowdy one on your shoulders. And, by chiggers, it really was fun! If this little feller was getting out of hand, just shove him at Cecilia and see what she could do with him!

Throughout this chaos the Endsruds remained unruffled and gracious. And the happiness of the Wilsons, especially the father and mother, broke out in a hundred little ways all afternoon.

The banquet was abundant and tasty. It was obvious to Steve that the Endsruds were enjoying it much more by sharing it with the Wilsons than if they had kept it all for themselves. His mind was formulating this into some kind of principle when a little rascal interrupted his thoughts by ducking under the table and pulling his shoelace loose!

When at last evening came and the Wilsons went home laden with "leftovers that will never keep," the Endsruds—of whom Steve by this time felt very much a part—were weary but happy. Slowly and warmly they set about righting the house again. But when the clock struck nine, Pastor called a halt to their labors and, gathering them around the piano, played a few Thanksgiving hymns while everyone sang. Then he suggested that tomorrow would be soon enough to take care of what work remained. Everyone agreed.

Before going off to bed, Steve and Cecilia wandered out onto the back porch. The heat from their flushed faces diffused into the cool night air. For several minutes they stood there side by side gazing into the night, their arms enfolding one another about the waist. Their grip was firm, their breathing steady. At length Cecilia looked up at Steve and whispered, "I hope all this fuss today didn't...."

Steve's index finger pressed lightly against her lips. Drawing her in to himself, he gently rested her head in his left hand and embraced her with his right arm. Long and tenderly they kissed. She clasped him tightly to herself, feeling and loving the strength of his sinewy body. They were enveloped in their love. Then, wordless but still heavy with love, he walked her to her bedroom door, squeezed her hand, and mounted the staircase to his room and a beautiful night's sleep.

The remainder of the week slipped swiftly by. They spent Friday morning cleaning the house and Friday afternoon retracing some of Cecilia's favorite pathways leading to the haunts of her childhood. In the evening they gathered around the hearth once again.

All day Saturday they either received friends at the parsonage or went out to visit those who couldn't come to them. A mere month before, this would have struck Steve as pure drudgery, but now he lapped up every moment of it in Cecilia's company.

On Sunday Mrs. Myrholm was at the organ for the first service and Steve and Cecilia sat with Ellie on the main floor. For the second service Cecilia was at the organ, doing her best to make it a vehicle for worship and prayer, not for performance. Her normal preludes were not designed to be showpieces but stimuli for prayer. She once told me that if you come to church and worship and pray and don't even notice that the organ is there to support you, the organist has done her job well.

After the second service, a number of people gathered up in the loft. They came to commune, if you will, with a dear friend. Nor was Cecilia a bit self-conscious about all of this attention directed toward her. These were her friends, after all, and she was as eager to be with them as they were to be with her.

For them she had to stay and play the organ for another half hour. She felt she owed these good people whatever she could give them for their generosity. As she was ending the last piece, old Mr. Andreason, who had directed the Christmas pageant for as long as anyone could remember, moved over next to her and said in his wavering voice, "You vill come back and play for us at Christmas, von't you, Cecilia?"

"Only God Himself could prevent me," she replied.

The train left in the middle of the same afternoon. There were tears of joy in Ellie's eyes when she kissed Cecilia farewell and pulled Steve down to give him a kiss on the forehead, too. Beneath his calm restraint, Pastor Endsrud also revealed his deep satisfaction with his daughter's choice. He blessed them both as they were about to mount the train and told Steve he was looking forward to their next opportunity to be together.

Steve and Cecilia boarded the train that day believing that life could not get any better. The Endsruds, for their part, remained on the platform and watched until the train disappeared into the distance, bearing their precious daughter and her dearest friend Steve, confident that the two of them were truly being guided in all things by the good hand of God.

XXXVII

The night Steve and Cecilia returned to St. Mark was blustery and stormy. By morning snow lay a foot-and-a-half deep on the ground, held in place for a time by the glassy gelidity that results in the early winter from a heavy wet snowfall followed by plunging temperatures. Overnight, life on the campus of Christiania College was fundamentally altered. Thick sheepskin coats appeared, and red noses and cheeks, and frozen fingers. The cold wind needed no more that the distance between two buildings to nip your ears good and proper. Folks hunkered down into their wraps and scurried as fast as they could between refuges of warmth. Work was accomplished mostly indoors; nature was admired mostly through the window.

A week later the severe cold relented and temperatures rose during the day to just below the freezing point. Steve and Cecilia resumed their evening strolls after her practice time. Not many couples dared to brave the elements after sundown, but they did.

It was consoling to me to observe their happiness from a respectful distance. As it happened, my own "romantic life" was going through some turmoil at the time, and they gave me hope for a brighter future in that department.

One evening when Steve was supposed to meet Cecilia in front of the women's dormitory and walk her over to the music hall, she failed to show up on time. This had never happened before. He waited outside for a few minutes and then went in and requested the receptionist to call her. But she was not in her room. What could have become of her? Anxiety gnawed at him, but he tried to reason it away with the thought that something important must have detained her somewhere. Confused and uncertain as to what to do, he instinctively headed over to the music hall and mounted the stairs to her organ chamber.

But it was empty! There was no sign of her anywhere. The whole thing was growing more worrying by the moment. More confused than ever, he started down the stairs. As he rounded the third landing, something on the ground down below in the trees just around the corner from the entrance caught his attention, barely visible in the moonlight. He stopped and peered out through the window into the night. Surely this wasn't.... Look again! Could it be?... It was!

He flew down the stairs to the entrance. It was cold and dark, but Cecilia, oblivious to all else, was sitting on the ground, breathing heavily and caressing an object lying in the snow. He ran over to her, but she did not look up. Cautiously touching her shoulder, he pleaded, "Cecilia, my love, what's the matter?"

She turned her head slowly up towards him. Her eyes were moist. Steve stared at her in astonishment. Then she sprang up and flung herself into his arms, burying her face in his shoulder and surrendering to her sobs. Opening his heavy sheepskin, he enfolded her trembling body into its depths and hung on to her.

Her sobbing eventually subsided to jerky little whimpers. She rolled her head weakly from side to side on his shoulder and whispered, "I am so silly, so very silly."

The whole thing took Steve right back to the first nocturnal visit from his Specter Maiden and her grief-laden tears for him and the ants and the world.

Steve looked down at the object in the snow. It was a perfect cardinal, very beautiful but very dead.

"No," Steve objected. "You are not silly. You are wonderful. You are an angel."

Steve took a deep breath.

Then he nibbled her ear.

"You are *my* angel."

She melted into his arms. They stood there in warm embrace. Both of them were panting.

"Let's go upstairs," he urged at length.

On the way up the staircase, Steve was doing a little calculating. Being the son of Julia whose menstrual periods were severe and inescapably noticeable, Steve was well aware of how fragile a woman's emotions can become once a month. "It has to be her time now," he told himself. "It's just the way of women."

When they reached the organ chamber, they sat down next to each other on the bench. Steve had not felt so desolate for over a month. Leaning into his shivering treasure, he lightly caressed her cheek and said, "Do you want to tell me about it?"

Without looking up, she moved in closer to him and began haltingly.

"It's nothing, really.... But then again.... No, it really is silly.... Still, I'll tell you about it because ... because you're my Steve and you won't think I'm crazy."

Steve nodded.

Reaching into the pocket of her coat, she pulled out a sheet of paper and opened it deliberately.

"This afternoon in the library, Paul gave me the German part of what's on this paper. He was feeling kind of down in the dumps and just wanted someone to share it with, I guess. It's a little poem by Goethe called *Wanderers Nachtlied II*. He wrote it on a mountaintop in the evening when he was an old man. Something in it spoke to Paul's sadness, I guess. After he gave it to me, I think he felt better.... Well, then for some reason I began to get silly over it, too. It's been going through my head all afternoon, as if I were the old man! I even made a translation of it for you so you could see it too. I knew you wouldn't get silly.... Then I came across that poor little cardinal lying in the snow and oh, I don't what came over me...."

She handed him the paper and repeated the poem softly in German as he read it silently in English.

"Ueber allen Gipfeln	"Over every mountain crest
Ist Ruh';	Is peace;
In allen Wipfeln	In all the crowns of trees at rest
Spuerest du	Thou seest
Kaum einen Hauch;	Scarcely a sigh;
Die Voegelein schweigen in Walde;	The little birds are hushed now;
Warte nur, balde	Only wait, soon thou,
Ruhest du auch."	Thou too shalt die."

"Only he doesn't say 'die' in the last line. He just says 'rest,' but you know he means 'die.' It isn't supposed to be sad, just accepting of the inevitable, almost embracing it. Still, when I saw that beautiful cardinal lying dead in the snow and thought of the words 'Die Voegelein schweigen im Walde,' something just snapped inside me. I can't even tell you what it was! I broke out in tears and sat down next to the bird and ran my fingers over its soft feathers and just cried and cried and cried. I lost all track of time. It felt like I was crying for the whole world, Steve—all because of that little cardinal and that poem.... Now you know what I mean by 'silly.'"

Far from being put off by this bizarre account, Steve's heart nearly burst for love of his precious Cecilia. He laid his hand on hers. It was warmer now and she was shivering less. He kissed her on the temple and slid off the bench and onto a chair.

"Won't you play something soft and peaceful, my angel?" he whispered.

She nodded. Selecting just the right stops, she began playing from memory.

The serene harmonies and poignant melody of Bach's "Komm, suesser Tod" settled over the chamber and tenderly enfolded the two young lovers. Steve leaned back in his chair and inhaled deeply. His lungs felt sore and heavy. Gazing into his angel's tear-stained face now absorbed into the remote world of her music, he knew he was bound in love to this amazing woman forever, not to cramp her or in any way to tame her spirit, but to treasure her and to keep an eternal vigil over her.

Getting out of his chair, he approached Cecilia from behind without interrupting her playing. Placing his hands lightly around her waist, he whispered into her ear, "What would life be worth to me without you, my treasure?"

Later that night I passed Steve in the corridor. He scowled almost fiercely at me, but did not say a word. I knew why.

XXXVIII

The following day Steve noticed that Cecilia was behaving very strangely. She cut all her classes and spent the morning alone in her room. The afternoon she passed in the solitude of her organ chamber. Whenever they were together she was especially loving towards him, but she seemed preoccupied and a little dizzy. Her thoughts wandered, her sentences trailed off, her words got all mixed up. He caught her humming to herself several times. But he was not perturbed by these eccentricities—after all it was her time, and this was Cecilia. Nevertheless he shadowed her throughout the day whenever he could with the dedication of a practiced sleuth. He was not about to permit her to fall into a repeat of yesterday's heart-wrenching episode.

During supper she scarcely uttered a word, but the furtive glances she tossed at him were like little jetting leaks of something big and powerful stored up inside her.

After supper she took him by the hand and led him to her organ chamber in the music hall. "I want to show you something," she said. She seated him in the chair and climbed onto the organ bench, spreading out on the music stand before her several sheets of staff paper covered with handwritten words and notes. Steve was mesmerized by what she was doing.

Her hands came down on the keyboard in a powerful opening declaration. Then the music receded into overlapping waves of a simple fugue which gathered momentum to an intense climax before melting away into a lovely choral figure. This turned into another fugue, more subdued than the first one but just as intense. It too faded off into a quiet denouement that lingered just long enough to bring the music to a perfect end.

When she was finished she closed her eyes tightly, tears squirting out from under her eyelids, and let her fingers float over the keyboard in a soft reprise of the main themes, finally allowing her hands to drop to her lap. Then she raised her head, swung around on the bench, and looked straight into Steve's gaping eyes.

"My love," she said. "This is part of yesterday. It is for us. I want it to surprise you. You won't forget the name 'Susan Dahl,' will you?"

"Susan Dahl," he repeated. "No, I won't forget it. Ever."

A smile toyed with the corners of his lips at the thought that she had written this wonderful music for them. But in Cecilia's eyes there was only pleading. After staring into her eyes for a long moment, he stepped up to the bench and kissed her on the forehead. Then he turned to go.

"You won't forget?" she asked again, the pleading still in her eyes.

"Susan Dahl. I won't forget, my dear angel. I'll come back later as usual."

Steve felt much better as he descended the staircase. So, she wanted to surprise him! He was still humming the melody of the second fugue, experiencing once again its intensity and beauty. So, this was a part of yesterday, was it? What might that mean? He would have to wait until his Cecilia decided it was the right time to unveil her surprise for him. But it would be worth the wait!

She was something else, his Cecilia!

XXXIX

The weekend was soon upon them again. The temperatures had steadily fallen all week long. Friday night the wind blew with slicing sharpness as soon as the sun fell below the horizon. Except in the small patches where the sun had melted it a little, the fine powdery snow shifted and drifted back and forth. Steve and Cecilia decided to spend the evening in the lounge of the women's dormitory with a few other people listening to phonograph records on the new Gramophone which had recently been donated by someone.

More amusing than any vaudeville act, especially for Cecilia, the odd-looking machine ground out in squealing bursts of noise something that vaguely resembled Beethoven or Tchaikovsky or Bach. The foibles and distortions produced by those early attempts at recording tickled Cecilia's funny bone all evening long. Steve was just as amused by her reaction to these puny sounds as he was by the sounds themselves. When the anemic strings in Cesar Franck's "Symphony in D Minor" struggled and surged upwards toward a thin climax, with the great brass choir making its pompous entry sounding more like a collection of Cracker Jack whistles than the trumpets of doom, she nearly broke up.

By 9:30, however, she was looking all tired out. Noting this, Steve, to ensure that their time together was always a blessing for her and not a burden, took her hands in his, raised her up off the davenport where they had been seated, and suggested that she go right to bed and sleep in as late in the morning as she wanted to, since he knew she had no classes on Saturday. She lay her head on his shoulder (you couldn't really kiss romantically in public in those days), squeezed his hands, and said she would.

Steve, for his part, on leaving the dorm, did not feel at all like going to bed. The biting antiseptic air cleared out his head and aroused within him the desire to tackle something really challenging. The library was still open, he noted. He might just find something suitable to his mood in there. So he detoured into the library and headed for the "stacks" which, though formerly so repellant to him, he was now often finding strangely attractive. The only nook in the whole entanglement that was familiar to him was Stack Five, northeast corner. Here was deposited a collection of treatises on mathematics and physics to which he had infrequent recourse. Surveying the offerings on the shelves, his eyes were arrested by one that read *The Collected Mathematical and Scientific Dissertations and Treatises of Blaise Pascal*. He pulled it out, blew the dust off, opened it, and observed on the checkout card that no one had ever taken it out. An inscription informed him that it had been a part of the private library of one "Hjertaas Jensen" which had been bequeathed to the college in 1897.

"Hmmm," he muttered, fondling the heavy relic. "You ought to do the trick."

He sat down in an unoccupied carrel and was soon absorbed in the first chapter: "Dissertation on Conic Sections Presented to les mathematiciens parisiens at Sixteen Years of Age." He followed the youthful Pascal around in this admirable essay until he picked up on the direction of his thought and then sailed on ahead of his words to stand back and watch Pascal drift by just as he knew he would. He enjoyed playing this game with essays like this one. First, you had to bend your mind to follow the hand that wrote the work and the eyes that were now reading it; but once your mind caught the scent, so to speak, it could race on ahead and claim the quarry before the author got there. It was real fun.

About that time the lights in the "stacks" blinked on and off. Just as the thing was getting really interesting! So creeping down the narrow circular stairwell to the desk, he checked out the volume and trotted off to the dorm with it tucked safely under his arm. The wind, he observed, had grown milder now, almost balmy, in the short time he had been in the library.

The corridor was deserted and Ted was in bed. So Steve sat down at a table in the lounge and opened the book. Glancing at his watch, it was 10:15 p.m.

The next time he looked at his watch it said 3:35 a.m. Ridiculous! The thing must be on the blink! It couldn't be more than midnight. Well, he'd just finish the chapter he was on and call it a night.

When he finally rolled into bed, his eyes were starting to ache. That fool watch said 4:20. He'd have to get it fixed.

Two hours later the washed-out grays of dawn seeped through the window, unnoticed by Steve.

An hour after that, Steve was faintly conscious of Ted stirring around. He groggily replied to his roommate's libelous conjecture as to why he had got in so late the night before.

An hour and a half later he bounced to life when Ted strode into the room and slammed the door.

"What's the matter?" he almost shouted in alarm.

"The matter? Nothing, Casanova. Nothing except the snow is melting, that's all! Another two or three days of weather like this and we'll have the robins back!"

"Dang! What time have you got? I can't trust my watch."

"It's 9:00 Saturday morning, in the year 1920. Don't ask me the date. All I know is that spring is early and you're still in bed."

Steve gazed glassy-eyed into the quilt on his lap.

"O rats," he muttered, seeing that his watch had been correct all the time. Good thing he'd told Cecilia to sleep in late. Otherwise she'd have expected him to meet her for breakfast and be worried about him by now.

He touched his eyes. They were tender to the touch.

"But it was worth it," he told himself.

XL

In his 10:20 physics class, Steve nearly dozed off several times. He would like to have called the whole thing off and gone back to bed. The soreness in his eyes had reached the point that when he closed his eyes it would creep forward and escape through his eyelids, but when he opened them it screwed itself slowly further back into his head. He knew from experience that the more deeply it entrenched itself in his head, the more difficult it would be to rout. If only he could come by a couple of hours of sleep right now, he would have a normal day.

Somehow he managed to stay awake through Dr. Brockhaus' class. Fragments of the formulae and segments of the lines of reasoning which had absorbed him the previous night kept floating through his mind, drifting round and round in lazy spirals. They kept swarming around him like yellow jackets at a garbage pit—which was a pretty good description of what he was feeling like. Their monotonous buzzing drilled itself into his brain. Normally he enjoyed this kind of stuff, but when your eyes and head feel like they are about to pop, a fellow can't even enjoy what he usually enjoys the most.

Now hold it a minute! It was Cecilia that he "enjoyed" the most, and he could enjoy her anytime.

I wonder, though, if my angel Cecilia were sitting beside me right now, he asked himself, *how much would I be able to actually enjoy her through this lousy headache and these aching eyes? They say England lost America because of someone's gout.*

Lunchtime gave him a chance to move around a little. Distractions pulled his mind away from Pascal's theorems and his own throbbing headache, especially the distraction of Cecilia. He thought she had never looked so lovely as she looked as she was coming down the walk in front of the dormitory to meet him for lunch. There was an almost unreal airiness about her.

"Good morning, my love!" she exclaimed. "Isn't it a beautiful day?"

Squinting fiercely he scanned the bright sky, inhaled the fragrant air, and pressed her hand in his.

"Yes," he said. "It sure is."

And maybe it would be, after all.

After lunch they stepped out onto the veranda of the cafeteria. It was deserted. Beneath them lay a sweeping view of the countryside to the south.

Suddenly Cecilia lit up!

"Why don't we go for a motorcycle ride this afternoon? It's so warm and sunny. We could take a picnic and ride over to that hill way over there and have an early supper outdoors right under those trees and be back before dark."

She was pointing to a wooded bluff just a few miles away where they had gone once before in the fall.

"*This* afternoon?"

"Why not?" There was that sparkle in her voice again that he hadn't heard for a several days.

"Well, for one thing, we'd get plenty wet going and coming."

"We could dress for it. We could take some spare socks and build a fire when we get there. Wouldn't you love to do that? It'd be a real adventure."

"That it would," Steve agreed.

"And for another thing?" she teased.

"For another thing…," he began hesitantly.

He looked into her eager eyes.

"You're right. Let's go!"

XLI

Eagerly they walked over to the women's dorm. Steve's headache seemed to disappear while he was waiting for Cecilia. What wonders that girl could effect! She had chased away his pain as easily as dawn scatters darkness. He felt game for anything. And that was a good thing, because here she was, coming towards him all dressed up for riding and holding a small bundle in front of her.

"There's a picnic lunch in here for us," she said with a smile, handing it to him.

Next they walked over to the men's dorm. Steve could feel her hand trembling just slightly in his. There was something a bit light-headed about her today which made her all the more attractive to him. Probably she was not entirely herself yet. Was it wise for him to yield to her impulsive request and take her out into the country today? She might regret it tomorrow.

Ah well, he concluded to himself. *Once we get there both of us can relax and rest. That's as good a place to do it as anywhere, I suppose.*

His few moments of worrying about Cecilia's condition had just refanned the smoldering embers in his own head. He would need that rest!

It took him no time at all to get into some thick warm clothes and put on his cycle jacket. He, like Cecilia, brought along an extra pair of dry socks. Soon they were sputtering down the hill toward the wooded bluff in the distance.

The roads in town were, of course, in fairly good condition. The current of springlike air rushing past Cecilia's bared face and through her blond hair lifted her heart right out of her up towards the sky. She clung to Steve, inhaling deeply and soaking in the vernal delights all around her. She marveled at the gleaming purity of the snow shimmering under the noonday sun.

Steve too was marveling at the snow. He had not expected it to be so dazzling. The shafts of sunlight glancing off the glossy surface of the snow drove themselves like daggers through his squinting eyes into the most sensitive part of his headache. The ointment of Cecilia's delight in the ride had no effect on this acidic onslaught. Things had better improve once they got onto the country roads. He didn't know why they should, but they had better!

In point of fact, the situation deteriorated even further when they left town and turned onto the road leading to the bluff. Steve now had to cope not only with glaring snow but also with demanding road conditions. Normally it would have been great fun for him. But today it was pure torture. On all sides the blinding sea of fire stretched out all the way to the horizon, implacable and inescapable, daring him to slice his way through it over the lacerated and sloppy roadbed. Under the slop, the ground was still frozen solid, forming a hard surface slickened by the slush and half-melted mire. Defiantly Steve propped open his protesting eyelids and clung to the handlebars to keep the machine on the road and prevent it from spinning out of control. On and on it went. It took everything he had to break through the red wall of pain in his eyes and force himself to react nimbly to the challenges of the road—here a deep rut, there a treacherous mudhole, here a large rock, there a fallen branch. On and on and on.

Poor Cecilia, enjoying every frolicking moment of it and assuming that Steve was enjoying it too! He was in his element, after all. How could she know that the tenseness in his body was different today from every other day? How could she know that this was proving to be pure torture for him, not the thrill he usually experienced in overcoming challenging road conditions?

Steve made a firm decision to resign himself to the struggle. That helped. No point in fighting the pain. There was enough to fight on the road.

Just open your eyes wide and let it come, he lectured to himself. *You've got mighty precious baggage here to be worrying about your eyes. Just get her there safely*, he told himself over and over again. He had to remind himself constantly that his baggage was precious because even with her arms around his waist, she didn't *feel* precious. His feelings were consumed by the massive ball of fire stabbing him in both eyes and sending explosive throbs into his head. By sheer force of reason he flung his feelings aside and focused on Cecilia and the challenges of the road.

At last, the struggle ground to a jerking halt. Steve turned up a little pathway leading to the place where they had come earlier in the fall and pulled up beside a great oak tree. Cecilia jumped off the cycle and danced around to the front, but Steve remained anchored to the seat gunning the engine, his eyes pressed tightly shut. He could hardly believe it was all over. Slowly he let the roar of the engine which had become synonymous with life die away.

Here they come, he shuddered to himself, anticipating the stabbing pains in his head which he had been holding at bay. She was standing in front of him grinning spritely. He looked up.

"That was quite something, wasn't it," he heard himself remark.

She nodded abruptly.

"Let's go take a rest under that tree. A drive like that sort of takes it out of a fellow for a while."

He fumbled his way over to the tree and sank into a bed of warm dry leaves trapped in a hollow between two big roots and bathed in the afternoon sun. The old oak clung to the hillside near the top of the windward flank of the bluff. The prevailing wind had sent most of the snow skittering over the top of the bluff to the leeward flank.

Steve shut his eyes, his head propped solidly between the two large roots.

"Cecilia," he said absently. "I think I'm just going to take a little nap for a few minutes."

"Sure," she said. "You've earned it."

In a moment he was unconscious.

Meanwhile Cecilia gathered some dry wood, cleaned out an open area in the leaves not far from Steve, and lit a crackling fire to help keep him warm. Then she poked around in his bag until she found his dry socks. Unlacing his left shoe, she eased it off without disturbing him and peeled off the wet sock. She touched his toes. They felt numb. So she massaged them and the rest of his foot briskly until his whole foot was pink again. She put on the dry stocking and, turning to the other foot, gave it the same treatment. The shoes she set closer to the fire to dry out. Then for an hour or so she sat below Steve, massaging his stocking feet and tending the fire.

Sitting there she gazed at the trees. A squirrel scampered back and forth between two nearby oaks, apparently just for the fun of it. A blue jay stirred up a racket high overhead.

They always sound like they're scolding someone, but I think it's just their way of laughing, she told herself.

For a long time she mused on these things. Then quietly, imperceptibly, an awesome sense of the vastness and providential goodness of Creation began to stir within her. It was the spotless fathomless blue of the sky and the endless whiteness of the earth. It was the time-warped gnarls of the ancient oaks in contrast to the fleeting nowness of the little woodland creatures scampering around in them. It was the fragrance-laden breezes and the cozy cushion of leaves. It was the sun's benediction and the earth's adoration. It was all of this and more, distilled in the all-embracing love of God and in Steve and Cecilia's blossoming love for each other. Her heart was bursting with joy. God had been so good to them!

At that moment Steve stirred. She looked up at him from where she was sitting at his feet. His eyes blinked and opened and then pressed shut.

"O Steve," she purred with quiet ardor. "Isn't God wonderful? I've just been soaking in this tiny corner of His vast creation and thinking of how great He is, and of all He's done for us."

Steve blinked again and pinched his eyes back shut, reeling from the brightness as from the door of a blast furnace.

"Mmmmm," he mumbled. "We are pretty lucky, aren't we?"

She looked at him a little crestfallen.

"Lucky?" she asked softly. "Wouldn't you rather say 'blessed'? God has blessed us, don't you think?"

"You sound just like my mother."

"Like your mother?"

She was still rubbing his feet. He didn't talk much about his parents.

"You must love her very much," she suggested.

"There is only one person in the world that I love very much," he muttered between his teeth. "Only one person I'd drive through a wall of fire with a splitting headache for, just because she wants to come out here."

Cecilia fell back in alarm.

"O my love! Why didn't you tell me you had a headache? We would never have come out here if I had only known! Why didn't you tell me?"

"Because," he replied slowly, opening his eyes a slit and wobbling his head drunkenly with each word, "because you're the one person in the whole world I'd walk through burning coals to reach if you were on the other side. That's why."

His head fell back, his eyes pressed shut again.

Cecilia turned her pleading eyes away and peered into the fire. All at once she felt like crying. She swallowed hard. Then she looked back at him. Her throat was tight. Her tongue felt swollen. She got up and sat down next to his head. Gently she rested her hand on his forehead.

"But … can you love me and not love everyone else too?" Tears were blurring her eyes now. She blinked and one big tear fell onto his cheek.

Steve was simply going to answer, "Of course I can." But something in her voice checked him before he spoke.

"Actually," he said very softly instead, "when I'm feeling more like myself and when my heart is full of you, I guess you could say that my love for you spills over to everyone else, too, in some sense. Yes, you could say that."

She leaned over and kissed him on the forehead.

Now she was lightly caressing his eyeballs through his eyelids. It felt good.

In the silence that followed, Steve mulled over what he had just said, moving from confusion to greater clarity.

Could a headache subvert his love for her? No, not really. But it could sure subvert his love for others beyond her. His love for her, based on a clear rational decision of his in response to everything that had led up to it, was an openly acknowledged factor in his life. It was his life! It was lodged just as firmly in his mind as it was in his heart. If pain drove her out of the feelings of his heart, she was still very much in his mind. His feelings for her could be, and almost always were, quite overwhelming, but his love for her was sustained by more than his feelings. It was sustained by his decision to love her and to believe in her love for him.

But what of his love for others beyond her? Had he ever openly acknowledged its existence or defined it as an important factor in his life? Let's face it: it was a by-product of his love for her, and entirely on the feeling level. He didn't even know he was doing it when he was doing it! No wonder it simply disappeared when something like a headache destroyed the feeling side of love. Now he had his finger on it....

Listen, old boy, he warned himself severely. *That's the way it's got to stay. If you experience this "love for others" as a spontaneous offshoot of your love for Cecilia, well and good. When it springs from your heart all by itself, no problem. But why would you ever let it get entrenched in your mind? It could make a real sucker of you if you thought you had to love others no matter how you felt about it. Loving Cecilia is so rewarding. It's worth any personal sacrifice on your part because of the returns it brings. If loving her flows over into loving even people you have every good reason to despise, then at least recognize the fact that you are under no obligation to love them when you don't feel like it, when it doesn't come naturally. What did you learn last summer? Two things at least: the joy of authentic companionship and the stupidity of clinging to an ideal, like wilderness living, when you have stopped desiring it. So, you can love others as long as loving Cecilia makes you want to. But careful about taking it further than that.*

At this moment he knew he was living on his decision to love her. His heart could feel almost nothing. It was as though reading the wedding notice of a couple of strangers in the newspaper, he could neither doubt their happiness nor share in it. Sheer reason would have to carry him through today. Here she was, loving him with all her heart and tearfully stroking his brow, while all he could do through his blinding headache was to calculate that he loved her.

Such pretty bits of insight, arranged so neatly and encased in my poor aching head. Why can you think *love when your head aches, but you can't* feel *it? You have to think yourself through the motions of love. Here is an angel sitting by my head, running her fingers across my brow, caressing my throbbing eyeballs, and letting her tears fall on my face. And here I lie, almost as unmoved as a stone. All on account of the fact that I am suffering from the worst headache of my life, which is all on account of one Blaise Pascal, which is all on account of my curiosity getting the better of me, which is all on account of my feeling so good last night, which is all on account of how high I was riding after being with her, which is all on account of how much I love her! How crazy is life! You can start out in heaven and wind up in hell! Well, thank God that with her I will be out of this hell and back up to heaven again tomorrow. So stick it out, man, and don't do anything stupid.*

He opened his eyes. She was looking down at him, questions written all over her face. He reached for her hand and pulled her down to his side. The effort itself pumped poison into his head, but he bore it without wincing. Taking her into his arms, he said, "All I know is that I love you more than life itself. Please believe me. I can't love anybody without loving you."

She rested her head on his chest. His heart was thumping beneath his shirt. *What a strange thing to say*, she thought. *Not that loving me makes him love everyone, but that he can't love anyone without loving me.... My poor Steve must be bearing a terrible wound in his heart.*

Lying there with her head on his chest, she felt his breathing become more regular, as though he were dozing off. She put her right arm around his rib cage and very gently drew him in more tightly against her.

"O Jesus!" she prayed softly under her breath. "How can I help You heal that terrible wound in his heart! I'll do anything You ask of me for him, dear Savior. Anything! Whatever it takes. I love him so much."

They lay there for some time without stirring. At length Steve took a deep breath and shifted his position.

"Cecilia, would you please get me the first-aid kit under the seat of the cycle? It's just a tiny box. There are two aspirins in it. I'm going to take them now."

She fetched it for him.

"Now a handful of clean snow."

She brought it. He placed the two aspirins in his mouth and swallowed them without water. Then he took some of the snow, melted it in his mouth, and swallowed it, too.

"That's what I get for being an amateur scientist," he said, laughing weakly. "Pills don't do much good without something to dissolve them in. Now we'll give them a few minutes to go to work. Then I have something to tell you that I've wanted to tell you for a long time."

She sat down next to him.

"No, here," he motioned, patting his chest with one hand and stretching out the other towards her. So she lay down again, her head beneath his chin and her slender body extended alongside his and enfolded in his arm.

They lay like that for several minutes, with their eyes closed. Then Steve opened his eyes. The headache had subsided to a mere annoyance. He inhaled deeply and felt her head rise with his chest. He gazed down at her golden hair. She went out of focus and in his mind's eye he beheld the indistinct form of his Spectre Maiden in all its tantalizing beauty. Love surged into his heart, warm and real.

"Cecilia, I want to tell you about the Maiden from Heaven that I fell in love with this summer," he breathed.

Her heart almost stopped.

"Mmmmmm," she purred. Was this his great wound?

Several times he opened his mouth, but nothing came out. "I don't know where to begin," he admitted.

"I want to hear it all, my love. So why not go back to where it starts?"

"To where it starts," he echoed. "That takes you all the way back to a big empty farmhouse in North Dakota and to a mother that was constantly nagging her husband and a father that paid no attention to his wife or his son. For each of them, life had become a self-inflicted drudgery, but for different reasons. It wasn't until their kid got away to school that he discovered that you didn't have to hate life every blessed moment of the day because there were some things you could do just for the fun of it.

"So what did the poor kid do? He got out of the house every chance he could. He raced horses, dreamed up ridiculous pranks, stormed the countryside in the Model T Ford his dad bought for him probably to make up for his neglect, wandered around outside all by himself, not joyfully like you used to do but restlessly, and spent his time figuring things out in his head that most people ignore, and generally raising Cain when he could.

"Everything he enjoyed, decent people looked down on. Everything he couldn't stand, decent people spent their life pursuing. He knew lots of people who hated what they said they liked and liked what they said they hated, so he took any advice from them with a grain of salt. First thing you know, his mother was pushing him off to college and his father was trying to palm off the farm on him.

"So off he goes to college, hating every blessed minute of it except when he can get away on weekends with the fellows. But pretty soon this goes sour on him too. He gets a bellyful of that kind of stuff and about goes crazy trying to figure out what there is in the world that's worth doing. Something inside him won't give him any rest. Everyone is trying to get him to amount to something, as they define it. His professors, his mother, his father all have a clear idea of what he should be doing. He just wants to break free and fly away while he still can. Where? Who cares! Just so it's away.

"Something about the wilderness attracts him, away from everybody and everything that could ensnare him and close to the creatures in nature who live by instinct and do only what they feel like doing. So he turns his back on all the rubbish people have dreamed up to turn their lives into pure drudgery in the name of duty, and takes off on his motorcycle for parts unknown, preferably in a forest somewhere.

"All right, fine and dandy. After nearly a month of disappointment and dead ends, he literally stumbles into a paradise in Upper Michigan.... A paradise, I tell you, Cecilia, a real paradise...."

His voice trailed off and his throat tightened up. Cecilia had been hanging onto each word. Her heart was bleeding for him.

"It was beautiful, my love, so beautiful. And perfect for my purposes. A lush basin in the silent hills just south of Lake Superior. Pines and cedars and great hardwoods. Dotted with sun-splattered glades. Bisected by a tumbling stream of pure cold water. Birds and animals. Everything I loved. Nothing I hated."

"O Steve," she interrupted. "Will you take me there sometime? I'd love to be in a place like that with you!... I'm sorry. Continue."

"Well, at first I was overjoyed. I tinkered around building a camp. It was great fun. Before long I had finished the campsite, finished scouting the area, finished all my preparations for the good life there. So I settled back and waited for happiness. Well, Cecilia,... you'll never believe it, but I had already had all the happiness I was going to get in that place. I'd already had it....

"Then one day as I was tramping around, I ran into a big silver dog that I named King. Or rather, he found me and decided I was his friend. He was very handsome, a husky, silver and white except for a patch of black under his neck. When he looked at you, you figured he understood you. His eyes were a little Oriental, made him look very wise. Well, he stayed with me all summer. And, Cecilia, that creature never got his fill of trying to please me, even when I was all wrapped up in myself and ignoring him. I tell you before God that he was the first living creature I knew who really loved me just as I was, and I guess I learned to love him in return.

"Early one morning I was awakened by his howling. It turned out that our camp was right in the path of a couple of huge warring ant colonies. A tree full of wood ants had fallen over a big mound of earth ants, and did they ever fight! All day long we watched them whittle each other down from two huge warring hoards to almost nothing, all over a misunderstanding. The only survivor I could see at the end of the battle was the queen of the wood ants, and she was maimed.

"Can you imagine what that left me feeling like? Why was I allowed to witness this? Would it all be to no purpose? What could *I* be expected to do about it, for crying out loud? I was all twisted up in a knot. From that point on, everything in the forest seemed to spell 'futility' to me. I was restless, closed off from the beautiful world around me, and terribly alone.

"Anyhow, an unbelievable thing happened to me that same night. I dreamed of the ants, of course, and of King and of my wilderness paradise. They were all tumbling around together in my dream, not making any sense. And then, all of a sudden…."

Steve paused. He choked up. He took a deep breath.

"This is the part you won't believe, my love. All of a sudden, in the midst of all that chaos, *you* were there!"

Cecilia's head jerked around. She looked up at him, her eyes as big as saucers.

"ME?"

"Yes, , Cecilia. All of a sudden there you were. And the moment you appeared in the distance, the world stood still. A hush fell over everything, and all I saw was you. But you were so far away. It was as if you had come to me, to us, from another realm because we needed you so badly. Your eyes were cast down and I can still see you in my mind's eye sobbing quietly over us. Yes, I knew somehow that you were weeping for me, for us all, for the ants, for this poor old world. I wanted to come to you so badly, but I couldn't move. You approached a little closer to me, your eyes still wet with tears, and then you disappeared. I woke up, all out of breath.

Steve tightened his grip on her. He was breathing heavily. She was speechless.

"I can't explain how it was that you came to me," he went on. "You seemed to just come down from Heaven. For me, everything came together in you, my love. I can't explain it. It just did.

"From then on I had everything in that paradise except you, and so I had nothing. All it took was a whiff of your love to reduce all my other loves to ashes. In the following days my Spectre Maiden—that's what I called you—would appear to me anytime, anywhere. She would tantalize me and then disappear into thin air. I became obsessed with her to the point where I despised myself for it. I knew no such person could really exist, much less for me; but in my heart and my sick imagination she was always hovering near me.

"To this day, my beloved Cecilia, I can only marvel at it, and I always will. You really do exist, and you exist for me. The only one of you in the whole wide world, in the whole universe! I love the real you, and—wonder of wonders—you love the real me. It's too much, too much...."

He burrowed his face into her hair. Both of them were now sniffling softly.

"You can't imagine what a shock it was to me when I first caught sight of you in the cafeteria. The Spectre Maiden I had fallen so crazily in love with was standing in front of me in flesh and blood, almost close enough for me to touch. I didn't dare to hope for more than to get a glimpse of you on campus from time to time, you were so beautiful. So heart-meltingly beautiful. And now this. Now this....

"Without you, my angel, I am not even half a man. But with you...."

"Yes, yes, my dear Steve. Without you I'm not even half a woman.

And both of us together, united with our dear Lord in love, will know pure joy. We're awfully close to it already. It is a wonder."

Steve was shifting around to feel her precious body against his in a new position. Drawing her tightly to him he whispered, "If you had been with me in the hollow this summer, everything would have been perfect. We would have soaked up the still moonlit nights together and taken great pleasure together in the events of each day. We would have been so happy. We would have figured out what to do about the ant war. We would have had a plan. You are close enough to God to make that happen, and I am close enough to you to let it happen. Our arms would not have been empty. I guess we'd have to be married to do that, wouldn't we!"

She snuggled up to him. It was her way of saying, "I guess we would."

She whispered back, "Jesus will give us everything we need for happiness on earth and in Heaven forever."

Steve winced. He was too vulnerable at the moment to hear that, though at other moments it made perfect sense to him. She filled him. Why couldn't he fill her? Why did she always have to have Jesus along?

And now his headache was recouping its strength. The dull smarting around his eyes was slowly spreading again and his eyes themselves were burning. The longer he lay there, the more spent he felt.

"Cecilia, would you mind if we waited until sundown to go back? It will be much easier for me to drive in the dark."

"That's just fine," she replied. "I feel so sad for persuading you to come out here when you are not well. I pray that you and God will forgive me."

"Supposing only I do?"

Cecilia started in surprise. *Supposing only I do?' Whatever could he mean by that?* She looked up into his eyes, confusion written all over her face.

Steve did not really expect her to answer such a silly question.

"I don't understand, Steve. What do you mean?"

"I mean, don't you ever feel as if you and I are the only beings in the universe and that the only love and forgiveness that really counts is yours and mine? Don't you ever feel that our love is just between us?"

Quite unexpectedly a lump formed in his throat and the dull throbbing in his head seemed to be sublimated into a real spiritual agony. Was he really questioning their love?

Immediately Cecilia caught on to his pathos. It was all related to what he had told her about his lonely childhood. As her heart went out to him, a light veil slipped down over it. She had suspected it before, but now she knew that to Steve, at the moment at least, for her to love God first was to love him less. She struggled to find the right words. She had never felt for one moment that God was any less close to her because she was in love with Steve, or that Steve was less close to her because she was in love with God. But obviously that was not how he felt, yet.

"Steve, my love. For me, it doesn't work like that. I have more love for you when I love God first than I could ever have if I didn't. His love for us, and ours for Him, kindles the fire of our love for each other. If I didn't love Him most, I would love you less. It makes me so happy to have such a rich source of love in the Heart of God, a source that never goes dry. Please believe me. My love for God takes nothing away from my love for you. It makes it all the stronger. Do you see what I mean? It all fits together."

Steve pinched his eyes shut. His dear little Cecilia! He would try to understand. But it felt to him as though everything about their love had to be censored by God before she could embrace it. That's not what she meant, he knew, but it was what it felt like to him. Would she always be like that? Would there always be that Third Person intruding into their relationship, from her side? Steve was too worn out to pursue this any further, but it continued to unsettle him.

Cecilia sensed he couldn't absorb what she had said in the shape he was in. She knew he was not feeling well and so she wrote it off to that. She lay by his side, saddened by their first little disagreement but confident that some good would come of it in time. A good night's sleep would heal the little wounds opened this afternoon. They had too much going for them to let a day like today put their whole future in jeopardy.

"I think that love is the private property of two lovers and resents any intruders," he muttered.

With that Cecilia patted him on the cheek and got up to fix a little lunch for them before sundown. But her heart was restless. She thought of all the things that had preoccupied her these past few days and silently she commended them all to God. She must try hard to help Steve to experience the love of God at first hand, and she must understand from what he had told her why it was not easy for him to enter into it.

As for Steve, he was still shaking his head. How could his splitting headache have wrecked a whole afternoon and left him feeling so unloved and so unloving? How could he have chosen to say things that obviously hurt his Cecilia so much? He must try to be decent to her now, try to be understanding. He needed her so badly. For God's sake, however crumby he was feeling, he didn't want to push her away!

I will be so glad to get back to the dorm, take a couple of aspirins, crawl in bed, and wake up to a new day and the prospect of a happy Sunday morning breakfast with my Cecilia, he told himself. *She'll look gorgeous in her Sunday clothes, and we'll be sitting side by side in church holding hands. Hang in there!*

He glanced at Cecilia preparing their simple supper. She seemed sad.

"My angel, I love you. Please forgive me."

"No. You forgive me."

She came over and knelt in front of him. Steve sat up. They threw their arms around each other and kissed and kissed.

"Let's not let this happen again."

"Never."

"We can't be afraid to be honest with each other."

"Not ever again."

They glanced at each other often as they downed their picnic supper mostly in silence. Love was in their eyes.

XLII

As they started down the road back to the campus, Steve began to doubt the wisdom of having waited until sundown to leave. Denied the mellowing rays of the sun, the earth snapped quickly out of its vernal interlude. It was more than a mere annoyance to bounce along on top of the newly frozen ruts chopping up the road. It was a real risk. Little canyons crisscrossed the hardening gravel and mud like a mad maze of railroad tracks all fouled up. To maneuver through them safely demanded unflagging concentration from Steve. For Cecilia, the ride home was the opposite of the ride out. It was pure agony for her to know what Steve was suffering for her sake. She had to hang onto him tightly just to prevent herself from being thrown off the cycle as it bounced and bucked along.

But there was one good thing about it: the glare was gone. Pain was no longer ramming itself into Steve's skull from the outside; it was just a dull ache seeping out from behind his eyes. It comforted him to know that it was not going to last much longer. He could feel the swollen arteries in his head throbbing on the sensitive membranes that surrounded them, almost sluggishly now compared to the punishment they had taken earlier. It was like a dull venom in his head, numbing his senses. As he swerved through and around the ruts in the deepening darkness, the whole exercise took on the feel of an interminable nightmare.

He was grateful to feel Cecilia's arms around his waist. They would get through this, and they would be happy again. Just knowing she was there made the struggle possible for him. He couldn't give up!

The roadbed was getting harder. Picking his way across it, Steve would skid the cycle along in one rut and then have to hammer it across into the next one to avoid a hash of holes ahead. He tried the middle of the road, but that was no better. Many of the ruts there were on a diagonal as though someone had skillfully laid them out to ensnare motorcycles. He was not moving very fast, but the whole thing was steadily grinding his nerves to shreds.

Soon daylight faded away and his dim headlight was all he had to go by. He sank into a kind of trance, lurching from one near disaster to the next. He tried to banish all thoughts and mental images that might distract him from concentrating on his driving, and mostly he succeeded.

Finally Steve turned a corner and the lights of St. Mark came into view, less than a mile away. The roads would be better there.

"We're almost home, my love. You're amazing!" Cecilia shouted into his ear.

A few minutes later they were in town and the going was much smoother. The cycle turned onto Christiania Avenue. It was in excellent condition. The wheels bit into the road surface with smooth traction and they roared up the gentle incline all the way to the base of the hill. There the road curved to the right. Steve gunned the engine to get them up the steeper incline.

At that very moment the cycle struck a patch of ice where melting snow had run across the road during the day. It spun out of control, skittering wildly off the road. An ominous crash sounded sickeningly over the campus. Then, more sickening still, silence.

Minutes later an ambulance raced up to the scene from the hospital. A motorcycle carrying two passengers had skidded into the retaining wall above the power plant at high speed.

The male driver was rushed to the hospital.

The crumpled form of his passenger, a young woman, was gently gathered up and taken directly to the mortuary.

Even the mortician wept when he wiped the congealed blood from her face and beheld her lifeless beauty.

XLIII

Some three months had passed since the tragic accident above the power plant. Most of the students and faculty members had forgotten about it. Mid-semester examinations were over, and everyone was gearing up for the final push.

The Christiania College Choir, having just returned from its annual concert tour, was to present its home concert tonight. Already the auditorium was filling up with eager concert-goers, anticipating a splendid evening of sacred music. The choir was riding on the crest of the high praise Eastern critics had lavished on its entire program.

As the curtain rose on the handsomely robed choir, a lone figure on crutches made his way to an inconspicuous corner at the back of the auditorium where he could remain standing without bothering anyone.

The first section of the program consisted of Bach's sublime Easter cantata, "Christ lag in Todesbanden," based on Luther's hymn, accompanied by an excellent small ensemble of string and wind instruments.

The second section was composed of shorter works of a meditative nature, such as Mozart's "Ave Verum." The last of these was a work entitled "Verily" in which the words of Jesus from the twelfth chapter of the Gospel of John were set to music:

"Verily, verily, I say unto you,

Except a grain of wheat fall into the ground and die, it abideth alone: but if it die, it bringeth forth much fruit."[1]

No information was offered in the program notes about the composer, Susan Dahl.

The music, a striking opening statement followed by two contrasting fugues, both intense and sublime, left the audience spellbound from start to finish, with the message of Jesus still ringing in their ears when the last chord faded away.

At the very first note, however, the young man at the back, leaning forward on his crutches, broke into convulsive sobs which he tried hard to muffle.

"Your surprise, my angel. Your surprise…."

When it was over, Stephan Pearson, tottering on his crutches and trembling all over, stood staring at his feet, his eyes awash in tears.

The audience was still applauding when he pulled himself together, lurched forward towards the door, and fled out into the cold and lonely night.

THE END OF BOOK ONE

---

[1] John 12:24 KJV

Book Two

I

The cold meant nothing to Steve, nor the heaviness in his chest, nor the sharp pains in his half-healed legs, as he stumbled his way back and forth in the snow under the moonlit trees behind the men's dorm that midnight, mumbling to himself the words on which he knew, to the core of his being, that his whole life would depend from this evening on. Coming as a total shock to him at the end of the concert, he could only hear them as Cecilia's parting words of love to him, direct from Heaven. He knew beyond a shadow of a doubt that he would either be living them out somehow in his remaining days on earth, bound through them in love to her forever, or he would ignore them and die a lingering and bitter death on earth, far from her and from her love for him.

But for the moment, they were confusing words to him. He didn't question their truth, but he was far from sure of their meaning. He didn't dare to let them slip away from him now. They were all he had left to live for. She had called them her "surprise" for him. She had told him this with tears in her eyes that night on the organ bench just as she was starting to emerge from those two shadowy days of mourning. He had felt so protective of her that night because she seemed so very vulnerable and so delicate and so possessed of a beauty and a sorrow that were not of this world. That night she had played him only the music, without the words. But tonight she had given him both the music and the words and they had hit him like a sledgehammer. Now they were tumbling round and round in his mind.

"Verily….

"A grain of wheat….

"Fall….

"Fall into the ground….

"Fall into the ground and die….

"Except it fall and die….

"It abideth alone….

"Alone….

"Alone….

"But if it die

"If it die….

"It bringeth forth much fruit….

"Except it die, it abideth alone….

"Alone except it die….

"But if it die….

"BUT IF IT DIE!"

Arrested by that single haunting detached phrase, Steve cried out into the darkness, "Better for me to die now, my angel, than to abide here alone, without you! Better, better, better for me to be with you where you are now than to be where I am, so alone, so terribly alone…. I told you. You do remember, don't you? I told you I'm nobody without you, my love. Nobody at all! And here I am without you, less than nobody. I never dreamed I would have to face life without you! Never!…

"You fell, and you died. But I am the one who is alone. You fell and died and now, according to Jesus' own words, you are supposed to 'bring forth much fruit'? How? How? What fruit can you bring forth now that you're gone? What fruit now?…

"All I want to do is fall and die, too, my poor sweet angel, after what I did to you! I just want to die now. O God, why can't I just die? Let me fall and die now! Just let me fall and die…."

Swaying back and forth on his crutches in the cold silent night, Steve sobbed his heart out. "Why can't I just die? Why can't I just die?..."

At length a picture began to form slowly in his benumbed mind, or rather several pictures. They were of his Cecilia back in Meadowville at Thanksgiving.

"But you were already doing it, my love. You were already falling and dying, and bearing much fruit. You were doing it right here. You didn't have to leave me to do it! You were always falling into the hearts of your friends, of anyone you met. You were always dying to yourself so that you could be alive for them. I could see with my own eyes all the fruit you were bringing forth in them. You were! My heart broke for love of you when I saw you creating all that love. You were just being you! I couldn't help it! I'd fallen in love with an angel, and by some miracle she'd fallen in love with me. God only knows why! You told me I would love all your friends. You made it impossible for me not to! I guess that's what happens when you are loved by an angel....

"Somehow, when you fell into my heart, it was different from all the other hearts you fell into. My heart was already a wide open cavern with a space hollowed out in advance just for you. Just for you.... You must have known this somehow, because you fell into my heart just as hard as I had already fallen into yours, and we filled each other's hearts to overflowing. You fell into my heart and died. You were willing to give me, the frog, everything you are. Everything! You held nothing back. Not a thing! You thought I was asleep under the tree when you told Jesus you would do anything for me. You said 'anything'! I heard you say that, drowsy as I was. I heard every word of it. Right there you were offering to fall into the ground of my poor heart, dear angel, and to die there for the love of clueless me! But for sure you had to be thinking of dying for me by living with me over the course of a lifetime together here on earth, right? That was what you meant by saying you would do 'anything' for me, wasn't it? You didn't mean......."

Once again Steve slumped over his crutches and broke into sobs for the umpteenth time since he'd regained consciousness in the hospital and was told by his parents what had happened two weeks earlier.

Teetering there in the cold, with the words of Cecilia's "surprise" for him still running through his head, a slender shaft of light pierced the darkness, as he later described it, and alighted on him. It came in the form of a voice in his head, her voice:

"Fall where you are and die there, Steve, my love, and you will not abide alone. I know you want to die and come to be with me. But if you stay where you are and fall and die, I will come to be with you. That is what I want. You will make me very happy, my love, if you fall and die and bring forth much fruit right where you are. You will make me very happy and I will come to you. I will!"

Silence.

The slender shaft of light suddenly brightened into a floodlight.

"You will? And it will make you very happy?" he almost shouted into the night. "I'll do it, then! I'll do it! I'll fall and die here. Just show me how, my love! I'll do it! Just show me what I can do to make you very happy with me!"

Silence.

The floodlight was now almost blinding him.

All at once Stephan shouted to the skies, "I get it! You want <u>me</u> to become the fruit <u>you</u> died to bring forth!"

He could hardly breathe.

Gathering all his strength he stood up straight and cried out, "O my God, if that's what she wants, if that's what my Cecilia really wants, You show me how to do it and I'll do it! I will do it! I don't care what it costs. I will do it for the angel You sent me from Heaven and I sent back to You in Heaven! I will give everything I have, everything I am, to become the fruit of her falling and her dying. So help me God, I will!...

"Only show me the ground, Cecilia's Jesus! Show me the ground that <u>You</u> want me to fall into and I'll fall into it all the way. I'll fall into it hard, and I will die there. So help me, I will die there! For her I will die there! Just show me the ground!"

Steve pulled himself together and went up to his room. Ted was asleep. In the dim light of his desk lamp he opened the top drawer of his desk and took out a plain envelope with his name on it. Opening the envelope, he carefully unfolded the single sheet of stationery it contained and read it yet again.

Dear Steve,

The Monday after Cecilia's funeral we boarded the train and came here to be with you. You have not regained consciousness, but your doctor says your vital signs are improving every day. We are so very thankful for this. We love you and pray for your full recovery.

We have to leave now to get back to Meadowville for Christmas services. We want you to know that we do not blame you for what happened. We know how much you love Cecilia and how much she loves you. We don't understand why Our Lord has allowed this to happen, but we trust that He means for something very good to come out of what seems to us such a senseless tragedy.

It has been good for us to meet your parents here at your bedside and to share with them many tears, but also our hope and our faith.

You have two homes now, Steve—your parents' home in North Dakota and our home in Meadowville. You will always be a son to us.

We know our Cecilia would have been a wonderful life's partner for you, and you for her. But instead God has given her to you to be your angel to go with you wherever you go, to intercede for you every day before the Throne of Grace, and to welcome you to your heavenly Home when that day arrives.

Please accept this portrait photo of Cecilia which we had her sit for at the time of her graduation from high school. She didn't do anything the photographer asked her to do to look glamorous, and so she looks like herself, don't you think?

God bless you, dear Steve! Steve, our son!

Love, Irv and Ellie

Returning the letter to the envelope, Steve whispered, "Cecilia's Jesus, You are too good! You're just too good!"

II

There was one man on campus to whom Stephan Pearson felt he could turn for help in understanding Cecilia's message to him, the Rev. Dr. John Engstrom, the college chaplain and a professor of religion. Although not yet forty years of age, he had earned three academic degrees and been honored with a fourth in acknowledgement of two groundbreaking books he had written in the new discipline of pastoral psychology. His classes were popular with the students and his chapel talks were brief and to the point, leaving you both challenged and inspired. Steve appreciated the way in which Dr. Engstrom never failed to effect an appealing tension and rapport between the everyday life of a student and life's deeper meaning in the will and purpose of God. The very next day Steve approached Dr. Engstrom after chapel and secured an appointment with him for the afternoon of the following day.

Dr. Engstrom had visited Steve several times in the hospital. He had witnessed Steve's incredulous stupor at what had happened and had suffered with him through the denial and turmoil it detonated in his mind and heart. He was aware that the doctors had released him sooner than usual for fear that lying longer in the hospital would break altogether his will to live. That same day he met both with the dean of women to learn as much as she could tell him about Cecilia and with Dr. Brockhaus, Steve's advisor, who left him in no doubt about Steve's towering intellect. He even made a special effort to call me into his office that evening to glean every insight he could from me about Steve and Cecilia's relationship. I have to say that he was deeply moved by what I shared with him from my perspective.

The next day Steve was punctual in keeping his appointment. His eagerness to plunge ahead with his midnight promise to Cecilia and to God was written all over his face. Still shaky on his crutches he appeared in the doorway. The pastor greeted him and beckoned him to come in.

Dr. Engstrom, aware that sitting was awkward for Steve, led him over to a high windowsill overlooking the campus and the countryside beyond. Beneath the sill was a bookshelf just the right height for Steve to lean on. Steve stood there for a few moments, not knowing exactly how to start the conversation. A faint hint of desperation passed over his face. Dr. Engstrom picked up on it and came to his rescue.

"I have a little confession to make, Steve. Yesterday I took the liberty of speaking with the dean of women and with Dr. Brockhaus and with Cecilia's cousin, Paul. I think I have a pretty good idea of what you and Cecilia meant to each other."

Steve's face relaxed and his eyes glistened. Gazing out the window, he remained silent long enough for a certain calmness to still his heart and cool his mind before he spoke. At length he turned to the pastor and asked, "Were you at the concert night before last?"

"Yes."

"Do you remember the last song, the one called, 'Verily'?"

"Yes. How could I forget it?"

"'Verily, verily I say unto you, Except a grain of wheat fall into the ground and die, it abideth alone. But if it die it bringeth forth much fruit."

"Yes, of course. I was very moved by it. Everybody else seemed to be too."

"Well … well … Cecilia wrote that song. The program said Susan Dahl. But that was my Cecilia. She wrote it for me."

Dr. Engstrom looked straight into Steve's eyes in extreme surprise. Then he closed his swelling eyes and lowered his head.

"That's why I'm here."

With that, the whole story came tumbling out, starting with his search for peace the previous summer and everything that had happened to him in his paradise, and especially the intervention of his Spectre Maiden. As detail after detail unfolded, right up to the accident, the good pastor's heart rose and fell with Steve's. They shared smiles and they shared tears.

"Pastor, she left me her life in that piece of music. It was the key to her happiness, and I now know that she wrote it to unlock mine. It would be so easy for me to fall into despair, and to stay there, over what I did to my angel. But that's not what she wants. She wants me to be the fruit of her death, to become what I would never have become without it, inconceivable as that may seem. That's the only thing I have left to live for. I have to find a way to fall into the right ground and die so that I can bear much fruit. It won't be the same as her way of doing it. But it has to have the same effect. It has to bring forth life and love and goodness in people. It has to bear fruit. Pastor, first I need to know what ground I am called to fall and die on, and then I need to throw myself down onto it full force, with everything I've got. I am here to ask for your help. What ground does God want me, Stephan Pearson, to fall and die on? How can I do what it will take to make my Cecilia happy so that she will smile down at me from Heaven?"

Steve choked up.

The pastor took a deep breath and stroked his chin for a few moments.

"Steve, you have well grasped the secret of Cecilia's life, what made her so beautiful and so deeply happy. And you have seen that Jesus is telling us in the words of the song that this is the key not only to her happiness but to the happiness of every other person too. Of all of us! Grasping this truth is already a first fruit of her death.... But you are challenging me to help you identify which specific ground God is calling you to fall and die on so that you can bring forth much fruit. I think I know the answer. Yes, I think I know...."

Dr. Engstrom folded his hands behind his back, paced to the other side of the room, and returned to the windowsill beside Steve. He fixed his gaze on the frosty Minnesota countryside. Then he turned and fixed it on Steve.

"Steve. Do you see that journal on my desk over there? It is called *The Christian Century*, as you can see. The best theologians of our time are telling us that we are living in the most promising era yet in human history. The Great War has rid us of political systems that have brought the world so much bloodshed and anguish in the past, while at the same time teaching us lessons we shall never forget about the futility of solving anything by war. Our best minds are sensing that the Gospel of Jesus is about to take root everywhere, leading the whole human race into an era of unprecedented peace in which entire peoples are lifted out of grinding poverty. Modern science is giving us ways to free people everywhere from drudgery and oppression, so that the human spirit can rise to embrace its full God-given potential. Sacred Scripture holds up for us a vision of the Peaceable Kingdom of God in which each man can sit under his vine and fig tree, secure and happy and productive.

"You ask me into which ground you are to fall, where it is that you are called to die to yourself and bring forth much fruit for others. I will tell you plainly what I think. Find the fertile field that beckons to you most irresistibly, the field that for you holds the most promise of yielding fruitful results for mankind in the era now on our doorstep. And then plunge in. Don't look back.

"Do you catch a vision, Steve, of what you can do? Let me sketch out for you our divine calling and see where that takes you. We are called to redeem our times, to strive for the sake of the race to advance significantly in every area of honorable human achievement, to conquer disease and ignorance, to grow in knowledge and especially in wisdom, to bring out the best in people and to eradicate evil from the face of the earth, to develop the full untapped potential of the minds God has given us. We are called to foster all that is good and godly in the human soul. The task of religion is to inspire man's devotion to the cause of peace and true progress as the noblest manifestations of the Divine Will here on earth. The task of education is to enlighten man for intelligently managing the opportunities afforded by democracy and liberty. The task of science is to be on the front lines, to break through our ignorance and uncover new and vastly more effective ways of eradicating evil and suffering from among men.

"And Steve, it is my firm conviction that you belong on the front lines. What do you think?"

Halfway through the pastor's fervent appeal Steve closed his eyes, dropped his head to his chest, and nearly suspended breathing. The pastor's words took on color, form, and action in his roiling mind. To use the resources of science to offer the destitute and suffering of the world a chance for a better life! Here was a vision of fruitfulness that fit him perfectly and would surely bring joy to Cecilia! A shiver ran through him at the very thought of it. He could hardly wait to get at it! Before him lay the broad and fertile fields of science. Here he could throw himself down and die and be consumed by the very work that attracted him most. He could bury himself in it, and his work would surely bring forth fruit, maybe even much fruit. And she would be so happy with him. Yes, there would be times when he would miss her terribly. But there would also be many times when he would know she was close to him, so close he could almost feel her.

Steve didn't have to say anything. Dr. Engstrom read Steve's reaction to his challenge all over his face.

All around Steve at this very moment could feel his Cecilia, and she was smiling at him through her tears. But this time it was so different from the first vision he had had of her in his night dream where he couldn't move. This time she was there waiting for him, *and he was coming.*

Minutes passed. The pastor could almost feel Steve's pulse throbbing in the air. He knew what was going through the young man's mind. He lowered his voice to a fervent rumble and said, "Plunge in, Steve. Plunge in!"

Steve smiled at him broadly and nodded abruptly.

"Even before I throw away these crutches."

Then Steve, flushed with grave and joyous enthusiasm, took the pastor's hand and shook it vigorously.

"Thank you, Pastor. I was sure you could show me my ground. Now I'd better get started or I'll keep somebody waiting."

So saying, he swung around and disappeared through the door.

Dr. Engstrom paced about in his office for several minutes, enjoying the afterglow, a thankful warmth in his heart. But the longer he paced, the cooler his heart grew. At length he said out loud in slight annoyance, "You might have clarified the issue for him a bit better.... Ah well, you can only do so much in one day."

Then he sat down at his desk and turned his attention toward tomorrow's chapel talk.

III

Stephan Pearson lost no time in falling into his ground once he had identified it. Actually, he took Dr. Engstrom at his word and plunged into it, relieved to have found a way to redeem his guilt, at least in part. Mathematics and physics had always exerted a powerful attraction on him, and now that he was armed with a worthy and impelling motive for it, he allowed their powerful magnetic field to draw him deeply into them. His genius was unleashed.

Even before his transformation in Dr. Engstrom's office that day, Professors Brockhaus and Larson had already been astounded at the facility with which his mind grasped the relationship and broad unity of concepts normally dealt with in isolation from each other. For all his outward nonchalance, his mind had never been an attic collection of miscellaneous data. For him, details fell into a picture already in place or else created a picture in which they made beautiful sense. They never stood alone. If pieces were missing in a picture, he postulated what they might be and then sought for them until he found them and inserted them where they belonged. His mind would often construct a pattern out of known data with a few blank spots in it which left him the fascinating challenge of locating the missing pieces. The professors' back-row student had caught their attention almost from the first day without even trying and had held it just by being himself.

Now, however, he suddenly moved figuratively from the back row to the front row for the simple reason that all of this mattered to him now. It was no longer just a game. Their delight in him was exquisite as they watched him come alive to his vocation. With a compelling goal ahead of him, fascinating mental challenges all around him, impelling memories behind him, and a holy motive within him, he was at long last striking a unique interior balance that even I had to admit was nothing less than a miracle.

Although his legs and rib cage bothered him for the next two-and-a-half years of his undergraduate career at Christiania, he did not let this prevent him from taking those long leisurely walks in the country which had become second nature to him from his childhood. I was grateful that he maintained his contact with me on a regular basis, bursting into my room from time to time and sharing with me something he found too exciting to keep to himself even though I often had no idea what he was talking about. I am also aware that he returned to Meadowville the following Thanksgiving to be with Irv and Ellie and a few of Cecilia's special friends, to inform them personally of everything that had happened to him after Cecilia's death, that is, of how constantly present she was to him in his own falling and dying. He told Irv and Ellie how much their love meant to him and he begged them to pray that he might become a worthy fruit of their daughter's death. After that, they never saw him again, as far as I know, but they never stopped loving him and praying for him.

Over time, I am aware that his vivid sense of Cecilia's immediate presence receded somewhat, but never disappeared, as did also to some extent his strong motivation to fall and die for the good of others. This was because he became caught up in the fascination of his work itself from day to day to the point where he needed no further motivation to be doing it. But Cecilia and the vision ignited by Dr. Engstrom remained within him as silent justifiers of what he was doing with his life even though his joy in doing it was becoming its own reward.

In those days, wherever he went, whether at home or elsewhere, Steve was met with enthusiastic approbation to which he appeared to be quite oblivious. He needed no external approval for what he was doing. There was little danger in those days that anyone would question his goals or seek to undermine his dedication to them. The ideals to which he was dedicated were being extolled everywhere. Chapel speakers heralded the dawn of the new age of peace and progress and urged students to take their rightful place as Christians in that imminent age. There was much to be done yet before the Kingdom of God could come fully here on earth, and Christiania students were to be among the first to lay the fruits of their efforts in the cause of peace-making and poverty reduction at the feet of King Jesus.

Even more influential on Steve than this overt assurance of the rightness of his course from those whose business it was to know was the tacit approval of it that charged the very air of Christiania College. The spirit of the whole place, from the administration down through the ranks, was vibrant with its own form of missionary zeal:

> "Hail to the brightness of Zion's glad morning,
> Joy to the lands that in darkness have lain!
> Hushed be the accents of sorrow and mourning,
> Zion in triumph begins her mild reign...."

The vocation of a Christian was, after all, no longer so abstruse as it had at one time been considered. Let a man line himself up with the tide of progress by associating himself with a useful occupation in harmony with the better aspirations of humanity. Let him find his own unique way of contributing to improving the conditions of life for his fellowman and he would not only find personal fulfillment but he would be discharging his duty to his Creator. Christ had been a man, after all, and as such had been vitally concerned about the total needs of mankind, both the spiritual and the physical. Why else would He have spent two-thirds of his active life in a ministry of healing? The trouble with past generations was that they had too often spiritualized the religion of Jesus, reversing the Incarnation so that they encouraged people to flee the world rather than face it. Improving living conditions in the world had been seen by them as a trivial concern compared to working to ensure the eternal life of the soul. But Jesus had taught us to pray, "Thy Kingdom come," had He not? How could God's Kingdom ever come into a world trapped in ignorance and poverty and suffering?

There were a few dissident voices that dared to question this updated version of the Gospel, but they were dismissed as reactionary and out-of-touch. The tide was definitely moving in one direction in the early 1920s, and if you didn't want to be labeled old-fashioned, you got on board and let the tide sweep you along with everyone else towards the paradise just ahead.

Although Steve was not especially interested in anyone else's dreams, the climate in the early 1920s insulated him from any serious misgivings about the rightness of the ground he had plunged himself into. The realm of theoretical physics, which at that time, as I understand it, was just beginning to split open a crack into the world of fundamental particles, held Stephan Pearson spellbound in its grip. Within his own short lifetime, the quantum theory of radiation had been propounded by Max Planck and clarified by Albert Einstein. Within the previous decade the nature of the atom had been determined and then defined by Bohr, and the character of X-rays had been established by Roentgen. In addition, Albert Einstein had reduced the relationship between matter and energy to the simple formula, $e=mc^2$. All of these developments, of course, raised more questions than they answered. The work of Planck and Einstein, for example, had seemed to indicate that light waves were of a corpuscular nature, at least in some important respects. Steve became very curious to discover exactly what is the relation of matter to energy in this marginal area in which one phenomenon partakes of the characteristics of both. And all of this was fermenting in him while he was still at Christiania. He and I talked about such things often in those days.

In spite of the accident and his lackluster record in his freshman year, he graduated with his own class *magna cum laude*, majoring in physics and mathematics and minoring in chemistry. His parents were both extremely proud of him on graduation day. Old Lars managed to camouflage his disappointment that he would have no successor and heir to the estate. Julia, on the other hand, could not contain her joy. Steve had already shared with her what Cecilia's death had done for him. To her it was a miracle. Her Stevie was going beyond her wildest dreams for him. He was on a course that was sure to make God very happy.

IV

Like the Magi of old whom a star drew irresistibly into a distant land, Stephan Pearson followed the brightest star on his horizon for the next two years. His professors had secured for him an appointment to a postgraduate position within the circle of aspiring young physicists that surrounded Dr. Albert Einstein in Germany. On the day after graduation, his last in St. Mark before setting sail for Europe, I happened to pass by the open door of his room while he was packing his suitcase. He saw me.

"Paul! Please come in for a minute."

He stood there looking at me a little oddly, clasping a handful of clean socks which he was about to set into the opened suitcase on his bed.

"You know why I am going to Europe, don't you?"

I nodded.

Steve swallowed hard.

"She didn't die for nothing, Paul. There are moments when I feel so alone, even useless without her. But then I look at her portrait. See? There it is."

It was lying on a bed of underwear in his suitcase.

"Then I remember that she is always right here with me, encouraging me to get back to work when I am discouraged, to accomplish something really good, and to find happiness in doing it. I just wanted you to know for sure. And I want Irv and Ellie to know. She didn't die for nothing, by God! She didn't die for nothing."

"I know, Steve.... God is with you."

Now I was the one having a hard time holding it together. We stood there looking at each other for a long moment. Then both of us instinctively stepped toward each other and ended up in a bear hug.

Nothing more was said.

And with that we parted for many years.

It is difficult to reconstruct Steve's two years in Germany. While there he acquired considerable stature as a promising physicist and mathematician. His relationship with Dr. Einstein weaned him still further away from what some might call his "ulterior motives" for devoting himself to science. There was an extraordinary fascination for him in the mixture of mystery and certainty that composes theoretical physics. He found himself near the very center of that tiny circle of men who were intent on prying their way into the atom, first to be startled and then to be baffled by the things they were observing. This was the gathering place for those imaginative men whose minds had reached the frontiers of the unknown by crossing the known on the solid ground of the mathematical unity and consistency of all creation. The sheer thrill of observing even from afar what few men had hitherto considered observable, of building constructs on the basis of demonstrable fact in a domain that had previously been the subject solely of guesswork and conjecture, of working with phenomena whose very existence had been unknown until then, of playing daily with the grand oxymoron of undeniable fact and pure fantasy which is the essence of theoretical physics—this exerted an almost hypnotic power over Steve and his colleagues. Theirs was the challenge of deciphering the mathematical symmetry necessarily inherent in all phenomena, even the least understood. Living and working within the field of a magnet as strong as this one proved to be, precluded the possibility for many years to come that Steve would wander off in any other direction.

In a seminar one day, after Steve had deftly displayed his gift for correlating several concepts by means of their mathematical interdependence, a feat for which he had had to call upon several mathematical disciplines simultaneously and in German, Albert Einstein remarked to one of Steve's fellow students: "Keep your eye on that young man."

Apparently he did not travel around very much on the continent while he was there, although his infrequent letters home indicate that he made at least two trips to Paris. These letters, which I have seen, were respectful, if uninformative, but their arrival at wide intervals kept his mother's hopes for him alive.

Returning to the United States somewhat reluctantly and for reasons that are not clear, he set about writing his doctoral thesis on matter and energy for an Eastern university. In 1926 at the age of twenty-five he received his PhD in theoretical physics and began a fourteen-year period of pure research under the auspices of the Eintvold Foundation near Boston, Massachusetts.

V

Industrialist Ivor Eintvold was something of an amateur scientist himself. He endowed the foundation that bore his name with ample funds for extensive research in the new physics. It occupied a large new building on the outskirts of Boston and was loosely affiliated with one of the nearby universities. Eintvold had established the foundation shortly after the Great War in an effort to give science a free hand to develop without having to fulfill military commitments. The only stipulation he made with respect to the investigations into the new physics pursued there under his auspices was that he be informed of any discoveries having commercial possibilities.

Originally Dr. Pearson's position in the foundation was designated as research assistant in which capacity he and other assistants worked with Dr. C. T. Lambertsen in his pioneer investigation into gamma rays. For three years they sought to unravel the basic nature and properties of these electromagnetic emissions, which are the primary and most obvious characteristic of radioactivity. As any radioactive substance breaks down into more stable elements, there is an emission of "pure" electromagnetic energy in the form of gamma rays that possess a remarkable penetrating power. For a long while scientists were unable to verify experimentally that any weight was actually lost in the reduction of radioactive substances, a weight loss which one would expect from Einstein's formula $e=mc^2$. Already Steve had, with others, postulated the existence of subatomic particles to account for this very minute weight loss and several other phenomena. The whole issue involved him deeply until 1929 when, partially as a result of their work, the government of the United States began using gamma rays to detect internal defects in opaque objects. In that same year Dr. Lambertsen died and Dr. Pearson stepped into his position as research physicist, heading a team of brilliant young assistants and dividing his time now between the study of cosmic rays and the study of the structure of nuclei. Their previous work with gamma rays had laid the groundwork for the field toward which most of the world's theoretical physicists were now turning their attention.

During Stephan Pearson's school years most physicists had assumed that cosmic rays were electromagnetic waves on the order of X-rays and gamma rays. But in 1927, just as Steve was beginning his research into gamma rays, an Amsterdam physicist proved that they were particles because they responded to the latitude effect. Around the turn of the decade a world survey was being carried out to determine the exact nature and intensity of cosmic rays and their possible influence on life on earth. Dr. Pearson and his team were major players in this survey.

The results of the survey were fascinating in and of themselves and led to several discoveries of special interest to nuclear physicists. Among other things, it was ascertained that cosmic rays are composed of 92% ordinary protons, 7.5% alpha rays (i.e. helium nuclei), and 0.5% heavier nuclei which all together impact on the earth's atmosphere with an energy equal to the average starlight. These rather commonplace particles are, however, traveling at accelerated velocities which to this day cannot be approximated even in the largest accelerating equipment made by man. Furthermore (and this was of particular interest to nuclear physicists), very few of these original particles ever reach earth because they collide in the upper atmosphere with other particles and produce a secondary radiation that does reach the earth. Today we know that the Van Allen Belt also runs some interference for the earth. At any rate, this secondary radiation revealed to scientists for the first time a number of previously unknown particles, including a positive electron (i.e. a particle with the same mass as an electron but having a positive charge), so-called "V-particles" which have a mass greater than the mass of protons, and later eight or ten varieties of mesons. In addition, these upper atmospheric collisions form free neutrons which bombard surrounding matter to produce radioactive elements such as H3 and C14. By this examination of the atmosphere, scientists were set on the trail of many phenomena later to be discovered also in the nucleus of the atom, and several possibilities for methods of examining nuclei were suggested to them. The cyclotron, for example, was a noteworthy result of observing the effect of neutrons on surrounding material in secondary radiation.

Dr. Pearson worked assiduously on behalf of this survey and followed its proceedings with keen concern. It occurred to him that whereas Dr. Einstein had associated particles (photons) with light waves, a wave nature now had to be associated with particles. Beams of electrons were behaving like light, responding to defraction and the interference effect. The more involved he became in his work with nuclei, the more he realized how indebted he was to his earlier study of relativity with Dr. Einstein in Germany. For the particles with which he was now dealing were moving at such high velocities that they required the correction of relativity to be analyzed accurately.

For fourteen years Dr. Stephan Pearson was on the front lines of research through his association with the Eintvold Foundation. His colleagues, especially Dr. A. E. Niessen, his only close friend during this period, all assert that he labored with undeterred diligence, as though driven by an inner compulsion. They say that although he was engaged in what could be termed "pure research," he never lost sight of the potential benefits for mankind of what he was doing. This perspective betrayed itself in virtually everything he wrote, even in unapologetically complex publications intended only for the eyes of fellow scientists. I certainly make no pretense of having unraveled the technical content of the main body of his works, but I can easily discern what I might call a prophetic tinge to them. In his three books and the numerous articles dating from this period in his life, he invariably gets around to a consideration of the practical application of their research to some aspect or aspects of human well-being. He did have the satisfaction of living long enough to see some of these projected benefits become realities.

Aided by his dedicated famulus, Dr. Niessen, and his entire team, he made bold strides into the unknown and probed into many mysteries that had beggared explanation until then. There is a bit of the romantic in every research scientist, whether he wants to admit it or not. And that element of the romantic is woven around the fact that the nature of his work demands the same unwavering devotion demanded by a true and lasting love affair.

VI

For those fourteen years, Dr. Stephan Pearson lived alone in a tiny house he had found about a mile and half out into the country from his place of work. He had purchased it with its acre of land from a retiring farmer who had used it to house his hired man. It lay back from the road a couple of hundred feet behind a thick untrimmed hedge of lilac bushes and maple trees. It looked very shabby indeed until Mr. Eintvold happened to drop in one day. The next day he sent over a painter and a repairman to spruce it up as best they could. But it was certainly more than adequate for Steve's modest needs.

From the doorway, nearly overgrown with grapevines, one stepped immediately into a 12'x14' living room quaintly crowded with a big old sofa on the inside wall to the left, an overstuffed chair in the front corner to the right, and an array of green plants stacked wherever there was room for them. In the front wall next to the door there was a window, and in the wall to the right another one. In the summer very little light made it through the big grape leaves into the room. Above the sofa on the wall to the left that partitioned the living room from the bedroom hung six medium-sized frames all in a row, side by side. Each contained a sheet of music staff paper scribbled with musical notations and words. Across the top of the first sheet was scrawled the single word, "Verily."

The kitchen and bathroom consisted of a small lean-to behind the living room that appeared to have been an afterthought. A cast-iron wood range, a bank of crooked cupboards, a new refrigerator, a hand pump over a porcelain sink, and a small table with two wicker chairs filled this room to capacity. A window that could be swung open looked out over the deciduous woods behind the house and included in its scope an unpainted plank garage in which Dr. Pearson kept his panel truck.

If a visitor turned sharply left on entering the front door, he stepped through a curtained archway into Stephan Pearson's bedroom, which is where guests were invited to put their coats. A single window on the far wall looked out through a mass of bushes into the open fields beyond and admitted a dim glow into the room with its simple furnishings: a single iron bed, a dresser, a kitchen chair, a lampstand, and a free-standing armoire.

In contrast to the drabness of everything else in the room, on the lampstand facing the bed stood a framed portrait of a very lovely young woman with tender features and soft doelike eyes. On the wall above the lampstand was a framed letter that began with the words, "Dear Steve," and ended with the words, "Love, Irv and Ellie." No one, as far as I could tell, ever managed to induce him to speak either of his unusual living room wall decorations or of the mysterious girl in the portrait. This silence of his, together with the "previously committed" indifference with which he treated all women, led to the general assumption among his colleagues that he must have sustained a great heartache at some point in his life. They wondered if he had been jilted.

Dr. Pearson's social contacts were rather rare during this period in his life. His only real friend was Dr. Niessen, and their friendship was on a professional level. As a matter of solemn fact, Dr. Pearson seemed largely oblivious to any other level. One could say that he abandoned the trivialities and dynamics of ordinary human life to take up residence in the mesmerizing world of theoretical physics with its inanimate mysteries and mathematical regularities. You yourself had to take up residence in that strange world if you wanted to meet the Stephan Pearson of those days, and Dr. Niessen had done that. They shared the keen delight of learning the secrets of this new world whose existence was not in the least dependent on theirs. As two of the very few spectators in the astonishing amphitheater of minute existence, they were welded by their mutual awe into an unseverable comradeship.

There were two exceptions to Stephan Pearson's seclusion from daily life. Each Thanksgiving he would invite Dr. Niessen and half a dozen indigent students from the nearby university to his home for turkey dinner, rearranging the living room to accommodate a table and chairs borrowed from the church he attended. This act of unfeigned goodwill was relegated by some of his associates to his increasing fund of eccentricities. It was noted that he even offered a prayer of thanksgiving prior to serving the food.

The other exception was his practice of attending Mass every Sunday at the church just down the road from his house. He normally went to the High Mass at 11:00 a.m. since the organist who accompanied that Mass knew how to bring sublime sounds out of the instrument.

One might suppose that these were lonely years for him, and it is true that they were pockmarked by occasional periods of engulfing sadness, especially at the approach of Christmas. Dr. Niessen also told me of one startling occasion that sent Steve suddenly plunging into depression. It seems that the two of them were working on an electronic device near a window when suddenly his mentor's eyes froze on the window and followed, as in a trance, the form of a slender blonde young woman passing in front of their building walking down the sidewalk. He began to tremble, like a man with the palsy, and was useless for the rest of the day. The effect of this incident was weeks in wearing off. During these rare relapses into what appeared to be a state of mourning, he became impenetrable and performed his work in the perfunctory manner of a machine.

But as a rule, his work was his wife, and the fruits of his work were his children. They made a good family—no quarreling, no dissension ever. It was a much happier family than he had known in his youth. The world of symmetry and orderly balance that had become his home must have led him by degrees to making the tacit assumption that the world of ordinary human intercourse could be expected to behave in a similar way.

He certainly displayed a kindly and generous attitude toward others. He had nothing against anyone, and he had no reason to believe that the daily occupation of most people was any less fulfilling to them than his was to him. Besides this, he had received directly from Cecilia a vocation to love the people he met. And so the taciturn scientist, normally all wrapped up in his work, would now and then demonstrate absurd extremes of personal sacrifice for the presumed good of someone else. The following anecdote was told to me by one of Steve's associates during my visit to Boston in the fall of 1938.

It seems a university student who had been hunting in the marshes of southeastern Massachusetts one rainy Saturday morning stopped at the research center on his way home to flaunt his string of ducks. Just before leaving, he took one fat mallard off the stringer and tossed it into the corner with the remark, "Here's a little fresh protein for you, Dr. Pearson." The doctor nodded without interrupting his train of thought.

That evening, donning the slick raincoat and fireman's hat and the floppy galoshes he had worn in the morning, Dr. Pearson noticed the duck sprawled out in the corner, its head tucked under its wing. Supposing that the student had forgotten the bird of which he had been so proud, he picked the thing up by the neck and trudged halfway across town under the bright moonlight to return it.

The student claimed that when he opened the door at 10:30 p.m. and saw Dr. Pearson standing there in fireman's clothes holding the duck out to him, his mind went blank. Then, quickly realizing what had happened, and not wishing to disillusion the good doctor, he thanked him kindly and asked him into the house. But his night caller politely refused, insisting that as it was past his bedtime, he needed to get on home. With that, he departed into the starlit shadows, raincoat, rubber hat, and galoshes.

From what I have gathered, it seems this is a fair representation of Dr. Pearson's infrequent excursions into the world during these years.

VII

The official reason for my trip to Boston in the fall of 1938 was an interdenominational missionary conference being held there, but actually I was more interested in seeing Steve than I was in attending the conference. I hadn't seen him in over fifteen years, and in the interim the few things that I had heard about him triggered my interest in reconnecting with him. Naturally, I was curious to find out what had become of his commitment to be the fruit of Cecilia's tragic death. As the evening approached which I had set aside to spend with him in his home, I found myself caught up in a tangle of poignant memories.

In a way, I suppose, I can be thankful that Steve's head was so full of the stuff of his daily work that evening because it afforded me an open window into his daily life. He gave me the impression that the prospect of my visit had had a sobering effect on him. To be sure, he was not unhappy to see me. He showed me through his house, including the bedroom, making sure that I took note of Cecilia's quite stunning portrait so near his bed and of the letter from Uncle Irv and Aunt Ellie in a frame on the wall above it. I would say that my visit had a religious significance for him which induced him to welcome me as far into the world of his research as he could draw me. I think he wanted me to experience that world for myself so that I would have some appreciation of how his work was allowing him to fulfill his mandate from Cecilia.

It was very clear to me that no day went by for him without his experiencing Cecilia's hand of blessing upon him. He even told me, with some hesitation, that his weekly contact with the Catholic Church down the road had helped him realize how strongly connected he and Cecilia were and would always be through the Communion of Saints. She remained for him, he assured me, the reason why he still had what he called "a firm grip on life," though he knew his grip on life would never match the grip she had had.

With that, he led me across the threshold into that world in which his grip on life was solid and firm, never to cross back over it again until near the end of my visit. And I simply followed meekly behind.

Over the next hour or so he touched on a number of subjects all related in some way to his daily work. His comments were dense and often suggestive of more than they actually described. I had no sense that he was trying to conceal anything. He spoke without affectation and with great, if quiet, sincerity. I believe the following observations are an accurate reflection of his convictions at that time.

It was evident that his current understanding of life derived from his implicit reliance on the mathematical regularity and simplicity of all relationships in the world of minute particles in which he was working every day. It is not too much to say that he stood in awe of this world. His grip on life amounted to his underlying confidence that all of life is necessarily as sane as the special sector of it into which he had so fervently plunged. The reason he could allow himself to make this assumption in good conscience was that in dealing with "fundamental particles," he was in constant touch with the amazing orderliness and consistency of the basic building blocks of every phenomenon in the created universe.

Leaning back in his armchair, he drew deeply on his pipe and declared, "Discovering that all of creation is founded on perfect and ultimately explainable regularity has profoundly affected my own attitude toward life. There is nothing in you, Paul, and there is nothing in me that is not systematically integrated into the forces of the entire universe. The gap between science and religion is fast closing."

As our leisurely conversation moved along, I saw that for Stephan

Pearson the gap had all but closed already, and by a process not by any means peculiar to him. In his own mind he could not conceive of the universe without a Prime Mover, to use a philosophical category of our forefathers. The daily applications of thermodynamics kept in front of him, he explained, the evidence that the universe can only have been initiated in an act of creation. It was not that he had intensely sought out an answer to a question that had been plaguing him, but rather that the answer confronted him wherever he turned in his work. There is a Creator, or little practical sense could be made of such demonstrable and useful principles at the Second Law of Thermodynamics. To him, one glance at the physical state of the universe, in which all components are racing away from a central point towards infinite space, strained to the breaking point any theory of origins other than an act of creation. And this, in a word, was to a large extent his God, tempered by the continuing warmth and wonder of Cecilia's Jesus. Requiring an independently existing Will for the satisfactory solution to the problem of origins, Steve tended to merge the Originator with that which He had originated once its existence was assured. I came away from my evening with Dr. Pearson with the impression that his own personal and practical trinity-construct consisted of the Creator God, the Systematic Unity of all Creation, and the Inevitability of Scientific Advancement. To this trinity he was dedicated heart and soul, and was serving it at this point in his life with a certain serene enthusiasm and peace of mind.

In short, during these fourteen years of relative seclusion, Dr. Stephan Pearson experienced almost nothing to shake the foundation of his faith in human progress as the vehicle for the coming of the Kingdom of God on earth or his conviction that Cecilia was happy with him for what he was doing with his life. The Great Depression served only to underscore for him humanity's need for the universal prosperity science was prepared to offer it. In addition to the lure of his work itself, he had, as it were, a divine mandate to forge ahead so that humanity would not dally on the threshold of its New Era. This too eventually settled down within him into a pervasive sense of combined urgency, vocation, and approval. With this support he lacked nothing to satisfy fully his impulse to "launch out into the deep." He was being borne on the crest of the rising tide of optimism. He was contributing in a major way to the spirit and substance of scientific advancement. He was heeding the call first heard at Christiania College "to eradicate the evils on earth in the name of God." And he was perfectly clear in his own mind that he knew exactly what that call meant for him.

VIII

One evening in the spring of 1940 as Dr. Pearson was in the process of typing the final copy of an article he had been asked to write for the *Scientific American*, he was interrupted by a sharp rap at the door. Answering the door, he was taken aback to see the uniformed figure of a special government courier standing erectly before him.

"Dr. Stephan Pearson?" the courier demanded.

"Yes."

"Please sign here," the courier ordered, thrusting at him a receipt snapped to a clipboard on top of which was a large envelope.

Dr. Pearson took the board and glanced at the envelope. The return address stated: THE WHITE HOUSE.

Quickly he scribbled his name on the receipt and the courier disappeared. Ripping open the envelope with trembling hand he withdrew a heavy sheet of paper, unfolded it, and read:

Dr. Stephan Pearson:

May I respectfully request that you present yourself in the Oval Office at -:-- a.m. on -------- --, 1940, to discuss a matter of the utmost importance, and may I further request that you inform no one of this meeting.

I am not at liberty to disclose further details. You will be fully apprised of the matter in the course of our meeting.

This letter will gain you admittance into White House and the Oval Office at the stated time.

Sincerely,
Franklin D. Roosevelt (signed)
President
United States of America

Steve refolded the letter and tucked it back into the envelope. He sank down on the sofa, his head in his hands. A wave of sickening loneliness passed through him. What in the world was this all about?

The meeting was only four days away.

He got up and stumbled into the bedroom. He turned on the lamp on the stand and then sat down on the bed facing it.

"Don't leave me now, my love!" he whispered.

Taking the frame containing her portrait in both hands, he looked at her long and hard and then clasped her to his bosom and hung on.

IX

Five days later a 1933 Ford light delivery truck drove into the driveway and stopped beside the house. A small man with graying hair on his temples got out and went into the house. Once inside, he methodically went from room to room, removing things from drawers and cupboards and putting them into packing boxes. He took only small and strictly personal items, such as clothing, and left nearly everything else untouched. And as he was doing this, he kept on muttering to himself.

"Barbaric forces have once again arisen in the world, forces bent on destroying all that is good and noble and hurtling civilization back into pre-Christian darkness. Gentlemen, to counter this evil and to come to the defense of human freedom and dignity will require the devotion and sacrifice of enlightened men everywhere....

"The cry of all humanity under siege for its very life is summoning you. Your country is summoning you. I am asking you in the name of all that is good and decent, in the name of God, to respond to the call of your country and dedicate yourselves without reservation to the cause of preserving democracy and freedom for our children and our children's children.

"This is what we are asking of you...."

And at that point the President spelled out in detail what was being asked of the handful of extraordinary human beings sitting across the desk from him.

Steve paused in his packing, sat on his bed, and bowed his head.

"Who would ever have believed that eradicating evil on the face of the earth would come to this?…"

Looking up into her innocent eyes, he stared at her and slowly shook his head. Hands trembling, his breath short and rapid, he took her picture and placed it in a large leather briefcase. Then he took down the framed letter from Irv and Ellie and inserted it into the briefcase beside the photo. He went into the living room and removed the six frames from the wall over the sofa. They just fit into the briefcase next to the other two frames.

Within an hour the truck was packed. On his final inspection of the house, he picked up a sign and a hammer and some nails that were lying on the kitchen table. Then, walking slowly through the house, he stopped at the front door and turned around. Lifting his arms into the air, he said out loud, "Thank you, Cecilia's Jesus, for giving me this little haven for all these years." Turning about, he emerged from the front door and with difficulty locked it with a rusty key. He nailed a "SOLD" sign beneath the front window, got into his truck, and disappeared from view for some five years.

Incidentally, I discovered after his death that he had not actually sold the house. He had given it to an elderly couple he had met at church who had fallen on hard times and lost their home.

At this point a dark and impervious veil falls over the life of Stephan Pearson. Rumor had it that he was in the Chicago vicinity for a time. Other rumors put him in Tennessee, and still others located him in the American Southwest. The fact is that for over five years neither former colleagues nor old friends heard a single word from him or received any news of him. Even his widowed mother, whom he had contacted just before disappearing, died in complete ignorance of his whereabouts. He ceased to exist for everyone he had known. The only creditable information about him was what he had shared with his mother. He had told her that he was safe and was involved with the government in the war effort. She had passed that on to Uncle Irv and Aunt Ellie.

X

If, during the course of World War II, someone had been sitting on the rocky eminence several hundred feet above the village of Ciel des Montagnes, Vermont, he would never have guessed that the nations of the world were engaged in mortal combat. Only the most astute would have taken note of the few hints of it that were visible there in those sorry years. Early in 1942 one might have noticed the drab brown US Army bus that wound up the road from Montpelier, stopped in front of the schoolhouse to pick up half a load of young men drafted for military service, and then continued on to the next village. Or one might have observed the flag that flew at half-mast much more often than usual throughout the next four years. And, of course, one could hardly have missed the wild jubilation that rocked the town in the fall of 1945. But never could anyone have culled from the changeless calm of the old rolling mountains and the picturesque rock-strewn farms dotting the valley any hint of the blood and gore of Iwo Jima, the suicidal assault on Anzio, or the monstrous holocaust of Hiroshima and Nagasaki. Yet, young men from Ciel des Montagnes and District were directly involved in all of these horrors.

No hint whatever would anyone have detected of the passions of racial hatred and blind patriotism that were driving presumably civilized men to acts of barbarous atrocity at the very moment the silent sun was sinking beneath these ancient undulations of rock, casting long lazy shadows and hazy shafts of light across their upper meadows. No notion would anyone have entertained of that new "conscience" which desperate circumstances were forging in the minds even of honorable and moral men that required them to invent horrors in the cause of safeguarding the world from the even worse horrors being disseminated by dishonorable and immoral men.

Such was the character of Ciel des Montagnes' immutable face. In the wake of the war, there persisted here behind this face something of the older and more innocent conscience that had been irreparably shattered in many other parts of the world.

XI

One might be tempted to say it was an exceptionally grand spring day in the year 1947, but spring days in northern Vermont are habitually grand. They are exceptional only for the urban visitor who ventures that far off the beaten path. It is more than just the fresh breeze bearing aloft the dank odor of the decomposing litter on the forest floor, more than just the crystalline sky drawing the souls of men and women, the young and the old, upward. It is also the breed of people who make this place their home, a folk whose steady slow pace of work is the natural result of their imperturbable temperament and the tranquil assurance with which they get things done. Watching these people patiently withdraw oozing sap from the maple trees and more patiently still let it simmer down into syrup and sugar can have a most calming effect on the harried city-dweller.

At any rate, the day we have in mind was just such a day. On it, a black 1933 Ford panel truck lumbered into Ciel des Montagnes from the direction of Montpelier, plastered with the mud and dust of a long trip. Its single license plate had been issued in the State of Pennsylvania. Although it hesitated several times while moving through the six or eight blocks that constitute the length of the town, it did not stop but continued on down the highway for about a mile, past the schoolhouse and out into the country. There it turned off onto a gravel side road that twisted northward up a small drainage and around some fields for another mile before disappearing into the woods and upper meadows. At the far edge of the woods, the truck stopped and turned in towards a small cabin tucked under the trees. Here, apparently, was its destination.

The unimposing man who got out of the truck and unlocked the cabin would have passed for around fifty years of age. He might well have been a migrant worker returning for another season's labor. His hair was a thick metallic gray except for a few dark strands across the crown of his head, and the skin of his not unhandsome face was drawn together in deepening wrinkles over his small features. A partial stoop marked his bearing as he walked, and a chronic squint pinched at his eyes. It was obvious that he had worked hard in his life, but some of his appearance of fatigue could probably have been written off to the long trip he had just completed.

Later that same day, Farmer Collins drove into the yard. He had been expecting the lone man's arrival and left some twenty minutes later with a fatter wallet and a broader smile.

The next morning, the visitor drove to town and came home with enough basic provisions for at least a month or two. For the first week he seemed quite content to stay in or near the cabin. He pulled a large wicker rocking chair out onto the veranda and spent long hours absently surveying the peaceful countryside from his comfortable vantage point and puffing on his old briar pipe. Now and then he puttered around a little in the wild yard under the trees, collecting dead logs and sawing them into usable chunks to be split for firewood. He seemed deep in thought most of the time, almost melancholy. There was also a mild agitation visible in whatever he was doing. He was definitely not a man at peace with himself.

By the second week he began to take two strolls each day, one in the morning and one in the evening. These gradually lengthened until they took on a definite pattern. Each morning he emerged from the cabin at around 6:00 a.m. and walked briskly up the road for a couple of miles to a point where it swung around the side of a low mountain and afforded a commanding view of the valley below. It was usually 7:30 before he took a last cold drink from the spring that spewed its contents out from the rocks above the road. Then he proceeded laterally on a path around the front of the mountain for another mile and a half until it intersected a trail which happily terminated in his own backyard after traversing stony meadows, leafy woods, and grassy glades.

The evening stroll usually began at about 4:30 and took him in a rectangle in the opposite direction. First he ambled down the road in front of his cabin to the main highway which consisted of a narrow, sparsely traveled strip of blacktop. Then he turned right and went past the schoolhouse into town. Usually he walked on through and headed out the other side, greeting anyone who greeted him. About a mile outside town, he crossed a gravel road that ran roughly parallel to the road running by his cabin. This he followed up the gentle incline of the mountain's lower slope before cutting across about two miles of open countryside back to his cabin.

These two daily hikes were distinct from one another in more respects than time and place. The one in the morning was invariably more buoyant. The hiker seemed positively eager to embrace the freshening day, to breathe in deep draughts of the cool clear air. The evening hike, by contrast, was slower. The hiker seemed weighed down by heavy thoughts and unresolved sorrows. No matter how splendid the sunset or cheery the birds' songs, he greeted them with a sigh. He seemed simply unable to get up and out of himself on his evening hike.

No doubt, many people's days begin and end like that.

Once his routine was established, the solitary man lived one day much like the next for several weeks. Every morning was a new beginning for him. Every evening saw him fall back into the same discouraging rut.

Then one day his routine evening pattern was upset by an unexpected intrusion, never to fall back into its old rut again.

XII

It happened on an ordinary evening as the solitary visitor was trudging along the road to town, his hands cupped behind his back and his head slumped forward, his usual evening hiking posture. For some reason this evening his mind was replaying some old "tapes" from his years in Germany with Einstein. And when it wandered off into other matters, it continued its internal monologue in the German language.

By now he was familiar enough with the course of his evening walk that he scarcely needed to look where he was going. Thus absorbed in his thoughts, he was crossing in front of the double row of ancient maples bordering the schoolyard when he was startled by the sound of a rapid movement, then a jolting thump and a shower of papers flying in the air.

"*Entschuldigen Sie mich!*" ("Excuse me!") he cried out in shock as the pretty teacher with whom he had just collided landed back down on the turf with a thud.

"*Einem, der so tief in seinen Gedanken verloren ist, ist viel erlaubt,*" ("A person has to make plenty of allowance for someone so deeply lost in his thoughts.") she replied almost coyly, brushing herself off.

"*Bitte, lassen Sie mich diese Schularbeiten fuer Sie sammeln,*" ("Please let me gather up all these pieces of homework for you.") he insisted, darting from one escaping sheet of paper to the next.

"*Ach, mein guter Herr! Seien Sie bitte nicht so verlegt. Es ist nichts. Regen Sie sich nicht auf. Niemand ist verletzt, und die Aufgaben werden nicht weithin fliegen.*" ("O my good man! Please don't be so embarrassed.

It's nothing. Don't get so excited. No one is hurt, and the lessons won't fly far.")

"*Nicht verlegt! Ich waere ein ganz tierischer Mensch, wenn ich nicht verlegt waere, eine so huebsche und schuldlose Dame niederzuschlagen.*" ("Not embarrassed! I'd be a brute if I weren't embarrassed after knocking over such a pretty and innocent lady.")

Scrambling after the sheets of paper, he began putting together in his head how it had happened. She must have been sitting on the ground hidden by this massive trunk and sprung up in surprise when he almost stepped on her. Himmel! This was unfortunate!

"Himmel?"

Why was he talking to her in German? And why was she answering him in German? What was going on here?

He gathered up the last of the errant papers and brought them to the teacher who was still brushing the leaves off her skirt.

"I … I don't know how to…," he fumbled around.

"So you speak English, too," she broke in playfully. "That's too bad. I was looking forward to practicing my German on you."

She sounded so disappointed by this latter misfortune that she made the poor man forget all about the former one.

"I'm sorry, ma'am," he tried again.

"Oh, that's all right," she softened. "Are you a native of Germany, or did you have to learn the language?"

"No," he replied ambiguously. "I'm a renegade Norwegian-American who lived in Berlin many years ago."

A strange vagabond, this, thought the young teacher to herself. *He can't be a seasonal laborer, though he's dressed like one…. I wonder from what he has fallen….*

Whether it was female intuition that aroused her sympathy for this apparent drifter or scholarly instinct that detected something deeper beneath his effective camouflage, she found herself filled with a lively curiosity to learn more about him.

"I was with the Red Cross in Bremen and Hamburg after the war until this fall," she offered. "That taught me a few idioms you won't find in grammar books."

The older man lowered his head and gazed a hole through the leaves on the ground.

"They tell me the destruction of those two cities was nearly total."

"It was," she affirmed. "There wasn't much left. Just a lot of lost waifs standing in a state of shock on heaps of rubble. The rebuilding has already started, but it will take years."

"It must have made you feel good to pitch in and help."

"In a way, I suppose. In a very little way. Mostly you felt dejection. I am sure it would have got to me if there hadn't been so much to do. You felt—you couldn't avoid feeling—the remorse of those who realized they were getting what they as a nation deserved and the shame of the victors who had doled out such terrible destruction on so many innocent people."

She hesitated. Clearly, the memories were painful for her.

Then she stood up straight, threw off her heaviness of heart, and announced, "My name is Katherine Kunstler. I teach grades five through eight at the school here."

"And I'm Dr. Pearson," echoed the sad little man. For the past six years that's all he had heard: "Dr. Pearson, would you have a look at this?" "Dr. Pearson, what do you make of that?" "Dr. Pearson, this…." "Dr. Pearson, that…."

Immediately he added, "Stephan Pearson."

She held out her hand and he shook it a little limply.

"Katherine," he said. "I do hope we can meet again under more … more propitious circumstances."

"I would like that."

They smiled at each other. Dr. Pearson arched his back, cupped his hands, and resumed his evening stroll. Miss Kunstler sat back down under the tree to think. Her eyes peered through the treetops. She was mentally going back over her chance encounter with this most unusual little man to see if she could glean from it a few more scraps of information about him.

XIII

The following evening as Dr. Pearson was passing in front of the school, it happened that Miss Kunstler was sitting beneath the same trees working on another set of papers. Approaching the spot where the collision had occurred, he looked up and saw her mild but resolute eyes beaming back at him. Mechanically he raised his hand in greeting, a trifle surprised but not unhappy to see her there again. Walking on, he felt a twinge of self-consciousness about what had just happened that was not unpleasant at all.

The next evening she was not there, but Dr. Pearson paused momentarily by "their" tree before moving on. A few hours later, when it occurred to him that it was Saturday, this realization seemed somehow significant to him, but he couldn't put his finger on exactly why.

Monday evening Miss Kunstler was back under the tree again correcting papers. Approaching the line of maples, the solitary hiker marked how cheerily she lifted her chin and smiled at him, so he ventured to stop and exchange a few words with her. Tuesday evening he arrived a little earlier than usual and traded a few more cautious banalities with her. The week went on in this manner from day to day until by Friday Miss Kunstler felt emboldened enough to invite him to sit down on the bank beside her "for a minute or two."

There was a rather deep grassy ditch running between the twin rows of maples that bordered the schoolyard and the road, forming an irregular slope, now gentle, now steep, under the trees. The spot which Miss Kunstler favored for correcting papers was almost like a sofa with a low back and a long foot stool. Four or five people could easily have been accommodated on it side by side.

The little teacher discreetly moved over to give Dr. Pearson plenty of room. Even though the evening hour had brought restful tranquility to the world around them, she found herself just slightly short of breath and she detected in the abrupt self-conscious movements of her new friend a similar trace of disquiet in him.

But through the trunks of the trees on the other side of the ditch they could look beyond the walls of the frame schoolhouse onto the patchwork of woods and pastures that rolled off into the horizon across the hunch-backed swells, and as they sat there taking in this ancient sight, they both grew more calm and composed. The sun, now spreading its diagonal rays over the lush vernal vegetation, had transformed the hills into a weightless translucent green, the color of sprouting life.

They took it all in without saying a word.

Eventually Miss Kunstler observed, "You can see why I prefer to do my work out here every chance I get. It doesn't really take your mind off Jimmy's poor grammar, but it puts it in a healthier context."

"That is worth something."

"In the winter I positively cringed before this stack of papers. Now I welcome it."

The gray-haired man was gazing into the distance and nodding his head up and down in response.

"It's fearful, is it not, to contemplate how much violence and suffering it took to preserve peaceful scenes like this."

Mildly startled by this strange comment, Miss Kunstler tried to imagine what kinds of violence had anything at all to do with the tranquility before them.

Sensing her confusion, he added, "The war."

Silence.

"Oh, of course.... It is fearful. But ... but if we think about it so much that it totally sours the sweetness of what we have fought for, then we might just as well not have fought for it, don't you think?"

He stroked his chin wearily.

"That is certainly true. That is exactly what it does."

"Very often I think of all the destitute and broken families, the shattered lives, I left behind me in Europe…."

"And doesn't it plague you to think that they are destitute and broken because we fought to keep this?"

"It does. And yet, though I can never escape it, I can vindicate it logically in the name of achieving the greater good. It doesn't make much sense, but every other choice makes even less sense to me."

"That's how I vindicate it too. But I only wish my heart would pay more attention to my mind…. Or maybe I don't wish that either. Lately my mind seems to be pulling loose from its moorings, too. I thought it was in a perfectly 'safe' harbor. But lately…. O well. It's time for me to be moving on. You'll be blaming me for not letting you finish your work."

"O no, Dr. Pearson. You'll be blaming me for distracting you from your serious work of coming to terms with all of this."

They smiled at their thin excuses, but understood. Dr. Pearson rose to leave.

"Please take care until Monday," she called after him.

"Until Monday," he repeated to himself as he trudged on down the road.

On impulse he glanced back over his shoulder. For the briefest instant their eyes made contact, but that fleeting moment of contact felt to him like glue.

It ensured that Monday would lead to Tuesday, and then to Wednesday, and then to Thursday and Friday, and then to the week after.

XIV

In a life that had been full of associates and devoid of friends, Dr. Pearson had not had the benefit of an earthly companion for many years. To be sure, he had never lost a sense of Cecilia's constant presence with him in the spirit. But even at best, that was different, and in recent years it had not been at its best. It was increasingly impossible for him to convince himself that what he was doing "for his country" was making her happy. Not his Cecilia who could be moved to tears over a dead cardinal!

And so, even that form of spiritual companionship with Cecilia had eroded over time to a mere memory, and a painful one at that at the thought that she must be feeling betrayed by him. Now, however, his long-forfeited need for female companionship was being stirred back to life. He was emerging from a very long hibernation. It was no longer good enough for him to sit on the porch in his wicker rocking chair and mull over the troubles in his soul all by himself. He was continually finding his mind being drawn down the road of its own accord to the double row of maples in front of the school and to the one person in the world with whom he had actually found it possible to share tiny but real pieces of the nightmare he couldn't get off his mind. In his imagination he sat there on the porch pouring everything out to her, and in his imagination she was taking it all in without rejecting him.

But his thoughts of her were not just confined to that role. His lonely heart was being drawn to this unexpected source of womanly warmth in his life. He was finding himself thinking about her outside of all reference to issues of any kind. When he pictured her pretty head cocked to one side and looking up at him from beneath the maple trees as he approached her, something stirred in his long dormant clay. It pleased him that her hair was always slightly disheveled because of the breeze and because of the way she leaned her head back on the tree trunk, but it was ever the same lovely satiny brown. Corresponding to her trim five-foot one-inch frame, her facial features were small and neat and her eyes were kind and twinkly. But what really got to him was the harmony between her heart and her voice, the eager generosity of her soul that expressed itself so perfectly in the clear smooth soft texture of her tone of voice. Perhaps this touched him so deeply because he had been so long deprived of the comforting sound of a woman's voice.

Although he held nothing back from the Katherine Kunstler of his imagination, he was careful to expose only bits and pieces of his thinking to the Katherine Kunstler he met under the trees, for fear of becoming too morose with her. He was thankful enough to have her as his confidante in the secret chambers of his mind. He had no desire to jeopardize their friendship by unloading himself on her out in the open. He was glad that she took the initiative in the short conversations they had under the trees. He was never made to feel that he was on the spot just because he couldn't think of something appropriate to say. What she said was sensible and pleasant to hear, never prying or threatening. He would stay with her there for only five or ten minutes each day so that she wouldn't tire of him and would welcome him back.

As the days went on, it became a struggle for Dr. Pearson to maintain the distinction between the two Katherines, the one to whom he unburdened himself entirely in his mind on the porch of his cabin and the one to whom he did not do so under the trees. It was hard not to discuss the one thing that was always on his mind with the one and only person to whom he regularly spoke about anything. And besides, he was beginning to believe that she could handle it, given her own experience. She always appeared judiciously open to him, as though she were gently inviting him to dive into whatever it was that was on his mind and to make her a sharer in it. Furthermore, his leave-of-absence from his present employer was due to end in two more weeks, so it was now or never. With this in mind, he let small bits escape from his mind out into the open with her on Monday through Thursday.

And on Thursday she said to him, "Steve, you can come clean with me. Tomorrow is Friday. Why not spill it all out to me right here tomorrow, or as much as you can in one evening? We still have a whole week. You don't have to do it all at once."

He looked her straight in the eyes. "You really mean that, don't you?"

"With all my heart, I really mean it."

He turned his eyes away from her, took a deep breath, got to his feet, swung around and headed back home by the way he had come. He had gone about ten paces when he stopped to have another look back at her. She hadn't taken her eyes off him.

"Tomorrow, then," he repeated.

She nodded. Twice.

The next day he arrived early. Miss Kunstler was already sitting in their usual trysting place beneath the maples, but this time she had no papers.

"I have the whole weekend to correct them, and that gives us the whole evening together here. All I want now is to listen to you. I trust your wisdom."

"My wisdom?" Dr. Pearson shook his head. "Wisdom is based on having a well-chosen standard and consistently orienting one's thoughts and actions toward that standard. At the moment, I have neither. No standard and no sure orientation."

"There is little certainty anywhere in the world today. I don't think most of us are sure we have legs under us to walk on any more."

"Or any place to go if we did have."

"True."

Staring off into the distance, Dr. Pearson shook his head and marveled,

"Isn't it a wonder that we can even talk like this? What is wrong with us humans? Just look at that peaceful panorama right in front of us. So orderly. So calm in its sprouting, growing and dying. So sure of itself. If it weren't for us humans, the world would be a paradise. Only man, of all creatures, can touch everything around him. No other creature can do that. But our touch is so often the touch of death. Instead of letting ourselves be shaped by the goodness of the created world, we give free reign to our twisted wills and we destroy it. Why are we so out of whack with the goodness all around us? Why? Miss Kunstler, I don't want to put you on the spot, but do you think that any permanent good was achieved by the war?"

Her head dropped into her hands. She took a long moment before responding.

Then she looked up at him and said, "We are being perfectly honest with one another, right?"

"Perfectly honest."

"When I was in war-torn Europe, that was the question I couldn't escape. The war was a total commitment, a titanic effort, on both sides. The price paid for it in human lives lost, and other lives destroyed, was incalculable. I was looking for some evidence that all of this was not a gaping waste. True, some love and some care came out of it, but they seemed to be overwhelmed by the emptiness, the hatred, the urge to get even on the part of so many, on both sides. Permanent good? Crazy as it may sound, I don't have an answer for you."

"That's what I mean, ma'am. There's a first difficulty, and then there's a second difficulty, and I don't know which is the greater. When your confidence in the rightness of what you are fighting for is strong and you are certain that goodness stands to gain from the expedients on which you are working to preserve it, it is hard enough to visualize the horrors you are creating for others—'the enemy'—in the service of your good cause. At least you have the Ultimate Good to rivet your eyes on, as each day you work with others to perfect the means of the destruction needed to safeguard it. But after the war is over and the dust has settled and cities are left in ruins and cathedrals are turned into heaps of rubble and families are shattered and lives are in shreds, then comes the second difficulty. You look around at the what is happening in the world you have helped to chastise so brutally, you look for evidence of lessons learned, and a terrible doubt invades you in the form of a question: 'Has the horrible destruction you created done anything to establish the good which was your only reason for creating it?' The question haunts you for an answer. You have brought harm to so many people. Have you actually helped anyone? You look around in the world, I say, and you cannot answer, 'Yes.' You cannot! You cannot...."

"But," she begged cautiously, "all humanity shares in the guilt. We must bear it together. It doesn't all fall on one person."

"But can we believe that? Do you really? If it were true, if we all really knew how guilty we are, something good would have come out of the war, a lesson would have been learned that would guarantee that such destruction and human tragedy could never happen again. People everywhere would find contentment in 'cultivating their own garden,' not envying somebody else's. War would never again be seen as a means to achieve anything good. Humanity would be in the business of learning how to love, not hate, if we all felt guilty for the war. If we humans really knew how to come to grips with the great evils of our past, those very evils would goad us on to better things in the future. We might even be able to pardon those who met one evil with another evil in the past, and left the world the worse for it, because they were not able to see clearly what we see. But, Miss Kunstler, I am coming to see with dreadful clarity that most people fight because they are cowardly, not because they are defending noble ideals, not because they are serious about replacing evil with good. One man kills another and another and another more to save his own skin than to save democracy. Men fight when their personal safety is threatened, and rarely otherwise. If the Japanese had not attacked Pearl Harbor and the Nazis had not festooned our seaways with submarines, we would have let the rest of the world solve its own problems. The true knight-in-armor was a rare fellow, even in the Middle Ages.

"You are too young, my dear little friend, to recall the first Great War.

For a good many years folks in this country sort of took it for granted that the forces of evil had spent themselves in it, and the world was now rid of them. It was thought that the horrors of that war had taught us all a lesson we would never forget. In fact, the whole thing had been such a revolting experience that we Americans all turned our backs on it in disgust. We were dead sure that we were now pointed in the direction of progress. I'll wager that this happens to people after every serious conflict. The rank and file just want to return to 'normal life.' Which just sets them up for the next war."

"Dr. Pearson, you may well be right. History, especially recent history, seems to bear out what you have just said, particularly now that the means of waging war have gotten so out of hand. I mean to say no one would march into battle unless he felt that his gains would outweigh his losses, except in self-defense. And he slinks away from the battlefield, if he is a man of conscience at all, whether victorious or defeated, under the accusation of his heart that no gains could have outweighed the losses. Yet, what is it about us human beings that allows that same soldier to haul out his old uniform and join the ranks again as soon as there is a new call to battle?"

"One could say," he replied, "that there is no such thing as a lesson severe enough to teach us mortals anything permanent. The forces of greed, cowardice, and blind passion, driven by some demagogue's megalomania, are more natural to our race than those favoring peace and good sense."

"So it seems."

"And therefore there is no excuse for those who, having learned nothing from the overwhelming evidence of our past, choose to sacrifice the lives of their fellowmen in a fruitless effort to cram good sense down the throat of a world that just vomits it back out."

"Except the excuse of ignorance. Our ignorance before the fact of what we learn only after the fact surely mitigates our guilt."

"Yes, yes. Mitigates it, perhaps, but it doesn't erase it. I have to tell you exactly how I see it on the basis of what I have been put through these past few years. It may sound extreme to you. Do you mind?"

"Of course not," she said, reaching over and caressing him on the arm.

"Our trusted leaders are guilty of thinking they can control history without understanding it. If they had any misgivings at all, they beat them into submission with a totally inadequate and simplistic rationale that appealed to the fears and loyalties of their followers. They chained their minds to the fate of a larger soulless cause whose course and result were a foregone failure. They refused to give reason the freedom it requires to be reasonable. It was tailored to solicit the public support needed to pursue their cause. They foresaw the horror of what they were concocting and chose to close their eyes to the sight of it. We cannot call them, or any of their co-opted associates, guiltless. All of them closed their eyes, knowing full well what they would have seen if they had opened them. Now, after Dresden and Nagasaki and Hiroshima, the force of circumstance has pried them open, and what a bewildering mixture of responses we see in them! Artful justifications abound, at every level. But bitter remorse is gushing into the heart and conscience of some of them, especially into the co-opted associates, who are now compelled to call into question everything they were taught to see with their eyes shut. They regard themselves now as having been dumb oxen treading round and round a millstone which they were told not to examine. 'Just keep on grinding away, and leave the results to us,' they were told. And now that the grinding is done, most of these poor oxen have lost their ability to walk in a straight line. They chose to be dumb oxen in 'a worthy cause.' Of course, being dumb oxen carried with it a lot less personal responsibility for what you were doing than being real men would have. The men up there, who had the full picture, were constantly singing assurances into our ears: 'You're doing beautifully. Just keep on walking round and round that millstone and keep on giving us what we need in the name of rescuing humanity, civilization, and progress. Let us worry about whom we are supplying as grist for your mill.' No, all of us who allowed ourselves to surrender our own moral sense to the will of our leaders, to be their dumb oxen, are far from guiltless. For me, Miss Kunstler, it meant sacrificing eventually, by slow and painful degrees, the one real treasure in my life. Can you imagine what it has cost me to give her up?… I don't expect you to understand. But sacrificing her to the cause of the war has left me bereft of everything. I have nothing left."

Dr. Pearson had said everything he could say at that moment. He stared dumbly into the ground in front of him.

Miss Kunstler was left speechless. Seeing his ashen pallor sent a wave of cold fear through her, leaving her trembling and shivering. He saw that.

"Please forgive me, Miss Kunstler. I really don't want to put you through all this. I am being selfish and old and terribly unkind."

"Please, sir. I would consider it an honor if you would call me Kay."

Dr. Pearson's eyes rose to meet hers. He looked at her, puzzled, even confused. Her eyes were aglow with expectancy.

"Kay," he replied. "Yes, of course…. Thank you! And I am Steve for you from now on, a strange old man to come and darken your youth with such deep shadows before your time."

"Steve, you're not old, not at all. You have lots of life in you yet."

"I wish you were right, my little friend."

Steve got up to leave even though the evening was young. Kay seemed a little disappointed.

"You don't know what it means to me, Kay, that you have given me the opportunity to do this with you this evening. I am so grateful." He hesitated, clearly wishing to say more.

"It feels like … like poison has been drawn out of my system."

"Steve," she said, rising to her feet. "If you don't come back here on Monday to release more of that poison, I'll die of anxiety for you. I really will."

"You needn't worry about that."

She took his hands and squeezed them.

And he squeezed hers.

She thought she noticed a slight spring in his step as he left her, a spring she had never noticed before. There was a definite spring in her step as she set out for home.

XV

Over the weekend all the issues that Dr. Stephan Pearson had been accustomed to dealing with one by one came avalanching down upon him all together. He was in the hurry of a conscience-stricken man who, having found at long last someone with whom he felt free to share his crushing load of sin and guilt, was impatient to connect with her again to unload the rest of it.

He skipped his usual Saturday and Sunday hikes, and also his Monday morning hike, and instead paced round and round his cabin as the pressure built up inside him.

Monday evening came at last. He left early on his hike and arrived early in front of the school. Just the same, he was relieved to find his little friend there already under the trees waiting for him and beckoning him to come and share the bank with her. As he took his place beside her, he greeted her self-consciously and struggled to think of a pleasant way to begin their conversation. Kay shared his nervousness, wondering what to expect and how to respond helpfully.

It was a different sort of day. Clouds had been building up since noon but had never quite reached the stage where their clean-cut towering billows fan out on top in broad indistinct anvils of ice and snow. Billow had simply been piling up on billow and swell on swell until they were balancing precariously high in the air, ready to topple over at a touch. But now the sky overhead was clear and blue as the clouds had moved off to the south and west directly in Steve and Kay's line of vision.

"You know, Kay, I can never look at massive clouds like those without thinking that what nature does so peacefully, we do so violently. Those massive clouds bless us with cooling rains, a few puffs of wind, and a little harmless lightning and thunder. The mushroom clouds we have created rain down fire and destruction and human misery."

They studied the imposing and ever-shifting cloud formations in silence. Kay's heart was so full of confusing hopes and contradictory feelings that she scarcely dared to open her mouth for fear of what might come pouring out of it. Carefully now she planned each word she would say.

"Educated people keep telling us that man's mind has been set free at last from the ancient taboos that once prevented him from investigating whatever he felt like investigating. Now he may venture anywhere he pleases without running into man-made road blocks. I suppose that's basically good. But there is something to be said for the taboos if they were holding us in awe of forces that are too big for us to control properly, if they were sparing us the global menace we're facing now."

"Ah, but Kay, it's inevitable. We are naturally curious creatures, and so our knowledge is bound to expand in all directions. Some people are content to learn what is already known, but others have to push beyond the current limits to our knowledge and venture into the unknown. The urge in them is so strong that they would die if they didn't. It's inevitable, Kay, inevitable.... But *is it good*? That's what plagues me. *Is it good?*"

"You mean, what if it's inevitable and *evil*?"

Kay's eyes were as big as saucers.

"Yes. You can call it potentially good, which implies that we can't just expand our knowledge without also taking responsibility for how it will be used. But who's doing that? And based on what criteria? Or else you can call it always evil, which implies that the more we learn, the more trouble we get ourselves into. Or you can dodge the issue and keep plunging blindly ahead, hoping for the best. My dilemma is this: I can see what we need to do to make it good, but I can't see any sign that enough of us are willing or able to do it to make a difference.

"What we call 'progress' is exciting and inevitable. How can it not be of God? Or, as one of my mentors would have put it, how can progress not be in harmony with the Creative Force of the universe? Now, if God is good, if the Creative Force is orderly and constructive, who would not conclude that progress, that is, the gradual evolution of man's knowledge and his ability to put it to use, must also be good and orderly and constructive? Who would not equate evil with ignorance and the obstruction of progress? Who would not be honored to devote himself to the cause of progress, to lose himself in the world of research and discovery? But with my own eyes I have seen highly educated and brilliant men seize the fruits of progress, the cream of our discoveries, and fashion them into weapons of mass destruction.

"No! I unmask myself—I am … one of them!"

Steve hunched over, collapsed, and covered his face with his trembling hands.

Kay almost threw herself at him. She wrapped her arms around his chest and hung on, stroking his right cheek very gently with her soft hand. Slowly his trembling subsided.

Steve pulled himself together and sat up straight. She released him, still facing him squarely. He turned to face her.

"Now I put it to you. Progress is inevitable. Progress has been the cause of an evil more heinous than any evil created by men in the past. Tell me: *Is progress of God*? I cannot believe that it is not, yet how can I believe that it is?…"

"But Steve, think of advances in medicine, in labor-saving machinery, in comforts that make life for so many people more than just bearable."

"I know. But that doesn't begin to offset Hiroshima and Nagasaki. What do you make of what those two bombs did?"

Kay's tongue went hot and dry. She dreaded what a truthful answer might do to Steve, but she dreaded even more what a dishonest answer would do to him. She closed her eyes.

"I try not to think of it, Steve. I try desperately not to think of it. I just want to dismiss that horrifying chapter of our recent past and move on into a better future. But I know that is not the right way to look at it.... Some of our Red Cross workers in Europe had spent time in those two vast crematoria after the war. Who was left? Human wrecks, crazed, crippled, gradually falling all apart from a creeping untreatable new disease created by us. Disbelief and despair were everywhere, they told us.... Steve, do you know why our leaders didn't just drop those bombs over the ocean a little ways off the coast if they wanted to demonstrate their power, where a west wind would carry the fallout away from the people? Why, oh why did we have to match their treachery at Pearl Harbor with an act of even crueler treachery of our own?"

Steve's eyes turned to glass. His body crumpled together, as if pounded down by a jackhammer. He was trembling again, all over. Kay clasped her arms around his shuddering shoulders.

"Steve! Steve! Forgive me! There are enough terrifying things in the world. I do not have to become one of them! O, forgive me!"

She moved her hands down to his arms and gripped them tightly. He pressed his hands together in a vise, closed his eyes, and bit his lip to regain control of himself. Somehow he must tell her the whole truth about himself right here, now, in real life, not just in his mind. But first he must stop shaking. Then he must find a way to wipe the vision of horror from his thoughts long enough to formulate for her what he needed her to know.

It took a long time, but eventually a measure of calm returned to him. Kay's tight grip on him helped. As his tremors subsided, she relaxed her hold. Neither of them said a word, or even moved. At last he reached out for her hands, falteringly, and cupped them within his. He looked into her tear-stained eyes.

"May I tell you why I am so crushed?"

"Please."

Once more his head and shoulders slumped down almost to his knees. A tide of sorrow engulfed him. Then he sat up straight, took a deep breath, and said without looking at her, "I share with a small handful of colleagues the chief responsibility for creating those bombs. I was at the center of the Oak Ridge work from its inception. Only I know how much I contributed, how terribly much. And why? Why did I do it? To defend the good, to protect civilization, to halt the barbarians. And by what means? By creating a barbarous monster on the end of a paper leash and turning it over to our leaders who turned it loose on mankind. That's how we did it, Kay! We brilliant scientists!"

Kay gasped. "Was it *that*? O my poor, poor Steve…."

He shook his head hopelessly, staring dumbly between his drawn-up knees.

She stared at him and marveled. He was a little man. Just a kindly, harmless, sensitive little man. In his striped coveralls, he could have just come in from haying. Any farmer in the area might have borne his small head with its nondescript features and metallic hair. Only occasionally had his mannerisms betrayed to her anything noteworthy about him. To look at him, you would take him to be as common as a weed in the ditch.

So it is thanks to men like him that the world is hovering on the brink of global holocaust, she gasped within herself, shaking her head.

She leaned back on the bank right next to Steve, suddenly weak all over. He leaned back limply, too. His heart was still thumping.

How can he be any guiltier than I am? she thought.

And how guilty are you? came a voice from somewhere within her.

XVI

Those imposing clouds that had been standing guard in the eastern and southern skies were now silently dissipating. Their scattered remnants were catching the last flashing shafts of sunlight and diffusing them over the earth in a cool amber glow. Cowbells tinkled in the reigning stillness as herds wound down the mountain paths homeward from the upper pastures. A few dull sounds from town indicated comfortingly that the steady pulse of human life was beating on. Perched high in the maples in front of the schoolyard several robins were closing a busy day with torrents of cheerful music. Beneath the maples two people, so very dissimilar in appearance, were going through a silent confluence of spirit that he had not experienced for over twenty-five years and that she had never known.

At first they lay there exhausted, as if they had just crossed the finish line of a strenuous race. The last lap had left them gasping and panting and limp as rags. In a motion of pure weariness Kay's hands tugged slightly at the cupped palms in which Steve had them enclosed, but they did not come free. This caused a strange ripple of relief to pass through her. She let her head fall onto the rough fabric covering his shoulder and arm.

They lay there in silence. What might have looked awkward to an onlooker felt smooth and soothing to them. The longer they lay there, the more their shock and sorrow melted away, as though a skillful surgeon was removing sharp fragments of shrapnel from their wounded spirits, one by one. Each of them could sense that this little miracle was happening to both of them at the same time, and there was comfort in that knowledge.

The guilt was still there, and the issues around progress and evil were still unresolved, especially for Steve. But a "higher force" was now bathing them in the balm of forgiveness and respite. What was this force? Was it love?

As calmness slowly replaced anguish, they got back in touch with their immediate situation. There they were, lying in the deepening twilight of this warm spring evening with her head on his chest and her hands locked in his. The last glimmer of sunlight was playing on the edge of the vanishing clouds, streaking the sky gloriously through the dense crowns of the maples.

"The little birds are hushed now," murmured Steve as he often did at the onset of darkness. His throat tightened at those words, as it always did. Tonight it was as if nothing that had happened in the last twenty-five years had dulled his memory of Cecilia in the slightest, and nothing had even begun to fill the aching loneliness that never went away.

What was this soft warmth he felt enclosed in his hands? After so many years of empty hands? Was this really a pretty little head on his shoulder? Were these satiny strands of dark brown hair really brushing gently on his cheek? Was he—old, gray-haired, worn out—really basking in the aura of a lovely young woman who was also now a trusted friend?

He did not know what to make of it. All he wanted was to stay there forever, absolved in the forgiveness of one who insisted on sharing his guilt though she was innocent. The very thought of going back into the world that had claimed his soul for the past six-and-a-half years sent a shiver through him. In response to this dreadful thought, he slid his free arm under Kay's shoulders and drew her closer.

Meanwhile, Kay had also returned to the present moment, marveling first at the strangeness and then at the ease of their nearness. In her mind's eye she envisioned the inside of the schoolroom and all thirty-two of her precious charges gawking at her. If they could see her now, most of them would react with glee, a few with horror, a very few with malice, and a few with that same blank expression they always wore. But she would not really care what they thought. In fact, she wouldn't care what anyone thought. She'd just close her eyes and think of, well ... she'd think of Steve, of course! What else had she been thinking of lately?

A dearly puzzling, tragic man. So great and so miserable, so high-minded and so crushed, so brilliant and so taken advantage of, so kind and so treacherous. Treacherous? No! Not Steve. Out of the fruits of his genius others had wrought treachery, but still he claimed the guilt. He was only as guilty as any other American who had believed in the cause of the war and supported it with all his strength. The nobility of his character, the impunity of his motives, were they not self-evident in all he said and did? Just take a look into his eyes! All you can see in them is depth and honesty.

Presently a thought crossed her mind. It had flitted across it before, but now it strode across it.

I have to marry this man! I could never be happy with anyone else. All I care about now is his happiness, helping him put his life back together. He needs me. I can't imagine life without him. I have to marry him.

This led her to reflect on the various GI's and others she had dated in Europe, and a few back in America. All the decent ones had been insipid, and all the rest thought that every woman they ran into was starving for sex. Any girl who resisted their advances was subjected to verbal humiliations such as, "So you're saving yourself for Mr. Right, are you!" How often she'd heard some version of that line! She'd always reply, "Yes, that's exactly what I'm doing." It was so demeaning!

But Steve was altogether different. She had had to pull herself away from the clutches of the others, but she had clung to Steve and sunk into his arms. She had had to spurn the others, sometimes aggressively, but she encouraged Steve. She had cringed at the thought of a future with any of the others, but was excited at the thought of a future with Steve. As she turned it over in her mind, she realized that she was just as saddened by the thought of his future without her as she was by the thought of her future without him. She had invited him into her heart, and now he was about to leave. How could she let him go?

That was the moment when his arm slid under her shoulders.

"How comes it," Steve said in a whisper, "that such a wonderful and lovely young woman like you is not married?"

The question didn't come as a surprise to her at all, given where her thoughts had just been.

"I guess it's because the right man has never asked me."

She was satisfied with the way that sounded.

Almost at once, a grimace bit into her face.

"What is it, Kay?"

She balked and, withdrawing momentarily into herself, she replied haltingly, "That's not the only reason. You see … I'm very diabetic. The doctors tell me I have to give up any idea of having children. When some men discover that, they don't want me."

"They are very silly," Steve asserted, squeezing her hand.

Once again they lapsed into silence. An owl was hooting in the top branches of one of the trees. The air was still warm.

"Steve?"

"Yes?"

"Why is it that a man as kind and brilliant as you are is not married?"

He was half-expecting the question and had no idea how to answer it.

"Someday I will tell you the whole story."

Kay's heart stopped. "*Someday*? Does that mean?…"

"Twenty-five years ago I had a very great love … and then a very great sorrow, of my own making. She died in an accident. And I have never tried too hard to recover. I've just wanted to make her happy with what I was doing with my life, to know that she didn't die for nothing. That's why."

Kay held her peace for a long minute and then asked, "Wouldn't she be happy to see you recover?"

Steve looked at Kay and blinked hard.

"Yes, I know she would. I have never really wanted to 'get over her' for all these years. But my misery and loneliness can't be making her happy, any more than my work on the bomb made her happy. I know she wants me to accept forgiveness for my guilt and to get over my despair. I just know it. But I can't do that at the institute. Everything I'm asked to do there is making matters worse for the world."

Kay's brain was in high gear. Steve had so much hanging in the balance at this very moment. Whatever he was being asked to do at the "institute" was eating away at his soul. Surely that's why he had taken a leave-of-absence and fled to the hills of Vermont. If he went back to the "institute" now, it would kill him. But what could she do about it?

Well, he must not return to the "institute," and that's that! But what else could he do? After all those years in the front lines of research, who could use him outside of that field? She had never known anyone who was so brilliant and yet so gentle, so wounded himself and yet so considerate of others. To her, he represented at heart the noblest in man. His sharply analytical mind, his sensitive soul, the natural way in which he combined his dedication to science and his relationship to God, his way of integrating the rational and the spiritual—this must fit him for something more fulfilling for him to do than what he was doing now. Whatever it would be, it would have to combine the coldness of pure science with a warm concern for the well-being of people. The absence of that combination is what has been killing him. He would also need to be in an environment in which he would have a chance to figure out how God relates to all of this, and how he relates to God.

Now, where might he find a workplace that would satisfy all these requirements?

"Come on, little brain," she urged herself. "Show me what Steve can do next?"

As she pressed all these factors together in her mind, a recognizable shape came together. She smiled to herself, first broadly, then a little anxiously. Her heart was fluttering with excitement. What would he make of it? Would he go for it? Oh, just maybe he would!

She lifted her head and whispered eagerly, "Steve?"

"Yes?"

"Have you ever thought about switching into teaching? At a college in a little town somewhere?"

This idea took Steve squarely aback.

Teaching? A few of the men he had worked with during the war had gone into teaching, but he along with a few others had been swept by Uncle Sam from Oak Ridge straight to Pittsburg. "We must keep our superior minds working for us," was what they had been told. He shuddered to think of what they might be planning to do with his research of the past eighteen months. "We must maintain our decisive lead to preserve peace and guard our freedoms." They had left him no time to think about anything other than the government's program to develop the next generation of bombs.

Teaching.... How could anyone pervert and twist that? In teaching you could speak your convictions and shape young minds into pursuing only beneficial uses for developments in science. You would have the time and leisure to give serious thought to the emerging problems of the postwar world. You could probe the heart of modern society and your own heart, too. You would certainly not have the latest equipment to work with, as you do at the institute, but you would be marvelously free!

"Mmmmmm," Steve responded. "Did you ask that of yourself, Kay, or did a great good Spirit prompt you?"

"I think it must have been a great good Spirit," she replied, giving him a squeeze.

She could tell the idea was already taking root in him and germinating. She knew that what was going on inside him right now would probably affect the course of her own life forever. Limp with relief, she buried her head deeper into his rejuvenated breast.

"I will try to return to Christiania," he announced at length.

"Christiania? That sounds exactly right," murmured Kay. "Isn't that somewhere in Minnesota? What made you think of that college?"

"That's where many years ago it all happened. It won't be easy to go back there and relive everything. But that's also where I was sent off on my life of research with such enthusiasm. And I have a feeling that that's where I'll discover where and how I went off track. Not to mention all the eager young minds I'd have to work with in a place like that."

"Steve, I'm so happy for you, so very happy."

The joy of her relief was almost too much for her. She brushed back some stubbornly persistent tears and buried her head once again in Steve's chest. Feeling her warm little body rise and fall with an irregularity that betrayed its secret, Steve realized how deeply she must care about him. Was he filling an emptiness in her life the way she was filling an emptiness in his? Clearly his future was also hers, and his fulfillment could only happen in her. Without her the darkness would swallow him up again. He held her close. She was warm, she was life, and she was sniffling with happiness. She was caring, she was sparkling, and she was lovely to behold. She was a little treasure of untold worth.

"Kay," he said. The words stuck in his throat. Then, bursting through under their own pressure, they came rushing out. "Will you come with me to Christiania? I can't face the future without you."

Her only answer was a tighter squeeze, a more audible sob of joy, and a jerking nod of her head. He clasped her to himself. He would not be alone anymore, no longer a lonely figure in a callous world. Not alone anymore!

When eventually they loosened their grip on each other, they laid their heads back in peace, side by side. They were englobed by a serene thrill, cupped in the soothing hands of the life that lay ahead of them. The moon inched above the horizon and soon was showering them with its cool beams. The air was getting chillier now, but they weren't ready to move away yet.

"Kay, how old are you?"

"Twenty-six last April."

"I was forty-six last January."

"See, I was right. You're not old."

"I don't feel very old right now."

"To me you feel very strong," she remarked, running her hand up and down his chest.

"What will people say? The hoary-headed professor with the beautiful young wife. And newly-weds yet!"

"It will be fun for me to hear what folks have to say. I won't care. Will you?"

"Let them talk."

Then he took her by the hand and lifted her to her feet where, for the first time, they kissed each other standing up, a long and love-drenched kiss, bathed in bright silvery moonbeams.

Just then an elderly spinster, a member of the local school board, happened by. She gazed at them from a little distance with her hands planted on her hips until she had had too much.

"Well, I declare, Miss Kunstler! I'm sure the board will be interested in a report on the nocturnal activities of its young grade-school teacher and her affairs with tramps!"

Steve and Kay fell apart like two positive magnets. But Kay speedily recovered her poise and retorted cheerily, "Miss Hinckel, I want you to meet my fiancé, Dr. Stephan Pearson."

The old lady's eyes nearly popped out of their sockets. She looked Steve over from head to toe.

"Well, I declare! *Doctor* Pearson! Well, ah.... Congratulations, that is!"

And she bustled off to town to spread the news.

XVII

The very next day, Dr. Stephan Pearson sent two letters. The first was to Christiania College, informing them that he was available for appointment to a position on its staff in any of the Departments of Physics, Mathematics, or Chemistry and briefly outlining his activities since graduating from that institution. The second was to the institute in Pittsburg, resigning his position there and requesting that they make all the security arrangements necessary for his departure. Then in the afternoon he put on his best clothes, drove down to pick up Miss Katherine Kunstler after school, and with her paid a visit to the county clerk to buy a marriage license and then went on to Kay's minister to make arrangements for a simple wedding the day after school was out.

Christiania College had, of course, followed Dr. Pearson's career with some interest. Upon receiving his letter, the administration was so elated that it found it hard to sound professional in the return letter. It offered him the professorship of physics that had for two years been in the hands of an acting chairman. This would involve not only the duties of the chairman of the Department of Physics but also the responsibility of serving as head of the entire faculty of science and mathematics. When Steve showed the letter to Kay, he beamed and said, "Who would ever have thought I would become another Brockhaus?" Then he entertained her with some tales about his old teachers at Christiania.

And so in the fall of 1947, Dr. and Mrs. Stephan Pearson gratefully and joyfully took up residence in the little town of St. Mark, Minnesota. For nearly a decade, the black storm clouds in Dr. Pearson's soul receded to the distant horizon, all but obliterated by the brilliant sunlight shining directly overhead.

THE END OF BOOK TWO

Book Three A

I

There is really no need to enter into a detailed explanation of why the mantle of serenity dropped around Dr. and Mrs. Pearson for the next decade. A newfound love, a newfound mission, and a renewed faith in God for both of them combined to hold at bay the menaces of doubt and guilt and a deteriorating world situation.

Easily the most prominent stabilizer in Dr. Pearson's life was Kay. She must have known her heart well when she married Steve. The life into which he led her was wholly compatible with all she held dearest and best, and in return she gave him the vicarious pleasure of living with someone who was as adoring and playful as she was basically happy.

In their first year at Christiania, she witnessed the healthful effects which the radical change in his life was working on him—the disappearance of his morbid imagination, the restoration of his gentle humor, the regeneration of his faith in the good of what he was doing, the personal investment he was making in his students. Witnessing the rebirth of the new man out of the old stuff, she could scarcely contain her joy. She virtually bubbled over in her own cleverly educated way. Steve knew that the reason she was so happy was because of what he and his work meant to her. And that made him very happy in turn.

During the first year of their marriage, Kay derived all the sense of fulfillment she required from supporting him in his rehabilitation. It helped that the college administration made no secret of their satisfaction with every aspect of how he was discharging his many responsibilities, whether in the classroom, in the laboratory, or in his administrative roles. It was enough for her to be at home when he came home, to pour him a glass of sherry and make him comfortable when he was bone-weary, to offset his habitual inclination to work too hard, to serve him delicious meals, to go to church with him and to hold his hand as they worshiped, to massage his shoulders and back in the evening to help him relax, and to love him with all her heart at night.

Steve had been right, too, in his early estimation of her grace. She had a genius for being able to surprise him with just the thing he needed but would never have asked for on his own—a favorite meal at just the right time, a comfortable pillow as he was dozing off in an awkward position, a choice comment to put a strained situation into a better perspective—in short, a host of thoughtful little gestures which only love can see clearly to do. This same loving discernment of his mind and heart prevented her from getting underfoot—if that were possible!—when he seemed deeply lost in thought. And she appreciated that the accumulated quirks of a solitary middle-aged bachelor were not going to vanish overnight just because he was now married.

Nor was the concern all on one side by any means. Steve was not being doted into presenile complacency by his pretty young wife. On the contrary, their relationship was fully interdependent, for Steve soon discovered that Kay had not been exaggerating when she called herself very diabetic. Her balance between the semblance of perfect health and a state of desperate illness was as precarious as Steve's had once been between apparently sound mental health and periodic dips into depression. But she was one of those remarkable people who make this fact difficult to detect. She never complained of it, never even spoke of it. Of course, she watched her diet even when she prepared a hearty meal for Steve, but one might have attributed this to the self-discipline that kept her trim and in good physical shape. Her long walks while Steve was at work and their lengthy strolls together on the weekends could just as well have been seen as rooted in lifestyle practices, not health issues. There was little external evidence of the delicate blood sugar/insulin balance she always had to be on guard to maintain.

Nevertheless, Steve was never unaware of it. From the day not long after their arrival when he returned home to find her slipping into a diabetic coma resulting in a very quick trip to the hospital, he appointed himself her defender and guardian. This accounted for the fact that he would phone home two or three times during each work day unless she had planned in advance to be gone for the day with a friend. No matter how much she did for him, he never saw himself as a passive recipient, but always as the special protector of his lovely but fragile wife. This prevented their relationship from growing lopsided. They both knew how much they depended upon one another. Each loved the other dearly and was dearly loved in return.

In the first year of their marriage, they experienced only one serious disagreement. Kay, who had been orphaned at the age of ten, had received a good but firm upbringing at the hands of her maternal grandparents. They had taught her by example the worth of affection and concern for others, devoting their last and weakest years to her with singular unselfishness. She especially remembered their tender vigil over her when at the age of fifteen she slipped into her first diabetic coma. After the war broke out, it seemed that the spirit of these patriotic octogenarians broke with it. Both died within months. As soon thereafter as she was able, Kay applied to join the Red Cross, keeping a commitment to her grandmother which she had willingly made. As a diabetic, she was automatically rejected. But being Kay, she had persisted until they gave in and accepted her with certain restrictions. Soon she found herself near the thick of the fracas, giving of the love that had been given to her. We have already caught a glimpse of how the plight of war orphans unhinged her. This, together with her not fully accepted inability to have children of her own, earned her the nickname Mother Katherine from her coworkers. None was so dedicated to these waifs as Mother Katherine, none so patient with them, none so sympathetic to their acting out, none so able to draw them out of themselves. She could put smiles on empty expressionless faces and even bring tears of love to long-shriveled eyes.

For her, there was no question of what she must do after returning home. Already possessing the basic formal qualifications of a grade school teacher, she had no trouble securing a suitable position in Ciel des Montagnes, forty miles from where she had grown up. Grateful as she was for this, and much as she enjoyed her pupils, she sensed deeply that something was missing from her life—the love of a man, of the right man. As we have seen, when Steve came along, he was her man. And the joy of having a man like him to love eclipsed for a time the pain of knowing she must remain childless. But after several months of marriage, her longing for children resurfaced. This was the cause of their first and only serious disagreement.

Even before their wedding, Steve, once he had grasped the seriousness of Kay's condition, immediately set to work to find out how they could consummate their union safely. He began his research in the local library in Ciel des Montagnes and then consulted the local physician who lent him some medical books which proved helpful. Based on what he learned, he drew up a chart that told them which days in the course of her menstrual cycle were absolutely "safe" for intercourse. The main complication was the irregularity of her cycles caused by her diabetes and by the insulin that kept it in check. But Kay and Steve resolved to work together on it to ensure that they would make love only on those days when they could be absolutely sure that she could not get pregnant. To be on the safe side, the chart Steve drew up gave broad leeway for error. This turned the few "safe days" available to them every month into a veritable monthly honeymoon.

Condoms were out of the question. Steve's research told him they could not be trusted. Their failure rate was much too high. Both Steve and Kay had friends whose experience attested to that fact.

In any case, one evening when they were still five days shy of her "safe period," she came after Steve with an aggressiveness normally reserved for the "safe period." He backed away from her in confusion.

She pressed ahead. He rolled over and exclaimed in alarm, "What are you doing, sweetheart?"

"My love," she pleaded, "let's either try to have a child, someone to call you Daddy, or let's give up this rigmarole."

She had been acting funny ever since he'd got home. Now he knew why. Her hormones were raging. This would be the absolutely worst time to make love!

"A child? You and I? So that's it.... You know we can't have children; we can only have each other. Isn't that enough? Are our intimate times nothing but rigmarole to you?"

Steve was both frightened by her actions and deeply hurt by her words. Lying beside her in bed under the dim light, he broke out in a cold sweat. In the pit of his stomach, it felt as if his world was caving in on him.

Steve's crestfallen questions cleared Kay's head in a matter of moments. It dawned on her all at once how badly she had wounded him by what she had said without thinking, and she shrank back in shock from her own words. Watching him before her very eyes wither away into the shadow he had been before she came into his life, she felt like a fool, ashamed and sick at heart. What could she do now to heal the wound she had just ripped open? Painful as the truth was, Steve was absolutely right. It was a matter either of nurturing what they were able to have between the two of them and being thankful for it, or of having nothing at all.

Steve turned and looked at her in dismay. Disillusionment was etched all over his face. Looking back at him with flushed cheeks, her eyes brimmed over with tears. They hesitated for the merest instant. Then they flew into each other's clutches.

"This must not happen again!" whispered Steve, nibbling her ear.

"Never again!"

This was a promise she strove never to break, especially as the aftereffects of that evening lingered like a cloud over Steve for several weeks.

She had a great man to love and sustain. What more could she ask for? She had better set her whole heart on loving him well.

Despite this temporary setback, Steve's general progress was upward, decidedly. One of the evidences of this which encouraged Kay was his desire to make and keep new friendships. The fact that he had returned to Christiania in search of some answers spawned in him a motivation to make the acquaintance of those who seemed to have found some of them. Such a man was Dr. Harold Thorsheim, chairman of the Art Department, and such a woman as his wife, Mary, twenty-one years his junior. The Pearsons and the Thorsheims met at the president's reception for new faculty members. Their mutual delight in meeting another couple with a similar age-spread piqued their interest immediately. Dr. Thorsheim, at sixty-two years of age, looked more like his wife's father than her husband, and more like their children's grandfather than their father, even though both of their children were already in their upper teens. These two couples sensed a deeper affinity between them than the circumstances of the reception allowed them to explore. Soon they were gravitating toward each other and spending time together of their own accord.

Dr. Harold Thorsheim was widely admired in the field of church architecture for his resourcefulness in weaving traditional Christian symbols into the idiom of contemporary construction techniques. Readers will no doubt have been exposed to his inspired and inspiring architectural masterpieces, churches of his design found throughout the Midwest and beyond. He had the ability to penetrate below the surface of a simple object and fashion it to make it speak to you through your eyes. The way he disposed a bare row of joists in the nave of a church, for example, would set the mind of a thoughtful worshiper to meditating on spiritual truths. This sensitivity of his to how the Word of God is always visually communicating Itself throughout creation enabled him to design many churches whose apparently effortless architecture is in reality an inexhaustible fund of triggers for the fertile imagination of the prayerful. There was something about the wedding of scientific principles and spiritual insight in his work that struck a chord with Dr. Pearson. And the artist, for his part, found in Dr. Pearson a similar marriage on a different level, the blending of an insistence on scientific objectivity with a lively concern for the human soul. In any case, here was a scientist who not only listened to him when he strayed off into a rhapsody on some aspect of church architecture, but who often encouraged him to expand on it! Not many of his fellow architects took that much interest in what he had to say!

Kay and Mary moved just as swiftly to close the gap between them. Kay could not hear enough of Mary's tales about the blessings of unity and mutual appreciation which the disparity in their ages had brought into their marriage. She could easily foresee many of these blessings in her future years with Steve. They had to concur that the maturity of their spouses added depth and poise to their marriages and counterbalanced their more youthful impetuosity. Mary was delighted to find out that Kay was a grade school teacher. She herself had just returned to teaching two years earlier, ostensibly to help put Carolyn and Peter through college, but really because she loved kids and the challenge of helping them grow into the persons God had created them to become. So there was always plenty of engaging conversation going on between those two women, while their husbands were solving "weightier issues" in the front room.

Soon after their first Christmas in St. Mark, the Pearsons moved into the house a little beyond the edge of town which was to be their home until the end. Harold Thorsheim had heard that the previous owner was intending to sell and had notified the Pearsons. They were on his doorstep even before he had put it on the market. The place extended an immediate invitation to both Steve and Kay, with its five wooded acres of land, its large garden where Kay could work off those dangerous excess calories, its arbored view of the calm pastoral landscape surrounding it, its invigorating half-mile hike to the hill, its proximity to the Thorsheims whose home was nestled in a secluded grove halfway between them and the college, and the quaint and cozy efficiency of the house itself. When Steve offered to pay the asking price in cash the next day, the seller's only question was when they wished to move in. If Steve's years of service to Uncle Sam had done nothing else for him, they had at least fattened his bankroll to the point where, mismanager and generous soul though he was, he was never short of money. Kay never did find out where he had all his money invested or deposited or stashed. I am not sure he himself knew.

To complete the picture of the Pearsons' domestic life in St. Mark, it remains only to add that Kay began teaching grade school during their second year in town. Mary Thorsheim's intuition is to be thanked for this healthy turn of events. She sensed that once Steve was back on his feet and Kay's constant care of him was no longer needed, Kay would require some other outlet to express her caring nature. Her need to give would not decrease in proportion to his need to receive, a situation which the arrival of children would normally have rectified. As Kay's closest friend, Mary had more than hunches to go on that things could easily turn sour for them bit by bit. But she saw in Kay's qualifications as an elementary school teacher the perfect way to avert the danger of marital stagnation. As a teacher, Kay's capacity to love would never pile up behind jammed floodgates, but would keep right on flowing full, sweet, and fresh.

Inquiry was made, and on Mary's recommendation the principal invited Kay to start teaching the second grade class in the fall. Once Mary had assured Steve that his wife's classroom would be next to hers, he no longer hedged at the thought of her going into a coma undetected. He too saw the wisdom of the plan and could think of many factors in its favor. He even called it "perfect timing."

From then on, Steve and Kay settled into a very satisfying routine for some years that allowed them plenty of time to be together and gave them much to talk about and share with each other. Mary had detected and disposed of the worm of restlessness while it was still in the embryo stage. It is easy, then, to understand why Steve woke up each morning happy, why he labored each day contentedly, and why he returned home each evening with eager step. His precious little wife and the delights and challenges of his work were more than enough to hold at bay anything from the outside world that might have threatened his peace.

II

During the school year, from 7:30 in the morning until 5:00 in the evening, Monday through Friday, and all morning long on Saturday, Dr. Stephan Pearson could be found in one of five places—in his office in a turret atop the massive gothic-style science building, in his lecture hall, in the physics laboratory, in the chemistry laboratory, or in the chapel.

Although the science building was a massive structure, the faculty offices within it most certainly were not. Tucked under staircases, blocked off in dead-end corridors, and squeezed into turrets, they impressed one for their coziness if not for their convenience. Dr. Pearson had been ceded the use of the southwest turret, one of two medieval projections on either end of the south wall of the fortresslike structure. To reach it one ascended a circular staircase from the fifth floor where the impressive and up-to-date science library was housed. One then ducked under a beam and emerged onto a narrow covered corridor on a flat flanking section along the edge of the roof. This led to Dr. Pearson's turret firmly planted on the southwest corner of the building. It was about twelve feet in diameter on the inside and lined with an octagonal arrangement of bookshelves reaching two-thirds of the way to the ten-foot base of the conical ceiling. In the south-facing segment of the octagon was a tall window, the lowest section of which could be opened for fresh air.

Such an affair may seem cold and forbidding, especially during those long Minnesota winters, but in reality it suited the retiring disposition of the professor very well. Kay saw to it that the college provided him with a thick warm carpet on the floor and an electric fan-heater for use in cold weather. Twice a month she scaled the tower when Steve was in class to keep his workspace as clean and tidy as possible.

This last task might have overwhelmed a lesser woman. Every time she waded into the mess Steve could create in a couple of week's time, she had the impression that a cyclone had struck. Books, papers, pencils, refuse of every description were lying in the same comfortable positions they had landed after being tossed or lost. Soon, however, Kay learned on which shelves the most used and consequently the most abused books belonged. She developed a system of separating the scattered papers into three categories—definite scraps, probable scraps, and probable essentials. The definite scraps (relatively few in number) she herself threw away. The probable scraps (a veritable mountain) she placed in a neat stack on the left side of the great oak desk right above the waste basket. And the probable essentials she placed on the right side of the desk up against the wall. Because of her dedicated efforts, both professor and students recovered papers that may otherwise have remained lost forever.

The turret office did indeed well suit Dr. Pearson's disposition. He was the sort of scientist who, rather than involving himself deeply in particular laboratory investigations, had instead devoted himself to planning out his investigations' next steps, pencil in hand. Technicians enough he had always had to carry out his instructions and report on results. He had been accustomed to spending many hours in the company of his well-trained fertile mind, visiting the laboratories that reported to him as often as necessary to check on progress or, occasionally, to conduct an investigation which for some reason he felt he should do himself.

His move to Christiania had, of course, curtailed this sort of activity, but it had replaced it with an activity that quickly engaged him to the full—teaching. His first challenge was to meet students where they were and not overwhelm them unintentionally. He must have succeeded in this. Every student of his that I had an opportunity to meet and interview after his death spoke glowingly of his classroom style during these years. They spoke of his encyclopedic grasp of every subject he taught and his infinite patience with students who were struggling. He never consulted notes. It was all in his head, neatly arranged, they told me. Furthermore, despite his towering intellect and reputation, he was always accessible to his students and the soul of kindness in every situation. But what they recalled most vividly was his ability to fire their imaginations. In the course of his lectures, he would regularly digress to paint a vision for his students of how humanity's lot could be improved by the proper application the principles and the knowledge they were in the process of learning. He spoke of instant worldwide communication through a network of satellites (which he had designed on paper and illustrated for his students), of the elimination of famine and starvation through—among other things—the controlled culture of algae, of the potential of nuclear fission and atomic synthesis to produce limitless power for the benefit of all, and of a whole host of other possibilities he envisioned for a better future for the human race. He spoke with such radiance and confidence of this future, even in the face of the widespread panic induced by the threat posed by the Soviet Union, that the fear of nuclear war gave way in many of his students to enthusiasm for the many exciting prospects of nuclear peace. His first three years at Christiania saw the number of physics majors in the graduating class jump from five to twenty-seven and climb steadily from there.

He was not a dynamic lecturer, far from it. His voice did not even carry through the terraced lecture hall. It didn't take long for the electronics man on his staff to rig up a portable microphone which he could unobtrusively hang around his neck. He didn't try to be interesting. He just was, by virtue of what he said, not of how he said it. A principle could be ever so abstract, he almost always had a homely illustration of it at hand to make it easier to grasp and retain. Occasionally he would suddenly lower his voice and sever contact with the class, mumbling something to himself half aloud. This was an almost mystic moment for those in the class who were caught up in the spirit of the man. He never did lose his "romance" with theoretical physics and with mathematics especially, and their seductiveness could catch him at the most inopportune moments. The former students whom I was able to interview from this period in his life loved him for this and even held him in a kind of awe because of it.

Specifically, for what subjects was he responsible? A cursory reading of a number of the catalogues dating from these years reveals that he must have established a working partnership with the Departments of Chemistry and Mathematics, for he often moved over to teach one of their courses and was not shy about recruiting someone from their faculties on occasion to teach a course in his department. Each year he taught one class in general physics, a beginning course for science majors, but also available to fulfill the science requirement for nonscience majors. I am told that this class became very popular and was always oversubscribed. In addition, he regularly instructed a semester course in the three fields of thermodynamics, nuclear physics, and theoretical physics. Then, crossing into the Chemistry Department, he taught a two-year course in theoretical chemistry involving thermodynamics and molecular structure. And every year he taught one class in upper-division mathematics which included over the course of time such subjects as differential equations, advanced calculus, and theory of complex variables.

With all of these quiet endeavors lumped together in a pleasing and orderly fashion, Dr. Pearson's life settled down into a regularity that was far from boring or routine. His mere presence at Christiania attracted several outstanding new faculty members within a few years so that, in addition to the fine man in electronics whom he had inherited, there were now also first-rate teachers of inorganic and organic chemistry, a capable new electronic physicist, and a lightning-quick Hungarian mathematician, a refugee whom he had met in Germany many years before. The quality of work proceeding from little Christiania with its fifteen hundred students was commencing to attract some notice in the world.

In his office by himself or with his students one on one, in his lecture hall, in his laboratories, or at daily chapel, reticent and diminutive Dr. Stephan Pearson seemed the very embodiment of self-possessing unaffecting genius, moving with his own brand of quiet eagerness in the well-ordered orb of his lofty calling, his grace-filled wife, and his peaceable religion.

III

His peaceable religion. Without it neither his wife nor his new vocation could have brought Dr. Stephan Pearson so far from the brink of despair and held him aloof from it for a decade. For neither his wife nor his vocation would have been capable alone of stilling the clamor of extreme guilt in his soul. Only his peaceable religion could do that, most of the time. But even it was unable to ward off every shaft of accusation aimed at him by the events of those years. Had he been living in isolation from contemporary history, it might have been a different matter. But he was living in the world of the late 1940s and '50s, even though far removed from its crossroads.

He could not, for example, escape noticing that his most dreaded fears after America had dropped the bomb on Hiroshima and Nagasaki were now being realized. The secret of atomic fission could not be safeguarded by the United States but was being diffused over the whole earth. Very soon Great Britain possessed it, as Steve knew she would, based on England's involvement in its development. But Russia's announcement on the floor of the United Nations that she too had successfully exploded the bomb really staggered him. No one wanted to believe their claim. But in 1952 one was detonated which was verifiable to the whole world. The treasure had fallen into the hands of unscrupulous men, the very men who had sat behind those whose bloody duplicity had driven Chiang

Kai-shek from the Chinese mainland and instituted a reign of terror over more than four times as many people as lived in the United States.

But no less troubling to Dr. Pearson's peace of mind were America's own advances in the destructive power of the bomb, to which he himself had contributed at the institute in Pittsburg. One heard every day of the billions of dollars allocated to the military objective of staying ahead of the Russians, but no mention was ever made of developing the great potential of atomic fission and synthesis for man's welfare. He had been assured in the most solemn fashion that as soon as the war was won, his strenuous efforts during the war would be channeled into peaceful benefits for all mankind. He had been duped!

No sooner had he and Kay arrived at Christiania than he witnessed the total collapse of another of his cherished hopes. The horrendous price exacted of mankind by World War II had not purchased the treasure of world peace nor had it elevated freedom and democratic civilization above the forces of barbarian invasion. He had pleaded with his overlords not to withdraw troops from Europe until it was clear that the Soviets were withdrawing theirs. But domestic political considerations predominated, and our troops came home while Russian troops remained in Central Europe and tightened their stranglehold on the nations they had "liberated." And the whole world, wearied by the war, acquiesced. Dr. Pearson could only contemplate with appalled disbelief that four short years after the war to rid the world of the demonic barbarism of the Nazis, more people were subjected to a new and aggravated form of it than ever before.

So what had the war accomplished? Had it left the world at the mercy of two snarling monsters armed with inconceivably destructive weapons who were now holding the whole world hostage? Were all the Ciel des Montagnes of the world now in graver peril than ever? Was the threat of global annihilation preferable to the threat of subjugation to our enemies?

The state of Dr. Pearson's peace of mind was understandably dependent on the many joys and satisfactions he was experiencing at close range and on their ability to block out the accusing finger of deteriorating world events for which he knew he was in no small way co-responsible. In the face of this challenge, some answer had to be found for his most troubling question: Where was Cecilia's Jesus in all of this? How could he, Stephan Pearson, have fallen into the ground and died, as she had challenged him to do, and still have produced all the wrong fruit?

For this he had to be satisfied not with a direct answer but with a brilliant inversion of his question: If we know that God is good, why do we let the small pieces of the total picture which are visible to us destroy our faith and our hope? Why do we allow them to override our trust in God who has control of the total picture? Our trust is in Him who is, and who was, and who is to be. So let us persevere in seeking to do what is right and leave the sorting out of the big questions to Him.

For Stephan, this was a breakthrough which sustained him and animated him for a full decade.

IV

No one was more responsible than Dr. Harold Thorsheim for bringing about this inversion in Steve's view of reality. As the little physicist drew back from the epicenter of science's involvement in producing weapons of ever greater destruction, he lost that daily contact with the demands of the politics of survival which had driven him to the brink of despair. His great need now was for a sustainable sense of the goodness of Almighty God next to which the evils unleashed by men would shrink in importance. And the longer he was exposed to Harold Thorsheim's implicit confidence in just this, the closer he came to adopting that confidence for himself.

The Pearsons and the Thorsheims spent many evenings together until Harold's death in 1953. Kay and Mary would always retire to the kitchen where over a cup of herbal tea they could pursue in conversation the things that interested them, while Steve and Harold normally took control of the front room or, in pleasant weather, the front porch. Most often the men discussed some aspect of their respective fields that was of common interest to them, and frequently this led them into the spiritual dimension. As they spoke, Harold often glowed with humble admiration for the grand historic continuity of the Christian community as it expressed itself in her rich cultural and liturgical heritage to which the leaders at Christiania at that time were fully and intelligently committed. Steve, for his part, often found himself, as Harold spoke on, reliving his experiences of worship in the beautiful Catholic parish near his house on the outskirts of Boston before the war.

Dr. Harold Thorsheim was a man caught up in the worship of God. This was evident from their very first conversation. Steve discovered that life was for him a ceaseless act of adoration of the Almighty, alive with countless signs and symbols each directing the inner man toward the eternal verities which the loving Power beyond our history has graciously woven into it for our benefit. His religious posture might best be described as an acute awareness of the fact that although God has entered time to convey eternal truths to His time-bound creatures, still those truths themselves stand with God outside of time. Wherefore, although Christ died once in time to defeat the evil one and to atone for our sin, nevertheless His sacrifice goes on forever in the presence of God who knows not the restrictions of time. For Harold Thorsheim, this overarching reality made the Sacrament of the Altar much more than a mere memorial. It is God's means of uniting us with Mary and John and Mary Magdalene and, indeed, with all redeemed creatures of all times and places at the very foot of the Cross, since in the eyes of God, the eternal Father, the crucifixion of Jesus, His Son from all eternity, is never past history but always present reality. The consecrated elements of bread and wine which become Jesus' Body and Blood are God's way of uniting us to the death of Jesus in the closest possible manner. This awesome truth never failed to bring tears to Harold's eyes whenever he tried to account for it in words.

"The great Apostle Paul in his first epistle to the Church at Corinth puts it this way: 'The cup of blessing which we bless, is it not the communion of the blood of Christ? The bread which we break, is it not the communion of the body of Christ?'

"Salvation, it seems to me, is an ever-descending stream of grace from on High whose sole purpose is to reunite us to God and evoke from us a response of gratitude and love forming an ever-ascending column of incense from below."

"That's quite a picture," Steve replied with closed eyes to envision it in his mind. "But don't you think that such pictures might run the risk of restricting our concept of the Eternal Being?"

"Perhaps. No picture tells the whole story," replied the artist, leaning back in his easy chair. "As I see it, God's purpose in entering time and space through the Virgin's womb was to give us an authentic grasp of the intangible through the tangible, of the invisible through the visible. If we whose minds are capable only of making time-space associations are left to ourselves to fathom and then depict ultimate spiritual truths in our minds' eye, it is amusing—if not a little pathetic—to note what mental images of God we might come up with. I knew a man one time whose abstract concept of God was 'Sheer Power.' When I asked him what mental image he associated with that concept, he replied, 'Whirling electrons in infinite space, or a massive explosion.' It was news to him that the Eternal Word became flesh to give us a more accurate picture of who God really is."

Steve nodded and Harold went on.

"C.S. Lewis illustrates this in his little book on *Miracles*. As I recall it, he cites the case of a woman who, as a child, had been raised by parents who prided themselves on their enlightened understanding of God as Infinite Substance. In her child's mind this suggested a vast tapioca pudding, an image of God that was further tainted by the fact that she greatly disliked tapioca pudding. I suppose most of us in moments of honesty would have to say that we have at times entertained some pretty far-fetched images of God ourselves."

"Well," chuckled Steve, "I'll have to admit that your friend's picture of 'whirling electrons in infinite space' hit me pretty close to home, at least at one stage in my life. Not that I consciously thought of God in those terms, but I take your point."

"Well," smiled the artist, "no need to feel alone. It's a strange but self-evident fact that we've got to think of the Creator in the categories of His creation or we can't think of Him at all. So in the end it seems to be a question of discovering the most accurate way of applying the categories of creation to the Creator, always taking care not to confuse the two. The

Church Fathers were wrestling with an issue closely related to this when they sought to define the dual nature of Christ, human and divine. At any rate, let us suppose that in addition to being Power, the Supreme Being is also Love and Justice, and that He is all three of these in relation to His creation, and especially to us mortals created in His likeness. What image do you think would capture this reality for us?"

"Father, of course. Or even Almighty Father. Or even 'Our Father who art in Heaven.' The word 'Father' is drawn from our human categories, and the word 'almighty' or the words 'who art in Heaven' lift us beyond the human to the divine, beyond this creation to its Creator."

"Precisely. And the moment one understands both the necessity of calling God 'Our Father' and its inherent limitations, one is ready to enter into the rich adventure of becoming acquainted with how the Church over the years has appropriated suggestive imagery to embody and proclaim spiritual truths. We say, for example, that our prayers 'ascend' to God simply because we associate dignity with height. If we said our prayers descend to God, this would inevitably suggest to us that He is an inferior Being, someone we could step on and walk over. Nor could we say that our prayers fan out to God without suggesting that He has little more status than we have, that we can look Him almost straight in the eye."

Harold drew on his pipe, now gone dead, and went on.

"That's why Christian symbolism is ageless. It evokes associations in the human mind that do not radically change. Symbolism by definition is a representation of truth, even of very Great Truth. No one in 1948 need recoil from referring to prayer as ascending to God any more than a person in AD 33 needed to recoil from it, even if in those days people thought of Heaven as located directly above earth, since the main point then and now refers to God's superior dignity and power. It is likely that the words 'up and down' in the context of human society will always mean the same thing whether we're standing on earth, landing on the moon, or dangling in space somehow."

"Besides," added Steve, "changing it to 'in and out' would be no more accurate geographically and no less accurate spiritually."

"Right. So that to speak of God's mercy as an ever-descending stream from on High and of our response as ever-ascending incense from below serves only to wrap a wonderful spiritual truth in easy-to-grasp imagery."

"All right," Steve responded playfully. "But you'll have to forgive someone like me for finding it a little difficult to picture how the source of a column of smoke can survive directly in the path of a stream pouring down on it from on High."

"Ach, you scientists!"

And the conversation moved into a lighter vein until they parted company for the evening.

The discussion that night led to Steve's attending Matins with Harold the following morning in the side chapel before classes began. This daily event was open to all, but attended mostly by faculty members. In this way Steve gradually succumbed to the joy of adoration. It was a slow process, akin to the healing effect of medication on a serious wound. And then one day he found himself caught up in the serene thrill of blending his voice with the voices of worshipers from all ages and places in a single act of praise and thanksgiving rising to the Throne of Grace.

But there was even more than this to his joy.

Harold's unblushing love for the liturgy of the Church, in which for nineteen hundred years Christians the world over had been expressing their faith toward God in one tide of praise and supplication, soon affected Steve's struggle against his postwar fears that events in the world were making it impossible to believe in a good God. Here he was in the midst of a formidable army of men and women, many of them sufferers, martyrs, victims of injustice and disease, all praising God in the most consistent terms for His great goodness! Nothing gave voice to this miracle more effectively than the great "Te Deum Laudamus!" sung nearly every day:

"We praise Thee, O God: We acknowledge Thee to be the Lord.
All the earth doth worship Thee: The Father everlasting.
To Thee all angels cry aloud: The heavens and all the powers therein.
To Thee Cherubim and Seraphim: Continually do cry,
Holy, Holy, Holy: Lord God of Sabaoth;
Heaven and earth are full of the Majesty: Of Thy Glory.
The glorious company of the Apostles: Praise Thee.
The goodly fellowship of the Prophets: Praise Thee.
The noble army of Martyrs: Praise Thee.
The holy Church throughout all the world: Doth acknowledge Thee.
The Father: Of an infinite Majesty;
Thine adorable, true: And only Son;
Also the Holy Ghost: The Comforter....
Lord, let Thy mercy be upon us:
As our trust is in Thee.
Lord, in Thee have I trusted:
Let me never be confounded...."

Through wars and treachery, plagues and famines, in good times and in bad, the Church had faithfully raised these strains to God, entrusting Herself to His perpetual care and then boldly going about Her mission. The fact that She was still here singing these same words to Her eternal God, was this not proof that She had indeed never been confounded despite Her faltering steps? And were not Steve's steps Hers?

In short, Steve came to believe that the goodness of God means that evil is transitory and must be seen in its limited role in the mystery of His broader plan, never in isolation. Thus, when he thought of his own past and the evil he had helped to create, or when some evil from the wider world caught his attention, he repaired to the liturgy of the Church and immersed himself in its authoritative constancy and calm assurance within which evil appears as a passing shadow, a spent force. And this kept him from coming unraveled.

"In Thee, O Lord, have I trusted: Let me never be confounded."

This was Dr. Stephan Pearson's peaceable religion. It was his solid wall to lean on when he was world-weary, his assurance that Providence would honor his efforts to guarantee that science would in the end serve to eradicate poverty and evil, not to promote them. He had little faith in human beings to achieve this. He knew far too many scientists who went about their business totally unconcerned about the long-term effects of their work. For him, on the other hand, everything now began and ended with prayer. And as a teacher this meant above all to instill the right motives in his students so that when they lost themselves in the pure allure of science, they did not abandon their moral sense. Liturgical prayer did this for him, leading him to have peace in doing his best and leaving the rest to God.

This transformation in Steve did not, of course, happen in a day. It grew in him slowly but surely as the Church's liturgical celebrations came to provide the consolation and hope which the world could not. Kay, too, shared in Steve's gradual recovery of reliance on God as the Ultimate Unifying Force. She was mindful of how healthy it was for Steve to have a place of refuge from the storms of life, a rock on which to stand in the shifting sands of world events, a last court of appeal to which to take his case. And as he was restored in spirit, so was she. Discovering the riches and depth of true liturgical worship was a real eye-opener for her. The church of her youth had had little commitment to liturgy. Worship was a free-for-all much of the time. Everything depended on the personality and gifts of its ever-changing ministers who ranged all the way from devout to flippant in their conduct of worship. In the changeless but prolific traditions of the Church, she found something much truer, more authoritative, more enduring, than anything she had known before. And her drifting soul found a mooring place.

The respected professor's blend of brilliance as a research scientist and mathematician and his humble devotion to God did not fail to leave its mark on both students and colleagues. If a man of his caliber could excel in both science and religion, how could anyone question their compatibility? Both must be essential in the pursuit of truth. Even the students who were the most indifferent or even antagonistic to religion could not avoid the message implicit in his daily routine of removing his white laboratory coat at chapel time and making his way across the campus to the church. It didn't matter if he were right in the middle of something, such as assisting a student. When the moment came to leave, he excused himself and left, transformed in an instant from master to servant, from academic to mystic.

The disputes of the renowned theologians of that time meant little to him. It was not that he disdained them. It's that he found himself in agreement with Harold Thorsheim, who was better acquainted with them than he was, that most commotions in the specialized arena of theological combat affect the basic genius of the Church's faith about as much as a few noisy splashes on the surface of the ocean affect its changeless depths.

It took almost two years for Steve to feel at liberty to share with his friend the exact nature of his burden of guilt, his direct personal responsibility for contributing to the development and successful production of the atom bomb. It happened near the end of one of their cherished evenings together as couples.

"Harold, you need to know something about me. You have generously shared with me from the very depths of your heart and soul, and I have been greatly blessed by that openness and candor on your part. I now need to share with you something from the depths of my heart and soul, but it will not come as a blessing to you."

And he spilled it all out, all the way from the circumstances surrounding his love for Cecilia and her death, to the letter from President Roosevelt and its consequences, to his providential encounter with Kay, and everything in between.

The shock and wonder of it did leave Harold quite stunned, at a loss for words, but not for long.

"Steve, I have come to know you well, and I have come to love you. You are my brother in Christ. Nothing can change that. God is bringing some great good out of all this, of that I am certain."

Steve looked at his friend through the tears in his eyes.

"I can't thank God enough for you and Mary. You won't know until you are in the presence of God Himself how much you have blessed us."

It remains only to take note of a little ritual that developed whenever the Pearsons and the Thorsheims spent an evening together. They would end it by singing a hymn which Steve found very meaningful. Its words were by John Ellerton and its hymn tune was by John B. Dykes. All four of them sang well, and in four parts, Mary informs me. I would love to have been there. This is the hymn:

Behold us, Lord, a little space
  From daily tasks set free,
And met within Thy holy place
  To rest awhile with Thee.

Around us rolls the ceaseless tide
  Of business, toil and care;
And scarcely can we turn aside
  For one brief hour of prayer.

Yet these are not the only walls
  Wherein Thou may'st be sought;
On homeliest work Thy blessing falls,
  In truth and patience wrought.

Thine is the loom, the forge, the mart,
  The wealth of land and sea;
The worlds of science and of art
  Revealed and ruled by Thee.

Then let us prove our heavenly birth
  In all we do and know:

And claim the kingdom of the earth
For Thee, and not Thy foe.

Work shall be prayer, if all be wrought
As Thou wouldst have it done;
And prayer, by Thee inspired and taught,
Itself with work be one.

These were very happy years for Steve and Kay. They knew the peace of being reconnected to God, of thoroughly enjoying one another, of loving their work, and of having close and trusted friends. In addition, they enjoyed the respect of the broader community, Steve from his colleagues on campus and Kay from her colleagues at school. One might call it an equilibrium of soul that was theirs in those years, a state of great blessing which allowed their energies to flow outward for the benefit of people around them rather than being sucked inward by their own neediness.

V

Like college campuses all across the United States in the fall of 1942, campuses in 1950 also bore mute testimony to the fact that our country had been drawn into yet another war. Whereas the women's dormitories were filled to capacity, the men's dormitories were almost empty. Only the lower floors were occupied. The shades were pulled down and the curtains were drawn together on the upper floors. The nations of the Free World were rushing to the aid of the beleaguered South Koreans, aware that Moscow was the force behind the aggression of North Korea. Once again all able-bodied American young men had been summoned to fight the enemy on foreign soil, spilling their blood and the blood of the enemy for the imperiled cause of freedom. The world was tense, watching its two opposing nuclear giants spar at each other from behind the thin masks of the United Nations and North Korea. Mortal fear gripped everyone. What would happen if these giants threw off their masks and faced off against each other directly? Gory as this war had become, it had so far remained within the arbitrary bounds of conventional weaponry. Would it at some point break loose and engulf the whole world in a nuclear holocaust with unthinkable consequences?

But this unwanted interruption in normal scholastic activities seemed short-lived. Already in November the United Nations' forces had routed the aggressor. Our boys would be home for Christmas, ready to resume their education after a six-month hiatus that had added years to their stature. Soon the musty rooms would be aired out and life would be back to normal. No one anticipated the enemy's next move that would result in the return of the Korean peninsula to much the same state it had been in before the conflict began and would prolong the bloodshed fruitlessly for another two-and-a-half years.

Shortly before Christmas, a scrambling torrent of ill-equipped Chinese soldiers poured into Korea from Manchuria, sending the UN forces reeling backwards. The human avalanche kept coming and coming, overrunning the very men whose gunfire was mowing it down in waves. It rampaged onward until it ran up against a line deep in South Korean territory where UN troops had had time to dig in their superior equipment. From there, at great cost in terms of time and lives lost, our men fought their way back to the thirty-eighth parallel.

There were no boys home for Christmas that year.

Nor the next, except for a trickle of wounded veterans.

The peace talks dragged on and on. The Communists were waiting for a withdrawal of Western troops, much as had happened in Europe after World War II, and were poised to capitalize on it to recoup their losses. Not until July of 1953 was an Armistice finally signed, and even then it created a frontier and a no-man's-land which American soldiers are still obliged to guard.

In the fall of 1953, life at Christiania took up pretty much where it had left off. But it was a much-altered lot of male students that filled its classrooms. In some ways they were serious about making up for lost time and moving ahead with their lives, and in some ways all they wanted to do was have fun, fun which had been denied them for some three years. They wanted to lay the groundwork for a successful life, but they decidedly wanted to have a good time in the process.

Dr. Harold Thorsheim passed away late that fall. An old chest injury of his was blamed for giving rise to complications from a cold that lingered for several weeks and then suddenly brought on the end. His death left an emptiness in Dr. Pearson's soul that nothing else seemed quite able to fill.

VI

Throughout this trying period, Dr. Stephan Pearson clung to his hard-earned balance with the tenacity and integrity we might have expected of him. There was no reason why his convictions should be any less valid in wartime than they were in peacetime. He had never denied that the world is evil: he had merely affirmed that God is good and that He strengthens and vindicates His people in the face of evil. It was God's business to do whatever He chose to do with man's sincere and honest efforts to serve Him and his fellowmen. With this stalwart faith firmly implanted in his soul, he was able to find relief from the tensions of the world in his cozy office, in his ever-fertile mind, in his vocation as a teacher, and above all in Kay.

It would have taken more than a distant war to break Kay's gracious hold on him. She remained first and foremost the rejuvenating elixir of his life, his daily contact with a world of tenderness and care. When they were alone with each other in the world they shared between them, it was as if no other world existed. Of course, these hours of deep happiness came and went, but they were always there to return to on a regular basis.

He loved her more each day and wasn't shy about saying so. As the days stretched into years, his admiration for her grew apace. He found her quick mind ever more able to pick up the thread of complex concepts he happened to drop in her presence, sometimes of a technical nature, sometimes of a metaphysical nature. In this way, little by little, she developed into a partner with whom he could share many things he would otherwise have had to keep to himself. He probably never realized what effort this took on her part, the library books and articles she studied in order to communicate with him more nearly at his level. But his obvious delight in her in this facet of their relationship was reward enough for her.

His ongoing concern for detecting positive results from scientific progress opened a door in his mind which, if Kay found it ajar, was receptive to any insights she might supply him from her daily life as an elementary school teacher. Sometimes he was even aggressively curious about the details of what to her seemed like an insignificant incident from her day which she happened to mention to him in passing, as though he could not hear enough from her about the mind-set of the younger generation. When he was in that our-hope-lies-with-the-younger-set mood of his, she would have to tackle all sorts of questions from him about the attitude and values of her students. She enjoyed this, as it made her think, even as it drew her more deeply into the soul of the man she loved.

Moreover, each day Kay grew more beautiful in his eyes. Her sparing table habits, her enforced exercise regimen, and her overall enthusiasm for life surely contributed to this. Her bright and hopeful spirit made her a delight to be around and indicated an underlying reserve of courage which she could call on to get her through tough times.

No, the war did nothing to loosen Kay's gracious hold on Steve.

Nor could the war undermine the joy and consolation he found in worship and adoration. The deeper the world pressed him into the bosom of the Church, the more he encountered Her rock-solid foundation and Her sublime constancy. Let the world disembowel itself in its madness and fury! In its very midst stands the Church, steadfastly looking to the eternal God whose goodness always has the last word. The world must stand speechless before Ultimate Truth as expressed, for example, in Bach's "St. Matthew Passion" or in his "Mass in B Minor," both of which were gloriously presented at Christiana during the Korean conflict. The world was powerless before that which it could neither fathom nor produce of itself—pure adoration of God from a people He would never allow to be confounded.

And in that faith in God and that hope for the future, Stephan Pearson went on teaching and inspiring his students year in and year out.

VII

For more than a decade life moved along from day to day with few bumps and much satisfaction. It is true that the return of the veterans from the Korean War brought with it a tiny worm that burrowed itself into the new core of Stephan Pearson's soul, but this worm was so often content just to lie dormant that it escaped detection. Since he himself was so slow to acknowledge its presence, we too shall disclose it gradually by describing one particularly annoying Friday late in the spring of 1956. Kay must have unloaded it on Mary who took me through that day as I was preparing this book.

The day began in a most promising way. The sun rose glorious over the freshly sprouting cornfields. Steve and Kay were out in the yard by 5:30, cleaning dead leaves from under the shrubbery. They loved this sort of work at this time of the day when the air is fresh and the smell of human activity is faint, a time of new beginnings and hopeful prospects.

At 6:30 Kay went into the house to change clothes and fix breakfast. At 6:45 Steve went in to change clothes and enjoy breakfast. At 7:00 Steve suggested to Kay, "Why don't we flick on the radio for a few minutes and get some news about the convention in Minneapolis. Cecil Hartman should mention it."

"Good idea. Maybe something has been decided about the merger."

She reached back onto the counter and turned the knob. Within a few seconds the urgent voice of an announcer was summoning the two tranquil breakfasters to rally round the cause:

"Mr. and Mrs. America! How are you able to live without ABLE? ABLE! The brand-new, all new, dependABLE washday product you have all been waiting for! ABLE, friends, is capABLE of washing any washABLE with remarkABLE ABILity. With your dainties it's adorABLE, with your work clothes it's unbeatABLE, with your dishes it's irreplaceABLE, with your floors it's unscuffABLE, with your walls it's unmatchABLE!! I repeat, friends, how are you ABLE to live without ABLE? The **only** washday product that is all seven in one—dependABLE, remarkABLE, adorABLE, unbeatABLE, irreplaceABLE...."

-Flick-

"...deplorABLE..."

"...and insufferABLE!"

"My gracious, dear! Now we know what's wrong with our marriage!"

"Just think! Without ABLE we've missed out on what could have been ten years of bliss!"

"I shall pick some up on my way home from school this very day. Fear not, my dear! From this day forward, we shall no longer be disABLEd!"

Kay flung her arms out theatrically in a sweeping gesture of triumph, sending Steve's glass of milk caroming to the floor with a crash.

"Well," he replied sardonically, observing the milk creep out over the linoleum. "The first thing to which we can apply its magic touch is the floor next to the table."

They burst out laughing as Kay scurried to get the mop and bucket to clean up the mess. In a moment she was back at the table with a fresh glass of milk for Steve.

"Do you want me to turn the radio back on?" Kay wondered.

"No. How can they expect a person to recover from that torrent of asinine verbiage in time to listen to the news with dignity and discernment?"

"That's a good question," Kay replied, taking a bite of toast.

Dr. Pearson's first class was not until 8:50 on this particular day, and there was no Matins because of the convention, so he decided to spend the first hour in his office on campus. There was a little stack of papers he had to get around to marking one of these days, but first, he reasoned as he walked up the arbored lane to the hill, he'd have to try to settle some knotty problems that had been on his mind lately. There appeared to be a relationship between those two.... But was it real or just coincidental?... No.... No.... The graphing was too consistent to be accidental. Perhaps the key lay in the—

SCREECH! - HONK! HONK!—BEEP!

What in the...?

Dr. Pearson swung around to face the racket. A car had come speeding over the rise just as he was stepping into the lane, had swerved violently, and screeched to a halt to avoid the professor sunk deep in thought. Two more had barely escaped colliding with it from the rear. There he stood, surveying the chaos occasioned by his mere presence on campus: one car skidded sidewise directly in front of him and the other two gunning their engines impatiently behind it.

"Er, G'morning, Doctor. Sorry for the ... ah ... close call," flustered the blond Nordic specimen in the first car. "Kind of on pins and needles, I guess you'd say. Big race this afternoon."

The professor was going to tell him not to worry about it when someone hollered from the last car, "What's the hold-up? I've got to make a 7:50 class on the other end of campus!"

Instantly the first car peeled off, leaving him standing in a cloud of blue exhaust. The other two whizzed by in bright blurs before he had time to collect himself. Gathering up his shattered train of thought, he retreated to his turret.

"A man takes his life in his hands walking across campus these days," he muttered.

Normally the noise from below did not bother him, but today he had to shut his office window to cut off the distraction of passing cars.

"Every useful invention is subject to travesty," he mused as stock cars, presumably gathering for the "big race," roared by showing off their skillfully mutilated mufflers.

But it is man's good fortune to have pleasant moments interspersed in the most annoying of days. The rest of the morning passed without incident except that in place of the regular chapel period, someone had managed to schedule a twenty-five-minute harangue from a special itinerant speaker warning everyone about the dangers of creeping socialism.

At noon as he was eating lunch in his office, one of the papers on his desk caught his eye. Sparing as was his normal use of the red pencil, this paper was so decorated with scarlet that it looked as though he had sliced off the end of his finger over it. It was that poor Gary Amundsen's last test paper! The professor had promised to return it so that he could study for the big test on Friday afternoon, and today was Friday! Well, there were still three-and-a-half hours left before the test. The young fellow would certainly appreciate getting that paper back now so he could see where he went wrong. There were several errors he had consistently committed throughout the test which five minutes' attention would rectify.

So he left his half-eaten sandwich and clambered down the staircase to the administration offices located on the main floor. There he learned that Gary Amundsen resided in Kildeer Hall and that his entire afternoon was free to study for the test. Paper in hand, Dr. Pearson penitently headed for Kildeer Hall.

It was not that the young man was incapable of the work. From the way he talked in class, he evidenced the commendable ambition of qualifying as an engineer like his father and joining him in the family business. Besides, he would never have got as far as differential equations if he had not shown some native intelligence along the way. True, the course was giving him some difficulty, but Dr. Pearson did not regard his problems as insurmountable. With a bit of application, he had it in him to become a fine engineer. In class he always had such an earnest look on his face, as if he'd do anything to please you.

"The poor fellow is probably studying his head off at this very moment, and here I am with this paper that could be a real help to him."

Dr. Pearson swung open the big glass door and entered the reception area of the new dormitory where he ascertained the number of Gary's room. He mounted the broad staircase to the third floor, Room 317.

These are magnificent accommodations they're building for students these days, he thought. *I understand Harold had a hand in this one. If he were here now, he'd be explaining to me the scheme of this structural feature or the meaning behind that fixture. You could count on that. Good old fellow....*

Here he was in front of Room 317. He knocked. No answer. Again he knocked. Again no answer.... Of course! He'd be over in the library. Why hadn't he thought of that before?

"Good afternoon, Dr. Pearson," he heard from a door not far down the hall.

"Hello, Len." It was one of his chemistry students.

"Are you looking for someone?"

"Gary Amundsen. But he must be over in the library."

"Before you go over there, sir, it might be a good idea to check the lounge to the left of the reception desk as you come in the main door."

"Okay, Len. Thank you."

There had been a large, yes, a very large open area to the left of the reception desk, he now remembered. Strange he hadn't thought to look in there before trudging all the way upstairs. Time was of the essence for the young man.

Descending the last flight of stairs, he was able to see through the glass wall into the lounge from above. There were perhaps a dozen men gathered around a TV set watching a baseball game. Not much chance he'd find Gary among them when so much was at stake for him in this test. Still, Len had said to check there.

The puzzled scientist slipped into the lounge. The TV set was in the far corner. The young men had their backs to Dr. Pearson as he cautiously entered and approached the group for a better look. Scanning the back of their heads, he was about to turn and leave when a mop of red hair resembling Gary Amundsen's popped over the top of a roomy upholstered chair. Moving closer to the chair, he angled off to one side for a view of the young man' profile. It was Gary! His elbows resting on the arms of the chair with his head propped up in his hands, he was peering at the screen with rapt attention. A few moments later he gave a little jerk and slouched way back into the chair, staring distractedly at the ceiling. His eyes wandered over to the windows and gazed into the distance, finally roaming back to the TV screen.

A man in the TV announced, "The score at the end of seven innings is Milwaukee nine, Brooklyn one."

Gary Amundsen stretched and yawned.

The little professor was nonplussed. Was this the lad who in class seemed so eager to learn, almost too eager? Was this why his eyes were always watery and more or less bloodshot? Was he totally unaware of his plight? Didn't he care that three hours of studying could make all the difference between a pass and a fail on that test?

He walked meekly over to the lad and held out the paper.

"I told you I'd get this paper back to you before the big test today. You still have time to make good use of it."

"Wha.... What?" Gary jolted around in his chair, coming to abrupt academic attention.

"Oh, hello, Dr. Pearson. What was that?"

That earnest look came over his face.

"This last test. There are some mistakes on here that you could easily avoid repeating later this afternoon."

"The test? Oh yes. For this afternoon. Thanks a lot. I'll look it over as soon as this game is over. Only two innings left."

Dr. Pearson was pensive as he left the plush lounge.

"That lad doesn't know what's good for him, that's all."

The embracing spring air rushed through the doorway and met his warm face. Right next to the dormitory he spotted a large empty baseball diamond spread out under the sun.

"At least he might have been out here," he said to himself, shaking his head.

Then he ambled slowly back toward his office.

On the way across campus, he stopped at the post office to collect his mail. The box was stuffed with envelopes of varying sizes. Among them were two letters of departmental interest, one personal reply from a colleague in Milwaukee, and half a dozen advertisements. Two of the latter were addressed to "Box Holder" and were soliciting subscriptions to third-rate magazines. Another was an invitation from a Book Club to purchase $52.49 worth of books for $0.99 complete with a ten-day trial period with no obligation if returned within the ten days. The other three he tossed into the overflowing wastebasket without bothering to look at them.

That evening, Kay noticed that he was having a hard time being cheerful. It was as if something was eating him.

"Are you feeling well, my dear?"

"Not exactly. Let me explain why."

Then he told her of his experience with Gary Amundsen and finished by remarking that the results of his test that afternoon made it clear that he had paid little, if any, attention to the returned test paper. And he had arrived to take the test with those same bloodshot eyes that had previously given Dr. Pearson the impression he burnt the midnight oil studying.

As he talked, Kay grew sullen.

"Marvelous as this TV is," she put in, "I sometimes wish it hadn't invaded every home the way it has. In the last few years I've noticed a marked—you could say—regimentation in the way children respond in class. They all seem to be thinking the same thoughts in the same patterns. How is Dandy Duck going to get out of the mess he got himself into just as yesterday's program was ending? We'll know at 4:00 if we rush right home after school. And isn't Mr. Filibuster awful? He wouldn't let Johnny Squirrel set up his acorn stand so he could earn a thousand dollars and retire. All this sets off alarms in some of us teachers, who grew up in an era when children made and solved their own adventures, to listen to this kind of thing all day long."

"Well, honey, don't you know that those programs sell Choco-Milk Sweetener by the case? Isn't that all that matters?"

"It also sells a few other things, like TV teeth, for example. That's what Dr. Jensen called it the last time I was in to have my teeth checked."

"TV teeth?"

"Yup. There's something about the way kids hold their heads in their hands while watching TV that pushes the teeth out of place in their soft jaws."

"You don't say."

"But the worst part of it comes on a beautiful day like today when they've all got to run home so as not to miss *Hello There*! In the winter it's bad enough. But when *children* would rather sit indoors and watch TV than play outdoors on a glorious day like this, something is really all out of kilter."

"It probably keeps the kids out of the streets in the big cities."

"Maybe. But where is the corresponding decrease in the rate of juvenile delinquency? I often ask myself if all the violence on TV doesn't actually inspire lawlessness. The kids sure talk about it enough. TV almost normalizes it for them, I'm thinking."

They sat there in silence for some moments. Then Kay spoke up more cheerily.

"Gladys Evans told me today that they're moving into that big new house under construction north of town." All at once her voice dropped and a quizzical expression came over her face. "I wonder why…."

"They only have two children, don't they?"

"Yes, and they're about ready to leave home. I always thought their present house on Christiania Avenue was lovely, especially with that big fenced yard."

"Well, now that he's head of the Psychology Department, perhaps…."

"Perhaps. I suppose we shouldn't criticize or judge the motives of others. I wasn't sure what Gladys meant by 'We have to keep moving up, right?' but it bothered me, I'll admit."

Steve took a deep breath and said, very slowly, "One would hope that when folks have more than enough for their own needs, they would automatically start thinking of what they can do for others who do not."

Kay sensed the sorrow, almost the anguish, impregnating these words. Getting up from the chair in which she had been sitting, she crossed the room and sank into the sofa beside Steve.

"I love you," she breathed softly, pressing against him. "The world cannot be altogether bad as long as it contains a few men in it who quietly give away what they don't need, and even some of what they do need."

Then she kissed the man she was talking about and laid her head on his shoulder. He put his arm around her. It felt so good to be so close.

As they were sitting in the semidarkness of the room, three cars passed in front of their house in the full moonlight. Two of them were pulling large boat trailers behind them down the highway. Both Steve and Kay had the same thought. Those outfits were expensive!

The sound of the cars died away in the darkness.

The little worm was not dormant now. It was feasting on Steve's one great conviction. Not that he surrendered it! It just became more challenging for him to hang onto it when evidence of man's self-worship seemed to be growing out of control and evidence of God's overriding goodness seemed harder to find by the day. Thank God for the liturgy! It was the one source of sanity in an insane world.

"Honey," he whispered at last. "Let's go to bed. I've had enough of this day, haven't you?"

"Not quite, sweetheart," she cooed.

"Oh?"

"Do your math."

Pause.

"You're right! Tonight we can have each other completely."

"So, what are we waiting for?"

"Right! What *are* we waiting for?"

And they did.

VIII

It was a year and a half later, October 1958. Thoroughly troubling days had been comparatively few and far between for Dr. Pearson, but the number of petty annoyances within each day kept growing. As long as he remained absorbed in his teaching, his worship, and his domestic happiness, it was not hard for him to slough off these annoyances if they didn't come at him too thick and fast. Underlying his usual serenity was the conviction that advancements in science would ultimately serve to eradicate evil and suffering on earth and do more good than harm.

The Reedville Board of Education had invited him to be the principal speaker at their high school's annual "Looking Ahead Day," this year to be held on a Friday in October. His overall theme would be "Preparing for the World of Tomorrow." He would address an all-school convocation at 10:30 in the morning, spend the afternoon visiting several science classrooms, and close the day with a forty-five-minute speech before the Reedville Association of Parents and Teachers that evening. It would be a busy day, but it would offer him many opportunities to fire up the enthusiasm of students to dedicate themselves to the cause of peace and progress. And so he had accepted the invitation gladly, replying that he and his wife would arrive at the school library by 9:30 a.m. as requested. Thus, leaving behind their respective responsibilities for one day, they set off for Reedville by car.

Reedville was a town which, until the years after the war, had been located about fifteen miles southwest of Minneapolis. It had been the hub of a specialized truck farming industry. Now, however, its population had quintupled, its size in area had quadrupled, and its farms had mostly been parceled out into rolling estates. Two freeways ran through the municipality, spokes leading commuter traffic into downtown Minneapolis. In other words, it had become the ideal American suburb, less than half an hour from "the loop," spangled with shopping centers large and small, and blessed with a quaint old-fashioned downtown. The residents of its sprawling estates, which had been carved with some skill out of its wooded hills and its fields, enjoyed a broad selection of new schools, competing automobile dealerships, elite country clubs, and antiseptic churches.

The drive to Reedville was pleasant for the Pearsons. They considered their 1951 DeSoto a fine road car. The bumps melted away under its large shock absorbers, and its six-cylinder engine purred along on a minimum of gas. They left St. Mark at 7:30 a.m. in order to give themselves ample time to contend with the inflowing traffic. Arriving at Reedville at 9:15, they stopped at a filling station to get exact directions to the high school.

"Go straight ahead for two blocks and make a right," they were told. "Then go straight ahead for a mile or so until you hit Highway 17. It's just across the highway. You can't miss it."

Indeed not! Surrounded by a vast sea of cars, it spread out in all directions like a great island. At the first sight of it, the Pearsons were astonished by its opulence. But, scooting across the highway in the few seconds allotted by the stop-and-go light to allow lateral traffic to consume six lanes, their astonishment swiftly turned into bewilderment.

Before them in graceful curves and orderly rows were acres of automobiles of every imaginable color and combination of colors. Pink Cadillacs, purple Mercuries, green-and-gold Studebakers, fiery red Pontiacs, gaudy winged Plymouths and Chryslers, jet-black Buicks, tiny sports cars, lowered hot-rods, converted pickups, racy convertibles:

every sort of vehicle ever produced or crossbred was on display there, it seemed.

"What do they do, commute from Iowa?" Kay puzzled, stroking her chin.

"I don't know, but it's a good thing we're a little early. Where do you suppose we should park?"

"I'll bet there's a faculty parking lot closer to the school."

"Good idea."

Steve started off in the direction of the building as Kay kept her eyes peeled for the faculty parking lot. He got twisted up in the confusing maze of cars but eventually emerged under a broad overhanging carport measuring perhaps one-hundred fifty by three-hundred fifty feet in front of what appeared to be the main entrance. Windows overlooking the parking lot and the active highway occupied three sides of the single-story structure whose floor was the carport.

"Interesting," pondered Steve out loud. "Protection for people coming and going in inclement weather, with the roof space devoted to classrooms."

"I wouldn't care to teach in a classroom with floor-to-ceiling windows overlooking a freeway," observed Kay. "How would you ever hold the kids' attention?"

From there they clung to the side of the building until they came to the faculty parking lot. Their DeSoto looked a little more at home back there. Parking on the edge of the lot, they made their way back to the main entrance on foot, asking each other what that giant goldfish bowl on top of the carport could possibly be used for in a school.

No sooner had they reached the doors than they were greeted, all out of breath, by a buxom blonde whose school sweater, pulled painfully tight, left little to the imagination. Seizing the startled professor's hand, she blurted out virtually in one breath, "You must be Dr. Pearson, our special guest for the day! And this lovely lady must be your daugt … wife! I'm Sally Larsen! Welcome to Reedville High School!"

"How do you do, Miss Larsen," he replied calmly. "Yes, this is my wife, Mrs. Pearson."

"How do you do, Sally."

"Well, my job was to greet you and take you up to the library where Mr. Pfister (he's our real cool principal!) is waiting for you."

"Thank you, Sally," they said together, following her up the broad steps to the lobby.

This was to be a day of surprises, and here was one of them. The lobby was a cavernous space lined with ten-foot potted plants and inlaid with designs in exquisite ceramic tile. Leading off from the lobby were three corridors, each measuring some twenty feet in width and framed in the same ceramic tile as the lobby. Steve and Kay followed Sally to the flight of stairs on the left. The splendor of it all had a more pronounced immediate effect on Kay than on Steve who normally awoke more slowly to what was going on around him. As they reached the landing, Kay was moved to ask Sally a question that had been on her mind since their arrival.

"Sally, this fine school must serve a very large area, judging by all the cars in the lot, right?"

"Well, not really," she replied both tentatively and emphatically, stopping on the landing to gaze out the window. "It's really awful," she explained, trying to sound disgusted. "If you don't come to school driving at least a '55 Pontiac, you're totally out of it. It's so bad that our dads have to come to our rescue as soon as we turn sixteen and get our driver's license. Otherwise we'd just be humiliated, that's all there is to it."

Then suddenly she sparked up.

"My dear daddy gave me that pink '57 Oldsmobile convertible over there just last month!" she enthused. "And he pays for the gas, too! Isn't he just too cool? That's it over there beside the black rod," she said, pointing into the middle of the sea of cars. "It's the one, two, three, four, five, sixth one in the third row of the second section."

The Pearsons scoured the lot in vain for a few moments until Sally mercifully terminated the search with a flourish.

"Well, it's real neat anyhow. Wish you could ride in it. I'm already on my second set of tires." She paused briefly. "I'll bet you folks have a really neat car, too, eh?"

Before they could answer, she bounded up the stairs, beckoning them to follow her. At the top they turned to the right and—was it possible?—stepped out onto the carport through glass-paneled doors sporting the word LIBRARY in gold letters.

In a bit of a daze they followed her into the bright enclosure, glancing at the handful of students standing at the windows watching the cars go by on the highway.

"Dr. and Mrs. Pearson, may I introduce you to our principal, Mr. Pfister, and this is our librarian, Miss Hazelitt."

"Welcome and good morning to you, Dr. and Mrs. Pearson," exclaimed the principal, extending his hand to each of them alternately. "We are so honored to have you both as our guests for the day. I trust that your drive from St. Mark went well."

"Yes, very well, thank you," replied the professor.

"We're happy to be here," put in Kay.

The principal, a tall immaculately dressed man of about forty years of age, launched immediately into the business at hand.

"We knew you'd want to get acquainted with our school family before the all-school convocation at 10:30. So with your permission, I shall personally guide you on a tour of our modest facility and introduce you to a few people as we go."

"Thank you. We'd appreciate that."

"Yes," began the administrator as though reminiscing over a long and difficult struggle, "it took quite a while to get here, but now we can be rightfully proud of our little schoolhouse."

With that, he set out with them from the library and led them on a tour of the entire school with the exception of the science wing which, he said, "you will be getting well acquainted with before the end of the afternoon."

If they thought the library—with its window-walls, its poverty of shelf space, and its five exterior surfaces to try to heat in the winter—was the only extravagance in the new school, they were in for a rude shock. In the course of the tour they were ushered into the main auditorium ("for general use"), the music auditorium ("You'll be speaking in here. The acoustics are better."), and the smaller auxiliary auditorium ("to foster a more congenial atmosphere for smaller groups"). Next they visited a capacious vacant room which Mr. Pfister called the Band and Orchestra Practice Room. As they came through the door, a young man jerked his feet off the top of his desk, scattered out some papers, and snapped to attention in one smooth well-practiced motion. The next room down the hall was the choir room, a little smaller than its neighbor but equally empty. "Mr. Giles has only one choir at the present time, but he has offered to give private voice lessons for credit next semester," their guide clarified.

From here they passed by the Home Economics Department, "furnished with the latest culinary equipment," and entered the manual arts wing, darting in and out of the printing shop, the aviation warehouse, the auto mechanics garage, the sheet metal shop, the carpentry suite, and finally the large supply storage area.

Next they were directed through a complex of corridors ("English, history, social sciences, and language laboratories for French, German, and Spanish") to the one remaining unexplored section. As they approached it, Mr. Pfister's pace quickened, his back straightened up tall, and his chin rose. Turning down yet another corridor, they came to a large set of doors over which hung the sign "Women's Locker Room and Gymnasium" ("We'd better not peek in there"). Some distance down the same corridor they came to still larger set of doors that boasted the sign "Main Gymnasium" ("for spectator sports"). The last set of doors was, of course, "Men's Locker Room and Gymnasium" ("We promote the total person: body, mind, and spirit").

But the climax was yet to come, the crown jewel yet to be displayed. Up to the third story they climbed. Around to another wing they followed the beaming principal where, to their surprise, he led them up a narrow spiral staircase in the center of the roof, much like the staircase leading to Steve's turret office. At the top was a small door on which were lettered the words: "OBSERVATORY. No admittance without written permission from the Principal."

"Here, my friends, is our crowning jewel, our tribute to science and the future of our planet, and indeed of our race! You have no idea what it cost me to get this gem written into our blueprints for the school."

He unlocked the door with some effort and shoved it open.

"The second largest telescope in the Upper Midwest!"

Steve and Kay looked at the telescope and the room in which it was housed.

What a magnificent piece of equipment for a high school, thought he.

How dusty! thought she.

The principal casually sat down on one of the stainless-steel tables as though this crowded little room were truly home to him. In so doing, he raised a cloud of dust that made Kay sneeze. Aware of the splendid disuse of this room which the thick coating of dust betrayed, the principal hastened to add, "Ah, of course, we haven't yet got an astronomy instructor worthy of this grand equipment. But Mr. Walthers, our man in printing, has been dabbling with astronomy for years and gets up here now and then to play around with it. I hesitate to let anyone else in here. You can imagine what this gem cost our good taxpayers," he said, stroking its eyepiece affectionately.

"Indeed!"

Mr. Pfister glanced at his watch. "Ah! Twenty minutes until the convocation. We'll head down to my offices where you can collect your thoughts for a few minutes." He gestured toward the door and the Pearsons descended the stairwell. Carefully he locked his jewel up tightly—to protect the community's investment in the future.

Back down on the ground floor they passed through the lobby and took the corridor to the right which led to the administration offices. The main area of these offices housed a dozen or more clerical workers and secretaries, and beyond it along the same corridor were the private offices of the principal and the assistant principal.

"Here we are at my modest seat of operations," announced Mr. Pfister, swinging open the door to his plush office. A funereal hush came over him as he drew them over the thick carpet into his inner sanctum.

"I would have settled for something less, but the people insisted...," offered the principal, noticing not without delight the Pearsons' shock at the opulence and conspicuous extravagance of the room. Twenty feet wide and thirty-five feet long, its ceiling was overlaid with an exotic design of acoustical fresco and its walls subdued by full-length heavy gold-flecked draperies. The four bookshelves sported only neat symmetrical sets, mostly limited editions. The large oak desk was obviously made to order by a true craftsman, as were the other furnishings. When the principal deemed that his guests had sufficiently soaked up the evidence of the esteem in which he was held, he ushered them into a smaller adjacent office of comparable extravagance.

"This is our guest office, your home for the day. That door opens directly into a corridor leading back to the main corridor. And this door opens into your own private washroom. Let's see—we have twelve minutes. Shall I tap on your door in seven minutes? I'll take you through my private passageway to the music auditorium."

"That will be fine," returned Kay politely. "Thank you."

The principal smiled and shut the door. Steve sank into the nearest chair. Kay followed him into the one next to it. He had long since lost touch with the tour.

"Well, my dear Dr. Pearson. Do you want me to turn on the television set in the corner, switch on some piped-in mood music, or start up the stereophonic set over there?"

"Just hold my hand. I think I am getting old."

IX

Although Dr. Pearson's address that morning managed to hold the interest of the audience, Reedville High School never saw the visionary scientist who routinely fired up the imaginations of his students back at Christiania. He was simply not in a very visionary frame of mind when 10:30 rolled around. Nevertheless, the contents of the notes he had prepared proved exotic enough on their own to keep his listeners attentive, while his reputation and scholarly mien lent them a distinctive aura of authority. Around the core theme of the gradual elimination of the evils that plague human life on earth, he arranged and related many of the scientific advances then on the horizon, most of which have become commonplace since then but which were almost unthinkable at the time. Each advance, he declared, if properly harnessed and responsibly utilized, could address a real human need and could release for better things the time and energy presently tied up in trying to cope with that need. He then proceeded to use the emerging satellite technologies to illustrate this point. Already there were on the drawing boards satellites to provide instant communications worldwide through telephone and other means, to beam television and radio signals in every direction, to gather and collate weather data instantly for the whole world, to explore outer and inner space unencumbered by the earth's atmosphere and to track accurately military maneuvers anywhere on the face of the globe with extremely high resolution cameras. His description of his own projects involving both fusion and synthesis, with their many anticipated benefits, kept the audience spellbound. Some peaceful uses of atomic energy were right around the corner, he informed them, whereas other promising uses would take time to develop with adequate safeguards. He challenged the students to join in the crusade to rid the human race of the shameful elements of its sorry past and to become part of a universal positive energy which, under God, would be dedicated to "turning swords into plowshares and spears into pruning hooks," in the highly suggestive words of Sacred Scripture. This, he concluded, was not only the best hope for the future of mankind on planet Earth: it was its only hope.

After his forty-minute address, no one mistrusted the administration's decision to call upon Dr. Pearson to keynote this year's "Looking Ahead Day." He really was different.

That noon the Pearsons were the guests of Sally Larsen again. After showing them through the spotless cafeteria, she shuttled them off to a private dining room where they were scheduled to lunch with the student council. This body of leading personages about the school had prepared a list of questions to guide its informal discussion with their guest of honor during the meal. For the first several minutes, however, it appeared that the discussion would revolve around the food, not the other way around.

"Not this old stuff again."

"It's the second time this month."

"Chow mein on 'Looking Ahead Day'!"

"To serve to our guests!"

"The government must be unloading its surpluses on us poor students again."

When nobody seemed to be touching the food, Dr. Pearson quietly suggested that someone say grace. A lad at the far end of the table, who thus far had said nothing, obliged. And with that, most of the student councilors commenced to pick at their plate of food, some first removing the celery, others first clearing the "mess" off the rice before tackling any of it that was not contaminated.

"Dr. Pearson," spoke up the handsome football player on his right, reading from the prepared list of questions, "as president of the Reedville High School Student Council, I would like to throw open our discussion by asking your professional opinion on an issue that is quite a hot topic around here these days. Who will get to the moon first, the Russians or us?"

Someone snickered near the end of the table.

"That`s difficult to say at this point," ventured the professor. "In what way would this particular issue be of concern to the students here?"

"Well," supplied a redheaded lad jauntily, "if the Russians get there first, they`ll turn it into a Communist satellite."

A few suppressed chuckles showed that his wit was not wasted on everyone.

"Oh, they`ll never get there first," asserted a brunette with conviction. "There`s too much bureaucracy in Communism. We learned that in modern problems."

From there the conversation took off on everyone`s opinion of Communism, the race to the moon, and the armament race.

"They wouldn't dare pull anything on us."

"We'd clobber them."

"That Sputnik just caught us off guard."

Steve and Kay, and that quiet lad at the far end of the table, had cleared their plates long before most of the rest of the diners had made an impression on theirs.

With five minutes of the allotted discussion time remaining, the president offered another question for the consideration of the group. "Dr. Pearson," he read, "would you please tell us what your … your con—fession is of the supercity of tomorrow, its con—veniences, its … novelties, its general—"

He tossed the paper aside. "What we want to know is, what do you think will make it hop?"

"Here, let`s see that paper, Goofus," needled the girl sitting next to him. "That's 'conception,' Mr. Pearson, not 'confession'—'your **conception** of the supercity of tomorrow.'"

"Yeah, that's just what I said: 'your confession of the supercity of tomorrow.'"

"O stupid!" exclaimed the brunette, throwing the paper back at him. "That's 'its conveniences, its novelties, its general attractions,' sir."

The little professor looked up from his empty plate, a strained expression on his face, and asked, "That too, I suppose, is an issue of collective interest to all of you?"

"Everyone wants to know where tomorrow's kicks are coming from. Don`t you?" volunteered a long-haired chap on the left.

The guest of honor looked down at his plate. His mind was as blank as the surface he was staring at. His tongue stuck to his gums. But the proverbial bell came to his rescue. Sally Larsen jumped to her feet as most of the assembled gathering was making for the door, conveyed to him the group`s thanks for his time, and wouldn't he please come back real soon? In a flash the room was nearly deserted.

"I`ll just leave you two to wander around at your leisure," she said, patting Dr. Pearson on the arm. "We have a real keen school building, the keenest I`ve ever seen." And then she hastily added, "But I'll bet Christiania is even keener! Well, I've got to run along now to another one of those meetings. Sometimes I wish I weren't so popular. See you later!"

And she dashed out of the room.

The two guests of honor looked at each other. "We might just as well go back to our 'home for the day,'" Kay suggested. "It won't be long until they'll be wanting you for this afternoon."

They were about to leave when the quiet lad who had been sitting at the far end of the table cautiously approached them and, looking down through the floor, said, "I ... I'm sorry for this noon. I was hoping it would go in a better direction."

The contrast between these words and all the other words spoken during the meal gave the Pearsons quite a jolt. A moment of awkward silence followed. Then the gentle scientist walked over to the young fellow, who was now blinking fast, put his hand on his shoulder, and said, "I was hoping so, too."

The boy`s eyes rose and met Dr. Pearson`s. Nothing more needed to be said.

Kay sensed at once what was needed. "We are just heading over to a private office set aside for us today. Why don't you come and join us? Your teacher won't mind when you explain why you aren't in class."

The lad`s face lit up at the thought.

"Yes, of course," said Steve. "That's a fine idea."

On the way over to the office, Steve was surprised to learn that the young man had read virtually all of his postwar articles of general interest, and some of his prewar writings as well. Where had he got hold of them? Oh, the Minneapolis library had almost everything!

They entered the office from the corridor in order not to disturb the principal. Steve was as excited about having at last discovered a spark of real promise as his new young friend was at being in the presence of the great man he had admired for so long. Eagerly they drew their chairs around so they could talk facing each other. The boy`s mind was obviously teeming with questions he wanted to ask.

At that very moment, there was a tap on the door connecting them to the principal's office. It swung open and Mr. Pfister strode in. "I heard you come in and before you settle down, I was just going to mention....

"Rolph! How did you get in here? You're supposed to be in class, not pestering our guests in their private suite. Now run along!"

Dr. Pearson and Rolph stared at each other incredulously. Then the former stood up and turned toward the principal. "Really, Rolph and I were just about to have a little...."

"Yes, I know. I know. You're too gracious to admit he's imposing on you. But trust me, if you let one of them get away with it, before long they're crawling all over you. Now run along, Rolph. And don't forget to stop at the office for an admittance slip. You're already four minutes late. Run along now."

The crestfallen lad got up. "Thanks anyhow, Dr. Pearson. Thanks very much."

"We'll get our little talk in yet," the professor assured him.

And the young man disappeared.

"Give them an inch and they'll take a mile!" declared Mr. Pfister. "That Rolph Eriksen is one of the most maladjusted boys I've ever seen. He has no conception of how to behave in society. Everything Sally Larsen is, that poor boy is not. Sally can fit in anywhere, but that lad fits in nowhere."

"Indeed.... Everything that boy is, Sally is not," Steve intoned softly, as though to himself.

"Ah yes.... Well, I was just going to mention that we have some twenty minutes before we are expected in the science wing, so feel free to relax here for a little while. While you're gone with me, Doctor, Miss Bailey will introduce your charming wife to our girls in the Home Economics Department. We mustn't have you bored during your stay with us."

"That is very thoughtful," replied Kay politely.

The principal ducked back into his office.

They sat back down in silence for a few minutes. Then Steve stood up.

"I think it's more than my age."

"I`ve never felt more like a dinosaur," concurred Kay, stepping into the washroom. She decided not to avail herself of the bathtub or of the shower, or even of the collapsible massage table folded up against the wall, tempting as it was.

X

Fifteen minutes later there was a rap on the door and Mr. Pfister walked in followed by a pert young teacher. The Pearsons stood up to greet them.

"Well, I guess it's time for us to be getting over to the science wing. Miss Bailey, may I introduce you to Dr. and Mrs. Pearson?"

"Welcome to our school," she said, extending her hand first to Steve and then to Kay.

"Thank you," they replied together.

"I certainly enjoyed your convocation address this morning, Dr. Pearson. The girls in Home Ec are dying to meet the wife of someone as amazing as you. Won't you come with me, Mrs. Pearson? I'm sure you will find your afternoon with us most enjoyable."

"I'm sure she will," Steve put in quickly, winking at Kay. "But she's the amazing one, as you will see."

"Thank you, Miss Bailey," replied Kay, brushing off Steve's compliment with an affectionate wink back at him. "It will be good to meet you all."

The teacher took her arm and escorted her from the room.

"Well, sir," began the principal guiding Dr. Pearson out through the door. "The science wing is right this way. In the afternoon, we have five physics classes and two chemistry classes in session. Of course, three of the physics classes are what we call applied physics which is designed for those students who really do not need to know the fine points to succeed in life. It enables them to fulfill their science requirement and gives them a broad general exposure to the whole field. It's a shame that it's taking so long to convince good colleges and universities to give credit for this class. What can we do to convince them that not everyone who goes on into higher education is cut out to become a scientist? I had a bit of trouble myself with science courses back in my high school days, and look how well I've done! What does it take to overcome prejudice?

"Well, as I was saying, that makes four stops for us this afternoon. Right now there is one regular physics class and one chemistry class in session for us to visit, and one each next hour as well. We'll plan on spending fifteen or twenty minutes with each class. Our first one will be a physics class taught by Anthony Ivesson, head of the Science Department, a remarkable man. We're fortunate to have him. He's been offered collegiate positions all over the nation, but he stays right here with us. Of course, to keep men like him we have to pay them well. Our salaries are among the highest in the state. But the Board agrees with me—it makes no sense to have the last word in facilities if we do not have the last word in teachers to go with them. A small price to pay for the future of our youth, I always say."

By this time they had walked the length of the east end of the building and were rounding the corner into a long broad corridor.

"Here we are—our wing devoted to science. These first rooms on either side are biology and hygiene classrooms and laboratories. We have excellent instructors in these areas too, on a par with our men in physics and chemistry. Ah," he stopped and peered through a small window in a door marked *Biology Laboratory.* "From here you can see our roomy greenhouse on the other side of the lab, facing south. See?"

He gestured for Dr. Pearson to feast his eyes on the scene.

Looking through the window, Steve sensed that some words of admiration were due. "Most practical. Very nice."

"Well, on to the Physics Department. In erecting this precedent-setting school, we decided against constructing a separate physics laboratory. Rather, we incorporated a complete lab into each of our three classrooms. Of course, only two are in use at the moment, but one must always plan for the future. You should have seen the cramped space we had to put up with in the old school. As we enter Mr. Ivesson's classroom, the first thing that will strike you is the practical arrangement of things. At the front of each theater is a large demonstration desk, fully equipped, for the teacher's use. The theater is arranged in tiers to give every student an unobstructed view of the teacher's large desk while providing him with a smaller well-equipped desk of his own on which to replicate what the teacher is doing or to conduct his own experiments. Each theater is furnished with a movie projector and a pull-down screen just behind the teacher's demonstration table. I feel it is a capital arrangement. I might even have enjoyed my high school science classes in a well-conceived environment like this."

"It sounds as if you've foreseen almost everything."

"Yes, yes. I think we have. But we're always open to suggestions for improvements. Here we are. We're a bit early, but they'll be expecting us." He pushed the door open and ushered his guest into the theater.

Although Mr. Pfister had made no attempt to conceal the noise of their arrival, not an eye in the entire classroom turned to look at them as they walked in. Everyone's gaze was riveted on a very curvaceous blushing brunette in a tight fire-engine red sweater standing in bright lights in full profile at right angles to the screen behind the demonstration desk, motionless except for her batting eyelids and bright quivering lips. Dr. Pearson's first innocent impression was of the masterful discipline Mr. Ivesson maintained in his classroom.

As soon as he saw them, Mr. Ivesson, a young man of medium height and slight build, hastily tiptoed over to them and rasped in a semiwhisper, "We weren't expecting you quite yet. We're in the middle of an unforgettable—er—demonstration pertaining to our present unit of work on complementary colors. In exactly one minute and twenty seconds, Jean will duck down behind the desk and every eye will remain glued to the screen behind her. The students will then see her—ah—her generous natural endowments in blue against the pure white screen. Can you imagine a better way of impressing this unit indelibly into the eager minds of young students?"

"Ah, most effective, no doubt, Mr. Ivesson. May I present you to our special guest, Dr. Stephan Pearson, of Christiania College."

"Very pleased," rejoined Mr. Ivesson, extending his hand to their guest. "It is always a particular pleasure to meet someone whose level of thought runs parallel to one's own, as was clear from your talk this morning."

"Truly," replied Dr. Pearson.

"Only twenty more seconds to go," whispered the teacher. Silence hung thick in the air.

"Down you go, Jeannie!"

The thoroughly scrutinized girl sank to her knees out of sight behind the desk as ejaculations of glee erupted from the class.

"She's perfectly blue!"

"All of her but her head!"

"That leaves everything that matters."

"Don't give me that! Can't you see her lips there too?"

"Sure enough! Hanging there all by themselves detached from her pretty face."

Mr. Ivesson allowed these comments to run their course for a minute or so before stepping up to the front of the class.

"Okay, Jeannie. You may return to your seat. You get top marks for this experiment. No one will forget what you taught us. So, class, when the retina, that is, the end of the optic nerve, has been drained, so to speak, of its ability to perceive red, to what color does it necessarily turn?"

"Blue!" shouted those who had heard him over the continuing din.

"Correct. Now that you are aware of this fact, you will encounter it often in your daily life. That's why we call this course "applied physics."

He paused to let the full impression of what they had just learned sink in.

"Now, class, we have a special treat for you today.... Class, I am asking for your attention.... Your attention! You get to meet face to face our guest who gave us that amazing talk this morning, the famous physicist and author, Dr. Stephan Pearson. He has kindly consented to spend fifteen or twenty minutes with us this afternoon to talk about science's contribution to and role in our future, especially in response to your questions. I am sure he would be grateful to have you pelt him with those questions, whatever's on your mind. And so, without further ado, Dr. Pearson."

Two or three fellows in the last tier began clapping with mock enthusiasm, but they were soundly reproved for it by a couple of girls with horn-rimmed glasses sitting directly in front of them who turned around and scowled a hole through them.

Dr. Pearson cautiously advanced front and center, taking up a position behind the demonstration desk. The elegance of the room with its gleaming furnishings, its stainless-steel desktops and up-to-date equipment, and its custom-built lighting fixtures gave him a ray of hope that something good might come of the next twenty minutes. And so, with the room still buzzing in several quarters, he kicked off what he hoped would become a good discussion with the following words.

"Perhaps we could best use the minutes we have together to discuss any questions you may have about what role you can play as an individual in making tomorrow's world a better place. With nearly three billion of us on earth right now, and billions more coming within your lifetime, you will undoubtedly have some questions about the ability of developments in science and technology to meet the world's rapidly growing needs. Some of you may have questions about where you can fit in to help science meet these new challenges. If so, I'll try to answer those questions, or if I can't, to direct you to where you might find answers. I welcome your questions now."

For the first time since the visual "demonstration," there was total silence.

The better part of a minute passed. The students were getting fidgety. Then Mr. Ivesson broke the silence.

"They are always a little shy at first. But they'll warm up to you. So I'll just get the ball rolling by asking you a question that is directly in your line of expertise. Do you see any limit to the use to which atomic energy can ultimately be put? For my part, through its application I can see mankind ascending to currently unimaginable heights, solving one problem after another until we reach the realm of what I like to call 'pure life,' a truly worthy goal."

You could have heard a pin drop. Dr. Pearson lowered his eyes to the floor, trying to make sense of the words he had just heard. Then, as if to himself, but loud enough to be heard, he said, "Pure life? Where there are no problems left to solve? One wonders what would actually happen to people if there were no problems left to solve. Anyone I know whose life seems problem-free either invents problems to keep himself challenged, or he atrophies and dies a slow death. Man has had the means for millennia already to transport himself into a state of induced euphoria, if that's what life is all about. Alcohol, hallucinatory drugs, morphine, peyote cactus, just to name a few of them, all are perfectly capable of freeing a man from his problems by inducing in him a state closer to death than to life.... No, eliminating problems is not the road leading to a better world. Eliminating evil is that road. And they are not at all the same thing. As a matter of fact, right now...," he paused and looked around at the students and at the magnificent teaching theater, "right now I can conceive of no greater evil or curse on our race than to succeed in solving everyone's problems for them."

Even before he had completed that last sentence, a voice boomed out from the back of the room.

"Hey, Doc! What do you think of the brand-new fuel injection system like in the Rambler Rebel? I got one for my birthday last week and I'm betting anyone it's the hottest stock car on the road. You're a scientist! Tell these cruds here what a really good engine is, would you?"

He gestured toward two comrades flanking him on either side.

"Oh, get a life! Doc, tell this jerk once and for all that a double-carbed Rocket Eight will outdrag any old Rambler on earth!"

"Boys! Can't you forget your cars just once? That's not why Dr. Pearson is here. Now let's have some good questions. I told you to go home last night and bring a list of them to class today. Ruthie, read us one of your questions."

"Me, Mistah Ahvsin?... Me?" peeped an alarmed voice from the front row, long curled eyelashes batting. "Why, Mistah Ahvsin, ah just couldn't think up a really good one ... sir?..."

"Well, Ella, we can depend on you to have an intelligent question."

One of the horn-rimmed girls near the rear sat up straight, adjusted her spectacles, and read from her prepared list.

"All right, Mr. Ivesson. Dr. Pearson, what advancements do you foresee that will relieve the institution of womanhood of the drudgeries of her slavery to the daily chores of homemaking? Please be specific."

Ella looked up from her list and readjusted her spectacles.

Again the visitor faltered, shuffling his feet on the tile floor before venturing a response.

"Actually, Ella, I haven't given that issue too much thought, and I'll tell you why. It has been more my concern to extend the use of our present conveniences into the hands of the millions of women worldwide for whom housework is real drudgery. To do this we are developing a way to harness solar energy by panels for cheap electricity available to all and to produce simple electron stoves that will fry an egg in seconds without heating the top of the stove and will roast meat in a few moments. It's merely a question of making the roast complete a circuit. But considering the conveniences we already possess in America, will future refinements of them make that much difference for us in the years ahead? I doubt it."

Ella couldn't think of a response and took refuge behind the four or five hands that shot up in the air.

"Tom," acknowledged the teacher with pleasure.

"Sir, please don't get the idea we're just a bunch of complainers. It's just that there's always room for improvement. We wouldn't have progress at all if everyone was satisfied with things as they are. A man can never say that everything he has is the best possible or that he has the best of everything. Isn't that what tomorrow is all about? Working to improve our lot? Making life easier, safer, more enjoyable?"

"Tom," replied Dr. Pearson. "Let me just raise two points with you, two points we often leave out of our reckoning, especially if we are young or if we've never really grown up. In the first place, when you say 'improving *our* lot,' whose lot do you mean? When we pray 'Give us this day our daily bread,' who is 'us'?... And in the second place, do you think that everything that *improves* you always makes your life 'easier, safer, and more enjoyable'? By the same token, does everything that makes your life 'easier, safer, and more enjoyable' always improve you? My dear young friends, the men and women who have risen to the greatest heights, whose love of life has been the keenest and most contagious, have reached that point only through much pain and suffering and great difficulty, often voluntarily taken upon themselves for the good of others. They tell us it's the only way to true and deep happiness. You know whom I am talking about: Abraham Lincoln, Mahatma Gandhi, Blaise Pascal, Albert Schweitzer, St. Therese of Lisieux, St. Rose of Lima, Our Lord Jesus Christ, for goodness' sake! All of these marvelous human beings exuded great joy because they embraced suffering for the benefit of others. Each of them sought in a great variety of ways to relieve their fellowmen of crushing burdens, burdens of every description, for which even the strongest back was no match. When the burden you are bearing becomes bearable, that's when you can help somebody else with their crushing burden. And that's when you discover what life and joy are all about. Not just fun which comes and goes, but joy which comes and stays. A life without burdens is a life without love. And a life without love is death."

"Mary Sue."

"My daddy wouldn't like that kind of talk. He says that your only chance for happiness in life is to work for what you want and then go out and get it. He'd call what you just told us impractical. And I see his point. If he saw life as you see it, we wouldn't be living in our big beautiful house, we wouldn't have our fiberglass speedboat that's so much fun in the summer, I wouldn't have my show horse Sammy, we'd be down to one car, we wouldn't be able to afford closets full of really nice clothes to choose from, we wouldn't have friends that share our way of life. Heck, our life would be just the pits!"

Nods of agreement were seen on all sides.

"But wouldn't your father say that it is important to live in such a way as to make the world a better place for everyone, not just for us?"

Mary Sue balked and curled her eyebrows.

"I don't think he would say that. He'd say everyone needs to look after their own happiness. That's just the way things are. People are responsible for their own happiness or misery. That's not my daddy's problem. His job is to see that we have what we need to be happy. If he spent his time worrying about other people's misery when they should be doing something about it themselves, where would that leave his family? What else does it mean for us to be living 'in the land of the free and the home of the brave'?"

Silence descended on the classroom. A few people sitting near the front heard these words in a low murmur.

"The free and the brave? You've just described slaves and cowards."

Then in a louder voice, "Surely there are those among you who care about the grinding poverty, the destitution, the slavery of so many of our fellowmen, and who want to do something effective to give them and their children a chance."

"Of course!" declared a girl from the middle of the theater, glaring at him indignantly. "Almost every Sunday in church we are reminded of them, and we *give* 'as we are able.' My aunt actually works in a church refugee camp in Jordan."

Nobody laughed.

Things had come to an evident impasse. Mr. Pfister took out his gold pocket watch and decided it was time to be moving on to the next class. Mr. Ivesson thanked the visitor in some dismay and thought to himself that this man was surely the oddest atomic scientist he had ever run across.

For the remainder of the afternoon, Mr. Pfister made an attempt to guide the discussions along more fruitful lines, but certain elements could simply not be evaded—the rudeness that erupted unchecked in every classroom, the self-absorbed mind-set evidenced by most of the students, their assumption that any future worth having would necessarily include ever increasing prosperity, the extravagance of much of the underused equipment in each theater. It was a world filled with magnificent technology that very dearly wanted the people to match it.

Finally the ordeal was over. Grateful to be back in his "office for the day," Steve confessed his desire to take a little nap in one of the reclining chairs. Mr. Pfister responded well to the idea, stating that he had another hour's work in his office before he could leave the school and guide the Pearsons to "Seafoam" to enjoy dinner with his wife and him "in a quieter environment."

In a few winks Steve was sound asleep. When Kay came in a few minutes later, she placed a pillow under his drooping head and kissed him on the forehead.

"My poor dear Steve," she whispered.

The only other event of significance that afternoon occurred as they were leaving the school to follow the principal home for dinner. When they got into their DeSoto, something felt wrong right away. Then the engine wouldn't start. Steve went out and raised the hood. He had no trouble spotting the problem: all the spark plugs were missing.

There was no doubt about it as he slammed down the hood: the front end of the car was at the wrong angle. However, checking the front tires, he found them properly inflated. Then he bent over and took a good look under the car.

"Well, at least they could have got together on it," he told Kay, straightening up and shaking his head.

Under the rear axle were two cement blocks raising the rear wheels just off the ground.

"What a shame. One prank wrecked the other one."

Naturally Mr. Pfister apologized profusely and arranged for a nearby garage to repair the disabled car over the supper hour at the school's expense. Then, escorting them to his gleaming black Chrysler, he drove them to "Seafoam," his estate in the hills on the west end of the municipality.

"And what are you chuckling about?" inquired Kay of Steve from her place in the backseat.

"Reminds me of a prank I engineered in my high school days. But I'm sure it didn't take as many of us to lift the rear end of that Model T off the ground and slide a couple of blocks of wood under the axle as it took them to lift our DeSoto off the ground."

XI

Dinner was a relatively pleasant break in a day otherwise full of strain. The affair had all the calm and coolness of polite social decorum. The hosts made a point of steering clear of controversial subjects.

"We just want you to relax in your little interlude in our home," was the way Mrs. Pfister put it. "It's not often my husband and I have an evening at home together, but when we do, we like to leave our work at the door and enjoy the peace and quiet. I inherited a real estate company which I have been running now for about ten years. That means both of us are with people all day long. It's so nice to look forward to coming home to a clean house and a gracious and delicious meal after a full day at work."

Dinner was served by Sarah, a large jovial Black woman who, they were assured, was absolutely indispensable around the house, especially as both of them were much too busy to look after the place properly. Kay imagined that it must indeed be a challenging job to chase dust off everything in such a spacious house inhabited by only two people and their domestic.

Too bad they have no children, she thought. *He can't be much over forty, and she could be my age. What a difference children would make around here!*

After dinner they sat in the living room for half an hour, sipping expensive cognac. In the course of their conversation, they discovered that Steve was to be the last or "culminating" feature in a rather full program. The school concert band would be kicking the evening off with two futuristic pieces followed by three short talks of "no more than five minutes each" presented by three faculty members pertaining to future trends in literature, in South American politics, and in telecommunication. After that the Drama Department would be presenting a relevant skit, and then would come Steve's address which would "gather up the loose ends and present them in a sweeping diorama of the World of Tomorrow."

Dr. Pearson understood his task. He was far less certain of his duty.

"O yes!" exclaimed the principal. "There is a reception in your honor at the home of the Leif Landgrens on Merry Rose Lane in the Queen's Crest Estates. Leif is executive vice president of the Three-N Corporation and his wife is a renowned obstetrician-gynecologist who serves on the school board. They have a son in Harvard, a daughter who is a junior in our high school, and a son in grade school. They are a charming family. Other members of the school board and their spouses will also be there, as well as our senior administrative staff. It will be a delightful way to close our day of celebrations with you."

XII

If the size of the audience congregated in the music auditorium that evening was any indication, the Associated Parents and Teachers of the Reedville High School had more than a casual interest in the future. Only the last rows in the balcony were vacant. Dr. and Mrs. Pearson were accorded the honor of viewing the balance of the evening's performance from the Surveyor's Box, a comfortable elevated platform in the left wing of the stage just out of sight of the audience. The vantage point was excellent: they could see everything that happened on stage without being seen. There was room in the box for only two people, which limited their interaction with everyone except each other.

The first ten minutes of the program were consumed by announcements and business items concerning the APT, delivered out in front of the curtain by the president, the mother of one of the students. Meanwhile the members of the band were hustled to their places on stage. They and their director, the chap who had snapped to attention that morning, seemed unusually keyed up by the prospect of this particular performance. Kay thought she had never seen such handsome uniforms. In the spotlights from above, the shimmering hues of silky bright yellow and green blended in stunning harmony with each other in splendid contrast to the braided bright red tassels dangling from their epaulettes.

A weak applause was heard and madame president ducked backstage. A few moments of heavy suspense prevailed. The band director raised his arms. Then he plunged his organization into the crashing chords of the opening number at the very moment the curtains flew apart as if in alarm. Some applause greeted the band's appearance but quickly retreated behind the noise. The conductor was making powerful definitive sweeps of his arms in response to which the musicians were plunging ahead in muddled rhythmic lurches. "Modern harmonies" battered up against each other from all sides. At first a semblance of order was detectible in the belting discords, a sort of alternation between the sustained and the moving parts of the piece. From where they were sitting the Pearsons observed that this din seemed to be exactly what the conductor was expecting. He never once showed any sign of faltering as he pumped his long arms up and down in great pendulum strokes, giving the impression of exercising perfect control.

Before long, however, the cacophony became so tumultuous that this impression of control slowly disintegrated into the sham it was. The individual sections of the band were clearly now going their own stentorian ways, and even within each section there seemed to be little concern for presenting a united front. Steve noticed two trombonists who shared a music stand arguing over whether it was time to turn the page. The same issue was causing a furious debate in the flute section. About then, with a courageous display of self-assurance, the conductor flung himself at the tubas just as the piccolos pierced the air with a shrill squeal. Undaunted, he turned and made a commanding gesture at the clarinets just as two of them laid their instruments across their laps, only to be stabbed in the back by a deep blast from the tubas.

"Subtle signals, these!" Kay shouted into Steve's one uncovered ear.

"How will this ever end?" he called back.

She shrugged her shoulders. "The uniforms look nice."

Steve was now covering both ears. The tears were rolling down their cheeks.

The poor conductor's face had turned a gorgeous vermilion. He looked like a man on his forty-ninth push-up whose capacity is fifty. Finally, with a look of desperation on his face, he held his arms aloft straight up into the air until he thought that every last player had seen them and had settled down on one note. Then he triumphantly dropped them and the battle came to a halt—except for one lone guerrilla, a third saxophonist whom news of the armistice did not reach on time. She continued to fire away after everyone else had laid down their arms. The startled conductor attempted to redeem the situation by pretending this was intentional and directing her into a proper closure. But the moment she realized she was all alone, she stopped playing in midair. And the farce was over.

Steve and Kay couldn't tell whether the clapping or the laughter was the louder.

"That was a work of the Hungarian composer, Bela Bartok," announced the conductor facing the audience. "He is considered the most representative composer of the modern school of anharmonics. He also founded it."

"That was Bartok?" stammered Steve.

"And now on the lighter side, we play the familiar theme from the television show, *Flash Gordon,* composed by Willie Smith."

There followed a tremulous, fragile rendition of those familiar notes that are supposed to suggest travel through the asteroids out toward the galaxies and stars of outer space. The tone poem is intended to make the listener feel as though he is dangling in space without support, a feat even more successfully achieved by a poor rendition of the work than by a good one. The audience clung to their armrests from start to finish.

During the applause, Kay leaned over and said, "Take your choice of futures—will it be chaotic self-confidence or terrified suspension in outer space?"

The stage was swiftly cleared. Everyone in the band seemed eager to get out of there. A lectern was set up front and center on the stage and Mr. Hoopes from the English Department walked over to it, flanked by the next two speakers. He summed up the five minutes allotted to him with these words at the end: "The literature of tomorrow is being forged in the classrooms of today and will take on the salient characteristics of the men and women who produce it."

The next speaker was Mr. Jennings of the Department of Business and Commerce who elected to spend his five minutes about the future of South America, issuing an urgent warning to any businessmen in the audience not to overlook the growing menace of Communism across that continent. He summed his message up in these words: "From the point of view of business, we must face the fact that our investments in most countries on that backward continent will be severely jeopardized in the years ahead by those Red tentacles which are even now getting a stranglehold on the poor. So you are well advised to make most of your foreign investments in safer places, like Canada and Western Europe, where there is still room for expansion. No one who, for short-term gains, puts his whole nest-egg in South America has taken the risks into account. The enemy could end up with every cent of his money."

The final speaker, Mr. Armstrong, the electronics teacher, called the attention of his hearers to the diverse applications of television technology in the future. "The day is just ahead when we will find television screens hanging from the wall of every room like pictures or mirrors. Women whose housework takes them from room to room will be able to keep track of their favorite TV serial." The merger of the telephone and television industries too was right around the corner, he assured them, first for industrial purposes and later for everyone. TV monitoring systems would soon be protecting homes and businesses and apprehending criminals. From there he rambled off into certain technical issues not included in his notes and finally jarred to halt when he noticed that he had overshot his time limit by a good ten minutes.

The audience politely clapped the three teachers off stage and settled back to enjoy the skit.

The skit was entitled *1984 Revisited*, obviously intended to satirize the excessively pessimistic outlook of *1984* by George Orwell. The narrator opened with the timely reminder that most of the exotic amenities which the audience was about to witness in the skit would be commonplace by the time the students of Reedville had reached middle age, a thought calculated to be at once startling and exciting.

The personages in the skit were the members of the Johnson family, a happy group of Reedvillites consisting of Dad, Mom, Marjorie, and Johnny. The plot consisted of a typical Wednesday in their lives some twenty years hence. Dad, who was a branch manager of Wickle Bickle Pickles, Inc., customarily checked with the IBM machine in his office on Mondays, Wednesdays, and Fridays. So this morning he got out of bed at 10:00 and pushed the breakfast button which activated a number of lights next to his bed and one minute later served up two fried eggs, a cup of coffee, two slices of toast and raspberry jam, and a glass of freshly squeezed orange juice. Then he got dressed and stepped out the front door onto a covered conveyor belt which took him to his office two blocks away. The IBM's were fine, and he was home from work in time for lunch.

Mom had got up a bit earlier to clean the house. This little trick was facilitated by a robotic noiseless vacuum cleaner that you simply started up and turned loose on the house, eliminating all strenuous bending and dragging. Her several other chores required equally little effort on her part and were attended by Mr. Armstrong's omnipresent wall screens affording her a morning of nonstop entertainment. At noon she faced the challenge of deciding which buttons to push to serve up four different lunches, according to each one's personal preference.

Marjorie determined, so to speak, to stay in bed all morning in the company of Prince Charming. So she hooked her head up to her Dream Guide into which she inserted a disc involving the celebrity of her choice, and settled back to become the star of her own romance. Thus she sailed off into a state of bliss that lasted all morning.

Johnny, somewhat younger and uninterested in such pursuits, chose to spend the morning with his Personality Developer. This handy device relieved parents of most of the annoyance of having to raise children since it was guaranteed to produce the results programmed into it, or your money back. It played with Johnny, taught him to read and write through games, erased undesirable blemishes from his character "four times out of five," and provided all the companionship a child needs to grow up secure and well-rounded. Up to six hours a day could be spent in the company of your Personality Developer before undesirable side-effects became noticeable.

That afternoon the family decided they were in the mood for some "kicks." So they took off in their family pulse-jet helicopter and whisked up north to the Lake of the Woods, landing near the boathouse where their atomic speedboat was housed. What fun they had, making breakers and crashing back into them at an angle, racing with other boating enthusiasts, water-skiing and swimming and diving, and using the Devapor-Heater to avoid the chill of having to dry off in the breeze!

That evening at the pavilion onshore there was a big party attended by hundreds of people. Four different kinds of dance bands played in different areas of the mammoth pavilion. Food and drinks abounded, everything it takes to make a good party. Afterwards, tired but happy, the Johnsons returned home in their helicopter, with controls turned over to the auto-pilot which took them straight to their house while they were all sound asleep.

The curtain closed to enthusiastic applause and many comments.

"Just imagine! Only twenty-six years from now."

"Fantastic!"

"Maybe it's rubbish, but in 1932 who could have imagined our world of 1958?"

"You're right."

"I'm glad that Personality Developer is extra equipment. I wouldn't want my Johnny exposed to one of them."

"Maybe not, but the Tollefsons could sure use one."

"Do you think it would lower the crime rate?"

"You must admit that's the way things are heading. You can't turn the tide of progress. I hope I live to see some of it."

"Yeah! Imagine owning a pulse-jet helicopter instead of a car."

"They must have put a lot of work into developing those props."

"Pretty ingenious, all right."

There were a few demurrals in the audience.

"I'm not sure I like the younger generation's *summum bonum*."

"Work is the elixir of life. If this is what our kids are learning at school, it's no wonder I can't get Bruce to lift a finger in the yard."

"If *that* world ever comes true, I'll be the first to volunteer to colonize the moon."

"You won't have to go to the moon. South America will be far enough."

"Bertha, where do God's plans for the world fit into a picture like that?"

Backstage Dr. Pearson was slowly rising to his feet. It was his turn now. His eyes were pinched into that glassy squint of his. He made his way down to the stage level and waited for the lectern to be placed back on center stage. Mr. Pfister was on the other side of the curtain introducing the speaker to the audience. He gave them a brief account of their guest's life and accomplishments and of his present position at Christiania College.

Kay's heart was pounding. She had squeezed Steve's hand as he was leaving the box. It was ice cold. But he had squeezed her hand back and their eyes had met.

"Pray for me," were his only words as he turned to go.

Now the curtain was opening to polite applause. Dr. Pearson made his way to the lectern. Kay closed her eyes and prayed for him with all her might.

Providence has graciously preserved for us a tape recording of Steve's entire speech that evening, as well as all the rest of the program. I have listened to these words of his many times, to that gentle voice trembling under the weight of the things he had to say, forming each thought as carefully and as clearly as he could.

And I am still moved by them.

XIII

"Mr. Pfister, our gracious host, Associated Parents and Teachers of Reedville and those of you serving on the school board:

"My wife Katherine and I thank you for your kind hospitality throughout the day.

"This evening I was to talk on the world of tomorrow. But after having spent a day in your midst I have discovered, my friends, that for all practical purposes that world is yours today.

"Or what more do you really want, do you really need? And if you had it, what would you do with it? Is it more satellites whirling around you overhead that you want, more buttons to push to rob your hands and your heads of what little skill is still required of them in our day, more silken cushions to lie on while your three score and ten years slip meaninglessly through your idle fingers? Do you really want to be spared life's trials, when it is in struggling with these very trials that all the great men and women of our past have been forged from the soul breathed into us by our Creator and from the raw materials of our human clay?

"I realize that the skit we have just witnessed was a clever spoof. Or at least so it seemed to me. I hope to God it was! Because I saw in it also something dark and disturbing. I saw in it a depiction of the troubling mind-set we encountered today in unchallenged control of far too many of the young people we met. I will describe this mind-set now as a tantalizing mirage that has so overpowered them that they fail entirely to see the two obstacles over which all who chase this mirage will inevitably stumble and fall.

"The mirage itself is nothing more or less than the illusion that as science solves man's problems one by one, it draws us ever closer to a state of bliss, a utopia, a kind of ersatz heaven on earth. The reasoning behind this illusion runs something like this: Problems cause anxiety and anxiety is the enemy of bliss. Therefore, eliminating problems guarantees a state of virtually continuous bliss.

"But who in their right mind would ascribe to science the power to eliminate all problems? We all face sickness, aging and death, with or without science. Anyone can experience the devastating and irreversible consequences of a tragic accident that can come out of nowhere, with or without science. Science cannot prevent the terrible curse of an upbringing that creates narcissists of our children who become adults that never grow up and are never really able to see beyond themselves, which, as we all know, is the very definition of hell. Do you really believe that these huge problems whose solution is always spiritual, and before which science stands helpless, will simply go away if we subject ourselves to a continuous lifelong barrage of entertainment as depicted in the skit?

"So expecting science to solve all our problems is truly a mirage, a substanceless chimera that must always remain out of reach. And here we have also touched on the two obstacles I drew to our attention a few moments ago.

"To understand the first obstacle, we must understand the radical difference between working to eliminate evil, which is our divine vocation, and working to eliminate problems, which, as we have just seen, is impossible."

Here he paused and bowed his head.

Then he repeated very slowly:

"We must understand the radical difference between being rid of evil and being rid of problems. They are emphatically not the same thing. Judging from our experience in your midst today, we have a long way to go to get this straight, and there is no time to lose. Most of our youth

have got it all wrong. Most of our youth are hypnotized by the mirage I have just described to you which will kill them if they don't get free of it.

"There is a note of irony here. What is it that motivates a scientist to tackle a difficult issue? It is the satisfaction you experience when you work hard and rise to the challenge of confronting and solving a particular problem. This makes your life meaningful, even exciting. Now every human being experiences a similar need to be motivated at some level to confront and solve problems if his life is to have any meaning at all. So what has the scientist actually achieved if he has resolved some of the very problems you *need* in your life for your own well-being, and left you with little or nothing left to challenge you? Without realizing what he is doing to you, he is depriving you of enjoying the very thing that he enjoys so much. Now, in science, the challenges of problem-solving are limitless, so there is no chance that a scientist will ever run out of problems to enjoy solving. But he could very well be depriving you, in the course of your everyday life, of having to tackle the problems that have inspired and challenged our forebears and made them strong and generous and good in years gone by. When science does that, it is not eliminating evil from the face of the earth. It is multiplying it. And the evidence of this has been all around us here today. My friends, happiness is not found in the momentary thrill of getting something we think we want, still less in giving something that does others more harm than good. Happiness is found in the lasting satisfaction of giving something that reduces evil in someone's life and meets someone's real need. If science cannot distinguish between eliminating problems and eliminating evil, it is no longer serving God's purposes but the enemy's.

"This is important because it is so easy to bury this question until it is too late. The types of problems that challenge such scientists as nuclear physicists, medical researchers, geneticists and biologists are highly specialized. As a result, you can have only a tiny percentage of the human race enjoying the privilege of tackling such problems, whereas the consequences of their work can at times have a revolutionary effect on the entire human race, often in areas totally unforeseen by the researchers themselves. All the amenities I mentioned in my talk this morning, plus some of those that we saw in the skit, and many more besides, are in one way or another the outcome of their work, and all of them have a potential for great good if they become our servants in the higher cause of eliminating true evil, but also a potential for producing great evil if they become our masters and enslave us to themselves for their own sake. We delude ourselves if we think that the average person, if he is no longer ***required*** to work hard to meet basic needs, will automatically blossom forth and replace that hard work with such ennobling pursuits as reading, studying, praying, meditating, caring for his neighbor in need, engaging in public service, or contributing positively to our cultural heritage. Too many of our own children are the proof of it. Rare is the young adult in our midst today whose mind and spirit are not at this very moment drowning under a tidal wave of perpetual entertainments and whose only goal in life is to keep it that way.

"But the scientist is not wholly on the wrong track. Mark this. In the life of every man, woman, and child there is a definite point that distinguishes the excessive problems that burden us from the manageable problems that challenge us and give us a reason to get up in the morning. It is the point that separates our *oppressive* problems (such as totally lacking the means to feed your starving family) from our *stimulating* problems (such as raising enough food for our family on our plot of fertile land). The greatest service, perhaps the only service, science can render mankind is to decrease the incidence of oppressive problems while *increasing* the incidence of stimulating problems. The moment science starts attacking our stimulating problems, it is robbing us of one of the ingredients that have been essential to a meaningful human life ever since God turned the Garden of Eden over to Adam and commissioned him to 'till and keep it.' If this happens, we will have destroyed our own future as surely as any hydrogen bomb could. How? By producing a generation of vegetating sluggards unable or unwilling to use their freed-up time and freed-up energy in productive and healthy ways for the good of others and to 'till and keep the Garden.' Imagine the capacity for mischief-making and worse represented by such a collection of raw directionless energies turned loose on society. With no moral sense other than the incessant craving for personal pleasure, I can see us now on the verge of an 'anything-goes' society in which the good and the beautiful become the enemy because they stand in the way of the 'rights' claimed by a culture in which raw narcissism has become the new norm. Is this the future we want? Is this what we are asking of science? If not, then we must address head on the fact that this is beyond a shadow of a doubt the society of tomorrow which we are producing right here today.

"This leads me to assert here and now—in acknowledgement of the great company of men and women who have risen through the heat of tribulation and been refined in the furnace even of oppressive problems, and in confessed fear of the hoards of flabby directionless energies which our extreme surfeit is producing this very day—that no science at all is much to be preferred to science improvidently and indiscriminately squandered on all sides with no regard to its devastating effect on people. Is our entire civilization doomed to degenerate into a mob of effete eighteenth-century French noblemen? Can you imagine what a whole society of sinecures would look like, or how it would survive?

"I see clearly, therefore—and I trust that you do too—that there is a point up to which the gifts of science can be a blessing and beyond which they are an incalculable curse. For who can attach a price tag to the unique properties of the human soul, forged through eons of meeting and overcoming the challenges which life on earth has placed in its path? Who will dare to assess the extent of our loss if these properties should wither and die *because science has rendered them useless?* This very day Katherine and I have seen with our own eyes the rusting away of human resourcefulness, and with it we have heard the death rattle of human inventiveness. On top of that, we have observed that the most elemental human expressions of generosity and mercy are being trivialized, *if not entirely lost*, by our next generation of leaders, driven as they are by their insatiable demands for stuff, stuff, and more stuff, for fun, fun, and more fun. And—I must be frank—this loss terrifies me…."

His voice broke. The audience was dead silent.

"You see, eradicating all evil is indeed man's greatest problem, but eradicating all problems is turning out to be one of his greatest evils. Left with no basic needs to be met by their own constructive efforts and energies, what will people do with those energies? Will they turn to crime, to cheap thrills at the expense of others, to unimaginable behavioral perversions to relieve the tedium of their life, to aphrodisiacs of all kinds to fill the emptiness of a life without love, to attachment to fanatical ideologies to vent their frustration, to pure sloth as the *summum bonum* of the *nouveaux riches*? I do not want to believe that this generation is becoming a monstrosity created in large measure by a few men and women of science who 'know not what they do'!

"Yet, this outcome is virtually inevitable unless we all understand what is at stake here and take decisive action to ensure that we constantly aim only at overcoming man's oppressive problems without robbing him of his stimulating problems. If we can't achieve this, we face an unenviable future in which the immense power for good or evil created by today's highly motivated scientists is left by default in the hands of the unmotivated—of our youth—who seem to have lost all capacity to distinguish good from evil. Have we created a monster we can't control and turned it over to those who are even less able to control it than we are? This is the grim prospect we face in the near future.

"This then is the first obstacle we stumble over in chasing the mirage: life without trials is not bliss. It turns out to be the greatest of trials.

"The second obstacle preventing us from reaching the mirage which has spellbound our youth, and some of us as well, is that chasing the mirage excludes by definition all concern for the well-being of anyone whose well-being does not directly affect ours. Seeking a worry-free life automatically excludes worrying about others. As logical as this may be, it is also extremely perilous. Creating a large island of unspeakable luxury in the heart of a much larger world of unspeakable poverty, and believing that it is possible to protect the former while ignoring the latter, is a formula for disaster. How?

"Here we are, perhaps five hundred of us congregated in this one auditorium. For most of us, science has long ago alleviated most of our oppressive problems, the ones that are not spiritual in essence, but it has also deprived us of many of the stimulating problems we actually require to stay healthy in mind, body and spirit. The results are obvious—a great increase in the nervous tension of a society in which far too many people know of nothing they really *must* do. It's not that there are no stimulating problems left in the world to motivate us: God knows there are! Herein lies the baffling paradox. While we are chasing one mirage after another to relieve our boredom with a life that lacks stimulating problems, two out three persons in the world are struggling under the burden of their oppressive problems, untouched by the science that once fed us, then satisfied us, and now is overstuffing us and killing us. Our virulent superfluity which we are tempted to hang onto for dear life is the answer to their desperate necessity! What is killing us by degrees could be saving them!

"Thank you, my friends. Until today, I myself refused to see this clearly enough. I must have thought that any *peaceful* use to which developments in science are put is automatically a good use. How little I understood its potential to corrode the human soul.... It must have been," he said as if to himself, "that I was too insulated in my own satisfying little world to notice the effect our achievements were having on real people. I thought people would be inspired by them to help others. But just look at what we are facing instead. I did not know Man. And I think I may also have greatly underrated the hold which the evil one has on our race.

"Now I see that if the great strides in science are to count for good, they must be diverted not only from the suicidal armaments race (and there seems to be little prospect for this), but even more from the suicidal demands of the gluttony that rots the human soul from within (and there seems to be even less prospect for this).

"Is there any way forward?

"There is but it requires a conversion, a conversion we may or may not be capable of making as a nation. We must commit ourselves to work, to work hard and single-mindedly, to bring relief, immediate as well as permanent, to our brothers and sisters worldwide who lack adequate food, medical care, gainful employment, personal shelter, and security. We whom gluttony imperils must share generously with those whom starvation threatens if there is to be healing, both for us in our need and for them in theirs. The glutton who refuses to be converted is consigning himself, not just the neglected poor, to a life of prolonged misery. The misery of the poor is largely physical and easy to relieve with a little effort, whereas the misery of the wealthy, of many of us, is spiritual and impossible to relieve despite recourse to alcohol, drugs, unfettered gluttony, pleasure-seeking, easy sex, a life of luxury, psychiatric care, and on and on and on. Without a deep conversion, our misery will go with us all the way to the grave.

"The indolent wealthy unusually don't even notice the poor, but you can be certain that most of the poor are well aware of the wealthy. I know next to nothing about the world of international business, but I do know that it is easy for the wealthy to toss a few crumbs at the poor and make off with huge profits. I do know that international businessmen who are truly concerned about working conditions, worker safety, fair wages, reasonable hours, and product quality control in the foreign countries where they do business are few and far between. Most businessmen pay attention only to the bottom line, the ease with which they and their stockholders can make bigger profits where workers are so helpless that they are forced to take what's given them, even if it is shamefully less than they need and deserve. We have a friend who has bucked the tide. It has not been easy, but he can point to three notable successes in India, Ethiopia, and Malawi, along with several failures elsewhere. Could we survive the tide of ill-will aimed at us from all sides if the rest of the world were to see us only as exploiters lacking a conscience, not as partners in eradicating the evils of destitution? We need to remember Our Lord's reminder that greed always turns back on the miser, ravaging him first from within and then from without.

"Thus it should be plain to all here this evening that our only hope lies in cultivating in ourselves and in our youth a deep commitment to what I will call having a 'toiling plenty,' an attitude toward our wealth in which we retain only what we actually need, and we find effective ways, perhaps through our churches and other well-placed organizations, of using the rest of our resources to lift unbearable burdens from the shoulders of our fellowmen wherever they may be found. For if mankind, that is, if *you and I*, with our strong Judeo-Christian heritage, are not moved by the freedom which the bounty of science has given *us* to a truly effective charity and a truly loving regard for the bitter needs of so much of the rest of the world, *no nation on earth will ever be so moved*, and our doom is sealed. If you and I are not so moved,"—his voice faltered—"you force me, you force me to conclude that our achievements in science have been a colossal disaster for the human soul, both yours and mine. If these achievements serve only to inspire in us a greed that knows no bounds even when we are already satiated beyond sensitivity, if these achievements cannot evoke in you and me a love for the needy and a passion to use our plenty to address their poverty, then you could not make me *give* our glorious 'achievements' away to the poor for fear that surfeit might do to them and their societies what it has done to us and ours. Better by far for the human soul to be faced with grinding poverty than with runaway prosperity. The soul can survive poverty but, in the words of Our Lord Himself, few souls can survive the ravages of wealth."

He paused, stunned by his own words.

Then he gathered his thoughts together and concluded his address with painful slowness and intense passion.

"Now go home, all of you. Make today your tomorrow. Figure out tangible ways to share your abundance with our brothers and sisters where the need is greatest. Be the beginning of the conversion of our nation from a community of grabbers to a community of givers, remembering always that if we fail in this, far from eradicating evil through the advancements of science, we will be entrenching it. We can't let this happen!

"God help us."

Dr. Pearson nodded his head. He was done. A pervasive hush descended on the auditorium. Then someone from the balcony began to clap, detonating an explosion of long swelling applause.

Kay was standing in the wing waiting for him as he left the stage. She threw her arms around him.

"O Steve," she whispered, brushing back a tear, "you were wonderful."

XIV

Queen's Crest Subdivision where the Leif Landgren estate was located had been a less choice farm a mere decade earlier, owing to the tortuous wooded ravines that carved it up. But the expansion of greater Minneapolis proved to be a bonanza for the elderly couple who had spent nearly half a century wresting a living from that piece of land. Its secluded valleys and rolling hills were ideal raw material for a land developer to turn into an exclusive gated community. The couple took the money he gave them and retired to Arizona, free of financial worries for the rest of their lives. The lots carved from the farm never did go "on the market." They were parceled out by "insiders" passing on a hot tip to wealthy industrialists. The only nonindustrialist in Queen's Crest was the noted brain surgeon, Dr. Emmanuel Kaufmann.

The homes in this exclusive maze of glens were worth five to ten times the value of a new home in any other district in Reedville, sprawling insects of glass and stone hugging the hillsides. The Pearsons, following Mr. Pfister's new Chrysler in their repaired DeSoto, were privileged to behold these dwellings in their full splendor as many of them were ingeniously floodlighted to highlight their most flattering attributes.

"Do they keep those lights on all the time, or are they doing that just for us?" Kay wondered out loud. "Makes me appreciate our cozy little house. I wonder what floodlights would do for our place...."

"You sweetheart," Steve responded, reaching over and squeezing her hand.

Merry Rose Lane wound through several gorges before it brought you to the Landgren home. Their broad driveway was lined with prestigious cars, but a widening in the road just below their house was obviously intended to accommodate an overflow of the parked cars of visitors. So the Pfisters and the Pearsons turned their cars in on an angle next to a few vehicles that were already parked there. It was just after 10:00 p.m. The Pfisters escorted Steve and Kay along the one hundred yards or so up the sloped driveway to the front door of the Landgren home.

"Why, if it isn't our guest of honor and his charming wife, and our beloved principal and his dear wife!" exclaimed Mrs. Landgren. "Do come in. We've all been waiting for you."

She was a stately woman of about forty-five years of age. She had tastefully applied makeup to her eyes that gave them the merest hint of Oriental mystery, perfectly matching her tight silk evening gown and the fluidity of her mannerisms. With grace she showed them into the foyer and helped them off with their coats, handing them to their Finnish maid whom she didn't bother to introduce to them. Then, taking Steve by one arm and Kay by the other, she led them toward the spacious living room in which about forty people were already comfortably seated. As they appeared under the hallway arch, the men all rose to their feet and the women all smiled politely at the persons of their guest of honor and his wife.

"Friends, friends," announced Mrs. Landgren. "May I have the honor and pleasure of presenting to you our guests, Dr. Stephan and Mrs. Katherine Pearson."

Then she released their arms, turned to face the self-conscious scientist, and said on behalf of everyone present, "Sir, we are indebted to you for your address this evening and welcome you into our home."

Turning back to the main body, she took Steve and Kay by the arms around the entire room, introducing each couple by name and position. The only couple who rang a bell with the Pearsons was "Dr. and Mrs.

Rolph Eriksson. The good doctor is everyone's favorite general practitioner in Reedville and a valued member of our school board."

The introductions completed, she conducted Steve and Kay to an elegant love seat behind a coffee table and invited them to be seated, adding with a touch of finesse, "Don't worry, my friends. You won't be lonesome. Many of us are eager to spend a few moments with you. I'll leave you right here where we can all reach you," she said, pulling two chairs around to the other side of the coffee table.

"Ingrid will see to it that you are offered plenty of hors d'oeuvres. Can I offer you something to drink?"

Stephan looked straight up at their hostess for the first time.

"Would you have a gin and tonic for me and a glass of sherry for my wife?"

"Certainly," she replied.

Kay looked at Steve. The strain of the day had heavily sapped his strength. She could see that he was already bending under the weight of the challenge he had urged on everyone else that evening, the challenge he would now be obliged to face himself. The pallor in his face, the trembling of his hands, and the retreat into himself that she sensed was happening already frightened her. She was all too aware that something was crumbling inside him, that he was in the early stages of caving in.

"Yes, thank you," she said. "A gin and tonic and a glass of sherry would be just right."

Mrs. Landgren vanished to fetch their drinks. Another woman immediately took her place. Her perfectly coiffed hair was purple-white. Her suit was haute couture. Her cheeks showed the flush of the three or four martinis she had already consumed. She was at no loss for words.

"Dr. Pearson! It is such a pleasure to meet you and your wife. I'm Lucille Maaker. My husband is the superintendent of schools. I so admired your address tonight, your composure, your self-possessing assurance, your oracular confidence in the truth of what you were conveying to us. You must have great faith in what you believe."

"I'm glad if you found my words beneficial," he returned.

"Beneficial? Inspiring, I should say. What particularly, shall I say, 'invited' my keen attention to the rest of the insights you shared with us was the allusions to the Deity you made early on in your address, and several times thereafter. Am I right in concluding that much of your assurance comes from your faith in the Almighty?"

"Yes," he answered. "That is true. To carry on from where we are now, we need hope. And that hope can come only from Him. Only He can bring about the conversion of our society. We can't do it. It has to come from Him."

"O Doctor, just to have faith that something is true behind it all. It must be wonderful! Do you mind if I ask you a rather personal question?"

She was working herself into quite a fit of excitement.

He nodded his head.

"What is your religious persuasion? That is, what spiritual collectivity do you affiliate with? For years I've been looking for one that really meets my needs, but I can't seem to find the right one. I need a spiritual connection that can give me your kind of faith. What form of spirituality do you practice? To whose belief system do you subscribe with confidence as a man of science and culture?"

"Actually, I have found at various times in my life great strength in the Lutheran and the Catholic...."

"*Lutheran*?" she broke in. "Why, every second church here is either Lutheran or Catholic! I was raised Lutheran. O doctor, NO!"

She staggered back.

"I can't believe it. Lutherans and Catholics are so ... I just can't believe it...."

"I find a depth and a truth and a timelessness in it that...."

"O Doctor, NO! Don't let me hear it again. If *they* had anything to offer me, I'd have found it long ago. O Doctor, I'm so disappointed!"

The poor disillusioned woman took a long draught of the martini she was holding and collapsed into a nearby chair, a glassy look in her eyes.

For the next two minutes nobody else ventured over to the sofa except Mrs. Landgren with their drinks. Gratefully Kay took them and gave the gin and tonic to her husband who had yet to regain his balance after his encounter with Mrs. Maaker. She almost had to fold his fingers around the glass to make him realize what it was. In so doing, she noticed that her own hand was unsteady and her own heart was fluttering. The room was abuzz with conversations, but directly across from them the voices of two impeccably dressed middle-aged men stood out.

"But is it good business? That's all I ask."

"That's the clinching argument. You can't run a business on noble thoughts and stay solvent for long in this world. How long would you stay in business if you paid no attention to profits and losses?"

"That's just what I mean. My company has a factory in Venezuela. *Yo mismo hablo un poco español. Es muy necesario para las negocias.* Sure, there are problems. The communist menace is real. But if it weren't for us, hundreds of men would have no means of supporting their families. When we transfer a plant manager from here to go there, we have to provide a home for him on a par with what he is used to here. That's only fair. But often the locals don't see it that way. They hold it against us, even though we are giving them jobs they wouldn't have otherwise."

"And a man has an obligation to his stockholders. What in the world would you tell them if you spent their retirement dividends on a charity in some foreign country? That's the church's and the government's business, not ours. We donate to the church and pay big taxes to the government. Fair is fair, I say. What's wrong with letting them look after that?"

"Besides, it wouldn't work. If you gave workers there even half of what our workers here demand, they wouldn't know what to do with it. Probably drink it all up, and then where would they be?"

"You'd have to charge more for your product here in the US."

"And your profits would plunge."

"And you'd be out on your ear after the next stockholders' meeting."

"You couldn't stay in business without massive revisions to import duties."

"The only person qualified to advise a businessman is another businessman with a good track record. And if he is a competitor, you do the opposite of what he tells you and you can't go wrong."

The two men chuckled.

"No, a man makes a fool of himself when he tries to tell a businessman how to run his business. After all, we hire the scientists not as business advisors but as employees to make our products more saleable."

"They're good men, most of them. Just ignorant of what makes the world go round. When you build them a well-equipped laboratory, give them some work to do for you, and turn them loose, they're as happy as kids in a sandbox."

"And think of all the great publicity you get when you award a post in your business to some kid graduating from your alma mater!"

"There's all too much truth in that," moaned Steve, reaching for Kay's hand.

"They belong in the laboratories we build for them, not on center stage," concluded one of the men, getting up to refill his martini goblet.

Just then a pert young woman of about thirty years of age flew up to Steve and declared, "Dr. Pearson! I just *have* to tell you how much I enjoyed your address. I confess I took offense at some of your remarks, but I can overlook them especially since you really didn't say a word against enjoying life. In fact, as I heard it, everything you said could be construed as your idea of how to really enjoy life."

"I guess you could put it that way."

"Yes indeed. I simply cannot suffer those prophets of doom who are constantly harping about our imminent destruction. What are they missing? I'm sick and tired of their whine. The doom they predicted years ago is no closer now than it was then. But still they don't change their tune. Why should we all hate life the way they do? If God wanted us to hate life, why would He have created us? So if, as they say, it is inevitable that we will destroy ourselves, shouldn't we be enjoying ourselves all the more between now and then? *Que será, será*! Why shouldn't we all enjoy life while we have it, you in your way and I in mine?"

Then, looking straight at Kay whose flushed cheeks enhanced her youthful attractiveness, she added, "I can see you also believe in enjoying life while we have it. Your wife is very lovely. Don't tell me that's totally accidental. Well, thank you for your time. My husband gets so jealous when I spend a few minutes in conversation with another man."

She vanished into the guests as quickly as she had appeared from their midst.

At that particular moment, Dr. Pearson must have looked unwell because the couple now approaching him backed away at the sight of him. But he looked up just as they were retreating and said, "No, Dr. Eriksen, Mrs. Eriksen. Please do be seated. We would be honored to get to know the parents of such a fine son."

He stood up, and Kay with him. They shook hands with the Eriksens.

Dr. and Mrs. Eriksen, aware of how depleted Dr. Pearson was, were especially moved by his cordial reception of them by name.

"Thank you very much. My wife, Ann, and I will bother you for only a few minutes."

Gesturing for them to be seated, Dr. Pearson said, "We are very glad for the unexpected privilege of meeting you this evening. Meeting your son, Rolph, gave us a bright ray of hope earlier today."

"That doesn't surprise us. God has given us a son whom Jesus possesses."

"A miracle of grace," Steve responded as Kay nodded warmly.

"I suppose, Dr. and Mrs. Pearson, that you have had your of fill of vapid compliments by now. However, driving here from the auditorium, my wife and I agreed that you converted what could have been one more disastrous evening into just exactly what our school and community need to hear now."

"Thank you. Kay and I felt disaster in the air, too."

"Our son, Rolph Jr., told us of his aborted meeting with you this noon, but he glowed when he told us you said you'd see him again."

"Yes. We are determined to see him again, God willing. I am at a loss to explain why Mr. Pfister was so eager to curtail our time together when we, not Rolph, were the ones who initiated it."

Mrs. Eriksen broke in. "Now you know what my husband's constituency had in mind when they elected him to the school board. They thought that because he had already single-handedly reconfigured our hospital board to be more oriented toward patient care than toward profit-making, he could turn our gaudy high school showpiece into an actual institution of learning."

"I don't mean to be too critical," commented Kay, "but how would you have found enough people around here to elect someone on that platform?"

"You wouldn't have," admitted Mrs. Eriksen. "I'm sure he was elected on his reputation."

"Well," explained Dr. Eriksen, "you see, the movement for my candidacy was initiated by a handful of sincere people who adopted the slogan 'From an empty showcase to a real schoolhouse.' They approached me and almost forcefully drafted me to run for the school board. The slogan may have won the election for me. In principle, who would not want a showcase turned into an honest-to-goodness school house where the students actually learn something useful, not just have a good time? In any case, I was elected by a slim margin, and, much as I am verbally respected, I have made almost no headway in converting our slogan into any kind of a plan of action."

"It sounds to me as if it amounts to resolving the tension between the spirit and the flesh simply by guaranteeing that the spirit will always be subservient to the flesh," observed Kay. "I don't envy you, but I deeply admire you."

"That is the issue in a nutshell. Those of us whose spirit is still willing are finding our flesh growing weaker and weaker. How do you face the same intolerable abuses day after day without finding yourself starting to tolerate them little by little, just to survive, just to stay sane? Some days I see myself as a living contradiction, saying one thing and doing something else, 'warring in my members,' as St. Paul says, against what I am firmly convinced is true. On the positive side of the ledger, a few really good teachers have joined our staff mainly through our efforts. But how does even a good teacher motivate the spoiled, lazy, self-serving, offspring of affluence? For every victory you win as a good teacher, they tell me, you suffer more defeats than you can count. The administration sees me as a curiosity at best, an enemy at worst, because in their view I am stuck in an outmoded and far too regimented view of the purpose of a high school education. Strides have been made since my time, I am told, in the psychology of education. The idea now is to encourage individuals to discover their own strengths and then to give them plenty of room to develop them on their own. It's called 'respecting each person's individuality.' To me, this is a recipe for disaster in an affluent and self-indulgent society like ours, where our children face so few real challenges and material deprivations. You said it so well. Trials and tribulations produce strong people. Their absence practically guarantees atrophy. I often ask myself why an approach so clearly doomed to failure has taken over our school. The answer, I greatly fear, lies in the fact that the healers of the disease are themselves too stricken by it to be of much help to the sufferers."

The man had spoken cautiously, unburdening his conscience to someone he knew would understand. Dr. Pearson heard him out, his back rigid and his eyes fixed on the troubled physician. Kay's heart was also aching for him, but it was aching even more for Steve as she watched her husband get caught up in the man's dilemma.

"But you have a son of whom you can be justly proud. He hasn't caught the disease," Kay interjected with a note of hope.

"Only by virtue of his strong mental and spiritual health which *they* seem intent on destroying," declared Ann. "If he were not so well grounded in our family values and our faith, so singularly able to avoid succumbing to the general plague, we would flee this place tomorrow. Even so, I wonder how much abuse any one student can take without caving in."

"Mental and spiritual health," repeated Dr. Pearson slowly, leaning forward. "Without that team, that inseparable team, a man is dead. And they must be robust partners, not fragile, not barely clinging to life. Or else, I say, a man is dead.... I would so appreciate the opportunity to speak with your son, as we had hoped."

"That opportunity may well arise, Doctor. Christiania is one of our church's colleges and it is Rolph's great desire to continue his education there, mainly because of you."

"I can think of nothing I would consider a greater privilege as a teacher than to have your son in my class."

Just then a plump colorfully attired woman of about fifty dashed up to the physician. Her puffy face was darting between a forced smile and a bona fide frown.

"Gentlemen, do excuse my interruption. But I just said to myself, 'Anna Wellington, while it's on your mind you get right over there to your old friend, Dr. Eriksen, and have him write you out the prescriptions for your pills before you forget and run out.' And so here I am with less than a week's supply left. Could I trouble you to do that for me now?"

"I believe so, Anna. Just a moment."

He took a wad of blank prescription forms from his vest pocket, scrawled something across three of them, and handed them to her. She was perfectly delighted. Her intermittent frowns vanished. She pranced off to a group of ladies conversing near the hors d'oeuvres and deposited the slips conspicuously in her purse.

"It's a web, my dear professor," said the physician sadly, "and I'm as entangled in it as anyone. You described Anna Wellington perfectly this evening, and she heard every word of it without batting an eye. There isn't a thing wrong with her that a little genuine affliction couldn't cure. She has every material possession she wants and has no idea that's why she's so 'sick.'"

"Just look at those poor creatures over there," said Mrs. Eriksen, gesturing toward that group of women. "They are talking about the only problem they know—their own precarious health. And they can go on and on about it."

"My dear," said the physician, "I will tell you how grave a problem that is from a purely medical point of view. Two of those prescriptions I wrote out for Anna were for different strengths of colored sugar pills and the third was for a plain iron pill like those we give to pregnant women. She's been taking those pills for five years now, and to them she ascribes the delicate balance of her health which, as everyone knows, is on the verge of collapse. I wouldn't be surprised if they were discussing another favorite topic of theirs at this very moment—tranquilizers. You see, only people occupied with really important matters require a chemical to keep them on an even keel."

"To them she ascribes...," intoned Dr. Pearson as if in a trance.

"And 'our virulent superfluity is the answer to their desperate needs.' Dr. Pearson, you see why we thank God you had the courage to say what you did." Mrs. Eriksen was almost in tears.

Dr. Pearson looked back at her and slowly shook his head.

"Look around you, my friends. All of these poor dear people who have so commended my address—do you see among them *one lasting achievement of my 'courage'?*"

Only then did they note the ashen pallor of his face and the palsied trembling of his hands. Kay grasped them and hung onto them tightly, terrified by the vacant look in his eyes. For fully a minute he sat there stiff and erect. No one stirred as the party went on gaily about them. Then his eyes dropped to the floor in front of him and he muttered half aloud, "I'll be quite all right. It's been a long day. I think we ought to start for home."

Kay swallowed hard. "Yes, it's past midnight. We need to be on our way."

Hasty, startled farewells were said. Mrs. Landgren looked roundly offended when she saw her guests of honors leaving before the party was over, but one look at Dr. Pearson told her why.

Just before leaving through the front door, he turned and let his eyes float around the front part of the living room visible from the doorway. Near the archway he caught sight of Dr. Eriksen gazing at him intently and perhaps remorsefully. The two men exchanged a knowing nod.

And the Pearsons stepped through the door out into the cold dark night.

XV

A car moving down the highway that winds between Minneapolis and St. Mark after midnight is a very lonely thing. The black anonymity of the passing countryside is briefly relieved only by the dim lights of several sleeping villages. Bearing its own source of light, it purrs along, steadily slicing its way through the darkness.

Tonight it was the Pearsons' turn to be traveling in such a car. Steve had silently brushed aside his wife's offer to let her drive them home. He had planted himself behind the steering wheel and maneuvered their DeSoto out of Reedville, by some miracle finding the right road that led them to St. Mark. Drawn into himself, he had said scarcely a word since leaving the Landgren home.

Kay, sitting close beside him on the cushion seat without quite touching him, felt her heart slipping into that state of panic which she had not known for over a decade. She wanted desperately to enfold in her arms the grieving man she loved, but she didn't dare touch him for fear he'd crumble. So she sat there, frozen in place beside him.

They were ten miles north of St. Mark when their car slowed down and swerved uneasily onto the gravel shoulder on the right where it came to a halt. Kay looked into Steve's expressionless face in the dim glow from the headlights and held her breath.

For a few moments he remained motionless and erect behind the wheel. Then, as she looked on, a wince snarled his features. He fell forward onto the steering wheel and broke into sobs.

"I can't go on! I can't go on! It's all a farce, a terrible farce! They're all dying right in front of my nose. They're dropping like flies and we scientists are the ones who are killing them! Hope? Progress? Eradicating evil? Rubbish! If our science blesses one, it curses ten, in peace as much as in war. It kills, it maims, it cripples—the soul in peacetime, the body in wartime. So I gave everything I had to producing *this*? To make my Cecilia happy in Heaven? And my Kay on earth? What kind of a fool have I been? This is the bottom of a pit I've got myself into! God! What's gone wrong? What have I missed? Why did it take 'today' to show me this? O Kay! What have I done to you? You trusted me, and look where I've dragged you! Look where I've dragged you...."

"No, Steve! No! No! Everything I cherish has come to me in you. You are the wisest, and the bravest, and the most wonderful person I have ever known. No, Steve! Come to me. I love you. Don't leave me alone. Don't go away from me!"

She pulled his limp body towards her and he received her, pressing her head against his chest with his left hand.

She clamped herself around him.

Trembling he stroked her soft hair with his hand and fingers, back and forth, back and forth. And in her embrace and with his gentle stroking in her hair, his tremors slowly died away.

"Kay," he said, breathing a little more normally. "You are the only good I know for sure. Where did you come from? How did you get here? I think you came straight from Heaven, sent to me by the good God. Why aren't there more of you? Why isn't the world full of you? Then we'd have hope. Can you tell me why the good God is letting the world destroy itself? Can you, my love? Why?"

"O Steve!" Tears were streaming down her cheeks. "Let's just start all over again, just with each other, like we did before. Let's let everything else go. Let's just start with loving each other and go from there."

"My love, I couldn't go on for another day without you."

Kay's heart was pounding, her breast was heaving up and down. Pulling herself even closer to Steve, she pleaded, "Love me! Love me!"

"Always I love you."

"Steve," she whispered fondlingly. "Love me here. Love me now. Love me!"

He ran his fingers through her silken hair.

"You know I love you always."

"Love me *here*! Love me *now*! Now…."

He understood. His loins were awaking to her touch.

"But it isn't safe now," he objected weakly.

"Love me here, Steve! Love me now!"

A good half an hour later the DeSoto crept back onto the pavement and slowly made its way back toward St. Mark.

XVI

After the disastrous day in Reedville, Dr. Stephan Pearson was a changed man. His colleagues attest to this with one voice. It was incredible, they claim, how his quiet assurance crumbled overnight. Though he continued to go through all the well-ordered motions of the past eleven years—lecturing regularly, assisting students in the laboratories faithfully, attending chapel daily—there was now a perfunctoriness in it that dismayed those who had known and admired the zestful sincerity that had once been his. His lectures were in the main lifeless and stripped clean of any visionary rambling. His assistance in the laboratories was reduced to the role of a walking computer. His attendance at chapel was devoid of the prayerful spirit that had once been its hallmark. Something had indeed happened to him at Reedville, and his associates experienced it as an emptiness where he had once been so full, a dryness where a well-spring of joy had once overflowed in him.

There was one relationship, however, that suffered no loss as a result of the Reedville crisis. Steve and Kay now found themselves back in the position they had been in eleven years before, with Steve hovering on the brink of collapse and Kay as his sole reason for hope and his sole support. The cloud of disillusionment and apathy that hung over him everywhere else was mercifully absent from his home. His awakening to the fact that the very uses, the good and peaceful uses, to which he had trusted that God would ultimately put the fruits of science, were themselves the catalyst of immense personal and societal degeneration had him backed into the same corner that its wartime uses had backed him into eleven years before. But now there was no obvious escape route, no clear recourse to a better alternative. If a good God was directing human destiny above the stage of human folly, where was the evidence of it? Surely He could not be guiding and blessing advances in science if they were destroying man both from without and from within! So once again Steve found himself falling back on Kay and starting all over from there. She, after all, was the very embodiment of goodness, a goodness which if it had been the common property of the human race would have taken the world in a completely different direction.

Kay, for her part, fully grasped how much he needed the soothing effect of her love and affection now. She nourished within herself those qualities she knew he cherished most, creating for him a sanctuary within their home where hope could be reborn in him. She sought to distract him from pondering the issues that had brought him down so low, not by artificially trivializing them but by creating an atmosphere in the little world of their home that superseded them. She knew of no other way to prevent the man she loved from falling to pieces, and her with him.

Firmly she resolved to devote all she had to sustaining her husband. She considered for a time resigning from teaching, but thought better of it. Mary Thorsheim, to whom she confided everything, helped her to reason that Steve ought not to be aware of any special or forced efforts on her part to buoy him up, but that she could help him best just by being her winsome self.

So she made a point of enriching their home life with things that make life worth living. Almost every day she brought home with her from school a tale about something especially fine which a pupil of hers had done or said during the day which she managed to inject skillfully into their conversation. Sometimes she would relate how she had tried to bring out the best in a challenging situation, and occasionally even Steve would cite something encouraging from his day. She purchased a set of devotional books written by a popular pastor from Minneapolis.

The message drawn from each day's anecdote always affirmed the divine order of things in some way, and Steve found them good therapy. In addition, Kay's sense of humor, always one of her assets, sharpened and lightened things up in response to life's little anomalies day by day, providing unexpected little turns in their conversation that made them both laugh.

And, of course, he got to embrace her every night and hold her soft warmth as close to himself as he could. And she loved it, and let him know it.

Naturally, Steve was not unmoved by the peace and loveliness that radiated from his wife and greeted him whenever he came home. They were so genuinely the products of mutual admiration and love, and so perfectly the expression of what he was seeking on a universal scale, that he would now find himself being drawn home every day the moment classes were over. There he could wash off any "radioactive fallout" that had alighted on him during the day. And there he could rekindle whatever ray of hope remained in him that God might yet turn things around in the world.

Thanks to Kay, home was a refuge and sanctuary for Stephan Pearson in the months following the debacle in Reedville. Reluctantly he left it in the morning and eagerly he retreated to it at the end of the day. It was his one hallowed spot on the face of the earth. It kept him going from one day to the next. The goodness he experienced in his wife had to come from somewhere, he told himself.

But why, he asked himself over and over again, *aren't there more people like her in the world? Why can't every home be like ours?*

XVII

Toward the end of November, Kay began to suspect that something was wrong with her. At first she thought of many reasons besides the obvious one why she should not be all right: The strain of coping with Steve's neediness was telling on her more than she realized, or perhaps as a very diabetic thirty-seven years of age she was prematurely losing her youthful regularity, or … or…. But when she started having serious problems with the delicate balance of her insulin dosage, she was forced to ask for an urgent consultation with Dr. Pederson. And when she returned home from her appointment (it was two days before Christmas), she was a different woman.

In those two days she did more concentrated praying and thinking than she had ever done in any other two days in her life before. Weighing all aspects, she concluded that the best time to break the news to Steve would be after the midnight carol and Communion service on Christmas Eve.

If initially the news had left her aghast, what would it do to Steve? It negated all of his careful efforts over the past eleven years to avoid just such a thing. It had ripped open all those longings within her heart which she had stubbornly held in check because she didn't want a repeat of the painful "clash" that had settled the issue once and for all at the beginning of their marriage. There was no doubt in her mind about when and where the breakdown had occurred, or about who was responsible for it. But now that it was a reality, fear and hope were at war with each other in her. Tears of joy mingled with tears of apprehension. She found herself returning again and again to the information Dr. Pederson had shared with her moments after breaking the news to her.

"There is something you and Steve should know," he had begun. "But first let me review a few things you may already know. As soon as your baby's pancreas becomes large enough to function, it will begin supplying both the baby and you with natural insulin in ever increasing amounts. As a result, your insulin dosage must be decreased proportionately, as you may already be discovering. I will have to monitor this frequently if you decide to keep the baby. Towards the end of your pregnancy, the baby's pancreas will have become so overdeveloped that you will not be taking any injections at all. At the moment of childbirth, this creates a double crisis. The baby must immediately undergo an operation to reduce its oversized pancreas before the baby succumbs to a huge overdose of the insulin you can no longer use. And your dosage also has to be immediately restored, but to what level? All we can do in these circumstances is to guess at the right amount. On top of that, any bleeding induced by childbirth can become very dangerous to a diabetic mother whose blood doesn't clot normally.

"That leaves us with three possibilities at this point. Sometimes the baby dies in the womb. This can happen at any stage, resulting either in a D and C or a stillbirth. Sometimes the baby is born alive and rapidly succumbs to an oversupply of insulin. And sometimes an operation on the baby to remove the excess pancreas allows the child to develop normally in every way. Of course, there are risks to the mother in all three possibilities.

"What I am driving at is this: the last alternative has enjoyed a growing success rate in recent years. There are specialists who have become highly skilled at performing the necessary surgery on the baby and others whose skills focus on the mother's urgent needs. Even so, a large risk remains, but it has been reduced enough so that at this point physicians are tending to present the facts to the parents and leave the decision in their hands.

"Of course, much as I respect the sacredness of life in the womb, there are times with a certain severity group of diabetic mothers when failure to terminate the pregnancy early is a virtual death sentence both for the baby and for the mother. And you, Kay, taking account of your age and your medical history, could very well fall into that group. I shall send all your records to specialists in Minneapolis this very day for assessment. Their assessment, together with my advice, will give you and Steve something to base your decision on."

Kay had gone home spellbound by the thread of hope held out to her by Dr. Pederson. He spoke as though there was a real chance that she and Steve could have a baby who would "develop normally in every way"! This would unite them in a new world, the world of a living soul of their very own whom they could love together and in whom they could inculcate the goodness the world needed so badly. How a child would bless them both at this point in their lives! Steve would surely not yield to despair when he had in his own arms a precious life to protect and guide. All they had to do now was say yes to the decision lying before them. The risk involved? Steve himself had drawn the conclusion that a life without risks is just about the worst thing that can happen to the human soul.

This was the thread of hope on which Kay strung her heart. Steve might well shrink back at first, but now she was armed with a *fact* for him to take into account, not just her feelings. That fact would stand, given any amount of encouragement from the specialists in Minneapolis, and it would stare him in the eye no matter what he said. Its power would work on him with time. Yes, it would work on him! And she and Steve would have their baby!

The Midnight Service on Christmas Eve was exhilarating. The whole church was illumined only by the soft radiance of the candles on the altar, the white bulbs on the Christmas tree in the chancel, dim recessed lights in the vaulted ceiling, and at the end by candles held by all the worshippers. The sweet tangy scent of pine needles was the incense offered to the newborn Savior on this night of nights as men and angels strove to sing His praises.

"Hark, the herald angels sing,
'Glory to the Newborn King!'"
"What Child is this who laid to rest
On Mary's lap is sleeping,
Whom angels greet with anthems sweet
While shepherds watch are keeping."
"Ah, dearest Jesus, Holy Child,
Make Thee a bed, soft, undefiled,
Within my heart, that it may be
A quiet chamber kept for Thee."
"Silent night, holy night,
All is calm, all is bright
Round yon Virgin Mother and Child,
Holy Infant, so tender and mild,
Sleep in heavenly peace."

As the story unfolded in song and words, Kay held Steve's arm in hers as in a vise, tugging on it every time shivers ran up and down her body. During the sacred moment of the Holy Childbirth itself, as the choir was singing the third stanza of Phillip Brooks' sublime carol, Kay heard every word as if addressed to her and Steve:

"How silently, how silently
The wondrous Gift is given!
So God imparts to human hearts
The blessings of His Heaven.
No ear may hear His coming,
But in this world of sin
Where meek souls will receive Him, still
The dear Christ enters in."

By the time they arrived home, a sort of beatific afterglow of peace had settled over Kay. Fear and doubt about what lay ahead of them had melted out of her heart. She had assumed until now that she and Steve would deal with this somehow by sitting down, coolly calculating the risks and mutually agreeing on the right course of action. Now this assumption was miles from her mind.

The aura of the Holy Night had had a soothing effect on Steve, too. As they entered the tidy intimacy of their living room at about 1:30 a.m. where only the lights on the Christmas tree were glowing, he put his arm around his wife and drew her down into the big soft davenport facing the tree. This tender gesture was all Kay needed to unlock her hallowed secret. Just a moment or two of silence, of soaking up the gentle mists of love, and she could hold it in no longer.

"Steve, my love. I have something wonderful to give you for Christmas this year."

She paused. Then without lifting her head from his shoulder, but squeezing his hand a little tighter, she said, "We are going to have a baby."

Steve's jaw dropped. He tried to say something that didn't come. Kay sat up straight and turned full toward him, clasping both of his hands in hers and beaming brightly into his eyes.

"What on earth do you mean by that?" he gasped.

Kay's grin broadened and became as contagious as she could make it.

"I mean that next July you are going to be a father and I am going to be a mother. Dr. Pederson says there are doctors these days who specialize in this. So now we can have our own baby, and it is already inside me."

It came at Steve too suddenly to grasp. He nodded slowly, said nothing, and sat in a daze for a very long moment. Then he reached out and took Kay by the arms. He drew her in to him again and, assured by the warmth of her body against his and the feel of their arms tightly wound around each other, he tried to absorb the reality of what she had just told him.

For a full half hour, this embrace of theirs in the soft light of the Christmas tree was their only communication.

Then Steve took a deep breath and conceded, "We'll have to look into this."

XVIII

"Looking into this" took the form of a visit to Dr. Pederson's office the day after Christmas. All day long on Christmas Day Kay had dropped little hints, as discreetly as she could, about the joys of parenthood and how grateful they could be that medical science had greatly reduced the risks in it for them. The only thing that had kept Steve on an even keel throughout the day was his phone call to Dr. Pederson at his home that morning and the physician's willingness to meet with them the very next day.

It was no secret to Steve that Kay had been suppressing and sublimating her strong maternal instincts for the past eleven years. This was clear in her devotion to her students and in the way she talked about them to him. He admired her greatly for letting her students be the outlet for these instincts, but he never lost the sense that way down deep she was always poised to take advantage of any unforeseen opportunity to have a child of their own. Now all of that was history. Kay was pregnant, and in a moment of weakness he had allowed it to happen. To be sure, if she was right that the danger was all but gone, that could alter everything. But he would have to have that on the best authority.

Kay's irrepressible joy and fearless assurance were infectious. He had never experienced her so assertive. Her mind was racing ahead to all the blessings in store for them by becoming parents, and what she had to say about it was persuasive indeed! All day long he wavered between being caught up with her in her enthusiasm and coping with his fears, fears first of all for her safety, and then also fears of how to go about raising a child well in a decadent society in an increasingly dangerous world. He even caught himself wondering if anyone had the right to bring children into a world like this at all.

In view of all this, the strongest affirmation she could get out of him was, "We'll see, we'll see…."

The next morning, Dr. Pederson, who was also a personal friend of theirs, wasted no time in taking them into his confidence.

"Yes," he answered with reserve when Steve asked him about new developments. "Some real progress has been made in this field in recent years. Some diabetic women are giving birth to several children, some are content with one, and some are advised against child-bearing altogether. It all depends on the history and the severity of each case."

"And in Kay's case, what would be your advice?"

"Well, I am not a specialist in this field. That's why I sent copies of all my records on Kay to a specialist in Minneapolis. His reply came in the morning mail, and I have taken the time to examine it carefully. He says that her history is in her favor. She has controlled her condition very well over the years. But her age and her severity index are not. Piecing it all together, he says that many women in Kay's category have one baby, but seldom more than one. And, he adds,"—the doctor's voice dropped—"it is not unheard of to lose a patient and/or her baby in Kay's category."

"Not unheard of!" cried Steve. "I hope he appended more specific statistics than that!"

"Six percent," replied the physician slowly. "Six percent in her category don't make it, according to the figures I have right here. Which is, of course, a great improvement over what it once was."

"Well, that settles that!" exclaimed Steve. "We can't play with that kind of a risk."

"But Steve!" cried out Kay. "Only six percent! I would have been happy with a 10 or 20 percent mortality rate. Only six percent! Darling, I'll be all right."

The physician lowered his head as though he were examining the report even more closely.

"And the primary reason for losing the patient is blood loss?" demanded Dr. Pearson, unheeding.

"Yes. Blood loss and failure to reestablish quickly and correctly the dosage of insulin the mother requires, suddenly deprived of the insulin she has been getting from the baby's pancreas. Blood loss becomes a major issue if there are complications in the delivery that create excessive bleeding."

"And you think I could actually consent to let you take that kind of a risk?" Steve demanded, turning to Kay. "These data speak for themselves. No husband in his right mind would choose to put the life of his beloved on the block like that!"

Kay was blinking fast. She had braced herself for a rough struggle, but it all seemed so unreal to her at this moment. Still, she was clear-headed enough to realize that this was neither the time nor the place to settle the matter. She hesitated and, ignoring Steve, she asked the doctor, "And how long is it before you have to have an answer from us?"

"Well, your serious problems will not begin for several weeks yet. After that, there will have to be constant vigilance, on your part and on mine. Every change in your condition will require an appropriate response. We will take nothing for granted. You will need to notify me of even the slightest change. And you should also know that if you decide not to carry the baby to term, we will need to perform a therapeutic abortion within the next month to six weeks, to minimize the risk to you."

"Then we shall take it home for at least a week before we give you our decision," Kay stated flatly.

Steve was about to object when, glancing at his wife, he bowed his head and nodded his agreement.

"Can we make an appointment for next week at this time?" he inquired.

"Certainly."

As they were getting up to leave, Dr. Pederson rose from his desk, walked over to them, and laid one hand on a shoulder of each of them.

"As a physician I can only present the facts in a case like this and leave the decision to you. And one of the facts in this case is that we have right here in St. Mark two diabetic women who have given birth to babies recently, one of whom experienced some complications in the delivery and recovery. Her name is Lena Nyberg. She was thirty-five years old at childbirth and has a seven-month-old tot. She lives with her husband and son in the last house on the left on Oak Street as you leave town.

"And as a friend I can only say, may God be with you!"

Kay looked up at the tall physician and smiled.

"Thank you," she said.

"Yes, thank you," echoed Steve vacantly.

And they left for home.

XIX

On their way out of the doctor's office, Kay said with some conviction, "Even before we discuss it, we should get all the facts in front of us. We need to pay Mrs. Nyberg and her son a visit."

"And Mr. Nyberg too, if we can catch him at home."

For Steve, this visit was a long shot, a mere protocol. His mind was closed to any alternative but taking the safest way out of the mess they had got themselves into. For eleven years virtually everything that made life worth living for him had been enshrined in his Kay, wrapped up in that precious little body of hers. Now they had carelessly undone eleven years of diligent self-discipline, and the only course of action that made any sense to him was to fix the problem, not to cave in to it.

But because he loved her so much, he was vulnerable to her pleading eyes and to those flashes of ecstasy that lit up her face at the most unexpected moments. They took the heart right out of him. Her persuasive tone of voice and her quiet confidence when she spoke of their baby were impossible to dismiss. It was not easy for him to stand up to her, particularly since she cherished the notion that this baby was her present to him, well worth any risk to herself. Even before the day was over, Steve came to appreciate fully the terrible price a therapeutic abortion would exact from her. But what choice did they really have? He shrank back in horror from the thought of a future without her. Good sense would have to prevail. He must remain inflexible.

In consenting to visit the Nybergs, Steve did not consider that he was giving in an inch to Kay's agenda. But he had to agree that it was only fair to exhaust every angle before making their decision. In the end he would remain firm and clear-headed.

Two days after their appointment with Dr. Pederson, they pulled up in front of the Nyberg home. "I'd love to show you our little Jimmy," Lena had exclaimed over the phone when Kay called and explained the reason for their request. "If you come at 3:30 tomorrow, he should be waking up from his nap. And I'll see if Larry can be here then too."

Kay was so worked up when they arrived at the Nyberg residence that she could hardly sit still. Mrs. Nyberg answered the door with a half-dressed Jimmy in her arms. "He just woke up," she tenderly explained. "He'll be a little owlish for a few minutes, but you won't mind if I finish dressing him in front of you here in the living room, will you?"

"Oh no," assured Kay, already taken in by the child's big blue eyes which he was clumsily rubbing with two sleep-drugged little fists.

They all sat down in the living room, Mrs. Nyberg in a large upholstered chair and the Pearsons opposite her on an old-fashioned davenport.

At thirty-six, Lena was an attractive woman, just an inch or two taller than Kay and perhaps fifteen pounds heavier. Her complexion was dark and her face was a bit more lined than usual for a woman of her age. But she radiated youthfulness as she bounced her beautiful baby on her knees. You could tell that she loved showing him off.

Jimmy was a doll, to be sure. In about five minutes his big blue eyes were twinkling playfully and he was amusing himself with his mother's wristwatch. Then he cocked his round slightly oversized head topped with a thick frosting of curly blond hair and rocked back and forth in his mother's arms as if to say, *Down, down.*

"Yes," Mrs. Nyberg said, laughing. "Once they start crawling, nothing is safe. You learn to put all movables out of reach. My husband, Larry, is an electrician. He fixed up the sockets so Jimmy can't stick his finger in them."

She stopped and watched the little tyke crawl awkwardly lickety-split across the rug after a ball. "They do keep you on your toes," she added, shaking her head.

Both the gracious woman and the energetic baby had won Kay over and even Steve could not help but feel happy for this woman. The scene reminded Kay of something out of the various *Madonna and Child* paintings of Raphael. The more she watched Lena and baby Jimmy, the more she pictured herself and her own roly-poly bundle of life in their place.

"You wouldn't trade him for anything, would you!"

"We certainly wouldn't." Lena glanced out the window over their shoulders. "Here comes Larry now, just pulling into the driveway."

Moments later the Pearsons stood up to meet him.

"Larry, this is Professor Pearson and his wife, Kay."

"Steve," said the professor, extending his hand to Larry, a tall blond Swede of about forty years of age, attired in work clothes.

Larry took a seat near his wife and everyone sat down again.

"Lena tells me you are facing the same thing we were facing a little over a year ago—an unexpected pregnancy and all the risks that go with it for a very diabetic woman."

"That's exactly it," nodded Steve.

"Well, we weighed all the factors as best we could. I was very hesitant. We had a good marriage even without children. I was quite prepared to keep it that way if it meant risking my Lena's life. But in the end the decision had to be hers, one way or another. I couldn't see myself forcing my will on her. And the rest is history."

"Was it really difficult, I mean the actual pregnancy, labor, and delivery?" Kay asked, leaning forward.

"Yes, I'd have to say it was." replied Lena. "Once I'd made up my mind to go ahead with it, Larry supported me all the way. We went ahead and trusted in the Lord. Frankly, when our baby started to show, Larry strutted around here proud as a peacock. 'That's our son or daughter in there,' he'd keep saying, patting me on the belly. The last six months of my pregnancy were touch and go with my insulin dosage all the way to the end when I didn't have to take any insulin at all. I felt real good then, considering. The ordeal began when I went into labor, but most of the time I was so groggy I didn't know what was happening."

"Was that from the anesthetics or from loss of blood?" Steve wanted to know.

"At first it was the anesthetics they gave me, but later it was also loss of blood. The child-bearing itself was not much different from usual, I was told. Once they've got your baby, you've just got to trust them to fix you both up as quick as they can. There isn't nothing you can do but hope and pray. It's in their hands and in the Lord's hands then."

"It must be a comfort to know how skilled those hands are," Kay added swiftly.

"It is. You keep telling yourself, when you're clear enough to think at all, 'They know what they're doing. They've done it all before.' The one doctor quick goes to work with a team and operates on the baby before the pancreas can hurt him, and the other doctor and a whole lot of nurses flock around you to stop the bleeding and give you transfusions and figure out how much insulin you need. It took me about four months before I began to feel myself again. But, you know, the whole thing teaches you an awful lot. It's brought Larry and me even closer together. And after what we went through for Jimmy, I think we have both learned a lot about what it means to love…."

Dreamily she looked at her labor of love creeping over the floor toward Steve's legs. "He's given Larry and me a whole new lease on life. Nine years we were married before Jimmy came. They were good years, but nothing like the last seven months."

The little tyke was grabbing hold of Steve's trouser legs with his fists and trying to pull himself up. "Here, let me help you," offered the amused and slightly flattered professor.

"Isn't he awfully precocious for seven months?" Kay marveled.

"That's what they tell us," chimed in Larry, beaming with pride.

But the little fellow was too wobbly-kneed to stand without support, so Steve reached down and braced him behind his back. In so doing, he leaned over and his necktie brushed across Jimmy's face. Jimmy giggled and gooed gleefully, throwing his arms around in the air chasing the soft swinging stripe of color. Now Steve was supporting him entirely.

"All right, then," he chuckled. "Come on up."

With that he hoisted the baby onto his knee and gave him the end of his tie to play with.

"Gaa, gaa, gaa, gaa, gaa," cooed Jimmy, stuffing the tie into his mouth. Steve extracted it before he could gnaw on it and dangled it above and behind and beside him in a variation of hide-and-go-seek.

Yes, Larry and Lena were truly blessed, Steve mused. Fine simple folk that they were, Jimmy was just the thing for them. But he and Kay had other things to make their lives worthwhile.

Kay, meanwhile, had made up her mind while listening to their story and observing Steve's response to the child's ingenuous attentions. Destiny had charged her with bringing this joy into the life of the great man she loved, and great joy would also be hers in doing it! This was Steve's one chance, risks and all, to procreate the goodness he was stunned to find in such short supply in the world. How could he in good conscience turn away from it?

About then Jimmy grew fidgety and restless. He wanted to get down, but whimpered when Steve set him on the rug.

"What he needs is his bottle," declared Lena with the authority of experience. "I have one ready for him in the kitchen. Would you like to feed him?" she inquired of Kay.

"I'd love to."

"Okay. I'll be right back."

She left the room. Kay nestled in close to Steve and beamed up at him. He took one look at her, drew a deep breath, and lifted his eyes to the ceiling as if to say, *Oh, good grief!*

"Lena wanted to nurse our baby," Larry noted, "but her recovery process was too long and complicated to allow it. The bottle has one advantage. Dad can do his share of the feeding too, and I do, especially at night."

By that time Lena had returned with the bottle. Gently Kay took

Jimmy in her arms and offered him the nipple. He went for it eagerly and settled back in her arms in perfect contentment. The quiet rhythmic "tk, tk, tk, tk, tk, tk, tk, tk" of his sucking filled the room. His blue eyes rolled around wide open, unsuspiciously surveying his spectators as he dined. Kay's heart was pounding at the feel of little Jimmy pressed against her bosom. Even now a little treasure much like Jimmy was forming in her womb. And it would stay there!

Steve was not unmoved by the maternal love expressing itself so beautifully at his side. In that instant, his objections seemed downright foolish to him, face to face with the blissful impulses with which the God of Nature has endowed every normal woman. *But*, he told himself, *there are many beautiful things in life that we simply cannot have. And this is one of them!*

Even so, when his wife looked up at him, her eyes glistening with hope and joy, his heart melted. *This feels like a losing battle*, he told himself. *But it can't be.*

XX

That night the showdown came. It had to. Kay would have burst if it hadn't. Her emotional pitch was so high that Steve realized there was no putting it off.

Washing supper dishes, she let two of them slip through her unsteady fingers and crash to the floor. In spite of himself, Steve couldn't help but smile. "The dear things that make up a woman," he whispered loud enough for her to hear as he gathered up the fragments from every end of the kitchen floor. This reminded him of the day they first "ran into each other" and he had scrambled around to gather up off the ground what she had dropped due to the impact.

But it was Kay who now, on her own, picked up the thread of that thought and said, *Alles was ich fallen lasse, dass nimmst du immer auf, du lieber Mensch, du!* ("Still trying to pick up the things I'm always dropping, you dear man, you.")

As she watched his steady hands gather up the broken pieces, she saw in her mind's eye the trembling hands of the man in coveralls she had taken for an itinerant worker, scrambling around in the leaves beneath the maple trees. That man had seemed so much older than this man, though this one was now bereft of all dark hair. What had made all the difference was the rebirth of hope in him and the impetus it had given him to apply his genius to something he could truly believe in.

That this man should never become a father would be a crime against humanity, she told herself, *and I've had eleven years to know what I am talking about. He'd be the last one to see it, but having his son or daughter in my womb is like having a bright light for this dark world right here inside me*.

"Steve," she said simply. "Don't you see why we *must* have the child I am carrying?"

Steve emptied the shards into the waste basket and stood up straight. He looked at her face, strained with the certainty of her irresistible logic, and shook his head.

"And why is it now 'must'?"

But Kay was too full and her voice was too near the breaking point to answer him properly. So she just stood there looking at him, blinking hard and nodding slowly up and down before turning back to the last of the dishes. When she was done, Steve moved up to her and gently took hold of her upper arms, turning her around. Then he took her hand in his.

"Come on now, Love. Let's go into the living room and work this out together right now. We can't go on this way. Come on."

Tears were streaming down Kay's cheeks in earnest. Tenderly Steve led her into the living room and seated her on one end of their loveseat davenport, seating himself almost beside her on the other end, but facing her.

"My darling," he began. "Can't you see that it would be insane for a woman of your age and in your condition of health to place your life—and your husband's life—in such jeopardy? For eleven years of happy married life we have worked so diligently to avoid exactly this dreadful prospect, and now just because of a moment of reckless weakness on my part, should our motives be any different?"

"Yes, Steve, we have been happy together. I can't imagine how I could have been happier for these eleven years than by being your wife. And you were wonderful to go to all the trouble right from the start to figure out how we could make love safely several times a month without risking my health. But that was eleven years ago. There were no Lena Nybergs back then. What happened to her and Larry was unimaginable back then. But now it has become a priceless blessing even more available to us than it was to them a year ago. It is one of those peacetime miracles of science that you have been inspiring your students to strive for year after year. What was impossible eleven years ago is almost routine now, they tell us. In view of this, how can you ask me to surrender the holy child, *our* child, who is within me, our own flesh and blood, at this very moment?"

She unbuttoned two buttons lower down on her blouse and reached over to him. Taking his right hand, she drew it into the opening and held it flush against the skin of her womb in total silence.

"Our flesh and blood," she whispered.

Minutes passed.

"O my angel," Steve whispered at last. "You are just too beautiful. I can't bear the thought of losing you."

He moved in closer to her and took her in his left arm. She was holding the palm of his right hand pinned flat against her womb with her left hand.

"You do realize I am fifty-seven years old. What counsel can a seventy-five-year-old father give his troubled teenage daughter? And what are my chances of living long enough to see her or him out on their own?"

"Very good," responded Kay faintly. She sensed it was "now or never." It was the moment for her to give it all she had. She braced herself for the impact she knew her words were going to have on Steve, and then she pronounced her judgment on his position.

"Your maturity is all the more reason why we must have this child. Your life has taught you more than most people learn in ten or a hundred lifetimes, and God has endowed you with a matchless mind and heart. Cecilia has shaped you to find true joy in self-giving. So help me, Steve, you owe it to God, to your fellowman, to Cecilia, to me, and to yourself to transmit that God-given mind and heart to your own offspring before you leave this earth. What hope is there for the world if men like you choose to lie fallow while degenerates reproduce their own kind by the millions? It is the offspring of men and women like you and me who are the hope of the world. And now you want to snuff out that hope, that light, before it even has a chance to dawn? *What are you doing?*"

Kay had been right. That did jolt Steve. It jolted him right out of himself back into the auditorium of the Reedville High School and to his own address.

"But do we have a right to bring a child into a world that persists in turning every good thing into an evil?" Steve mumbled.

"It goes deeper than that, Steve, and you know it. We should rather be asking if we have a right to deny to the forces of Good and of love in this world a strong and honest advocate. Steve! Think what you are saying! Are you willing to surrender all hope for the triumph of good, of the Kingdom of God, in the world? You keep challenging people wherever you go to confront evil in the world, and you yourself falter before making the small sacrifice now being asked of you. This could be your opportunity to make your most lasting contribution of all. You are a strong and courageous man, Steve, a man of faith."

She nestled in even closer to him.

"Imagine the potential for good whose fate is lying squarely in your hands at this very moment. And look, just look at when it all came about. Just look at when it happened!"

Kay was done. She had nothing more to say. It was all in Steve's lap now.

Her last words stung him, though he wasn't sure quite why. She was clearly making a connection he had not yet made. "Look at it. Look at when it happened!" she had said. Look at *what?*

They held each other tightly in their arms, his hand still resting on her warm womb.

The picture was gelling in his mind. When had this baby been conceived? On the same occasion on which he had challenged everyone to seize the initiative in the fight against evil, especially in its peaceful guises! That is exactly when he had planted the seed in her womb, the seed that was now their child. The Reedville challenge had withered and died, bearing fruit only in the Eriksens. The Pearson challenge had immediately borne fruit in Kay's womb. But was it also destined to wither and die, and not just to wither and die, but to be killed in her womb? Kay was telling him that to kill it would be worse by far than to let it die. In her mind, aborting their baby was the equivalent of conceding to the enemy, of giving up any claim to integrity in offering the world a better way.

Long minutes ticked by. At stake now was more than health, more than age, more than marital happiness. At stake now was life itself, the very basis of Steve's hard-won sanity. It was wrong to tempt God, but it was wronger by far to fail to rise to life's challenges. It was wrong to cower from the truth, but it was wronger by far to live in contradiction to known truths. Steve had challenged his audience at Reedville to a life of self-giving love in all circumstances as the only hope for the world and the only source of lasting happiness for anyone, especially for the affluent like themselves. This was his chance to live up to his own challenge. Self-giving love! He was looking it straight in the face.

Ruthlessly, as was his manner, he drove himself to the only possible decision. The signs of his inner struggle united Kay's heart with his in these moments of eloquent silence.

At last he tightened his embrace of her and said, "Thank you, my love. We are in the hands of greater forces than ourselves. What else can we do but give our baby a chance to live? I shall have to be braver than you."

In the morning he called Dr. Pederson's office and canceled their appointment for the following week.

The trial had begun.

XXI

The die was cast. Steve was now decidedly involved in a personal way in the implications of his Reedville address. And the more he thought about it, the more he saw it Kay's way. It was indeed the only way, he concluded.

In his own mind he was very clear about certain features of human nature. He had no doubt that as long as the human race survived, there would always be those dedicated to expanding the horizons of knowledge and gaining ever greater mastery over the forces of nature. No human life on earth would be unaffected by this. He was also convinced now beyond a shadow of a doubt that this would have a deadly effect on people as a whole unless love took over from Sin as the dominant force in the human soul, unless Cecilia's Jesus could do for the whole human race what He had done for her. Only then would man's innate bent toward self-gratification as a way of life be superseded by a divinely inspired thirst for the well-being of others. This passionate thirst was as needed for survival on the national and international levels as it was on the level of each individual person, and it represented the precise reversal of what was commonly understood as the process of evolution, the survival of the fittest. Somehow, people's loyalties had to be raised above the levels of chauvinism, blind patriotism, and all the many seductive forms of hedonism, raised to the level of a passionate concern for the well-being of others. If all we care about is our own personal well-being, we are on the road to disaster as a race. The chain of the survival of the fittest had to be shattered link by link through the victory of love, or else no one would survive. We would end up destroying ourselves as we destroy others. The strongest would annihilate one another and the weakest would be their helpless victims. Without love, scientists would continue to operate in oblivious isolation and people everywhere would suffer as a result. Love, and love alone, was the key to humanity's future. Without love, and all the risks it entails, humanity had no future.

For Steve, Jesus had said it all in enjoining us to "do unto others as you would have them do unto you" and to "love one another as I have loved you." Our failure to take Him at His word in the past had had catastrophic results at every level. Failure to take Him at His word now in this new age of science would lead inevitably to our annihilation. What was once prudent advice had now become humanity's recipe for survival.

But no one can be forced to love, he realized. We must be taught to love, inspired to love, reformed to love. We must be enveloped by love until it becomes our nature. This can come only through a spiritually transforming encounter with God who is Love, an encounter most often facilitated by people who have already been transformed by their encounter with Him, people like Cecilia and Kay.

The irony is this: the Cecilias and the Kays are the most authentic people in the world, the most honest, least devious, most fully alive, and most happy people in the world. What or who is preventing everyone else from making it their life's goal to be like them? What or who is blinding people from embracing what so clearly serves in their own best interests? Can it really be that "an enemy has done this," as Jesus said? What did He mean by that?

It encouraged Steve to see evidences of love operating here and there throughout the world in people who still believed that "it is more blessed to give than to receive," even though sometimes these evidences appeared in less than perfect expressions—like the teacher devoted to cramming a cherished principle down the throat of a student who has no possible use for it, or a nation urging self-sacrifice on its citizens for its own sake with no concern for the well-being of anyone beyond their borders. But the impulse for goodness was almost always detectible in many places and guises, however imperfect, and Dr. Pearson was quick to take note of it with a sense of relief.

During the months of Kay's pregnancy, Steve frequently spoke of these things with her. The conversation of a typical evening ran something like this:

"How did you feel today at school, sweetheart?"

Steve had been using more terms of endearment lately.

"Quite well. Dr. Pederson has cut my dosage of insulin down to forty-five percent of normal. And recently I've had more candy than in the rest of my life all put together. Life is pretty good."

"Well, just so we keep everything in balance. I think I like you a little plumper, anyhow."

"That's not me, Funny Face. That's our Little One."

Then they would just sit there in silence and stare at each other, soaking it all in.

"We've got to take really good care of him or her, Kay. If it's a girl, I hope she'll be just like you. If it's a boy, we'll do our best to help him to be a better man than I am. You have always blessed our home with kindness and love, and that will give our little one such a good start in life, a good basis for being generous and loving toward others, a good attitude toward others and just the right heart to communicate that attitude to them, especially if they are very broken. Just like you, it will come naturally to our child to be like the man Jesus told us about this morning in our devotions who gave the thief his cloak after he had already stolen his coat and who carried the soldier's backpack two miles when he could have quit after one."

"O my darling, that's you, not me!"

"No, it's you. It's only thanks to you that I bounced back from despair and found a reason to live again."

Steve was speaking in low ardent tones.

"The very night I was forced to despair of man's ability to see beyond himself and to love others, that's when we, you and I, brought together the elements of this work of love who is in your womb. Not progress, nor culture, nor solving problems, nor unraveling mysteries is the Cause of God on this earth, Kay, but simply love without which all of these other endeavors will lead only to disaster. But with love, all of them can be purified and sanctified and turned into something good. Love requires us always to take into account the full effects of everything we do on the basic well-being of people. 'God *is* love,' the apostle tells us, and he should know. That means that love is divine, and this gives us a firm basis for hope. Jesus' resurrection means something after all. It means that life on earth at its darkest does not have the final word. The little ones who live by faith in Him and are filled with God's love have the final word. You and Cecilia have it. And the precious little bundle in your womb will have it too, please God!"

"Yes, Steve. He will. God is at work so that through our child He may bring peace on earth, goodwill to men."

Steve closed his eyes and rubbed them with his fingers. His pipe had gone out while he was talking.

"It is all so clear. Love is the only force that can work this miracle for the human race.... And God is totally Love. Let Him use us and our little one as He will as instruments of His love."

"He will, Steve. We are giving Him what we can, and He is accepting it. I feel His strength in me. I really do. And I hear Him saying to us, 'Blessed are the peacemakers, for they shall be called sons of God.'"

"O my dear Lord!" Steve sighed. "How I long to be a true peacemaker, a true son of God!"

XXII

The night of June 29, 1959, was unseasonably warm in Minneapolis. Without a breeze to freshen it, the sultry air of the day was now smothering the city in its heavy blanket. The air conditioning fans in the general hospital were laboring to relieve suffering patients of the added burden of the heat. A faint light was glowing in a window on the seventh floor, one of the few still burning at 2:00 a.m. The seventh floor was the maternity ward.

An infant son had been born the previous morning to Dr. and Mrs. Stephan Pearson. The baby, whose delivery was complicated by its greatly enlarged pancreas and by other congenital issues, died before they could get him onto the operating table. A nurse had quickly baptized him as "Baby Boy Pearson, in the name of the Father, and of the Son, and of the Holy Spirit" just before he expired.

The mother's condition was so critical that the news of her infant son's death had been withheld from her. She had, in fact, regained consciousness only twice.

Dr. Pearson, though prepared for an ordeal by the unexpected complications of his wife's last month of pregnancy, was in a state of shock. Mary Thorsheim had remained with him all day and into the night and had heard from his lips little more than the words, "She has to pull through! O God! She has to pull through!"

At 2:05 a.m., the physician who had attended her all through her labor and delivery stepped into the waiting room. Steve shot to his side. "She has regained consciousness, Dr. Pearson," he said wearily, "and is asking for you. Mind you, only a minute or two."

Dreading and hoping, Steve opened the door and tiptoed into the room. Above the white curtain drawn around Kay's bed hung two inverted bottles of blood and a series of tubes. Quickly he moved to the side of the bed where the curtain was open. An oxygen tent had been removed from around Kay's head. Their eyes met. A weak smile broke out on her face at the sight of Steve. He laid his hand on hers, gazing in disbelief through the paraphernalia surrounding her.

Her breathing was faint and fitful. But her eyes gleamed with joy. She looked steadily at her wretched husband. Her lips parted a slit and closed again. Steve bent low over her, so low that his ear was almost touching her mouth. Her breathing grew even more rapid and fluttering. Her lips parted again and, in the barest whisper, scarcely audible, but clear as crystal, Steve heard, "It's a boy. Are you happy, my love?"

Her breathing grew even more shallow, as if her soul were barely clinging to her body.

"Oh yes, my beloved!" Steve choked. "My dearly beloved Kay!"

Tears were streaming down his cheeks. He was trembling uncontrollably.

"Then don't cry, darling.... I'll be all right...."

Her voice died to a whirr.

"I am ... very happy ... too.... Jesus just...."

Her eyes closed. One of the attendants firmly pulled Steve back and with one motion, drew the oxygen tent down over her head again. Petrified, Stephan Pearson watched the flower of his life wither away before his eyes.

A few long moments later, Kay opened her eyes for the last time and looked straight into Steve's eyes. A deep smile settled over her face, a smile expressing all the joys of a battle well fought and won. When she closed her eyes, the smile remained.

They tried to get Stephan to leave, but he insisted on remaining at her bedside, holding her hand. Mary joined him in his vigil.

The gentle smile was still on her face at 2:38 a.m. when Katherine Pearson took her last breath.

Book Three B

XXIII

The funeral for Katherine Pearson and Baby Boy Pearson took place at Grace Lutheran Church in St. Mark. Their bodies were laid to rest in the church cemetery on the east end of town, a short walk from the Pearson home. It was attended by a large congregation of mourning friends and colleagues. Neither Steve nor Kay had any immediate family members, no siblings, no parents, no cousins, to offer Steve personal support. Mary Thorsheim, sizing up the situation, decided to be his sister. And my wife and I, entering the church a few minutes before the Processional Hymn, became at her invitation the rest of his family. We followed the caskets down the aisle to their place at the foot of the altar and sat with Steve and Mary in the front pew on the left. The pallbearers, drawn from the faculty and administration of the college, followed us and occupied the first pew on the right.

The Lutheran funeral liturgy was conducted by the pastor with great reverence and restraint. To the surprise of all, he announced that instead of a sermon he was acceding gladly to the request of Dr. Pearson to celebrate Holy Communion so that Jesus might be directly present to all with a minimum of human intervention. My wife and I experienced this as a touch of pure grace. The first communicant kneeling at the altar railing to receive Jesus was Stephan. Mary and I needed to help him back to the pew.

After the lowering of the caskets at the interment in the cemetery, Dr.

Pearson graciously accepted the condolences of all who approached him at graveside. He had decided against a reception. As the crowd melted away, he turned to my wife and me and said, with a depth of emotion that almost got away on him, "Her last words to me were, 'I am … very happy … too…. Jesus just….'"

He choked up. Nothing more was said.

My wife and I choked up too.

With that, he took a deep breath and shuffled slowly over to his DeSoto. He drove the short distance to his home where, for all intents and purposes, he shut himself in for the rest of the summer. For the next two weeks, of course, he had a steady stream of visitors, including us, but after that his only consistent visitor was Mary Thorsheim who had promised Kay to "keep track of him in case something should happen to me." She felt it was only right for her to share this promise with Steve whose response was, "I guess we can't let her down then, can we?" And so for Kay's sake he welcomed Mary into his home twice a week so that she could "keep track of him" and do whatever cleaning up she could.

What did Steve do during those many hours and days alone in his house that summer? No one really knows. He let their lilac hedge grow wild all summer, he let most of the garden overgrow, and he let the lawn go to seed. He was seen now and then by passers-by on the front porch in a rocking chair, pipe in hand. Some days the shades on the windows of the house remained drawn all day. Mary sometimes found him, when she came on her regular visits, sitting in the living room in the semidarkness in a kind of daze. He seemed largely oblivious to dawn and dusk, to growth and decay in the world around him, perhaps because in his soul that summer there was neither dawn nor dusk, neither growth nor decay. There was just numbness.

When he happened to remember that it was Sunday, he would show up in church. When he didn't, his diligent pastor would pay him a visit, bringing him Holy Communion. Once Mary happened to be there when the pastor came, and they received Jesus together.

"Thank you, Pastor," Steve said. "Thank you for appreciating that I need time."

"Of course you need time, Dr. Pearson. When the time is right, God will speak to you as He knows best. Everything is in His hands."

"I really want to believe that, Pastor."

So existence dragged on for Steve, now feeling doubly forsaken. He was living in a vacuum. He lost all interest in the things that had once fully engaged him. They were all bloodless ghosts to him now. Nothing mattered anymore. Science? Dead! Learning? What for? Probing into the unknown? Who cares? Grief smothered his brain and all but gutted his will to live.

The only thing that seemed to lift him out of his numbness now, even if just momentarily, was the lingering memory of Kay's last smile and her mysterious last words, radiant with hope and promise while grief was devouring him.

The summer inched on, pulling the dead weight of Stephan Pearson along behind it. He told me on his deathbed that he had spent most of that summer milling about aimlessly like a corralled steer, plagued by images from his past that wouldn't go away, a collage of poignant scenes sometimes composed of elements widely separated in time. They often involved the interplay of his two angels. The sight of Kay's last smile, for example, would merge for him into the feel of Cecilia's first kiss, and then linger on and on. Or Cecilia's bending down low beside the dead cardinal, tears copiously flowing, would blend into Kay's heart-rending sobs at the mere suggestion of giving up her baby, and linger on and on. Or the feel of his hand pressed flat against Kay's warm womb over their baby would become the feel of Cecilia's warm body pressed against his shivering chest under the oak tree just minutes before she....

But invariably these scenes all eventually resolved into that last smile of Kay's, which also lingered on and on.

What tormented Steve terribly that summer at his darkest moments was the recurring fear that the Kays and the Cecilias of this world, beautiful as they are, might be pure illusion, leaving sneering chaos as the only ultimate reality. Though he fought it all the way, there were long hours, even entire days, when he was overcome with grief and despair. He was in a continuous state of mourning for what felt to him like the demise of goodness itself, the death of everything worth living for.

The long late evenings of that summer often found him alone in the little fenced cemetery, an easy walk from their house, kneeling in front of the raw dirt of two of the three plots he had purchased, or leaning up against a nearby tree facing them. It was almost as if he was enviously eyeing the one unoccupied plot, barely able to contain his longing to fill it.

XXIV

Before the fall semester began, the president of Christiania College reminded Steve that he was entitled to take a sabbatical leave of a year and that, although this normally required a year's previous notice, they were prepared to make an exception for him this year in view of the circumstances. But he replied that no, there was no way he felt he could profitably use such a year at this point. So the middle of September found him once again trudging up the hill each morning to spend most of the day in his turret, venturing out only to conduct his classes or to assist students in the laboratory or to attend chapel. It is quite possible that he would have spent the entire school year just going through the motions if something quite extraordinary had not occurred at the beginning of the semester.

Rolph Eriksen entered Christiania College in the fall of 1959 primarily because of Dr. Pearson. He had heard of the double personal tragedy that had struck his revered mentor, and this made him even more eager to be near him at this time. On the first day of class when he saw Dr. Pearson shuffle inertly into the room without so much as a glance at his students, he knew he was beholding a very different man. The renowned professor moved stiffly as if in pain. When he reached the lecture stand, he thumbed through the class cards without looking up. Absently he fastened the vest microphone around his neck, fiddling with it for a moment or two until it was comfortable. Then muttering between his teeth he said, "This is Physics 25, Lecture Section D. Please answer when I call your name."

One by one he went through the alphabetically arranged stack of cards until he came to the E's.

"James Edwards."

"Here."

"Harold Engquist."

"Here."

"Rolph Eriksen."

"Here."

"Donald…."

"Rolph Eriksen?" he repeated, puzzled.

Then, raising his eyes and removing his reading glasses, he said, "Rolph, would you please raise your hand?"

The lad, about halfway back on the right side, lifted his hand just high enough to attract the professor's eye. A furtive smile played on his lips.

"Hello, Rolph," Dr. Pearson said, warming up considerably. "I … I'm glad to see you."

He nodded his head in the young man's direction, replaced his glasses, and sank into the class cards once more. He had to clear his throat a few times before he could resume the roll call.

After four months of nonstop numbness, something had reawakened a bit of feeling in him. Something had found and touched a live nerve.

XXV

Rolph Eriksen, the quiet one across the long table who had said grace; the one who "with no conception of social behavior" had read most of Dr. Pearson's popular articles; the one who from his position of "strong mental and spiritual health" had apologized for his fellow students; the one whom Dr. Pearson had said he would be honored to have in class; this Rolph Eriksen was now in his class and in one of his laboratories, rubbing shoulders with him on an almost daily basis.

Who was Rolph Eriksen? In the days just before Dr. Pearson's death, I got to know him quite well. And this is what I learned in those long moments of quiet time which we shared during the vigil we spent together in the Pearson home.

At the age of twelve, Rolph had discovered the Minneapolis Public Library with its awesome treasures of the wisdom of the ages. At the age of twelve, he had also had his first mature spiritual awakening, precipitated by a chance encounter with an atheist at the library that drove him into Sacred Scripture and into Blaise Pascal. In his young mind, this unlocked for him what he came to understand as the "Higher Realm" in which all those who are serious in their quest for truth and beauty are to be found. This included for him the likes of John Milton and Isaac Newton, Ludwig van Beethoven and Johann Sebastian Bach, St. Teresa of Avila and Florence Nightingale, Louis Pasteur and Stephan Pearson, among others. All of these had in common an understanding of life as an upward quest, inspired by God, however diverse may have been their particular means of expressing it.

In the process of absorbing these treasures in his most impressionable years, a unique universe of relationships took shape in his mind. Its characteristics were garbed for him in terms that might have struck others as abstract but which for him possessed a concrete and almost personal quality: quest, higher realm, truth, beauty, revelation, holiness, and above all perception. Perception was for him the key to our ability to relate to the whole order of things, an order independent of man and contingent only on the Divine Will. Perception was an inner sensitivity to expressions of the higher realm not immediately apparent to everyone. One man, for example, might *perceive* a sunset, bask in it, be drawn into its mysterious and fleeting glory, while another man might just notice it and move on.

One day when Rolph was in the tenth grade, he decided it was time to try to put words to this. The result was a highly metaphorical and turgid *opus* in which none of the few people to whom he showed it, with the exception of his parents, saw more than a jumbled version of Coleridge's *Kubla Khan*, which is jumbled enough to begin with. Yet in Rolph's mind it was all crystal clear, the perfect blending of the natural world, the world of the human mind, and the world of Holy Scripture. His chief sorrow in these formative years of his life was the enslavement he observed in most of his fellow students to the cheap and fleeting pleasures of the lower realm when God had equipped them so well for rising to the higher realm and savoring its exquisite joys. All they had to do to attain the higher realm was to allow Him to be their Guide.

The quest for truth and beauty was the "Blue Flower" of Rolph Eriksen's adolescence, the vision that harmonized and sanctified everything for him. It led him early in life to attainments which for him were just the beginning, but for others already seemed like solid achievements. He soaked up everything he could lay his hands on in physics, chemistry, and mathematics, but he also devoured the complete works of Shakespeare, most of Calderon, Milton's *Paradise Lost*, the *Pensees* of

Pascal, significant sections of Aquinas, Kierkegaard, Ibsen, Goethe, and many others. In the privacy of his own room he lost himself in the Mozart and Beethoven symphonies and concertos, the great Bach choral works, much of Sibelius, Bruckner and Dvorak, and a smattering of many other composers, thanks to the long-play records he borrowed from the library. In all of these he discerned the outpouring of the souls of men who had been drawn by grace into the higher realm and were inspiring us and the whole human race to follow them there. All of this was for him an expression of the Gospel and he was not ashamed to say so.

In high school he fell in love with a girl from his church who respected him almost reverentially but found him a total enigma. His fascination with her began one night in a dream, his first of a tenderly romantic nature, and was fueled by his identification of her with the leading character in a historical novel he was reading at the time. At any rate, with the poetry he wrote to her, the short essays he submitted for her scrutiny, his social *maladresse*, his intellectual preoccupations, and his utter disinterest in the usual teenage activities, this two-year-long relationship was probably doomed from the start. Toward the end of their senior year in high school, she successfully killed it by telling him she was in love with someone else.

Thus when he enrolled in Christiania College, he had two compelling forces at work in him—his quest to live in and from the higher realm and his need to heal from the loss of the young woman he adored.

Now, Rolph was not a tinkerer who enjoyed fooling around with unknowns just to "see what would happen if…." In fact, his patience could wear thin in the laboratory. But he thrived on controversies surrounding such issues as the "what" and the "why" of the atom, the relationship of chemistry to biology, the whole field of quantum mechanics, and the like. He thrilled when he was in the presence of a mystery to be solved. Like the youthful Stephan Pearson, he was never sated with knowledge about anything because it was always leading him into more questions. He was in a virtually constant state of awe at the grandeur of God's creation.

Dr. Pearson observed him with mixed feelings. How would the God who was so very alive in him now survive in the face of the cold realities of life? He saw a forty years' younger version of himself in Rolph, and the sight quite frankly made him very uneasy.

Dr. Pearson's encounter with Rolph certainly succeeded in drawing him back at least partway into the stream of life. Because he cared for the lad so much, he had a decision to make: Should he encourage him to follow his quest, or would it be more charitable to dissuade him from it? Should Rolph be warned that he was probably heading for bitter disillusionment? Would such a warning do any good? And what if, in spite of everything, the lad was not all wrong?

There were moments, plenty of them, when the professor could barely stomach the blind enthusiasm of his pupil. Through him he was reliving his own days of blind enthusiasm. And look where they had taken him! He knew only too well where that special spark in Rolph came from and how easy it was to identify it with God's Will. Working shoulder to shoulder with the boy in the laboratory, he sensed in him the same awe which he too had once taken to be of divine origin. But he never had the courage to turn to him and say, "Be careful, Rolph."

Instead he let Rolph's budding genius grow and blossom out unchallenged. He let it open like a flower, delicate, exquisite, and quivering with life. He let it bathe in the sunlight and wave in the gentle breezes. He let its fragile petals unfold to the world, wondrous to behold. He could not bring himself to warn him that someday that flower would fall to the ground, those petals would scatter in the wind, and even that stem would be trampled into the dirt. He couldn't bring himself to do it even though he greatly feared that Rolph was setting himself up to be crushed as he had been.

It would be wrong to say that Steve had totally abandoned his faith in the goodness and ultimate victory of God over evil, but it would be correct to say that this faith was badly shaken. The prospect for him that Rolph in all his youthful faith and enthusiasm might well be on a collision course with calamity haunted him and expressed itself in some strange behaviors. Sometimes, while working side by side with him in the lab, he would suddenly turn his back on him and attend to another student. Or he would avoid him altogether, whether in class or in lab or anywhere else. They did have some good moments together, but Dr. Pearson's personal burden of sorrow and his anxiety for Rolph were never far from the surface.

Things went on like this until Christmas vacation arrived. He was at his wit's end over Rolph. He couldn't bring himself to come right out and disabuse the boy of his beautiful but hollow ideals, but he had to find some way to put him on guard. He decided that he would work this out in detail during the Christmas vacation, and then do what he needed to do for Rolph's sake first thing in the New Year.

Christmas itself was sheer torture for Steve. Mary offered to go with him to the Midnight Candlelight Carol Service, but he declined.

"I can't face it."

She understood.

Instead he spent almost the whole night of Christmas Eve slouched down in the loveseat where Kay had given him her present just one year ago, facing the tree and its soft lights which Mary had set up and decorated for him when he was away at work.

Pressing himself down into that hallowed spot where Kay had trapped him in the overflow of her love one year ago, now on that very same Holy Night one year later, Steve's grief overpowered him. The irony of Kay's last smile—could it have been caused by something as simple as her not knowing about their son's death, or was it caused by the wonder of what she was experiencing at that very moment?—this irony was altogether too much for him now, and in tandem with her final words, it broke him down into a night of anguish and nonstop tears.

"Oh my Kay, my angel, my love! Pray for me! Pray for me!" he sobbed all through that holy night.

XXVI

It wasn't easy for Dr. Pearson to sit down and figure out what to say to Rolph. The initial spadework was easy enough. It involved some data gathering, some attention to current events, some research into trends in history, and some reflection on the mystery and nature of evil. He saw it as his duty to present as balanced a picture as he could to Rolph and to let him take it from there.

But elements from his immediate past kept distracting and confusing him. Many of them inhabited the very house he was living in! They lurked in the Christmas tree and in the ornaments Kay had carefully chosen for it. They were hiding in the loveseat where Kay had revealed her secret. They were sprinkled all over the kitchen floor where she had dropped the two dishes. They mocked him from the kitchen table where they had shared devotions and prayer. They even nestled up to him at night in their bed of love.

By New Year's Eve, Steve was no closer to putting pen to paper than he had been at Christmas. He was starting to wonder if he had it in him to do it at all. Then it crossed his mind that someone in the early 1950s had given him a news magazine that had impressed him with its keen analysis of the trends of the time. He'd saved it with similar material somewhere in the attic. One more piece of data to consider before he'd have to get down to business! So he climbed the steep narrow staircase and crawled through the trapdoor into the attic. He rummaged through stacks of old material—journals, magazines, even newspapers. It was cold in the attic, so he went back downstairs to fetch a sweater. This whole exercise was starting to feel futile to him. It left him as cold in his heart as he was in his body. On his knees on the dusty floor, his fingers numb and stiff, he sorted through the last remaining stack of magazines in search of the article he was looking for.

He was about to turn and leave when he spied a tattered old briefcase in the corner, encased in cobwebs. He stared at it for a few moments. A faint smile of recognition played with his cheeks. This old friend had gone through college with him and accompanied him to Germany and to the institute in Boston. It had sat in his truck all through World War II and all during his time in Pittsburg. And now it had lain in the attic for some eleven years gathering dust. Fondly he reached for the handle and pulled the ragged object toward him across the rough timbers of the floor. His numb fingers fumbled to release the catch and open the flap. Dipping into the body of the case, he slowly retrieved one picture frame containing a yellowed page of manuscript music. The ink was fading on the paper and the frame was cracked and split. Steve set it down gently and drew out the next and the next until all of them were arrayed before him in a row. Then he reached into the side pocket and withdrew another frame. And there, suddenly, was his Cecilia, beaming at him across the years and through the veil between earth and Heaven. Trembling, he set it down carefully on top of the music frames at his knees.

Now he had his wallet in his hands and was fumbling with the picture section. He removed one of them, his favorite photo of Kay taken two years after they were married, and set it down next to the portrait photo of Cecilia.

The low sun was sending two dust-laden shafts of light gliding almost horizontally through the dim attic from the small west windows. They were intercepted by the form of a shivering old man hunched over some objects on the floor, sobbing his heart out.

That evening, pages from a small lined tablet flew in all directions. The scrawl on them is at times almost illegible, and their order is not always clear. I found them stuffed into the top drawer of an already stuffed desk. Rolph may have been the motive behind this outpouring, but he tells me that he never saw those pages until I showed them to him after Dr. Pearson's death.

This is what was on them, as best I could reconstruct it:

XXVII

Dear Rolph,

I am writing this to you because I care about you very much and I wish to spare you some of the agonies that have been my lot in life. I do not pretend to have all the answers. In some ways there are more questions in my life now than ever. It is almost as if the grace of God is forcing me at long last not to jump to conclusions too soon. Turmoil accurately describes my present state of mind, though I have come to some clarity about a few things. I am a man torn between the loves of my life that seem so Heaven-sent and the disasters in my life that seem to have come straight from hell. I am presently struggling hard to make sense of it.

When virtually everything you cherish is suddenly swept away, everything that speaks God to you vanishes, and when you realize that you yourself are the reason for its disappearance and that No One has intervened to prevent it from happening, the 'tiny hints' that all is not lost which you are given at such moments come to mean everything to you. I will tell you of my three self-created disasters and their subsequent "hints.'"

"When I was your age, I was hopelessly self-absorbed, but God gave me Cecilia Endsrud right here at Christiania. She, so close to Jesus, drew me from death to life. Before long we both knew we were destined to become husband and wife. But I killed her, and almost killed myself, driving a motorcycle recklessly just before Christmas. I can't describe to you the grief and remorse this plunged me into. But unknown to me she had left me a legacy, an anthem which she had written just for me, setting to music some words of Jesus that meant everything to her. She had played the music for me once on her practice organ, without singing the words, just days before her death. I found out what the words were only the next spring when at the end of their concert the Christiania Choir sang her anthem: *"Verily, verily, I say unto you, except a grain of wheat fall into the ground and die, it abideth alone. But if it die, it bringeth forth much fruit."* The anthem itself seemed to me—and to many others, I was told—to have come straight down to earth from the heavenly choir. Still recovering from my injuries I received it, in total shock, as my Cecilia's final farewell to me from Heaven. I was at first confused by her message and didn't catch on right away to what she was trying to tell me, but then all at once it struck me: she was telling me that *I, Stephan Pearson, am that grain of wheat* and that the way for me to make her very happy in Heaven was to fall into the ground right here on earth and die, and thus bear much fruit. Taking this message as my marching orders, and desperately needing to repair my guilt, I let myself go. I dove headlong into what I was told by a respected mentor was my 'ground' and I died. I surrendered myself completely to the worlds of science and mathematics. They had always held a powerful fascination for me, just as they do for you now. And so it was easy for me to dedicate myself heart and soul to the cause of human progress through the contributions that science was making to create a better life for people and to eradicate evil on earth. I was doing it for my Cecilia, and for Cecilia's Jesus, in a big way, so how could I go wrong? What further motivation did I need? You can see how the message she left me in that anthem moved me beyond despair, gave me a vision I could live and die for, and set me on my way. It was my first "tiny hint," and I clung to it for years.

The second disaster I brought upon myself was my direct involvement in the production of the atom bomb during World War II, for the noblest of patriotic motives, of course. Having to face up to the unimaginable suffering it inflicted on all those innocent people in Hiroshima and Nagasaki landed me in an inner hell I can't begin to describe. Kay was the source of my second 'tiny hint.' She brought me out of my long season in hell by convincing me to change my profession and become a teacher so that I could spend my energy inspiring students to use science only to make life better for people. (It also helped that she consented to be my wife!) For some ten years I was very happy doing exactly what she had suggested here at Christiania. Then came our experience on that fateful day at your high school in Reedville which disabused me of the notion that the peacetime uses of science are any less destructive of the human person than its wartime uses are.

And, of course, my most recent self-inflicted disaster was the sudden loss of both Kay and our son. When the baby I had planted in her womb was growing, we had many times placed our hands on that baby and consecrated ourselves and the little one to God whose Goodness and Love at work in people are the only force that can turn the world around and avert disaster. This bright prospect carried us through many trials right up to the day I lost them both. I know their loss would have plunged me instantly into a black hole from which I would never have emerged, except for the third 'tiny hint' that blocked that plunge. Kay had regained consciousness and asked for me. When I came to her bedside, she smiled at me weakly and proudly informed me that we had a son. Then she asked me if I was happy. I lied and said through my tears, "Yes, my beloved." Her face became the face of an angel and she said, looking me straight in the eye, "I am … very happy … too…. Jesus just…." Then her eyes slowly closed and she never opened them again until just before she died. Then she looked straight at me, smiled, and was gone.

Three beautiful promises, three crushing disillusionments, three sparks of hope.

I know there are multitudes of people the world over who have experienced similar disasters to mine. As a result, some have turned to God and some have turned away from God. As for me, I confess I am in a quandary. Sometimes the apparent meaninglessness of it all quite overwhelms me, the cruel heartlessness that can senselessly destroy the finest and best and equally senselessly allow the ugliest and worst to thrive. But then I see Cecilia and I hear her song, or I see Kay's smile and I hear her whispered words. And in those moments I see a flicker of light in the darkness!

But is it possible, I ask myself, that this light is nothing but a mirage, a delusion?

Yet Kay and Cecilia are the least deluded people I have ever known!

And still I wonder.

This has led me directly into wrestling with a related issue which has become a fourth "hint," so to speak. In my youth we spoke glibly about "the eradication of evil," as if it lay in our power to achieve it with a little hard work and dedication. But it dawned on me a few weeks ago in church as we were praying the Lord's Prayer that from the perspective Jesus gives us in this prayer, we have been terribly guilty of trivializing something He treats very seriously. By placing our whole life squarely between "Our Father who art in Heaven" and the "evil one" from whom we beg to be delivered, is Jesus giving us an indispensable key to a realistic understanding of the world we live in? If so, why are we ignoring it? Jesus presents the evil one to us in this prayer as a powerful enemy, an anti-God, bent on our destruction. And it is "the evil one," not just "evil," in German *"von dem Boesen,"* in French *"du malin."* Evil is a wicked superperson, not just a bad thing; an enemy, not a character flaw. Now, Rolph, if this is so, how can we ever be on the right track if we fail to take into account the evil one's determination to destroy the human race? We usually pray the Lord's Prayer as if the last line did not exist. That can't be what Jesus intends. I can see it so clearly now. By failing to take Satan and his wiles as seriously as Jesus does, I may have laid myself open to serving as his instrument for evil when I thought I was serving as God's instrument for good. If so, it is no wonder that the actual results of my work have been so horribly different from the results I expected. I fear I played right into Satan's hands by ignoring him. Like a rattlesnake, he kills you quickest when you don't know he's there. But we have no excuse. The Lord's Prayer is Jesus' continual reminder to us that the evil one IS always there, and that the earth *we* live and work in is a battlefield between Our Father and the enemy, and we are either on His side by grace or on the enemy's side by our fallen nature. Yes, Rolph, *this world is by definition a battlefield.*

Failing to reckon with the evil one is to court disillusionment and defeat from the very start. And I fear that I may well have spent my whole life doing just that.

All I ask of you, Rolph, is not to fall into the same trap I did. I am tempted to believe that Satan wants us to ignore him so that he can get us to give up on God. Then he has us. And I would certainly have given up on God long ago, and again in these last months, but for those two bright lights that I sometimes think He gave me just to pierce my gloom and never leave me in total darkness. Anyone who has had a Cecilia and a Kay in his life cannot ever be in total darkness. At times I have the distinct sense that my two lamps on earth have become my stars in Heaven.

Yet I must admit, I have my days when all truth seems to lie on the side of the darkness and everything else is illusion. But I always come back eventually to Cecilia's Jesus. Somehow, He strikes me as the One, the only One, who has it all together and under control, who sees the big picture, the only One who could have put that smile on Kay's face and those words on her lips, and the One who asks from me now nothing but my trust, and probably also my true obedience, since for years I thought I was being obedient to Him, but was not.

Your friend,
Dr. Stephan Pearson

XXVIII

Throughout January, February, and March, Dr. Stephan Pearson was little more than a walking shade. He seemed overwhelmed and powerless, like a man slowly dying. And he looked like one too. His cheeks were gaunt, his face was pallid, his stomach hollowed out. Most of his friends saw this as a reaction to his losses, but Mary Thorsheim suspected there was more to it than that.

His overall lethargy is doubtless to blame for the fact that his final illness crept up on him unnoticed. It blended in so well with his perennial disposition that neither he nor anyone else, apart from Mary, detected it. His spiritual nausea merged with his physical nausea and camouflaged it. The constant pain seen in his eyes could just as easily have had its source in a broken heart as in a broken body.

A number of humiliating but essential steps were under consideration by the college authorities. What could they do about their useless old wreck, too venerable to release and too irresponsible to retain? On the one hand, his reputation still attracted students to the college. But on the other hand, several were now threatening to leave on his account. His lectures were dull and disorganized. He always seemed a little lost. He never set foot in the laboratories anymore. The mathematics class he had scheduled himself to teach was in the hands of a member of that department. He ignored his duties as head of the Division of Science and Mathematics. In short, he was now a totally different man.

The administration's final decision, made in exasperation, was to raise his salary for the following year and strip him of responsibility for everything except the Physics Department. Everyone hoped he would snap out of it soon.

With speechless perplexity, Rolph Eriksen watched the man he revered shrivel up before his eyes.

"Is there anything I can do to help?" he pleaded one day after class.

"I wish there were," was the answer he got. "Thank you for asking."

He shrugged off the suggestions of Mary Thorsheim, who continued to visit him twice a week, that he consult a physician. Toward the end of March, she was considering taking steps independently to bring him under medical surveillance. She had prepared a fine dinner of easily digestible foods for him, some of which he had eaten with effort and regurgitated.

"I'm sorry," he said. "Seems like nothing agrees with me these days."

He himself did not suspect that something was physically wrong with him until a few days into April. The winter of 1959–1960 did not bring the customary drifts of snow and bitter cold to the St. Mark area, and the ground was fairly workable early in the spring. Now and then something like a fresh breath of air or the early morning song of a bird would stir something in Steve and inspire him to get outside. Accordingly one morning he got up early and went out to the garage. He took the spade down from its hook and went to the tiny plot he had tilled the summer before in the corner of the garden.

It took just one strong thrust of his right foot against the spade to double him over in pain. Grasping his abdomen with both arms, he gasped for air. The pain gradually subsided. He concluded that moping around all winter must have left him out of shape. He picked up the spade again and set to work. This time the pain hit him so hard it sent him reeling backwards. He collapsed on the ground clutching his stomach. And the pain hung on. Wheezing and panting and gripping his stomach, he staggered back into the house and fell into the nearest chair.

When he finally caught his wind, he cautiously sat up straight and admitted, "There is something to this."

As the days passed, the pain recurred at narrower intervals and with less provocation. Fortunately, he thought, it was very sporadic. He learned to avoid certain activities that strained the viscera. After he had experienced a stabbing pain two mornings in succession while walking to work, he drove his car from then on. It was with extreme care that he climbed the stairs to his office.

Somewhere in the neighborhood of April fifteenth, he noticed that he was passing blood. This may have been going on for some time already since he was slow to pick up on such things. Some level of pain was constant now, rising and falling. He pretty well knew what was wrong with him, but he just didn't care.

On April twenty-third as he was lecturing his Physics 25 class, Section D, he reached up with his right arm to pull down a chart. Before his fingers touched the string, his arm flew to his stomach. Clutching it fiercely, he groped for his desk chair with his left hand. Staggering forward, he slumped down into it. Instantly Rolph Eriksen was at his side. Several students ran to get help. Most remained riveted to their seats.

It took four or five minutes for Dr. Pearson to recover his wind enough to say anything.

"It will pass in a moment. I'm all right."

He requested that everyone still in the room kindly remain seated while he slowly rose and finished the lecture. The period was almost over. As soon as the dismissal bell rang, he sat down. Bedlam broke loose. Rolph and a handful of other students rushed forward again. Most of the rest of the students funneled out the door, bucking a torrent of Steve's colleagues who were jostling to get in. When they gathered around him, Rolph anxiously blurted out exactly what had happened.

The little physicist's condition was no longer a personal matter. In the company of an insistent Professor Amundsen of the Biology Department, he appeared in Dr. Pederson's clinic that very afternoon. The doctor admitted him to the County Hospital without further discussion. By suppertime half of the faculty had heard that Dr. Stephan Pearson was in the terminal stages of metastatic cancer.

XXIX

Dr. Pederson had driven Steve to the hospital in his own car and had stayed until he had seen him comfortably settled in a private room. He had also phoned Steve's pastor who showed up about an hour later.

"Would you like to receive Holy Communion, Dr. Pearson?"

"O yes! But I am not sure my stomach can handle the Host."

"I will dip my finger in the Blood of Jesus and lay it on your tongue."

Dr. Pearson closed his eyes and nodded gratefully.

At that very moment, Mary Thorsheim appeared in the doorway.

"Come and join us, Mary. Dr. Pearson and I are about to celebrate Holy Communion."

"Yes. Come, Mary," Steve insisted, beckoning to her weakly.

And so the three of them celebrated Holy Communion together.

When Communion was over and Steve and Mary had been blessed, the pastor said, "I have one more thing to ask you. Do you remember Dr. Engstrom? He was the college chaplain many years ago when you were a student."

"Very well."

"He is now quite elderly, a widower retired in Minneapolis," the pastor said, packing up his Communion kit. "He drove himself down to St. Mark to attend Kay and your son's funeral. I met him there afterwards for the first time. He seemed uncommonly concerned about you. He asked me to stay in touch, to let him know how you are managing. And so, of course, I phoned him as soon as I heard from Dr. Pederson. He said, 'I'll be there in the morning. I need to have some time with Dr. Pearson, if possible.' He wondered if you were all right with that."

"Yes. Of course. Yes."

"I'll let him know."

"Thank you, Pastor."

And now Mary was alone in the room with Steve. She sat down on a chair near his head. Silence reigned for many minutes until Steve, who had been staring at the ceiling, turned his head toward her and said, "Thank you for coming, Mary. I … I…."

"That's okay, Steve. Where would you expect me to be?"

Tears blurred the vision of both of them.

"Steve. You and Harold were such good friends. I have brought you something of his that I think may be of interest to you. It's his new Bible, the Revised Standard Version. It was published shortly before he died. He had it for only the last two weeks of his life. In those two weeks, he marked some passages that must have jumped out at him. Almost all of them deal with something I think he believed we had not given enough serious thought to. I know he marked them for me, but I have a feeling they might speak to you too. I have put bookmarks in place to help you find those passages, except where he left notes in the margin to guide us to the next passage. I'll just leave it right here in case you're interested in having a look at it," she said, placing it on his bed table.

"You are too kind, Mary."

Pause.

"I have appreciated everything you've done for me, you know, even though I haven't been very good at showing it."

"I know," she said, patting him on the arm. "Good night. God bless you! See you in the morning."

When Mary had gone, Steve lay there for a very long while inert, as the events of the day slowly seeped into his consciousness. They tried to serve him some Jello for supper, but he took only a little tea.

He was suddenly very weary. But he reached for Harold's Bible out of sheer loyalty and opened it to the first of several bookmarks.

> *The secret things belong to the Lord our God; but the things that are revealed belong to us and to our children forever.* (Deut. 29:29)

"They belong to us," mused Stephan as he gave way to sleep. "But what have we done with them?"

As he drifted off, he thought of Dr. Engstrom who for some reason was so keen to be there with him in the morning, and of Harold whom he would meet in his marked-up Bible in the days ahead, and of faithful Mary who had come on behalf of Kay just to be with him.

Despite everything, a deep and gracious peace enveloped Steve on his first night in the hospital.

XXX

Very early the next morning, Steve was awakened by a nurse who took his "vitals" and helped him to the bathroom. Once there, Steve was quite able to look after himself. When he emerged, he put on the hospital bathrobe and sat down in the armchair next to the bed. The nurse tucked a blanket around him and made him as comfortable as she could.

A short time later, Dr. Pederson, another physician, and the nurse entered his room.

"Good morning, Dr. Pearson. I hope you had a good night's sleep."

"I did, thank you. The staff here are very kind."

"This is Dr. Wallace, our surgeon. He's had a good look at your X-rays."

"I am afraid the news is not good, Dr. Pearson," began the surgeon. "The X-rays indicate that the cancer has spread out of control, eliminating surgery as an option. We will keep you here for the rest of the day and work out a plan for you to go home tomorrow for as long as possible."

"We can take that approach," added Dr. Pederson, "because Mary Thorsheim has already gone on leave of absence from her teaching, as of today. She insists on being with you for as long as you need her. We will give her some training today and I will be in touch with you in your home on a daily basis. If it gets to be too much for Mary, we will readmit you to the hospital. I am so sorry."

"You are very kind, Doctor. Mary and my wife were like sisters. I welcome her help. That woman is the soul of kindness."

"That she is. I will call in on you later. Remember that if the pain becomes more than you can handle, the nurses know what to do. Do not hesitate to alert them immediately. That's part of what we will train Mary to do for you when you get home."

"Thank you."

"So I'll drive you home in my car in the morning and make sure you have everything that you and Mary will need. She will be there, too."

An hour or so later, Mary showed up in his room with a thermos jug.

"Good morning, Steve."

"Good morning, Mary."

"I brought you some warm seasoned bone broth. Very nutritious and digestible."

"I'll enjoy that, sip by sip. Dr. Pederson told me what you intend to do for me. Mary! That's asking too much of you."

"No, Steve. It is not. I will be there for you for as long as you need me, but not underfoot. I consider it an honor, a God-given privilege."

"Dr. Pederson will be driving me home in the morning. He wants to make sure everything is set up properly. I am grateful you will be there with me, but after he leaves, I would appreciate a few hours home alone before you come. How about coming at 5:00 o'clock?"

"Of course. I understand."

Mary poured some broth into a cup with a straw. Steve slowly sipped at it and it stayed down.

"It's delicious."

At eleven o'clock, the nurse appeared and asked Dr. Pearson if he was prepared to receive a visitor, an elderly gentleman who identified himself as Dr. Engstrom.

"By all means."

With that, Mary gathered up her things and said as she was leaving, "I'll be back later this afternoon. Enjoy your visit."

A moment or two later, Dr. Engstrom appeared in the doorway, walking slowly with the aid of a cane. He stopped at the threshold, raised his head, and said, "Stephan Pearson. Is that really you?"

"Pastor Engstrom. Is that really you?"

A nurse was right behind him with another chair. She set it down facing Steve. He thanked her and motioned for the pastor to be seated. They took a few moments to absorb the marvel that they were actually in one another's presence. Then the pastor expressed his gratitude to Steve for his willingness to see him in the circumstances.

"I don't want to tire you out, so I will come right to the point."

"I'm very glad to see you. There is no hurry."

Dr. Engstrom stroked his chin.

"I remember so well that day when you came to my office on your crutches. I'll never forget my shock when you informed me that Susan Dahl was your Cecilia and that she had written that exquisite anthem just for you. I've heard it several times since then. As I recall, you had a question about what she was trying to tell you in it, and I had a ready answer. I watched you connect with my answer almost instantly. And from that moment on, your life took a dramatic turn in a new direction. We all saw it and celebrated it. I want to talk about that, Steve. But first I really want to learn more about your life, personally and professionally. And then I'll tell you some things about mine."

Dr. Engstrom was still that gentle unintimidating pastor he had been so many years ago. Steve gladly acceded to his request. Over the next half an hour or so, he drew the pastor through forty years of his life, as succinctly and truthfully as he could, right up to the present moment, omitting nothing of significance. The pastor was visibly moved, even shaken, at several points in his story.

When Steve was finished, there was silence for a long moment.

Then Pastor Engstrom spoke.

"Steve, you touched on something at the end there, when you were describing your recent insight from the Lord's Prayer, which directly relates to why I am here, to everything I feel compelled to share with you today. I know that it's too little too late, but still I want to compensate in some small way for what I should have alerted you to forty years ago, but didn't."

"Really?"

"Really. But I need to start from the beginning.

"To be completely frank with you, we got carried away, almost all of us, after World War I over the prospects of turning the world into an earthly paradise in the wake of that horrible war. The rhetoric that sought to justify America's involvement in an essentially European conflict was partly to blame, but we all bought into it. This, we were told by our leaders, was to be 'the war to end all wars.' It was 'the war to make the world safe for democracy.' Who could resist that kind of promise? And so we jumped into the conflict and tipped the balance of the war. When it was all over, as you well know, we were all looking forward to the paradise we thought the world was about to become, minus war and minus tyranny. This was to be *the Christian Century*, as it was already being heralded by leading Protestant theologians all across America. Both politically and theologically, we thought we were on the cusp of a Golden Age. And that, Steve, is the context within which I answered your question that day.

"Now, after you left my office that day, I immediately had qualms about what I had advised you, about its untempered optimism, about assuring you with some passion that this was beyond a doubt God's will for you. You see, I had never entirely lost my traditional theological bearings despite the spirit of the times, and I guess that's why I was feeling so uneasy about the adequacy of what I had just given you as a sufficient guideline for the conduct of the rest of your life. But I buried that feeling. I rationalized it away. I dismissed it.

"Then, in rapid succession, came Lenin and Stalin, Hitler and Mussolini, the Great Depression, World War II, Hiroshima and Nagasaki, and the Cold War. Some Golden Age!

"It was obvious that we had been wrong. But where had we gone off track so badly? It was only after World War II that I came face to face with what I now see was my major miscalculation, *our* major miscalculation, and in the strangest way. After my retirement from Christiania, my wife and I agreed that a term on the mission field would be a good way to put whatever was left in us to good use. So I offered my services to the Church and they assigned me to teach in a Lutheran seminary in Tanganyika for a term of five years.

"Here is what I want to share with you, Steve. During those five years in Africa, I learned more about God, about Satan, and about the actual plight of mankind than in all my years at Christiania. Our missionaries on the field, of course, were all trained in American, German, and Swedish seminaries, and most of them had imbibed the theology of Rudolf Bultmann. He is the one who attributed all supernatural phenomena recorded in Scripture, such as miracles and demonic activity, even the actual physical resurrection of Jesus, to an outdated worldview. His intention was to make Christianity palatable to modern man who, as he saw it, knew very well that miracles can't actually happen. Thus, if modern man is not to dismiss the Gospel out of hand, it has first to be freed from the shackles of the unacceptable prescientific mind-set of the times in which it was written down. Every supernatural phenomenon in the Bible must therefore yield to a purely natural explanation, and only then will its true meaning be revealed, a meaning which is often very different from its apparent meaning in a straightforward reading of the text. From this perspective, even God and Satan are treated more as abstractions than as actual beings. They are seen as ways of visualizing various aspects of purely human conduct for better or for worse. And Jesus, of course, was as much a child of his times as anyone else, according to Bultmann.

"Arriving in Africa with that mind-set, these missionaries were ill prepared for what they encountered. One day I received three of them in my office. They had come to me for advice. To make a long story short, Steve, they had taught the story of Jesus in several remote villages where the people seemed restless but very receptive. But when Baptism was offered, all hell broke loose. These missionaries witnessed phenomena before their very eyes which Bultmann had dismissively explained away—exhibitions of superhuman strength, levitation (this really threw them for a loop), instant personality and vocal changes from gentle to ferocious and back, impossible contortions in facial bone structures, threats against them delivered in perfect English from tribespeople who didn't know a word of English, and on and on. Everyone was affected, it seemed—men, women, and children—entire villages. It was pure bedlam. What should they do?

"Well, not sure myself how to proceed, I began by introducing them in some detail to the findings of Adolf von Harnack, the well-respected nineteenth-century German Lutheran historian, who had described just such phenomena in the life of the early church, especially in Asia Minor. This explained why candidates for Baptism in those days always underwent multiple exorcisms before they were baptized.

"I then asked the missionaries to return at the same time the next day.

"That very day, I paid a visit to the nearby Catholic seminary and located in their library a Church-approved manual describing the steps to follow in minor and major exorcisms. I also discovered that the Catholic priests at that seminary showed no surprise at all at what I shared with them. They had witnessed it often, they said.

"The next day, I gave the manual to the missionaries who lost no time in digesting it whole. They found it reassuring to know that other missionaries were experiencing the same thing. They returned to the villages affected and set about exorcising the entire populace one by one, which proved to be a dramatic reeducation for these missionaries. They were then able to baptize all of them in a most orderly and joyous way, stressing the importance of keeping Jesus at the center of their new lives to avoid falling back under the old tyranny of the devil. These villages were thereby transformed from places dominated by cruelty and fear into oases of peace, or, as von Harnack expressed it in relation to the communities in Asia Minor, from haunts of darkness to domains of light. One of the missionaries wrote a full account of these happenings which was published in our church's award-winning missionary journal.

"Since then, Steve, I have become much more aware of the malice of the evil one, more aware, as you pointed out from the Lord's Prayer, that our whole earthly existence is caught up between Satan's hatred for God and us, and God's love for us which frees us from bondage to the evil one. Where was this perspective in 1920? My experience in Africa catapulted it for me out of theory into fact, out of past history into present reality.

"And it's not just found in the Lord's Prayer. We have ignored, explained away, or trashed everything the New Testament teaches us so clearly about the enemy we are up against, the enemy Jesus faced from the moment of His birth until He harrowed hell between His death and His resurrection, about the one Jesus called a liar from the beginning, a murderer, the prince of this world, the great deceiver. We have had a far too superficial and tame notion of evil and as a result, we have laid ourselves wide open to it, and to the keen disappointment we experience when all our plans and ideals fall apart and we can't figure out why.

"And, you know, Steve, I knew better when I sent you off with only a partial vision of the 'ground' you were being called to fall into. I knew my Bible, but I chose to ignore what I didn't want to see. I was so carried away by the spirit of the times that I repressed the Holy Spirit. That's the only way I can explain it.

"So I have come to ask for your forgiveness. I don't know how much of the pain in your life can be laid at the door of the gravely defective advice I gave you, but I am sure that far too much of it can be. Please forgive me for all the disillusionment and grief I set you up for as the pastor you trusted."

The pleading in his eyes was almost desperate.

"O my dear pastor. Of course I forgive you, if there's anything to be forgiven. None of us paid much attention to the enemy back then. Who of us was really listening when Jesus told us, in reference to a world created good and then messed up, that 'an enemy hath done this'? There are never enough Cecilias around, intensely in love with Jesus and for that very reason intensely aware of the presence and workings of the evil one. She was radiant with beauty because she knew her Jesus was the winner, but oh, so easily heartbroken by any sign of Satan's cruelty to man or beast. She saw what I should have seen. It's not your fault, Pastor. I am the one who knew her and loved her. Believe me, when I was working on the bomb, I could hardly bring myself to think of her. I knew she was agonizing over what I was doing. It became perfectly obvious to me that I hadn't fallen into the right ground or died for the right cause, and that far from making her happy, I was torturing her. As we scientists maneuvered the elements of those bombs into place, and as the day of their deployment drew ever nearer, there were moments when I myself was perfectly aware that I was nothing but a pawn in the hands of the evil one. And I knew she was aware of it too! Nevertheless, I kept right at it.

"And when I think of how misguided I was a few years later in my unquestioned assumption that the peacetime uses of scientific developments would always benefit mankind, and that now at last I had fallen into the right ground, how that must have pained her, too! By making this assumption and embracing it so blindly, what was I really doing? I was justifying my own continuing love of science for its own sake, and I was paying no attention to what human nature and Satan's malice might do with it."

"Steve, both of us are on the threshold between this world and the next. I can assure you, being a theologian is not a safer path than being a scientist.

"But there is one more thing I want to share with you before leaving. Do you know anything about what happened at Fatima in 1917?"

"Not much. When I was in Boston attending the beautiful Catholic church just down the road from my house, somebody organized a pilgrimage to go there, I think. Something about Mary appearing to three children."

"Right. Well, when we were in Africa one of the faculty members at the Catholic seminary thrust a new book entitled *Our Lady of Fatima* into my hands and urged me to read it. When I saw that it was written by William Thomas Walsh, my interest perked up. Everything of his that I had read up to that point had been of the highest quality. Well, getting into that book really shook me up, but it made all kinds of sense. Let me say to you that I have no question about the authenticity of what happened at Fatima. It's hard to question it after God confirmed it through the dramatic miracle of the sun on the date foretold by Mary through the children months in advance and witnessed by some 70,000 people, believers and scoffers alike. Everything Mary said and did during those six apparitions is of the highest interest and importance, but the piece I especially want to share with you, Steve, is this: in 1920, you and I were dazzled by the dream of progress and wiping out evil. In 1917, Mary spelled out in unmistakable detail what the twentieth century would bring if mankind returned to God, and in equal detail what it would bring if mankind did not. And of course it did not, with exactly the results she had foreseen, including the rise of Russia by name and the horrors of World War II. But looking further down the road, she also announced that *in the end* what she called her 'Immaculate Heart' would triumph and there would be an 'Era of Peace' before the close of the age. To make way for this 'Era of Peace,' Satan's direct influence on the human race would be eliminated for a time, she said, and the human race itself would undergo a purging through chastisements, more or less severe, depending on our collective obedience or disobedience. So you see, the era we thought we were building in God's name will come about not on our terms at all, but on His terms, and not at all because of our initiative, but because of His."

"That does make all kinds of sense, Pastor. I'll have to let it soak in. You've given me a lot to think about."

With that, Dr. Engstrom shifted about in his chair, found his cane, and was about to stand up.

"I can't thank you enough for coming, Pastor. Would you please bless me before you go?"

Dr. Engstrom struggled to his feet, placed both hands on Stephan Pearson's head, and said very slowly:

"The Lord bless thee, and keep thee.

"The Lord make His face shine upon thee, and be gracious unto thee.

"The Lord lift up His countenance upon thee, and give thee peace.

"In the Name of the Father, and of the Son, and of the Holy Ghost.

"Amen."

Both men were too moved to say anything more. Steve looked up and smiled into the old man's squinting eyes.

Dr. Engstrom nodded, turned around, found his cane, and walked slowly to the door. There he stopped, twisted his head and shoulders around, and said, "Good-bye, Stephan Pearson."

"Good-bye, Pastor Engstrom."

XXXI

At 9:30 a.m. the following morning, Dr. Pederson's car pulled into the driveway of the Pearson home. With Steve clinging to the physician's arm, they entered the house through the back door. Steve found it very welcoming. Mary had cleaned and tidied it up in his absence. They made their way through the kitchen into the living room where with the help of the doctor, Steve installed himself in the big reclining chair which Kay had bought for him a few years earlier. Dr. Pederson covered his lower body and legs with a blanket. Then, on a side table to the right, he left two thermos jugs, one full of icy Seven-Up, the other of warm broth from Mary. He also set the telephone on the side table. He placed Steve's opened briefcase containing Harold's Bible on the floor to the left of the chair along with a hospital jar with a lid on it in case he had to use it. Mary had thoughtfully placed on the coffee table in front of the loveseat a wooden lap tray mounted on a cushion which Harold must have used in his last weeks. The physician put it on Steve's lap where it made a comfortable smooth surface for reading or writing or eating.

"Mary said you can phone her at home any time if you need anything. She'll be here by 5:00 p.m. If you need to take the edge off your pain, you may take as many of these pills as required, with liquid," he added, setting a small bottle on the side table next to the Seven-Up.

"Thank you, Doctor. I so appreciate your kindness. I think I have everything I need right here for the whole day. Would you please get

Harold's Bible and the writing tablet from my briefcase and set them on my lap tray before you go?"

"Certainly."

With that, he placed his hand on Steve's forehead.

"No fever. You should be all right. Have a good day."

"I'm sure I will. Good-bye, and thanks again."

As soon as he was by himself, Steve opened the Bible to the second marker. It was inserted at the beginning of the Book of Job. Chapters One, Two, and Three were highlighted in their entirety. Steve read through them very deliberately.

First he read of Job's blameless character, of his large and happy family, and of his great wealth. Then he read of a dialog between the Lord and Satan in which a wager was made over Job. Satan claimed that Job's faith was dependent on God's favoring him with prosperity and good fortune. The Lord gave Satan the power to take away everything except Job's life. As a result, in a single day Job lost everything—herds, servants, and family. But he did not lose his faith.

In all this Job did not sin or charge God with wrong.

Next, Steve read about Satan's response to this failure on his part. He asked for permission to torture Job's body, certain that this would make him curse God to his face. God gave him that power. *"Only spare his life."* Satan immediately went forth and afflicted Job with loathsome sores from head to toe. His wife counseled him to *curse God and die*, but *Job did not sin with his lips.*

"This reminds me of something I recall from my Boston days," Steve said to himself out loud. "Something about Pope Leo XIII falling into a trance just after celebrating Mass and witnessing a dialog between Jesus and Satan in which Satan claimed he could destroy the Church and Jesus gave him a century to try. That, we were told, was why Pope Leo wrote the St. Michael Prayer and commanded it to be prayed by all the faithful at the conclusion of every Mass. How did it go again?...

> St. Michael the Archangel, defend us in battle. Be our protection against the wickedness and snares of the devil. May God rebuke him, we humbly pray. And do thou, O Prince of the heavenly host, by the power of God, cast into hell Satan and all the evil spirits who prowl throughout the world seeking the ruin of souls.

"I must not have taken that prayer very seriously back then…."

Steve reached for a sip of Seven-Up and went on.

At this point, three of Job's friends joined forces *to come to condole with him and comfort him.* His misery was so great that it left them sitting beside him speechless for an entire week.

> After this Job opened his mouth and cursed the day of his birth, bemoaning the fact that he hadn't died in the womb.

In the next pages, Harold's markings highlighted Job's friends' insistence that some great sin had to be at the root of his misfortune, and that the only way for him to get better was to own up to it. This leads Job to protest his innocence with increasing vigor until he issues a challenge to God Himself to make sense of the cruel disasters that have befallen him for no reason, defying all logic. He wavers between his confidence that God will one day exonerate him and his despair at the prospect that it won't ever happen. It all comes to a head when Job protests his total innocence and his utter perplexity that God has allowed these calamities to befall him. Then along comes a young man who upbraids both Job and his three friends on the basis that God doesn't have to answer to any of them, but that if He did choose to answer them, it would silence them all.

And then, circled in red ink, these words:

> Then the Lord **answered** Job out of the whirlwind.

Steve read no further. Those words took his breath away….

Whatever the Lord may have gone on to say in His answer, the fact that He actually spoke to Job that He reached out to him at all, was what counted. It meant that Job was not abandoned to a meaningless fate, that there was an answer somewhere deep in the counsels of God! And this was all Job needed to know! It is all anyone needs to know! And it led Job to his final confession:

> Therefore I have uttered what I did not understand,
> things too wonderful for me which I did not know....
> I had heard of thee by the hearing of the ear,
> **but now my eye sees thee;**
> therefore I despise myself,
> and repent in dust and ashes.

"O Jesus! That could be me!"

Steve closed the Bible, folded his hands over it, and laid his forehead on his hands, rocking back and forth in silent wonder.

> Then the Lord answered Job out of the whirlwind.

Satan's game was over.

XXXII

It was an hour later, or perhaps two, when Steve woke up, his head still resting on his hands folded over the Bible. He straightened up, rubbed his eyes, and took a few sips of Mary's broth. Opening Harold's Bible to the next marker, he noted that he was now in the New Testament. Harold had highlighted the first eleven verses of Chapter Four of Matthew's Gospel, the account of the devil's stealthy attempt to co-opt Jesus at the very start of His public ministry. Steve read the passage attentively.

"What was Satan's strategy here?" he asked himself when he had finished reading. "In a word, to sever Jesus from His human nature so that He could not fulfill His mission. How? By enticing Him to use His power as the Son of God to serve Himself, not the Will of God. That would have put Jesus on Satan's side. That same strategy had worked with Eve. But now the devil has thrown everything he had at Jesus and failed. And then what?"

> Then the devil left him, and behold, angels came and ministered to Him.

Steve sat there pondering how easy it would have been for the average person to fall into Satan's trap. His enticements were perfectly in line with the cravings of fallen human nature: appetite, personal popularity, power—all self-serving. It reminded him of "the good life" as defined by most of the people they had met at Reedville. He sat there shaking his head.

Jesus knew what we needed to be delivered from, and He stuck to His guns. Those angels must have been a welcome sight when it was all over.

The next marker took him to Matthew sixteen, where only verse twenty-three was highlighted.

> But He turned and said to Peter, "Get behind me, Satan! You are a hindrance to Me; for you are not on the side of God, but of men."

Exactly! Apart from Jesus' influence, direct or indirect, human beings and Satan think alike! They're on the same side! The Lord's Prayer is chockfull of stuff that can put us on Jesus' side in this battle zone, but you have to build your whole life around it. Jesus really means business in the few words of this prayer. They're our defense against the evil one. Why didn't I see this sooner?

And Steve's mind wandered off into a tangle of events and choices that had taken him in the wrong direction over the years.

The next marker reinforced this one. It led him to John 8:44–45.

> You are of your father, the devil, and your will is to do your father's desires. He was a murderer from the beginning, and has nothing to do with the truth, because there is no truth in him. When he lies, he speaks according to his nature, for he is a liar and the father of lies. But because I tell the truth, you do not believe Me.

So here also Jesus says that the devil and the human race are on the same wavelength, that doing Satan's will comes naturally to us in our fallen state. I suppose that's what's meant by "original sin." He hooks us only to murder us, using clever lies and deceptions to suck us in. They become our 'truth,' and everything Jesus says which really is Truth, we reject because it doesn't match the devil's lies. Without God's help, we'll choose the murderer over the Life-Giver every time.

The last marker led him to John 14:30–31.

> I will no longer talk much with you, for *the ruler of this world* is coming. He has no power over Me; but I do as the Father has commanded Me, so that the world may know that I love the Father.

That is strong language.

A marginal note from Harold cross-referenced I John 5:19.

> We know that we are of God, and the whole world is in the power of the evil one.

That is even stronger language, and it sets us up for a lifetime of constant conflict if we are of God.

Another marginal note led him to I John 3:8b.

> The reason the Son of God appeared was to destroy the works of the devil.

That's the whole reason He came? Uffda!

From there to Luke 10:17–20.

> The seventy returned with joy, saying, "Lord, even the demons are subject to us in Your name!" And He said to them, "I saw Satan fall like lightning from heaven. Behold, I have given you authority to tread upon serpents and scorpions, and over all the power of the enemy; and nothing shall hurt you. Nevertheless do not rejoice in this, that the spirits are subject to you; but rejoice that your names are written in heaven."

And then straight to John 12:31–32.

> "Now is the judgment of this world, now shall *the ruler of this world* be cast out; and I, when I am lifted up from the earth, will draw all men to Myself."

So, even though the devil may win many battles, he has already lost the war. How many times have we heard in our Gospel readings about the demons' fear of Jesus and His absolute power over them? The demons are even forced to submit to the disciples! The Gospels are filled with Jesus' confrontation with Satan. And what about Pastor Engstrom's missionaries?

Harold's note now led him to Mark 16 where the first half of verse 17 and all of verse 20 were underscored.

> "And these signs will accompany those who believe: in My name they will cast out demons...." And they went forth and preached everywhere, while the Lord worked with them and confirmed the message by the signs that attended it.

Isn't that exactly what happened in the early church in Asia Minor, and in Tanganyika in our own time, and who knows where else?

So it seems to me on the basis of the evidence here that Satan and his hosts can control individuals and societies in two ways—by doing everything he can to get people to ignore Jesus and live by their own instincts which are the same as his, and by harassing and possessing and afflicting people directly for the sheer pleasure of torturing them and driving them and their loved ones to despair. Jesus not only exposes and defeats Satan in both of these guises, but He expects us as believers to be doing it too. I would say that the Beatitudes and the Sermon on the Mount give us the "new normal" for life in this sinful world for anyone living by faith under our heavenly Father, delivered from bondage to our infernal father. When I am done following Harold's trail, I will have to soak up everything I can find in Matthew Chapters 5, 6, and 7. Kay loved it so much, and she lived it.

Steve's eyes watered up at the memory of Kay sitting with him at the kitchen table. It had always made him happy when she took the lead in those few minutes of quiet devotion and prayer they spent together there each evening.

From Mark 16, Harold took Steve to two verses from Paul's Second Letter to the Corinthians (11:13–14).

> For such men are false apostles, deceitful workmen, disguising themselves as apostles of Christ. And no wonder, for even Satan disguises himself as an angel of light.

"Eve thought she was being enlightened by him, and she plunged into darkness. I did too."

From there Steve was led straight into Paul's Letter to the Ephesians, Chapter Six, verses ten through seventeen. He recognized the passage instantly. It was Paul's "Manual for Survival" in the battle for souls on earth between God and the devil. He read it slowly, reflecting on it verse by verse, as he and Kay had often done with similar passages over the years.

> Finally, be strong in the Lord and in the strength of His might.

A call to avoid from the outset the disaster of relying on our own strength.

> Put on the whole armor of God, that you may be able to stand against the wiles of the devil.

Without the whole armor of God, we would never be able to stand before the wiles of the devil. He will find any chink in our armor, Paul says, any unprotected spot, and move right in on us. Of course, if we are oblivious to the wiles of the devil, we won't pay any attention to God's armor. That explains a lot....

> For we are not contending against flesh and blood, but against the principalities, against the powers, against the world rulers of this present darkness, against the spiritual hosts of wickedness in the heavenly places.

Uffda.... Paul really lays it on thick. These enemies are nothing to be trifled with. They operate behind the scenes, manipulating "flesh and blood" to serve their treacherous purposes. They raise up a Stalin and a Hitler whose capacity for evil knows no bounds and they turn them into pathetic stooges of Satan. Men like them may act like gods, but Satan is pulling their strings.

> Therefore take the whole armor of God, that you may be able to withstand in the evil day, and having done all, to stand.

"Therefore!" he says. That is, making a correct estimate of the strength of the enemy and of the certainty that he will have his day, take what God is giving you to survive his assaults if you want to find yourself still on your feet at the end of the evil day.

> Stand therefore, having girded your loins with truth,

We've already seen that this is a basic difference between God and the devil, between the Father of Truth and the father of lies. I can see why God's truth goes on first, right up against my skin. Everything else builds on that.

> and having put on the breastplate of righteousness,

"That would be my commitment to making the Sermon on the Mount my whole way of life."

> and having shod your feet with the preparation of the gospel of peace;

That means that wherever we go, we will live and spread the gift of peace with God through Jesus in a world which has made its peace with Satan. If we don't, we've already fallen prey to the enemy.

> above all taking the shield of faith, with which you can quench all the flaming darts of the evil one.

Unshakable faith in God disarms the devil completely, as we saw in the failed attempts of his flaming darts to kill Jesus spiritually in the wilderness.

> And take the helmet of salvation

To protect your head. That's the helmet that makes victors out of martyrs.

> and the sword of the Spirit, which is the word of God.

Everything else about God's armor is there to protect us. The Word of God defeats the enemy, as we also just saw in Jesus' wilderness temptation by the devil. Faithfulness to God's Word in a fickle world full of words is the only weapon we have and the only one we need.

From there Harold directed him to 1 Peter 5:8–9.

> Be sober, be watchful. Your adversary the devil prowls around like a roaring lion, seeking someone to devour. Resist him, firm in your faith, knowing that the same experience of suffering is required of your brotherhood throughout the world.

Don't let your guard down, Peter is saying, because if you do, you haven't got a chance. The devil will swallow you whole. And he did. More than once. But Jesus kept fishing me back out of his gullet, and He still is. I am sure that the prayers of my angels in Heaven have something to do with this.... Only weeks ago I had all but given up hope.

The marginal note here said: "Now to the 'Revelation to John.' Read the marked passages aloud in rapid succession. Then ponder them all together."

Steve turned to the last book in the Bible. These were the passages marked by Harold:

> "Do not fear what you are about to suffer. Behold, the devil is about to throw some of you into prison, that you may be tested, and for ten days you will have tribulation. Be faithful unto death, and I will give you the crown of life." (2:10)

> "I know where you dwell, where Satan's throne is; you hold fast My name and have not denied My faith…." (2:13)

And a great portent appeared in heaven, a woman clothed with the sun, with the moon under her feet, and on her head a crown of twelve stars; she was with child and she cried out in her pangs of birth, in anguish for delivery. And another portent appeared in heaven; behold, a great red dragon, with seven heads and ten horns, and seven diadems upon his heads. His tail swept down a third of the stars of heaven, and cast them to the earth. And the dragon stood before the woman who was about to bear a child, that he might devour the child when she brought it forth; she brought forth a male child, one who is to rule all the nations with a rod of iron, but her child was caught up to God and to His throne, and the woman fled into the wilderness, where she has a place prepared by God, in which to be nourished for one thousand two hundred and sixty days.

Now war arose in heaven, Michael and his angels fighting against the dragon; and the dragon and his angels fought, but they were defeated and there was no longer any place for them in heaven. And the great dragon was thrown down, that ancient serpent, who is called the Devil and Satan, the deceiver of the whole world—he was thrown down to the earth, and his angels were thrown down with him. And I heard a loud voice in heaven, saying, "Now the salvation and the power and the kingdom of our God and the authority of His Christ have come, for the accuser of our brethren has been thrown down, who accuses them day and night before our God. And they have conquered him by the blood of the Lamb and by the word of their testimony, for they loved not their lives even unto death. Rejoice then, O heaven and you that dwell therein! But woe to you, O earth and sea, for the dragon has come down to you in great wrath, because he knows his time is short!

And when the dragon saw that he had been thrown down to the earth, he pursued the woman who had borne the male child.... Then the dragon was angry with the woman, and went off to make war on the rest of her offspring, on those who keep the commandments of God and bear testimony to Jesus. (12:1–13,17)

> Then I saw an angel coming down from heaven, holding in his hand the key of the bottomless pit and a great chain. And he seized the dragon, that ancient serpent, who is the Devil and Satan, and bound him for a thousand years, and threw him into the pit, and shut it and sealed it over him, that he should deceive the nations no more, till the thousand years were ended. After that he must be loosed for a little while. (20:1–3)

Hmmmm. Pastor Engstrom says that at Fatima Mary proclaimed that there will be an era of peace before the close of the age. Such a thing could never happen if the devil were still on the loose. But the conditions described here make room for it.

> And when the thousand years are ended, Satan will be loosed from his prison and will come out to deceive the nations.... And the devil who had deceived them was thrown into the lake of fire and brimstone where the beast and the false prophet were, and they will be tormented day and night for ever and ever. (20:7–8a,10)

> Then I saw a new heaven and a new earth; for the first heaven and the first earth had passed away, and the sea was no more. And I saw the holy city, new Jerusalem, coming down out of heaven from God, prepared as a bride adorned for her husband; and I heard a great voice from the throne saying, "Behold, the dwelling of God is with men. He will dwell with them, and they shall be His people, and God Himself will be with them; He will wipe away every tear from their eyes, and death shall be no more, neither shall there be mourning nor crying nor pain anymore, for the former things have passed away."

> And He who sat upon the throne said, "Behold, I make all things new." Also He said, "Write this, for these words are trustworthy and true." And He said to me, "It is done! I am the Alpha and the Omega, the beginning and the end. To the thirsty I will give water without price from the fountain of the water of life. He who conquers shall have this heritage, and I will be his God and he shall be My son...." (21:1–7)

Steve slowly closed the Bible. His mind was reeling. Suddenly he felt very very tired. He folded his hands over the Bible and once again laid his forehead on them. And that is how Mary found him sound asleep when she arrived at 4:45.

XXXIII

How long he had been sleeping she did not know. She saw that he had sipped some of the broth and most of the Seven-Up and had made use of his hospital bottle which she emptied and washed out. He stirred as she set it down next to his chair. He opened his eyes and sat up.

"I'm glad you were able to sleep."

"I was also able to follow Harold's trail through the Bible. What a ride that was! He's right. How could we think we were on the right track by ignoring the evil one when Jesus and the apostles were facing off against him and his minions constantly. And do you know what?"

"What?"

"That was Pastor Engstrom's message too, based on his almost direct experiences in Africa. It's why he was so eager to see me. He wanted to fill me in on what he considered a huge gap in the picture of my divine vocation which he gave me in 1920."

"So now you've heard it both from Pastor Engstrom and from Harold. Sounds like the hand of God at work. Do you have any idea where to go from here?"

"Well, this is not totally new to me. In my Reedville address I was forced, almost in spite of myself, to reckon with the evil one. And more recently the Lord's Prayer struck me in the same way. Now, with Pastor Engstrom's empirical evidence and Harold's massive scriptural evidence, I'll have to go somewhere from here. Right now I feel a very strong urge to go to chapel tomorrow morning. It's the last one this week and probably my last one ever. Will you help me get there?"

"Of course, Steve. We can work that out."

"May God show me how to make my last days count for Him somehow when so many of my other days counted against Him."

"We'll leave early and get there before classes dismiss."

With that, Mary helped him out of his chair and into the bathroom where he was able to manage on his own. His legs felt like rubber and the stabbing pains in his abdomen were just tolerable.

"I'll spend the night in the recliner, Mary," he said before she shut the bathroom door behind him. "I've done that a lot lately."

While he was in the bathroom, she straightened out his chair and furnished it with an additional blanket and a pillow. Then she waited by the bathroom door to help him back into the recliner. Once he was settled into it, she heated up some broth, putting more salt in it this time at his request, and sat with him until he had consumed all the broth that his body could handle, along with two pills for pain. It was getting dark.

"I want to be alert for tomorrow, Mary. Right now I am feeling quite depleted. Would you mind if I lean back and go to sleep? It won't bother me at all to have you moving around in the house. In fact, it will be a comfort."

"Sleep is a good idea. I'll put a school bell here on the side table. If you need me at any time, just ring it and I'll come. I'll move the floor lamp over on the left side of the chair where you can turn it on more easily if you need some light."

"Thank you, Mary. And will you also put the writing tablet and some pens on the side table within reach? I might just need them, too. And then let's pray the Lord's Prayer before you turn out the light."

Steve's voice tapered off mid-prayer. His "deliver us from the evil one" was the barest of whispers.

XXXIV

At some point in the night, Steve woke up, turned on the lamp, and jotted down notes on the tablet. They chronicled his odyssey through Harold's Bible and provided me with much of the contents of Chapter XXXII. There were also some jottings about Pastor Engstrom's visit which I fleshed out later in an interview with him. He started writing about something else, but his scrawl trailed off mid-sentence as drowsiness overcame him. Mary had heard him fidgeting. Noting that he had fallen back to sleep, she gently leaned him backwards into the recliner and lowered it, placing the contents of his lap on the side table. She turned off the lamp and went back to bed.

At 8:30 the next morning, the sun shining through the east windows reached Steve's eyes and woke him up. For a few minutes, he lay there bathing in its warmth. He soaked it up and for the first time since his double loss, he actually felt glad to be alive.

Mary, quick to hear the slightest rustle, tiptoed to the archway where she stopped and took in the scene before her—her dying friend reclining in the fresh morning light, a smile as deep and broad as happiness itself transforming his wasted face. Without turning his head, Steve sensed Mary's presence.

"Good morning, Mary," he said with some conviction.

"Good morning, Steve. How are you feeling this morning?"

"A little like those two disciples must have felt at the moment when Jesus broke the bread and their eyes were opened."

"Really!"

"And I'm about as eager to get to chapel this morning as they were to get back up to Jerusalem."

"That's shouldn't be a problem. We have an hour before we have to leave."

An hour later, Dr. Pearson's old DeSoto pulled up to the curb in front of the chapel. Mary got out of the car on the driver's side and came around to help Steve get out on the curb side. Leaning on her arm, he inched along the sidewalk to the steps where, grasping the handrail with both hands, he slowly pulled himself to the top. Once there, he grabbed the latch on the heavy door and hung on, wincing in pain. Taking a deep breath, he nodded at Mary who opened the door. From the narthex, it was a simple matter to reach a short pew along the wall in the left rear corner of the spacious nave. He eased himself into it and sat down. Mary leaned over to him as though asking a question. He nodded in return and smiled back at her. Then she went up the nearby steps to a seat in the balcony.

By now, students were trickling into the balcony. Dr. Halverson, the concert choir's renowned director and son of the choir's founder, was surveying these students. This would be a treat. The concert choir rarely sang for chapel.

XXXV

The bell rang, dismissing classes. Within minutes, students were pouring down the aisles. An usher, one of Dr. Pearson's students, noticed him sitting in the corner pew and gave him a bulletin, displaying no little astonishment as he did so. The bulletin was plain, a folded sheet of paper. There was a bold woodcut of a crucifix on the front, with Mary and John standing at the foot of the cross. When bulletins were distributed at chapel, it usually meant that there would be no sermon or meditation. Led by the campus pastor, the focus would rather be on prayer by word and music and on the Word of God, with periods of silence interspersed.

Now soft strains of organ music were rippling through the air and a hush descended on the assembly. Steve recognized the full-throated serenity of Bach's chorale arrangement of "*Ach Gott, vom Himmel sieh herab*."

The pastor stepped behind the lectern and intoned the Invocation: "In the name of the Father, and of the Son, and of the Holy Ghost."

"Amen."

"The theme interwoven into all parts of our worship this morning is dedication, and specifically the self-dedication to God asked of all who follow Jesus. We begin with Hymn 484, all stanzas."

Quietly the organ introduction rose out of the choir loft. This was going to be a prayerful service, all right, conducive of private devotions in the company of fellow disciples. Stephan Pearson's heart was in tune for a service like this. It felt about to burst from the pressure of its pent-up emotions.

Jesus, my Lord, my God, my all,
Hear me, blest Saviour, when I call;
Hear me, and from thy dwelling place
Pour down the riches of thy grace.
Jesus, my Lord, I thee adore,
O make me love thee more and more,

Jesus, too late I thee have sought;
How can I love thee as I ought?
And how extol thy matchless fame,
The glorious beauty of thy name?
Jesus, my Lord, I thee adore,
O make me love thee more and more.

Jesus, what didst thou find in me
That thou hast dealt so lovingly?
How great the joy that thou hast brought,
So far exceeding hope or thought!
Jesus, my Lord, I thee adore,
O make me love thee more and more.

Jesus, of thee shall be my song,
To thee my heart and soul belong;
All that I have or am is thine,
And thou, blest Saviour, thou art mine.
Jesus, my Lord, I thee adore,
O make me love thee more and more. Amen.

Cecilia loved that hymn. She used to hum it all the time.

The congregation rose and opened their bulletins to recite excerpts from Psalm 51. Steve knew the Psalm by heart, but never had he prayed it so fervently as now.

Have mercy upon me, O God,
according to thy lovingkindness;
according to the multitude of thy tender mercies,
blot out my transgressions.
Wash me thoroughly from mine iniquity:
and cleanse me from my sin.
For I acknowledge my transgressions:
and my sin is ever before me.
Against thee, thee only, have I sinned,
and done this evil in thy sight:
that thou mightest be justified when thou speakest,
and be clear when thou judgest.
Behold, I was shapen in iniquity:
and in sin did my mother conceive me.
Behold, thou desirest truth in the inward parts:
and in the hidden part thou shalt make me to know wisdom.
Purge me with hyssop, and I shall be clean:
wash me, and I shall be whiter than snow.
Make me to hear joy and gladness:
that the bones which thou hast broken may rejoice.
Hide thy face from my sins:
and blot out all mine iniquities.
Create in me a clean heart, O God:
and renew a right spirit within me.
Cast me not away from thy presence:
and take not thy Holy Spirit from me.
Restore unto me the joy of thy salvation:
and uphold me with thy free spirit.
Then will I teach transgressors thy ways:
and sinners will be converted unto thee.
Deliver me from bloodguiltiness, O God, thou God of my salvation:
and my tongue shall sing aloud of thy righteousness.
O Lord, open thou my lips:

and my mouth shall show forth thy praise.
The sacrifices of God are a broken spirit:
a broken and a contrite heart, O God, thou wilt not despise.
Glory be to the Father, and to the Son, and to the Holy Ghost:
as it was in the beginning, is now, and ever shall be,
world without end. Amen.

"O God, that's me! That's me! David fell for Bathsheba and killed Uriah. I fell for theoretical physics and killed two cities."

In the silence that followed the Psalm, Steve heard the clear tone of a pitch pipe blowing an "F." Then, like a thunderbolt:

VERILY, VERILY, I SAY UNTO YOU....

"O my God, you can't be doing this to me!" he gasped.

EXCEPT A GRAIN OF WHEAT FALL INTO THE GROUND AND DIE ... AND DIE, IT ABIDETH ALONE....

"It's too much, dear Lord, too much...."

BUT IF IT DIE, IT BRINGETH FORTH MUCH FRUIT....

"You're speaking to <u>me</u> out of the whirlwind, Lord! This is my whirlwind!"

EXCEPT A GRAIN OF WHEAT FALL INTO THE GROUND AND DIE.... AND DIE ... AND DIE.

Dr. Stephan Pearson collapsed forward in the pew as the last tones faded away. His head was in his hands. His shoulders were silently heaving up and down.

It's too much, Lord.... Too much....
How can I love thee as I ought?

He heard only bits and pieces of the rest of the service—his mind and heart were too full. The readings were all about the new creation we are in Christ, and the absolute priority of being reconciled to God before undertaking to do anything else in life. All of this now made enormous sense to him. It was either Christ or Satan, the Father in Heaven or the evil one. The failure to be reconciled to the Father, to the point of being a new creation in Christ, could have only one possible consequence, despite our best intentions. And Steve had lived it.

Floods of tears streamed down his cheeks.

"That's what you were trying to tell me, my angel Cecilia. I wasn't listening very well. But I'm with you now. It's taken such a long time, but our good and merciful God has finally brought me to where you've always been."

The pastor then offered a prayer of dedication and, glancing at his watch, announced the closing hymn:

"Number 463, Second Tune, first four stanzas."

Jesus, thou Joy of loving hearts,
Thou Fount of life, thou Light of men,
From the best bliss that earth imparts
We turn unfilled to thee again.

Thy truth unchanged hath ever stood;
Thou savest those that on thee call;
To them that seek thee thou art good,
To them that find thee, all in all.

We taste thee, O thou living Bread,
And long to feast upon thee still;
We drink of thee, the Fountainhead,
And thirst our souls from thee to fill.

Our restless spirits yearn for thee,
Where'er our changeful lot is cast;

Glad, when thy gracious smile we see,
Blest, when our faith can hold thee fast. Amen.

The chapel emptied quickly as students hurried off to their next class. When Mary descended the stairs from the balcony, she found Steve still rapt in prayer. She left him like that until he opened his eyes, looked up at her, and smiled.

"Well," he said. "I know what I have to do now."

As soon as Mary had delivered him home and settled him in his chair, he reached for the tablet and a pen. Out of the overflow of his heart flooded torrents of memories and insights covering the pivotal events of his life, mostly in chronological order. He was driven by the urgent need to use every fleeting moment remaining to him to respond to the question: "How can I love thee as I ought?" Filling the sheets of several tablets with words, sometimes barely decipherable, he was impelled to write in fits of energy from one relapse to the next over the entire weekend. When he felt his strength swiftly ebbing away and his goal only partially achieved, he confided his plight to Mary.

"How about contacting Pastor Mork? You've known each other for years. Wouldn't he be in a position to collate what you are writing and fill in some details?"

Steve was silent for a moment, a bit taken aback by her suggestion.

"Mary, I think you may just have given me the key."

He took a clean sheet of paper and wrote on it in large wobbly letters the contents of the telegram quoted in the Prologue.

And that is where I entered the picture.

When I arrived the next morning, the floor of the living room around Steve's chair was littered with several scribbled-on tablets and numerous loose sheets of paper. Mary had hesitated to disturb them, supposing they were in some kind of order. Steve was by now too weak to write, but my presence inspired him to unfold, often in amazing detail, the contours of the story you have just read. I assured him that, as I had already fulfilled the conditions of my sabbatical with several months remaining in it, I was in an ideal position to devote myself to telling his story.

"If you can only make something of all this, Paul, that may help someone to avoid the mistakes I made, by implementing earlier in life what it's taken me until now to learn...."

Two, three, four days passed. Pain did not seem to be a major issue as long as Steve did not have to move about. His periods of wakefulness and lucidity grew shorter and fewer. He was able to take no nourishment, and very little water. This gave me time to expand the sketchy notes I had scribbled down as he was talking. It also gave me the opportunity to get better acquainted with his one daily visitor, Rolph Eriksen, whose hour-long visits were greatly appreciated by all of us.

XXXVI

Stephan Pearson's last lucid moment came as a surprise on the evening of the fifth day. Rolph Eriksen, whom I had urged to stay longer that day, was alone with me in the living room at the time. Mary was in the kitchen. Although Steve had muttered incoherently at wide intervals throughout the day, he had shown no signs of consciousness since noon. We were not expecting to see any now.

But all at once he sighed loudly. We shot to his side. His eyes opened, big as saucers, peering straight up through the dim light of the room, as though there were no ceiling.

His breathing quickened. His lips quivered. His eyes fairly burst from their sockets. His head snapped up off the pillow.

"Look!

"Look!!!

"O my dear God!

"There they are!

"There they are!"

Awestruck, he held that position, eyes aflame, mouth agape, for several seconds.

Then his head fell back onto the pillow, his eyes closed. And with one deep final breath, he was gone.

Mary had joined us. We stood around him in silence. No one dared to move.

Then quietly I went over to the window and drew back the curtains. The setting sun dazzled my eyes. I stepped to one side, out of its direct light. From that angle, the bursting buds on the lilacs just outside the window looked like tiny flames of fire about to explode into life.

"Mary! Rolph! Look at this!"

Epilogue

This epilogue consists of the unedited contents of a few sheets of paper I found on the floor that didn't fit into the story line. Here Steve seems to have attempted to express succinctly and clearly what he believed he had learned in the last days of his life and what he most wanted to share.

1.

When Jesus says, "Verily, verily, I say unto you, except a grain of wheat fall into the ground and die, it abideth alone; but if it die, it bringeth forth much fruit," (12:24) He is stating a principle which can be applied in a general way to many situations, as I will illustrate from my own life. But in its context, it is obvious that He is applying it to Himself, to His own willingness to die to free the world from Satan, its present illegitimate ruler, and to draw everyone back to Himself. (John 12:31–32) It is also clear that anyone who claims to be His disciple must have the same end in view if his or her "death" is to bear the right kind of fruit. In the same chapter, He calls Himself "the Light" and says that the person who tries to live without Him "walks in darkness and does not know where he is going." (1 John 2:11) That is the literal truth of it.

When I enthusiastically fell into the ground of theoretical physics and died there, I also bore much fruit—two incinerated cities and an insane arms race. When I fell into the ground of promoting the peaceful uses of science, I bore much fruit then, too—countless souls of people destroyed by a life turned in on itself, made too easy and too comfortable.

In both cases, my dedication to science was co-opted by the evil one for his purposes because I didn't listen to Jesus carefully enough, I didn't pay enough attention to the ground I was falling into, the cause I was giving my life to.

Despite my betrayals and inexcusable shortsightedness, God's love has never left me, not even in my darkest moments, not even when I was on the wrong track altogether, woefully misguided. If Paul can tell my story for me, this will be evident everywhere in it. I was unworthy of God's gifts to me in the past, and even more unworthy of His gift to me in these last days. As filled as I am with regrets, He has bathed me in His costly love and forgiveness. I die a deeply happy man.

2.

God and Satan have been trivialized by Western civilization in our time. But God and Satan are not trivial, and by treating them as trivial, Western civilization has actually trivialized itself. Our culture thinks it has moved God from the center to the sidelines. But in fact He remains at the center, and the further our culture distances itself from Him, the more it sidelines itself.

Good and evil in our culture are then regarded in solely human categories. We define for ourselves what is good and what is evil, and we regard ourselves as fully competent both to achieve what we call good and to eliminate what we call evil. To maintain this posture, we ignore any evidence, however solid, that would suggest that we are wrong, that good finds its source and definition in our Creator, not in us, and that evil proceeds not only from us but even more from a creature of vastly greater intelligence and power than we have. Ignoring evidence is always dangerous, but especially in this case, because it leaves us exposed to powerful forces whose existence we do not even recognize. It leaves us utterly defenseless.

Even in some quarters of the Church, God and Satan are trivialized and humanized. Here we have a lot to learn from the early Church. How many ways do we have of understanding the Cross of Christ that do not take Satan into account at all, in contrast to Sacred Scripture, the Church fathers, and the early Church's experience? I believe that if we had the same consistent attitude toward Satan that Jesus had from start to finish in His earthly life, we would not be so naïve, so vulnerable to his wiles, so astonished and depressed by his victories, so available to serve his cause. We would be on guard, less exposed, and vastly more realistic.

If I were to point to one single element at the root of my wasted life, this would be it. You can't ignore what Jesus took to be the main issue—"The reason the Son of God appeared was to destroy the works of the devil." (I John 3:8b)—and still make sense of a life that claims to be following Him as His disciple.

I praise God for Pastor Engstrom's courage in coming to me. He supplied not just a missing piece to a puzzle. He gave me the grace of leaving this world at peace, much more appreciative of who Jesus is and of what His Cross truly achieved for fallen humanity—victory over Satan, triumph over death, full atonement for our sins, and a reopened gate to paradise.

3.

O Cecilia! You must have looked down on me for a very long time and wondered whether your death had been wasted on me. All the while I thought I was making you happy by giving myself away, I was actually torturing you because I was not giving myself away to Jesus. You hadn't told me to give myself away to just anything, to die in the service of science or progress or even education, to crawl outside of myself for just any old cause. You were telling me to die and come alive with Jesus, our Light and our Life. You were telling me to get as close to Jesus as you were, and to stay there, and to bear all the fruit that would come from that. You were asking me to die and rise with Him, to share in His victory over sin and Satan and the world. That's what you were telling me.

If only I had listened to you and Jesus! "Take up your cross and follow *Me*," He says, not "Take up your cross and follow your star." How different things would have turned out if I had paid closer attention to you! As it was, I made myself a tool of Satan thinking I was serving God and ended up making a major contribution to his agenda of destruction and hatred. If I had really been following Jesus, I would have joined the apostles and the saints in His mission to destroy the works of the devil, not multiply them! I was on the wrong side till the very end. I can't place the blame on Pastor Engstrom for misleading me. The choice was mine. It was all too easy to follow his suggestion and do what I wanted to do as if it were a call from God. I didn't look back. I kept your portrait and your music manuscript with me to inspire me, but I left your spirit and your deep and honest commitment to Jesus back in the organ room at Christiania.

Do they cry in Heaven?

If so, you must have cried for me a lot. And prayed for me!

Have you met Kay and our little son yet?

I stand in wonder that our gracious Lord did not give up on me. I'm sure it helped to have my three angels in Heaven praying for me. My heart is molten now. Even my pain feels good drenched in God's love and yours.

4.

What shall I say of my life?

As long as I, a grain of wheat, was living only for myself, I remained alone, terribly alone.

To sprout and come to life, I needed to relinquish my self-enclosed life and give myself away to something greater than I was.

But because that "greater something" turned out to bear evil fruit, not good fruit, in the end I was more alone than ever.

It was only when I finally discovered that the one "greater something" which bears only good fruit in abundance is actually a "Greater Someone," it is only as I have been giving myself away to Jesus in these last days that my aloneness has melted away.

Forever.

5.

I have very little strength left. Paul is coming tomorrow. I hope he can read this.

With my very last strength, I look back on my life and I marvel that God would send to a lump of clay like me a Cecilia, a Kay, and even a Rolph Eriksen. All of them crossed my path when I was most lost. All of them loved me when I was least lovable. They were angels sent to me from God when I most needed an angel and least expected one.

All eternity will not be long enough for me to thank You, O my God, for sacrificing Cecilia to rescue me, for sacrificing Kay to break me down and drive me into Your arms. Two angels of light sent to relieve my darkness.

O my God, I thank You, I thank You!

With my last breath I will thank you....

6.

Note from Paul: *There was one tiny scrap of paper that seemed important as it was probably his very last one. I stared at it for a long time before I deciphered it. Finally I made out these words in the scrawl:*

My son. I'll meet my son!

Our son!!